SHAKESPEARIAN AND
OTHER STUDIES

SHAKESPEARIAN AND OTHER STUDIES

BY

F. P. WILSON

Edited by Helen Gardner

OXFORD
AT THE CLARENDON PRESS
1969

Oxford University Press, Ely House, London W.1
GLASGOW NEW YORK TORONTO MELBOURNE WELLINGTON
CAPE TOWN SALISBURY IBADAN NAIROBI LUSAKA ADDIS ABABA
BOMBAY CALCUTTA MADRAS KARACHI LAHORE DACCA
KUALA LUMPUR SINGAPORE HONG KONG TOKYO

© OXFORD UNIVERSITY PRESS 1969

PRINTED IN GREAT BRITAIN

Preface

SOME years ago, at my suggestion, the Clarendon Press proposed to Professor F. P. Wilson that he should collect together his writings with such revision as he thought they required. I suggested this, and urged him to agree to the suggestion, because I knew that he was in the habit of annotating his own offprints, sometimes very substantially, and it seemed regrettable that this additional matter and his second thoughts should be wasted, and best that he should himself undertake the task of incorporating corrections and fresh information into the articles as originally published.

At his death, in 1963, Mrs. Wilson and the late Professor John Butt asked me to prepare the volume for the press and handed over to me annotated offprints, notes, and other material, such as letters from correspondents, which Professor Wilson had put together as material for the projected volume. It was at once apparent that he had not made any decision as to what the volume should contain and had not begun to make any formal revision of his articles. The task of deciding what fresh material should be incorporated and in what manner—whether into the text or by means of additional footnotes—was left to me, as was the decision on which articles should make up the volume.

The reasons why Professor Wilson had not been able to give any time or thought to the republication of his own papers were three. In the first place, he paid the inevitable penalty of being probably the most learned Elizabethan scholar in the world, of his high sense of professional obligation, and of his notable generosity of temper. He was endlessly consulted; his conscience made him unable to refuse help and counsel when it was asked; and his warmth of heart made him delight in giving his whole mind to other people's problems within the wide field of his own interests. Then, the death of his closest colleague and admired 'master', Sir Walter Greg, in 1959 laid on him the task of dealing with work Greg had in hand at his death. Lastly, and most important, he regarded as his first obligation the completion of what was to have been his *magnum opus*, the volume in the Oxford History of English Literature on Shakespeare and the Drama to 1640.

It had become apparent to him as he worked on this book that the material was going to prove too abundant for a single volume. I think also that as his health became more and more precarious he had realized that he was unlikely to live to complete the story to 1640. A little before his death, he decided to make a pause at the year 1600 and thoroughly revise what he had written up to that point, hoping that this could be published as the first volume of a work in two parts. This was feasible if he had himself been able to go on to write the second volume; but at his death the General Editors of the Oxford History and the Clarendon Press were faced with a painful and difficult problem. On the one hand it seemed impossible to ask a scholar of standing and authority to take over a history of the drama in the middle of the great age. Anyone attempting a full survey of the work of Shakespeare and his fellow dramatists would wish to make his own disposition of the material and could not be expected to adopt someone else's plan. Secondly, it seemed intolerable that Shakespeare, of all writers, should be arbitrarily split in half, and unlikely that any Shakespearian would be willing to accept a commission that restricted him to dealing with the second half only of Shakespeare's career as a dramatist. On the other hand, it was distressing to contemplate the suppression of two long and finely written chapters on the English History Play and Shakespearian Comedy. They had occupied Professor Wilson in the last years of his life; and he had, as his friends were well aware, found in the writing of them a reward for the long years in which he had toiled on the barren pastures of mid-Tudor drama. The solution of this dilemma that was arrived at was the decision to publish the narrative up to 1584 as Part 1 of the Oxford History, thus allowing the author of Part 2 a free hand to treat in unbroken sequence the history of the great age of the English drama, and to add the two long Shakespearian chapters to the projected volume of published papers.

This decision affected the composition of the volume. As originally planned, its main feature was to have been the extremely long article on 'Shakespeare and the New Bibliography' which F. P.

Preface

Wilson contributed to *Studies in Retrospect* (1945), the volume published to celebrate the fiftieth anniversary of the foundation of the Bibliographical Society in 1942. This article had been widely acclaimed on its appearance, and its author regarded it with justifiable pride. Soon after its publication many people urged that it should be republished in book form, and from the material sent to me it was clear that it had been fairly thoroughly corrected and revised, as if for republication, somewhere around the year 1948, the latest date to appear in any of the supplementary references. When it was decided to include the two long unpublished chapters from the Oxford History in the volume of collected papers, the balance of the volume as originally planned shifted away from bibliographical and textual matters, and this article, with its massive annotation, began to look like an odd bedfellow for the other studies. There was a further difficulty. Since 1948, the year in which it seemed as if Professor Wilson had made his own revision of an article first written in 1942, the 'newer' bibliography had developed. This article, therefore, required rather different editorial treatment from all the others. It had become a contribution to the history of scholarship, requiring some prefatory explanation and considerable extra annotation to call readers' attention to advances brought about by developments in analytical bibliography and to books and articles published during the last twenty years which bore on general and particular problems discussed. After much thought, and after consulting persons concerned with the bibliographical and textual study of Shakespeare, it seemed to me that the right course was to revert to the original plan of separate publication for this article. This has made the present volume more homogeneous, and allowed me, without making the whole volume too bulky, to include the last three papers, which I should have been loth to have had to exclude.

The first two items printed here required a good deal of surgery to turn what had been written as two chapters in a continuous literary history into two self-contained essays. I excised a certain amount of information—such as a brief summary of the known facts of Shakespeare's early life—necessarily included in what was to have been a standard work of reference but adding nothing to what is common knowledge. I had also to remove references backwards and forwards, in some cases supplying a sentence or two summarizing the passage in earlier chapters to which the reader was being referred. Very naturally, in what was to be an authoritative treatment, Professor Wilson had given at times the same examples as he had used in his published work, repeated information to be found there, and at times echoed his own phrases. Since these chapters were now to appear in a volume with earlier work which he was at times drawing upon and repeating, it was necessary to avoid this repetition of material. Then, the plan of the Oxford History allowed for no references. But Professor Wilson was a learned and allusive writer, and it seemed to me that readers would wish to have references supplied and quotations, as far as possible, identified. Luckily, he had pencilled a good many references in the margin of his typescript against the time when he would be reading proofs, so that the task of annotating was not too heavy. I felt at liberty to do this recasting because the last time I saw Professor Wilson before his death he asked me to undertake to see his work through the press, saying: 'You may correct me where I am wrong, rewrite me when I am clumsy or not clear, but I trust you not to make me say anything I would not have said.' It need hardly be said that there was little occasion to correct, or to rewrite on grounds of obscurity or clumsiness; but I took what he had said as a mandate allowing me to present what he left unpublished at his death in a form I thought he would have approved. Apart from some linking sentences and phrases nothing has been added to what he wrote.

The published articles presented a different problem. I had to decide whether the presence of additional matter should be indicated by square brackets or some other method. I came to the conclusion that this would distract readers and to no good purpose. Whereas Greg had provided a comment on his earlier work in the form of notes that could be printed in square brackets, Professor Wilson had made marginal corrections and added references which he had not written up in note form. It was clear that, in general, he had intended to incorporate these into the text. I have done so without indicating where expansion has taken place, merely informing the reader in the first note whether an article has been substantially

Preface

revised. For the sake of consistency, I have standardized all quotations from Shakespeare and all act, scene, and line references. They are taken from the edition of *The Complete Works*, by Peter Alexander, 1951. I have arranged the articles according to their subject-matter, not chronologically, to bring together the Shakespearian studies and, then, after the two memoirs of fellow scholars, to add two papers that are only marginally concerned with Shakespeare and the lecture on 'Table Talk' which is *sui generis*.

I have to thank the Secretary of the British Academy for permission to reprint the Academy lecture on 'Shakespeare and the Diction of Common Life' and the Academy memoirs of E. K. Chambers and W. W. Greg. I was grateful to the late Professor J. Dover Wilson for allowing me to reprint his contribution to the memoir of Chambers. I have to thank the Secretary of the Modern Humanities Research Association for permission to reprint the presidential address on 'The Proverbial Wisdom of Shakespeare'; and the editors of *The Library*, *The Huntington Library Quarterly*, *Shakespeare Survey*, and *Neophilologus* for permission to reprint articles from their journals. I have to record my gratitude to Miss Jonquil Bevan for patient and skilled help in tracing references and checking, and to Mr. J. C. Maxwell for his kindness in reading the proofs. Lastly, I must thank Mrs. Wilson for asking me to undertake this task and for all the help she has given me.

HELEN GARDNER

Oxford

Contents

PREFACE	v
1. THE ENGLISH HISTORY PLAY	1
2. SHAKESPEARE'S COMEDIES	54
3. SHAKESPEARE AND THE DICTION OF COMMON LIFE	100
4. SHAKESPEARE'S READING	130
5. THE PROVERBIAL WISDOM OF SHAKESPEARE	143
6. THE ELIZABETHAN THEATRE	176
7. TWO SHAKESPEARIANS	
I. Edmund Kerchever Chambers (1866–1954)	200
II. Walter Wilson Greg (1875–1959)	219
8. SOME ENGLISH MOCK-PROGNOSTICATIONS	251
9. THE ENGLISH JEST-BOOKS OF THE SIXTEENTH AND EARLY SEVENTEENTH CENTURIES	285
10. TABLE TALK	325

I

The English History Play

WHAT is a history play and how do you distinguish it from comedy or tragedy? In the century when the Rules were respected and often observed, Rowe said that Shakespeare's Histories were really Tragedies 'with a run or mixture of Comedy amongst 'em', a description to which there are obvious objections; for a run of comedy is not essential, and the nature and limits of the subject-matter seldom lend themselves to tragedy. Johnson found the distinguishing mark in the absence of any unity of action, the only one of the three unities he was prepared to accept. With inspired common sense he maintained that in his comedies and tragedies Shakespeare preserved 'well enough' the unity of action, but that nothing more was necessary to his histories 'than that the changes of action be so prepared as to be understood, that the incidents be various and affecting, and the characters consistent, natural and distinct'.

Johnson's comment takes into account the limitation that when a dramatist chose to write about a historical theme well known to his age, his theme, his chief characters, and the main sequence of events were given to him, and he sacrificed some of the liberty of manipulation. He was, in Sidney's words about poets like Lucan, 'wrapped within the folde of the proposed subiect', and could not freely take 'the course of his owne inuention'. 'If *Homer* wou'd,' the old rhyme said, '*Hellen* had been a hagge, and *Troy* had stood',[1] but this was no longer possible after Homer had made a history which no man can unmake. The authors of *The Mirror for Magistrates*, however, saw that there are some historical actions which can be composed into a unity more easily than others, and none more easily than those which lead up to the death of a king or

[1] E. Gayton, *Pleasant Notes upon Don Quixote* (1654), p. 10.

counsellor of state. Then History becomes almost indistinguishable from Tragedy. There are two such plays among Shakespeare's English histories, *Richard II* and *Richard III*, and Johnson's comment applies less well to them than to the other histories. The beginning of *Richard II* is the king in power and the banishment of Bolingbroke, the middle is the king's abuse of his power and the return of Bolingbroke, the end is the king's deposition and murder and the triumph of Bolingbroke.

When Heminge and Condell arranged the plays in the First Folio in the three divisions Comedies, Histories, Tragedies, they were not making subtle distinctions between the kinds of drama. The arrangement was dictated by its obvious convenience, a convenience of subject-matter; in one group they placed the ten plays on English history, arranged chronologically from *King John* to *Henry VIII*. If challenged, they might have admitted that the three Roman tragedies were also entitled to be called history plays, for they were based on Plutarch, an authority even more authentic than Hall and Holinshed. Nor would they have denied that some of the histories are also tragedies. *3 Henry VI*, *Richard III*, and *Richard II* were all first published as 'tragedies', though *1 Henry IV* was 'The History of...' and *Henry V* 'The Chronicle History of...'. Any play that ended with the death of the protagonist an Elizabethan would have thought of as a tragedy, especially if it exhibited what to Puttenham and others were the prime requisites of tragedy —the mutability of fortune and the just punishment of God in revenge for a vicious and evil life. If any play of Shakespeare's was written with this aim consistently in view it is *Richard III*.

When we attempt to define a history play by its subject-matter, however, we land ourselves in difficulties. Is *The History of Jacob and Esau* a history play? It is the earliest printed play to call itself a history in its head and running titles, and it records in dramatic form a series of events the historicity of which no man doubted. Are *Arden of Feversham* and *A Warning for Fair Women* history plays? The authors of these plays on contemporary murders prided themselves on their truth to fact, conceiving that by keeping to 'simple truth' they would bring home to their audience a sense of sin. Are we to disqualify these because though historical they present murder in low life, not in high? If we exclude all plays based on Holy Writ and insist that a history play is a play based on authentic history which exposes to our view the ways of men and women in power, then who is to be the judge of what is or is not authentic? Between the conception of history held by Lambarde or Stow or Camden and that of the groundling in a popular theatre there was room for innumerable shades of opinion. The plot of Greene's *Scottish History of James the Fourth, slain at Flodden* came from an Italian *novella*, yet might have been taken by many playgoers as an authentic episode in the quarrels between the two countries; but Sir George Buc, historian as well as Master of the Revels, indignantly altered the title of his copy[1] to read 'The Scottish Historie or rather fiction of English & Scottish matters comicall'. What of that period of early British 'history' to which Shakespeare and so many dramatists were attracted? Already in the early sixteenth century (Polydore Vergil, Rastell), and still more in the early seventeenth (Hayward, Selden, Hakewill), there were those who doubted the whole story of the Trojan ancestry of Britain and the historical existence of Gorboduc, Locrine, Lear; but such men would be rare in a popular audience at the theatre, and (let us hope) would be willing to suspend disbelief for the sake of the play. In any case British history was remote and shadowy as compared with English; otherwise, Shakespeare could not have departed so widely from earlier versions in the catastrophe of his *King Lear*.

A constant though not an essential ingredient of a history play on the popular stage is the clash of arms. The insignia of History in the Induction to *A Warning for Fair Women* are drum and ensign. Of Shakespeare's ten plays on English history and his three plays on Roman history only *Henry VIII* lacks a battle—if we except *Richard II* where there are alarums but no excursions, and in that respect, as in so many others, it is uncharacteristic. Dramatists may protest that they much disgrace the name of Agincourt 'With four or five most vile and ragged foils', but this does not deter them from overstraining the resources of their stage.

Another characteristic though again not a necessary one is the looseness of structure to which Johnson pointed. A sequence of

[1] Now in the British Museum.

events is chosen from some history or chronicle history, and the interest that was narrative is transferred into dramatic. The dramatist and the historian tell things in such order as they were done,[1] and where many actions happen at the same time they are forced to deal with them one after another. The loose structure of many history plays which present various scenes from a ruler's life or reign has been attributed to the influence of the morality plays,[2] but it is sufficient explanation that these plots could not well unfold themselves in any other way.

The chief interest in a history play is political or, with Shakespeare, in character revealing itself in politics. What is in question is good or bad government, and good or bad governors. We do not think of *King Lear* as political. It has a political interest, but it is there only to make possible the human interest. In this play there are souls to be saved, especially Lear's, and souls to be damned, especially Goneril's and Regan's. In comparison the political issue is a minor one. But *Gorboduc* is firmly political: indeed, if there is a protagonist, it is not Gorboduc, or Ferrex-cum-Porrex, but Britain or any state where civil dissension leads to civil war.

(i)

Perhaps we may best discover what enlightened Elizabethans expected of a history play by examining what they expected of history. The evidence is plentiful and comes not merely from the chroniclers and historians but from historiographers influenced by a new conception of history derived from Italian historians and historiographers. Of the absolute necessity of a knowledge of history to all kinds of men and especially to princes and men in authority all were convinced; and the knowledge was for use, not for ostentation. If it had not been so the great Burghley would not have advised a young Cambridge undergraduate (John Harington) to study Roman history, especially Livy and Caesar, 'which is exceedinge fitt for a gentleman to understande';[3] and Thomas Blundeville

---

[1] 'An Hystorye ought to declare the thynges in suche order, as they were done.' Thomas Blundeville, *The True Order and Method of Writing and Reading Histories* (1574), reprinted by Hugh G. Dick, *H.L.Q.*, iii (Jan. 1940), pp. 149–70.
[2] By G. Saintsbury, reviewing F. E. Schelling, *The English Chronicle Play* (1902) in *Eng. Studien*, xxxi (1902), p. 291.
[3] Harington, *Nugae Antiquae*, ed. T. Park (1804), i. 131.

would hardly have dedicated to Leicester his *True Order and Method of Writing and Reading Histories* (1574), translated from Francisco Patrizi and Giacomo Concio. Leicester, he tells us, read histories not as many do to pass away the time but the better to direct his private actions and his counsel in public causes, whether in peace or in war.[1] The belief was widespread that 'Like time bringeth forth like examples', a belief that has behind it the authority of Thucydides and in the nineteenth century was crystallized into 'History repeats itself'. Widespread also was the belief enshrined in one of the most popular proverbs of the sixteenth century, that it is good to beware by other men's harms, a saying as applicable to governments as to individuals, as conducive to public virtue as to private.

The number of historical works translated in the late sixteenth and early seventeenth centuries testifies to the importance attached to the reading of history. Philemon Holland, whom Fuller called the translator-general in his age, undertook his enormous labours partly because of the benefits Livy or Pliny would confer on such as could not read Latin, partly as a thank-offering for a life spent in peace and tranquillity, partly for love of the English language, partly out of a desire 'to do some good whiles I live to my sweet native country'.[2] Some translators added as a bonus a foreign disquisition on history. Walter Lynne in translating Carion's *Three Books of Chronicles* (1550) gives us Melanchthon's ideas upon history; North (*Plutarch*, 1579) gives us Jacques Amyot; Golding (*Trogus Pompeius*, 1564) gives us Simon Grynaeus, and so (without acknowledgement) does Thomas Lodge (*Josephus*, 1602); and Thomas Heywood (*Sallust*, 1608–9) gives us Bodin.

Many claims are made, and they are repeated by writer after writer. The good historian, who delivers with sincerity the truth, the whole truth, and nothing but the truth, enables us to compare things past with things present and gather easily what is to be followed and what to be eschewed.[3] Our life on earth is brief, and experience is the schoolmistress of fools. Although nature, art, and practice are all necessary to the conduct of life in peace and war,

[1] See Eleanor Rosenberg, *Leicester, Patron of Letters* (Columbia University Press, 1955), p. 62.
[2] Preface to *Livy* (1600).
[3] See John Brand's Preface to his translation of *Quintus Curtius* (1553).

yet from art (history) we may learn more examples in one day than experience can give us in a lifetime. And no case can arise in public affairs or private but may take light and counsel from history.[1] It teaches us how men prosper so long as they maintain justice, persecute vice, use clemency and mercy, and how bad men fall into manifold miseries and troubles. Therefore it teaches obedience to princes, for those who rebel *never* come to a good end.[2] In particular, if we read Appian on the Roman wars (in Henry Bynneman's translation of 1578) we shall profit from these lessons, all set out on the title-page:

Their greedy desire to conquere others. Their mortall malice to destroy themselues. Their seeking of matters to make warre abroade. Their picking of quarels to fall out at home. All the degrees of Sedition, and all the effects of Ambition. A firme determination of Fate, thorowe all the changes of Fortune. And finally an euident demonstration, That peoples rule must giue place, and Princes power preuayle.

And all these good lessons we may learn painlessly, since history is both more delightful and more effective than moral philosophy in that it teaches by examples not by mere precepts.

One of the sections on Ireland in the Holinshed of 1587[3] is dedicated to Raleigh, and there he is reminded of Cicero's famous definition of history as the witness of time, the light of truth, the life of memory, and the mistress of life. It appears in emblematic form in the frontispiece to his own *History of the World* (1614), and in the long Preface he sums up with unmatched eloquence all that his age could say in favour of historical writing. To him also its aim was to trace the workings of Providence in the deeds and characters of men, so that we may learn from times past 'such wisdom as may guide our desires and actions' in times present. No wonder his *History* was a favourite book with the Puritans and was recommended by Cromwell to his son as 'a body of history' which 'will add much more to your understanding than fragments of story'.[4]

[1] See preface to North's *Plutarch* (1579).   [2] See Brand, loc. cit.
[3] John Hooker's translation of Giraldus Cambrensis.
[4] *Writings and Speeches*, ed. W. C. Abbott (1937–47), ii. 236. The contrast between 'a body of history' and 'fragments of story' is made again in a speech to the Barebones Parliament, contrasting 'stories that do recite these transactions, and give you narratives of matters of fact' and 'those things wherein the life and power of them lay; those strange windings and turnings of Providence' (Abbott, iii. 53).

If history teaches more delightfully than moral philosophy, what of poetry? Amyot held that history had the advantage over poetry; for while poetry enriches things 'above the stars and their deserving' history tells only the plain truth. On similar grounds Bacon prefers history to poetry, poetry being an escape from the disappointing realities of life into an ideal world where actions are more heroical, and justice truly poetical with virtue rewarded and vice punished, whereas prose is obedient to the laws of reason and 'doth buckle and bowe the Mind vnto the Nature of things'. The great apologist of poetry in this age found it more delightful as a teacher than history or philosophy, but what Sidney says applies not to poets like Lucan, still less to poets writing for the popular stage, but to 'right poets' whose imaginations are not confined by historical trammels. To find an apologist for popular historical drama in sixteenth-century England we must go to one who himself wrote for the popular stage, to Thomas Nashe (*Pierce Penniless*, 1592):

In Playes, all coosonages, all cunning drifts ouer-guylded with outward holinesse, all stratagems of warre, all the cankerwormes that breede on the rust of peace, are most liuely anatomiz'd: they shew the ill successe of treason, the fall of hastie climbers, the wretched end of vsurpers, the miserie of ciuill dissention, and how iust God is euermore in punishing of murther . . . they are sower pills of reprehension, wrapt vp in sweete words . . . no Play they haue, encourageth any man to tumults or rebellion, but layes before such the halter and the gallowes.[1]

Some plays that just antedate, or coincide with, the beginnings of the English history play may be said to meet these requirements: *Titus Andronicus*, for example, and Greene's pseudo-historical plays about tyranny and treachery in high places. And if we could suppose that the only requirement of 'high and excellent tragedy' was (in Sidney's words) to make 'Kingis feare to be Tyrants, and Tyrants manifest their tirannical humors', how perfectly would *Cambyses* qualify, and Greene and Lodge's Biblical *Looking-Glass for London and England* and the anonymous *Selimus*. An apt example because it is founded on the translation of Appian just mentioned, with its

[1] *Works*, ed. R. B. McKerrow, revised F. P. Wilson (1958), i. 213–14.

moral title-page, is Lodge's *Wounds of Civil War*, acted *c.* 1589 and printed 1594. Unlike *Titus Andronicus* and the plays of Greene here is a play on a truly historical theme, a theme with all the prestige of ancient Rome behind it. Into five acts Lodge digests the quarrel of Marius and Sulla from its inception to their deaths. He does so seriously with little comic relief and with an emphasis on character and on dialogue plaintive, argumentative, and heroic rather than on murder and battle. Of the horrors of civil war, the mutations of Fortune—that 'blindfold Mistris of incertaine chaunce'—of the cares that attend ambition and great estate, the dangers of power that blinds 'the greatest wit with error', the play provides many an example. *O Vita! misero longa, foelici brevis*' the title-page exclaims. Here are sage and serious *exempla* set out in blank verse (with occasional rhymes for 'complaints', e.g. III. iv), a verse that never startles us by its imagery or melody yet sustains a good expository level. The play shows some knowledge of *Tamburlaine*, but how different is the treatment! The more Marlowe's play is seen beside its contemporaries the more astonishing it seems in its glorification of one whom any other dramatist would have held up to obloquy.

(ii)

However remote the period, the dramatist kept in mind that there are lessons in past history which the present would do well to heed. Yet one would have thought that a playwright who had this didactic purpose at heart would have seen that no theme could have so immediate an impact on his audience as one from the history of their own country. Thomas Wotton in an epistle prefixed to the earliest printed history of an English county, William Lambarde's *Perambulation of Kent* (1576), held that

(the sacred word of Almightie God alwayes excepted) there is nothing either for our instruction more profitable, or to our mindes more delectable, or within the compasse of common vnderstanding more easie or facile, then the studies of hystories: nor that studie for none estate more meete, then for the estate of Gentlemen: nor for the Gentlemen of Englande, no Hystorie so meete, as the Hystorie of England.

And yet there is no certain evidence that any dramatist before the

The English History Play 9

Armada dared to put upon the public stage a play based upon English history. We are even at a loss to find plays based on British history. Academic drama, which was not subjected to the scrutiny of the Lord Chamberlain and the Master of the Revels, had not altogether fought shy of these themes. *Gorboduc*, an Inns of Court play, is one example, and another is the trilogy of Thomas Legge, Master of Caius, *Richardus Tertius*, written in Latin and performed at St. John's in 1579. Legge's work is un-Senecan in presenting much spectacle, many characters and many episodes, but in language and sentiment it is most Senecan: and in subject too, for this tragedy, observed Sir John Harington, 'would moue... *Phalaris* the tyraunt, and terrifie all tyrannous minded men'.[1] But like Bale's *King Johan* the play remained in manuscript and in no way affected the practice of the popular stage.

Far more history plays have perished than have survived. Of sixteen plays written by Robert Wilson with others for Philip Henslowe between 1598 and 1600, all historical and most of them relating to English history, and of fourteen plays written by Richard Hathway with others between 1598 and 1602, and mostly historical, all are lost. At an earlier date the mortality was not less serious. The plays on classical history and legend acted by the Chapel children and produced at court by Richard Farrant in the fifteen-seventies are lost, as are the twenty-eight plays produced at court by the children of Paul's under Sebastian Westcott between 1560-1 and 1582. Yet in spite of these losses it is still most remarkable that in the plays and play-titles that have survived and in many comments on the subjects treated before 1588 there is no reference to any popular drama on English history. The only scrap of evidence relating to a play of this kind before 1588 is a reference in a jest-book concerning the comedian Richard Tarlton, who died in that year.[2] The play is either *The Famous Victories of Henry V* (printed in a bad quarto in 1598) or the play or plays upon which that ruin is based. But when we remember that the jest-book was not printed before 1600 and how in every age the snowball of a jester's reputation collects to itself all the jests that lie in its way, we may not attach much value to this evidence. Other early extant plays like

---

[1] Preface to *Orlando Furioso* (1591).   [2] *Tarlton's Jests* (1638), C2ᵛ–3.

Jack Straw, *The Troublesome Reign of King John* (printed 1591), *The True Tragedy of Richard III*, *Edward III*, Peele's *Edward I* all seem to be post-1588. Tarlton was the author of a lost play *The Seven Deadly Sins* (in two parts), of which we possess the plot as it was acted during a revival of 1589–92. In the revival, if not earlier, Henry VI presided over three shows presented by Lydgate, illustrating Envy (Ferrex and Porrex), Sloth (Sardanapalus), and Lechery (Tereus). But these were not *about* Henry: he presided as a type of kingly saintliness. In shows or entertainments, of course, as in street pageants, English kings and queens had long since been depicted. In Tudor London—to go back no further—William the Conqueror came into the London Midsummer Show of 1535, and before Elizabeth on her first ceremonial entrance into London a three-storeyed stage displayed her grandfather and grandmother, her father and mother, and herself with spoken verses on the union of the houses of Lancaster and York.[1]

If popular playwrights did not venture to produce plays on English history before the Armada the reason may have been a fear of censorship. Any subject, however ancient and however innocently intended, might be misconstrued with results disastrous to the dramatist. *Damon and Pythias* and *Gorboduc* were presented before private audiences; nevertheless, Edwards took the precaution of explaining that the court of Dionysius was no other court; and while Sackville and Norton presented a mirror for their prince, what their audience saw in that mirror was tolerated by the Queen and welcomed by the spectators. Daniel was not so fortunate with his *Philotas*, acted by the Queen's Revels children in 1604. Supposing that it 'could not but haue had an unreprouable passage with the time, and the better sort of men, seeing with what idle fictions, and grosse follies, the Stage at this day abused mens recreations',[2] he was much distressed when his tragedy was misconceived and wrongly applied to the Earl of Essex. The more recent the history the greater the danger; for, as Raleigh said, 'whosoever, in writing a modern history, shall follow truth too near the heels, it may haply strike

---

[1] *Malone Society Collections*, iii. 25–6; G. Wickham, *Early English Stages* (1959), i. 72.
[2] See the Apology printed after *Philotas* in the edition of 1623; *The Tragedy of Philotas*, edited by L. Michel (New Haven, 1949), p. 156.

out his teeth'. For whatever reason, after the Armada dramatists took the risk, and were licensed to take the risk, of writing plays on English history, and for some ten years the plays were acted which have provided many an Englishman with his only knowledge of medieval history. The popularity of this subject may be gauged by Shakespeare's devotion to it in his early years—nine plays out of eighteen by 1599—and by Nashe's eloquent praise of plays and especially of plays on English history in his *Pierce Penniless* (1592):

> What if I prooue Playes to be . . . a rare exercise of vertue? First, for the subiect of them (for the most part) it is borrowed out of our English Chronicles, wherein our forefathers valiant acts (that haue line long buried in rustie brasse and worme-eaten bookes) are reuiued, and they themselues raised from the Graue of Obliuion, and brought to pleade their aged Honours in open presence: than which, what can be a sharper reproofe to these degenerate effeminate dayes of ours?
>
> How would it haue ioyed braue *Talbot* (the terror of the French) to thinke that after he had lyne two hundred yeares in his Tombe, hee should triumphe againe on the Stage, and haue his bones newe embalmed with the teares of ten thousand spectators at least (at seuerall times), who, in the Tragedian that represents his person, imagine they behold him fresh bleeding.[1]

Here we may pause for a moment to examine some of the 'English chronicles' which raised our ancestors from the 'Grave of Oblivion' and gave the dramatists their history. Soon after the turn of the century historians like Hayward and Bacon were attacking the annalists for neglecting 'order, poise, and truth',[2] for the superficiality and partiality of their accounts of public affairs, for noting deeds and neglecting causes, for putting invented speeches into the mouths of historical persons, for including trivial reports of bearbaitings, fleas, mice, masks, mayings, and so on. With all these faults Holinshed may be charged. He did not look the gift-horses of the middle ages in the mouth, accepted the Trojan ancestry of Britain (according to Hayward a senseless fiction invented by

---

[1] *Works*, ed. cit., i. 212.
[2] Hayward's preface to Sir Roger Williams, *Actions of the Low Countries* (1618); see S. L. Goldberg, R.E.S., N.S. vi (1955), p. 237, for a discussion of the meaning of 'poise'.

Geoffrey of Monmouth), eked out the few facts known about Macbeth with a circumstantial romance composed by Hector Boece, and side by side with the death of kings, the carnage of war, the evolution of laws, he told of apparitions seen in the air, murders of private gentlemen like Arden of Feversham, disastrous fires, strange fish caught upon the coast, and the ingenious blacksmith who put about a flea's neck a golden chain of forty-three links with lock and key, which it drew with ease. In this world of fine fabling an Elizabethan dramatist may well have felt that Holinshed with his invented speeches and insistence on character was half-way along the road to romantic drama. Who would think that he was the source of the story of King Edgar's love for Alfrida, put upon the stage c. 1592 in *A Knack to Know a Knave*? The king's proxy plays a part similar to that of Lacy in Greene's romantic *Friar Bacon*; the dramatist (but not the chronicler) saves his life through the magic and mercy of St. Dunstan. It is not inappropriate that Robert Greene is cited in the chronicle's list of two hundred authorities.

Holinshed ought perhaps to be written 'Holinshed', so much is gathered from other chroniclers, dead and living. The first edition was in 1577 and the second and enlarged edition, the edition used by Shakespeare, in 1587. Among earlier writers who contributed directly or indirectly to what Professor Lewis called Holinshed's 'national stock-pot' are Froissart, Polydore Vergil, whose history of England was commissioned by Henry VII, Grafton, Foxe, Stow, Hall, and (for the character of Richard III) Sir Thomas More. Edward Hall's chronicle, posthumously issued by Grafton in 1548, Shakespeare knew directly and also indirectly through Holinshed. Hall is no impartial historian. He is biased against the Roman Catholics and the Scots, and he is biased in favour of the Tudor dynasty. His history is of men, especially kings, not of institutions or society, and here Shakespeare resembles him. His theme is expressed in his opening words, 'What mischiefe hath insurged in realmes by intestine deuision'; and beginning with the dispute of Hereford (later Henry IV) and Norfolk, which is the theme of the opening scene of *Richard II*, and to both writers the starting-point of the dissensions between York and Lancaster, Hall follows his

The English History Play

argument in lively prose through the 'unquiet tyme' of Henry IV, 'the victorious actes' of Henry V, the 'troubleous season' of Henry VI, down to the 'triumphant reigne' of Henry VIII. So doing he gives the ground to Shakespeare for all his history plays except *King John*. And he does it while always having an eye on character, while never neglecting to trace deed, cause, and effect, never forgetting that his purpose in writing is 'So that all men (more clere then the sonne) maie apparently perceiue, that as by discord greate thynges decaie and fall to ruine, so the same by concord be reuiued and erected.'

(iii)

Nashe's pamphlet with its testimony to the popularity of the Talbot scenes in *1 Henry VI* and Greene's *Groatsworth* with its splenetic attack on 'Shakescene' and its parody of a line in *3 Henry VI* are the first certain references to Shakespeare as a dramatist: the one was entered in the Stationers' Register on 8 August 1592 and the other on 20 September. How long Shakespeare had been in London before attracting attention the most diligent research has failed to establish. What little we know of his life belongs mainly to his later years when his fame was made and his mind and art formed, and even so the information is scanty and mostly of an official and legal nature. It is almost as if we knew Wordsworth only from his appointments as Distributor of Stamps and Poet Laureate. Very reasonably we can assume much about the conditions of Shakespeare's life as a dramatist and man of the theatre from circumstantial evidence, but no assured evidence helps us to such intimacies as his opinions on literature and the drama, his friendships and enmities, the women he loved, his religion. To write a full-dress biography of such a man did not occur to his age: if it had bred a Plutarch he would not have written about Shakespeare. When in the late seventeenth century the impulse came to discover what could be discovered about a man who was not a public figure but merely a poet and dramatist, all were dead who had known Shakespeare in the flesh. In consequence, for any important knowledge we have of him we must look not to his life but to his poetry; and there we are told not of his life but of what he made of life.

We do not know when he left Stratford or why, nor how he

occupied himself during the 'lost years' of the eighties. All or none of the early traditions may be true; but that which carries the greatest weight is reported by Aubrey. From the actor son of Christopher Beeston, a member of Shakespeare's company in the fifteen-nineties, he learnt that Shakespeare 'had been in his younger yeares a Schoolmaster in the Countrey'. And just so he may have spent some years of his early life teaching himself as well as others the logic and rhetoric which were as necessary to the Elizabethan poet as to the Elizabethan scholar, absorbing too the necessary materials for his invention, in particular the knowledge of Plautus, Seneca, and Ovid revealed in the *Comedy of Errors*, *Titus Andronicus*, and *Venus and Adonis*, and that knowledge and love of the history of his own country which led him to devote to this theme nine out of his first eighteen plays.

The dignity and seriousness of purpose apparent in Shakespeare's history plays are in sharp contrast to many of the productions by other hands. When the Privy Council insisted that players must be allowed to practise their art in order to prepare themselves for court performances, the City answered that many of the plays acted 'in open stages before all the basest assemblies in London and Middlesex' could not possibly be presented before the Queen.[1] *The Famous Victories of Henry V* is such a play. It is of incredible meanness in the form in which it has survived, but of course it may be a much debased version of a play or plays now lost. *The Life and Death of Jack Straw* has been ascribed to George Peele, but while Peele can write badly no play of his is so wholly destitute of poetry. But apart from the crudeness of the style how far do such plays meet the large claims made for history plays by Nashe? Spectators went away from *Jack Straw* with the knowledge that collectors of taxes are cruel and expendable, that rebels like Wat Tyler, Jack Straw (for in the play these are two, not one), and Parson Ball come to a bad end, that loyal hearts like the courageous Lord Mayor Walworth are the treasure of a prince; but to judge from the text of 1593–4 they were not once told that the king of the play is Richard II.

Rightly enough chronology was flouted for dramatic ends. Joan

---

[1] See E. K. Chambers, *The Elizabethan Stage* (1923), Appendix D. lxxv.

The English History Play

of Arc, burnt at the stake in 1431, gloats over the body of Talbot killed at Castillon in 1453; Somerset is slain by Richard Crookback then aged eight; Queen Margaret is made a contemporary of Dame Eleanor, Gloucester's wife, yet did not arrive in England till three years after Eleanor's disgrace; Margaret's 'lover' Suffolk was thirty-four years her senior; Hotspur is made coeval with Hal with brilliant effect, though the Prince was sixteen at Shrewsbury (1403) and Hotspur thirty-nine, older than the Prince was ever to be. But Shakespeare's departures from historical fact are venial compared with those of some of his contemporaries. His handling of the Buckingham scenes in *Henry VIII* has been praised by A. F. Pollard as 'remarkably accurate, except in matters of date'.[1] A good contrast is provided by Samuel Rowley's play about the same monarch, *When You See Me, You Know Me*.[2] John Day's reference to a puppet-play presenting 'the stabbing of *Julius Caesar* in the *French* Capitol by a sort of Dutch *Mesapotamians*' (*Blind Beggar*, IV. i) is no doubt merely satirical, as is Marvell's story of some Elizabethan strolling players who having worn out and overacted their London plays made a new one of their own in which Moses persuaded Julius Caesar not to make war against his own country or to cross the Rubicon.[3] But there are worse crimes than the flouting of chronology, for example the vulgarization of manners so apparent in a play like Rowley's. Shakespeare is at home in court, camp, city, country, and if in watching one of his plays today the manners seem confused it is not his doing but the producer's.

Henry VI, Part 3 is an obvious sequel to Part 2: without Part 3 Part 2 is actable, but inconclusive. But *1 Henry VI* may have been an afterthought, following on the success of Parts 2 and 3 and filling in the gap between Henry's birth and marriage. Here the centre of interest is in the French wars leading to the death of Talbot and the martyrdom of Joan of Arc: in 2 and 3 the centre of interest is the English civil wars. *Richard III* is almost as closely knit to *3 Henry VI* as that is to Part 2. In a recent performance of Part 3 Richard's opening soliloquy in *Richard III* ('Now is the winter of our discontent . . .') was spoken from the throne which his

---

[1] *Henry VIII* (1905), p. 182.   [2] See below, pp. 50-1.
[3] *The Rehearsal Transprosed* (1672), pp. 318-19.

brother Edward has just left and proved an effective epilogue, the last words being drowned by the bells celebrating Edward's triumph.

How far is this cycle—and especially *1–3 Henry VI* and most especially *1 Henry VI*—wholly Shakespeare's work? And if it is not all his work, then in what places and with whom do we find him as collaborator and reviser? The choice of Marlowe as a collaborator is not now so popular as it used to be—verse may be Marlowesque without being Marlowe's—but Peele, Greene, Nashe still have their advocates. The problem promises to remain for ever a matter of dispute. Those who maintain that because Heminge and Condell printed these plays as Shakespeare's, therefore they are his and all his are saved a world of trouble. Yet the 'disintegrators' have a case when they argue that there is nothing unlikely in the view that the young Shakespeare with his way to make and the credit of his company to sustain may well have employed a part of his time in collaborating or in revising and that if Heminge and Condell printed as Shakespeare's work that was only partly his they cannot be properly accused of bad faith, if judged by the standards of their age. To believe that *1 Henry VI* contains much that is not Shakespeare's is to relieve him of much flat writing. In his earliest plays the verse is stiff and unvaried, though showing already a command of the diction of common life; yet according to M. P. Tilley's admirable dictionary of proverbs the use of proverbial or semi-proverbial language is less than half as frequent in Part 1 as in Part 2 or 3 or *Richard III*, and the discrepancy is much more marked when allowance is made for the instances which Tilley omitted. This discrepancy is the more significant if we suppose that *1 Henry VI* is later than *2* and *3 Henry VI*, that it is the play acted by Strange's men as a new play at the Rose Theatre on 3 March 1592 and the play to which Nashe was referring in the summer of that year when he praised so notably the Talbot scenes. At the same time some allowance must be made for the absence of anything like the Cade scenes or the character of Gloucester (Richard III).

In the other three parts of the cycle there is nothing which the young Shakespeare could not have written and much that could only have come from his pen. In power and dignity they excel

The English History Play

anything in English historical drama up to that time; nor is it necessary to qualify that statement by excepting Marlowe's *Edward II*. The chief characters who embody the theme or themes which run through these early plays stand out sharp and clear, and the wealth and variety of vivid and consistent character which he can already present is remarkable. The Cade scenes in *2 Henry VI* have an earthy humour which Marlowe did not emulate and which give a foretaste of the comic scenes in *Henry IV*. In the (till recently) neglected *3 Henry VI* how few are the lay figures, and how sharply the chief characters are placed before us: the two kings Henry VI and Edward IV, Clifford, Warwick, Clarence, Queen Margaret, and, above all, Richard Duke of Gloucester. The scene is almost too crowded.

No succinct summary can attempt to describe the tergiversations and bouleversations of the many who in their ambitious struggle for power stop short of no brutality and no crime. The horrors seem to be doubled because they are horrors of civil war. The words of 'good Gloucester' to King Henry (*2 Henry VI*, III. i. 142) give a short view of the moral atmosphere:

> Ah, gracious lord, these days are dangerous!
> Virtue is chok'd with foul ambition,
> And charity chas'd hence by rancour's hand;
> Foul subornation is predominant,
> And equity exil'd your Highness' land.

Another short view is given in the two scenes in *Richard III* (I. iii, IV. iv) where Shakespeare, in defiance of history, preserves old Queen Margaret to face and outface Richard and to exchange sorrows with the widowed queen of Edward IV and the Duchess of York.

> *Queen Marg.* . . . I had an Edward, till a Richard kill'd him;
> I had a husband, till a Richard kill'd him:
> Thou hadst an Edward, till a Richard kill'd him;
> Thou hadst a Richard, till a Richard kill'd him.
> *Duchess.* I had a Richard too, and thou didst kill him;
> I had a Rutland too, thou holp'st to kill him.
> *Queen Marg.* Thou hadst a Clarence too, and Richard kill'd him.

This formal antiphon recalls past villainies and ties the plays together, a function also performed by the characters who murder in one play and are murdered in the next. A striking example most powerfully presented is that of 'false, fleeting, perjured Clarence'. His elder and younger brothers Edward and Richard fight beside their father in word and deed at the first battle of St. Albans (*2 Henry VI*, v. i), but Clarence makes his first appearance in *3 Henry VI* (II. ii). Here Shakespeare uses him to support Richard in taunt and innuendo in one of those scenes of high astounding terms which whip up the excitement of the audience before a battle scene. When Edward marries beneath him, Clarence forsakes his brother and puts his trust in the fortunes of Warwick, changing sides again before the battle of Barnet in time to stab the young Prince of Wales 'for twitting me with perjury'. But he is the most easily removed of all Richard's obstacles to the throne, and before the end of the first act of *Richard III* he has been murdered by two grimly comic murderers. It is the most dramatic scene that Shakespeare had yet written (I. iv), a scene almost wholly of his own invention in which the butt of malmsey of his source (Holinshed from More) is mentioned but not required.

This first group of history plays, like the second group, concerns itself with the rule and character of three kings of England. The least important is Edward IV, indistinguishable from Richard in cruel opportunism but distinguishable in that his consuming passion is not so much the ambition of power as sensualism and self-indulgence. Of Henry VI the portrait is full and never flattering. He plays a prominent role in all three parts, though it is not in the nature of this character to play a dominating role. If there is a centre in these plays it is historically England and morally the evils of civil discord. Henry's intentions are always good:

> Civil dissension is a viperous worm
> That gnaws the bowels of the commonwealth;

but he is powerless to do good, and with 'sad unhelpful tears' must watch the doom of the good Duke Humphrey of Gloucester. An infant when *1 Henry VI* opens he shows his helplessness before his discordant nobles in the very first scene in which he appears (III. i), and as the fortunes of quarrelling factions ebb and flow—Gloucester *v.* Winchester, Suffolk *v.* Gloucester, Warwick *v.* Suffolk,

York v. Clifford—he is humiliated again and again. Peace-loving but unable to keep the peace, here is a monarch whom the irony of destiny has placed in the one office where he cannot help but kill the thing he loves. Destiny has also given a termagant wife to the man least able to control her, a woman who 'works the easy-melting king like wax'. Whirling ambitions fight and intrigue about a man devoid of ambition. From the heat of battle he retires to meditate on the evils of high estate and the happiness of low (*3 Henry VI*, II. v). The elaborate formal rhetoric is interpenetrated and redeemed by lyricism. This lamb among wolves has the gift of compassion, a gift never more touchingly displayed than when his reverie is interrupted by the laments of a son who has killed his father and a father who has killed his son, and he becomes a chorus to the woes of his kingdom. But the saintly yet dangerously ineffective Henry is only dimly aware that but for him and his despairing goodness these cruelties would not be.

In the character of King Richard there are no enigmas. While some modern writers have held that Richard's character was butchered to make Tudor propaganda we cannot expect a Tudor dramatist to do other than present a character of unrelieved villainy. He plays a part in *2 Henry VI*, but Shakespeare does not show him in all his formidable self until the soliloquy which closes *3 Henry VI*, III. ii, where he announces his resolve to cut off all who come between him and the throne. The pith of the character is given in this speech, and what follows is so much illustration. So Shakespeare gives us his only play of which the hero is a villain, his gifts of intellect and will wholly turned to evil. The maturer Shakespeare might have seen him more intimately, less externally. Working through the less conscious levels of the mind he might have humanized Richard by making him less certain of himself, as he humanized Macbeth. But except in dreams Richard never falters in his determination to be a villain. In a later soliloquy (v. vi. 78) we find him blaming his evil upon his deformity—

> Then, since the heavens have shap'd my body so,
> Let hell make crook'd my mind to answer it—

an excuse not more convincing than Edmund's plea of bastardy;

for we are not left in doubt that man's will is free or that the evil he does brings retribution in this life.

The number of the soliloquies in which this engaging villain takes the audience into his confidence is as remarkable as their length and quality. In oratory he is a Nestor and in sly diplomacy a Ulysses:

> I can add colours to the chameleon,
> Change shapes with Proteus for advantages,
> And set the murderous Machiavel to school.

In artful humour Shakespeare plotted his play to show off his character's exceptional gifts, as in the wooing of Anne, widow of the murdered Prince of Wales, upon which Richard justly prides himself ('Was ever woman in this humour won?'), the serio-comic scene in which with Buckingham as go-between Richard affects reluctance in accepting the offer of the throne from the Lord Mayor of London and the citizens, the scene in which he succeeds (if he does succeed) in persuading Queen Elizabeth to further his suit to her daughter and his niece (wife-to-be of Henry VII). He is a play-actor who can be all things to all men and to all women too. Except in soliloquy he is always acting a part, even in the company of his confederate in crime, Buckingham, also capable of gracing his stratagems by acting the 'deep tragedian'. The consequence is, as Charles Lamb said, that we 'contemplate a bloody and vicious character with delight'.[1] His jocularity (Lamb's word) distinguishes him from the Senecan tyrants and Machiavellian villains in whom his origins have been sought. It is a jocularity that deserts him after the murder of the princes in the Tower (IV. iii). 'I have not that alacrity of spirit Nor cheer of mind that I was wont to have' (V. iii). This trait brings together two great artists, for in his unfinished life of Richard transmitted to Shakespeare by Hall and Holinshed Sir Thomas More had noted that after the murder Richard

> neuer had a quiet mind. . . . He neuer thought himselfe sure. Where he went abroad, his eies whirled about, his bodie priuilie fensed, his hand euer vpon his dagger, his countenance and maner like one alwaies readie to strike againe, he tooke ill rest a nights, . . . rather

---

[1] 'On G. F. Cooke in *Richard III*', *Miscellaneous Prose*, ed. E. V. Lucas (1912), p. 43.

The English History Play

slumbered than slept, troubled with fearefull dreames, . . . so was his restlesse heart continuallie tossed and tumbled with the tedious impression and stormie remembrance of his abhominable deed.[1]

In this play Shakespeare is following for the first time in the footsteps of a great writer. As the dangers close in upon him Richard's temper becomes shorter and shorter. But his courage endures to the end, shaken only momentarily by his dream. Perhaps it is the courage that believes with Seneca's Medea that 'Fortuna fortes metuit, ignavos premit', and with Machiavelli that Fortune submits to power, beliefs at odds with Innocent III's 'O Vanity, then, what reason has man to be so insolent?' There is no conflict of mind. Here is the only play of Shakespeare's of which it is possible to say that 'character is destiny'. Whatever Richard has sown he reaps with mathematical precision in that highly symmetrical scene in which the ghosts of eleven of his victims curse him and bless Henry of Richmond. There was never so moral an ending nor one that more faithfully observes the canons of poetical justice.

'A great sprawling melodrama' says R. L. Stevenson. Melodrama it is in action and in speech, but while the play is long, one of Shakespeare's longest, it does not sprawl. It is planned with as much artifice as (say) *The Rape of Lucrece* and *Titus Andronicus*. Artifice, audacious artifice, marks the three scenes which have been mentioned above. We may call them *tours de force* with all that implies of grudging admiration. Artifice is the mark of the ghosts. Artifice constructs the characters, with no half-lights, no enigmas, all brilliantly but mechanically conceived, all wrought according to plan, with plenty of surprises for the spectators but none (one imagines) for the dramatist. And artifice lies behind the verse. In this play and in *2* and *3 Henry VI* stichomythia, the formal antiphons, the elaborate examples of anaphora in Henry's soliloquy on the battlefield, the tangles of verbal wit, these and many other figures show how in these early years he dallied with words and word-schemes as if captivated by the shapes into which they might be made to fall. He had now learned a technique ready for any call

[1] Holinshed (1587), p. 735.

that might be made upon it. What remained was for technique to look like nature because it had become second nature.

Already images crowd upon him. Like his contemporaries he is fond of drawing homiletic similes from nature, some proverbial, some so used that they assume the authority of proverbs. 'Constant dropping will wear the stone', which he used no less than eleven times, 'Smooth runs the water where the brook is deep', 'Doves are driven from their houses by stench', 'Every cloud engenders not a storm'. Sometimes these come in clusters and seem to serve as mere amplification, not yet transformed into metaphor but hooked on with an 'as' or a 'so'. Yet in spite of artifice the verse seldom lacks life and movement. The diction skirts without loss of dignity the edge of popular idiom, and while this early verse is as yet single-moulded, how superbly within his limits can the poet manage a crescendo or a rallentando, enforcing his meaning upon ear and mind by transposition or omission of stress, and in the last line making 'the dead bones' live.

> Methought that Gloucester stumbled, and in falling
> Struck me, that thought to stay him, overboard
> Into the tumbling billows of the main.
> O Lord, methought what pain it was to drown,
> What dreadful noise of waters in my ears,
> What sights of ugly death within my eyes!
> Methoughts I saw a thousand fearful wrecks,
> A thousand men that fishes gnaw'd upon,
> Wedges of gold, great anchors, heaps of pearl,
> Inestimable stones, unvalued jewels,
> All scatt'red in the bottom of the sea;
> Some lay in dead men's skulls, and in the holes
> Where eyes did once inhabit there were crept,
> As 'twere in scorn of eyes, reflecting gems,
> That woo'd the slimy bottom of the deep
> And mock'd the dead bones that lay scatt'red by.
> (*Richard III*, I. iv. 18)

(iv)

Among the non-Shakespearian plays which belong to the early fifteen-nineties are several which in one way or another are related,

The English History Play 23

or may be related, to the work of Shakespeare. Of these the most interesting are *Edward II, Edward III, Thomas of Woodstock,* and *The Troublesome Reign of King John,* all anonymous except for Marlowe's play: to these must be added *Sir Thomas More* which is *sui generis.* It is believed that *Edward II* followed *2* and *3 Henry VI* mainly because the two passages in Part 2 and one in Part 3 which resemble passages in *Edward II* were suggested to Shakespeare by the chronicles for the reigns of Henry VI and Edward IV, whereas there are no corresponding passages in the chronicles of Edward II's reign which might have suggested these passages to Marlowe. If then *Edward II* was written between *3 Henry VI* and *Richard III* we may say that so far as we know Shakespeare was the first popular dramatist to give dignity and coherence to the play on English history, and Marlowe the first to choose an English theme which could be shaped into the pattern of orthodox tragedy.

When Marlowe chose Edward II for his protagonist, he chose a hero very different from his Tamburlaine or Faustus or Jew, very different also from the chief character in his play on contemporary troubles in France, *The Massacre at Paris,* a play so maimed in the reporting that criticism can only guess at the dramatist's intention and achievement. (But it is clear that the Guise, like other Marlovian heroes, was presented as a character of towering ambition and masterful intellect.) In *Edward II* Marlowe's purpose, like Shakespeare's in *Richard II*, was to illuminate weakness, not strength. Both kings expend themselves on unworthy favourites, forfeit the allegiance of exasperated nobles, are driven to reluctant abdication, and at the end are murdered in the prisons they are condemmed to. In both characters there is change, but the change is not so much in them as in our feeling towards them as we see them passing from the cruelty and selfishness of power to the helplessness and suffering of powerlessness. In Marlowe this switch to pity is not accomplished without some violence done to the character of Edward's queen as she becomes the *inamorata* of Mortimer, and the character of Mortimer is not revealed with that steady light which searches the motives of Bolingbroke from start to finish. There is much in the play about the divinity which should protect an anointed king, but it is less prominent and less effective than in

Richard II. Yet it would not be true to say that Marlowe was not concerned with moral issues. Both Mortimer and his love become 'Machiavels' in the fourth act, and Marlowe does not spare them. Mortimer alone calls upon Fortune. At the height of his power he boasts that he makes Fortune's wheel turn as he pleases, and quotes from Ovid the line *Major sum quam cui possit fortuna nocere*. And when Edward's murder is brought home to him and he sees that his end is in sight, there is no moral compunction but mere acquiescence in the decree of an arbitrary fate:

> Base Fortune, now I see, that in thy wheel
> There is a point, to which when men aspire,
> They tumble headlong down: that point I touch'd,
> And, seeing there was no place to mount up higher,
> Why should I grieve at my declining fall?
> Farewell, fair Queen: weep not for Mortimer,
> That scorns the world, and as a traveller
> Goes to discover countries yet unknown.

In *Edward II* the writing is more subdued than is usual with Marlowe, and there are few of the ardours and exaltations which distinguish his other plays. Here lies one of the great distinctions between *Edward II* and *Richard II*, the first play of Shakespeare's which is irrigated by lyricism. Not unrelated to this distinction is another: that Marlowe's is an altogether grimmer world, a world of evil and corruption deeper and darker than that of *Richard II*. Compassion did not come easily to Marlowe, and there is a cruelty in the last scenes not found in Shakespeare. In *Richard II* every sort of alleviation is offered. Richard is brought face to face with his accusers, and allowed to indulge himself in scenes which make him at once the playboy and the poet of the English kings. He takes affectionate farewell of his queen—a very different Isabel from Edward's. In place of Mortimer we have Bolingbroke. And at the end no passive submission, but death in courageous action. Shakespeare's compassion is nowhere more evident than in his invention of the faithful groom of the stable and the talk with his master about 'roan Barbary', when king and groom share a common humanity. There is no groom in Marlowe; instead, the invention

The English History Play 25

of a murderer, named Lightborn with a stroke of sardonic humour after a medieval devil, the quintessence of all that Englishmen had heard or dreamt of Italianate villainy.

Contrast a play written between 2 *Henry VI* (c. 1591) and *Richard II* (c. 1594) and variously known as *Richard II*, Part 1, and *Thomas of Woodstock*. The play is about the young king's extravagance and choice of unscrupulous favourites, and how evils flowing from the fountain-head, a vicious court, affect every subject in the realm. The leading figure is the king's uncle, Thomas of Woodstock, unhistorically presented as Protector, and the play leads up to his murder. The author is not known, but he is not Shakespeare or Marlowe or any other university wit, for he has neither eloquence (the rhetoric of the schools) nor poetry, and the little ornament is of the plainest kind, usually simple analogies between human and external nature. Woodstock is presented as Plain Thomas, plain in dress, plain and bluff in speech, obviously a character congenial to its maker: on one occasion Woodstock is mistaken for his groom by an Osric-like courtier. The bluff aristocrat is no show and all substance: the king's upstart favourites—Bagot, Bushy, Greene—are all show and no substance. Some scenes, especially those in which the unscrupulous Lord Chief Justice Tresilian's unscrupulous clerk Nimble appears—are indistinguishable from the morality-play scenes in which Lupton and others attacked bribery and corruption. In these scenes there is low comedy, but it is far from breeding laughter for laughter's sake. The dramatist's patriotism is in his social conscience, a conscience that takes stock of all classes of society, the farmer, the labourer, the Queen herself (Anne of Bohemia), who with the ladies of her court runs a sewing-meeting to supply garments for those impoverished by the king's extravagances. The manuscript in which the play survives is a prompt-copy bearing evidence of wear and tear in the theatre, and the popularity is not surprising. It is in no sense revolutionary, but its attitude cannot be reconciled with the view that opposition to any king, even a tyrant king, is wicked. It calls for fair play between king and subject, and does so in plain, lucid, and vigorous exposition. Other popular ingredients are the low comedy, the premonitions and omens of misfortune, battle, and two ghosts—Edward III and the Black Prince—who warn son and brother of his impending murder.

Very different is *Edward III*, no tragedy but a patriotic chronicle play which glorifies the success of English arms against Scotland and France (Sluys, Crécy, Poitiers, the siege of Calais). The last three acts are battle pieces in which the misguided French are punished for resisting the benefits freely offered by the invading English. The repudiation of the Salic law in I. i anticipates a scene in *Henry V* and serves, as in the later play, to justify invasion. In these scenes there are occasional parallels with Shakespeare's early work, especially in the passages where the alarums of war yield to moral comment and quiet reflection, yet they are not striking enough to be more than coincidental. The scenes in which the infatuated Edward woos the virtuous Countess of Salisbury in the absence of her husband at the wars (I. ii, II. i and ii)—the story is in Painter, from Bandello, from Froissart—break the back of the play, if a chronicle history can be said to have a back, and an occasional reference to Edward's amorousness later in the play does not bring them into a unity. But the fault must be condoned, for here (especially in II. i), in *Sir Thomas More*, and in *The Two Noble Kinsmen* we have, if anywhere outside the canon, the hand of Shakespeare.

This dramatist found this theme in Froissart and in Painter's *Palace of Pleasure* (novel 46), but the themes that military glory and love of women, and true kingship and adulterous love are incompatible were widely disseminated and had often been presented on the stage. If a historian wished to find an example of the different levels at which a popular dramatist might appeal to a popular audience, he could hardly find a better than the contrast between these countess scenes and the scene in *George a Green* in which King James threatens the wife of Sir John a Barley. The verse in *George a Green* is simple to drabness, and any dramatic effect the scene may have it owes to the situation, not to the words: the wife besieged in her castle, her young son in the king's power, the rescue in the nick of time. In *Edward III* the drama is fully expressed in the words and the suspense depends wholly upon character. The long II. i (459 lines) gives room for admirable play between the king and the king's poet vainly trying to find words to satisfy his master's conception of the countess's beauty, also for the indignation of the countess and later her father as intelligence of the king's meaning dawns upon them. The language is at times early Shakespearian, most strikingly in the line 'Lillies that fester smel far worse then weeds' (Sonnet 94). Images like

> Decke an Ape
> In tissue, and the beautie of the robe
> Adds but the greater scorne vnto the beast (II. i. 443)

which appear here and later in Shakespeare carry little weight as a pointer to authorship because they embroider ancient proverbial wisdom; but a few image clusters or groups of unconsciously associated words common to this play and Shakespeare are significant. What above all brings Shakespeare to mind is the moral tact with which a situation of great delicacy is presented. These scenes transport us from the history play altogether to that better land which lies on the border of comedy and tragedy.

Another type of history play which flourished in the nineties is the biographical play presenting scenes from the life of some famous Englishman not of royal blood. The chronicle history of a commoner is as episodic as the chronicle history of a king, for (as Aristotle said) infinite are the events which may be chosen from the life of one man. One such play is about the life and death of Captain Thomas Stukeley, a younger son of a Devonshire gentleman whose career reads like an improbable fiction.[1] The swaggering young spendthrift at an Inn of Court is well presented and his 'profluous prodigality' (as Thomas Westcote, the historian of his county, called it);[2] but the text becomes more and more incoherent as we follow his adventures from London to Ireland to Spain to Rome to Morocco. As in the slightly later *Henry V* a chorus apologizes for the limitations of the stage:

> Your gentle fauour must we needs entreat,
> For rude presenting such a royall fight,

[1] *Captain Thomas Stukeley* (1605) was entered in the Stationers' Register in 1600, having been acted by the Admiral's men *c.* 1596. Stukeley had already died on the English stage in Peele's *Battle of Alcazar*, a battle (1578) famous for the death of four kings, three *in re* (Barbary, Morocco, and Portugal) and one *in spe*, Stukeley.

[2] *A View of Devonshire* (1845), p. 271. In his London days he would, as Thomas Heywood put it, 'beat a street before him' (*2 If you Know Me*, 1606, l. 1317).

> Which more imaginatian must supply:
> Then all our vtmost strength can reach vnto.

Two other plays of this type are, one on the life and death of *Thomas Lord Cromwell*, and one on the life of *Sir John Oldcastle, the good Lord Cobham* (Part 1). Both plays have a strong Protestant bias and both get into the Shakespeare apocrypha. To ascribe the former to any known writer of the time was in Swinburne's view an unwarrantable insult, though it hardly deserves the six successive epithets he hurls at it.[1] There is more, but not much more, to be said for *Oldcastle*, written by Drayton, Munday, Hathway, and Wilson, the only one now extant of the twenty-five plays mentioned in Henslowe's Diary in which Drayton (that poet of all work) was concerned. The chief interest is that it is an attempt by the Admiral's company to present a rival piece to *Henry IV* and *Henry V* of the Chamberlain's men which should show Oldcastle not as Oldcastle–Falstaff but as a courageous and loyal subject of Henry V and a follower of Wyclif. The lost second part must have shown the death of Oldcastle whom John Bale in his Brief Chronicle of 1544 presented as a 'Blessed Martyr of Christ'. The most objectionable character in the play is the Bishop of Rochester. Comic scenes abound, and those in which Sir John the vicar of Wrotham and his concubine and Oldcastle's humorous servant Harpoole appear must have made the groundlings split their sides.

Of all these biographical plays *Sir Thomas More* is the most interesting, not so much for its intrinsic merit as for the three pages of it which are almost certainly in Shakespeare's handwriting. The scribe of the original play before it was tinkered with, and the author or part-author, was Anthony Munday. In *Palladis Tamia* (1598) Francis Meres called him 'our best plotter', but Meres was a euphuist without much discretion, though much must be forgiven him for his informative praise of Shakespeare. It may be that from the early eighties Munday had an important influence but the influence is now untraceable, and to cast Munday as a writer of

---

[1] He stigmatized it as 'utterly shapeless, spiritless, bodiless, soulless, senseless, helpless, worthless rubbish' (*A Study of Shakespeare*, 1880, p. 232). For a discussion of the play see Baldwin Maxwell, *Studies in the Shakespeare Apocrypha* (New York, 1956), pp. 72–108.

The English History Play

scenarios for Shakespeare is a flight of fancy beyond the evidence and beyond all likelihood.

Munday's play in its fair copy dealt with these themes: 'Ill May day' on which the people of London rose in anger against the foreigners in their midst and were pacified by More's oratory (six scenes), 'merry Master More' playing practical jokes on Erasmus and others, More entertaining the Lord Mayor at a banquet, More's fall and death.[1] More is presented most sympathetically— as a great Englishman, not of course as a martyr for his religion.[2] In the revision of the scene in which More pacifies the mob the quality of the writing is immensely superior to the banal simplicities of the original play, and several lines of evidence—handwriting, spelling, vocabulary, thought-sequences, imagery—converge to point to Shakespeare. To borrow a phrase applied by George Chalmers to the *Letters of Junius*, Shakespearian authorship is ascertained from 'a concatenation of circumstances amounting to moral demonstration'. The verse has the movement of dramatic speech and is written by a man who, at any rate for the moment, was a profound believer in an hierarchy of being, a divinely appointed order, and whose command of language and metaphor was such that he could even rejuvenate a proverb.

The manuscript of *Sir Thomas More* raises many difficult problems. There is some indication that it belonged to the Chamberlain's men and the most-favoured date for the original version is *c.* 1590-3 and for the revision 1594-5. About the same time as he was perhaps helping to cobble up his company's *Sir Thomas More*, Shakespeare was writing *King John*, basing it, so orthodox opinion holds, upon *The Troublesome Reign of King John* published in 1591 in two parts, parts which are not structural but a mere publisher's contrivance.[3]

---

[1] Henry VIII appears neither here nor in *Cromwell*. He is prominent in Samuel Rowley's play *When you see me you Know me*, but this was not acted till 1604 when Henry's daughter was safely in her grave.

[2] So, Gabriel Harvey could speak of 'owr Sir Thomas More' and bracket him with Tully as 'full of his conceytid jestes and merrimentes' and with Socrates as 'a continual Ironist . . . in the sweetist & finist kinde' (*Marginalia*, ed. G. C. Moore Smith, 1913, pp. 113 and 155); and still nearer to More's time Thomas Wilson, like Munday and Harvey an ardent Protestant, said that More, like Socrates, excelled in metaphor, 'a man for his witte very singulare' (*The Rule of Reason*, 1551, U5).

[3] This edition is exceptional in containing addresses to the Reader. Of plays written for the public stage *Tamburlaine* (1590) alone is earlier in this respect.

In style the play is pedestrian, being not so much a tissue of lines stolen from Marlowe and others as a composition embracing the clichés of idea and language common to all dramatic writers of that date, and indulging at some length the popular taste for debate and lament, with here and there a Latin tag. It boldly disregards historic time, and Holinshed's chronicle history of King John will be searched in vain for an Arthur who is a child or for the characters of Austria, Hubert, and above all Faulconbridge, the bastard of Richard I. The sequence of scenes is much the same in both plays, though the sequence of events within each scene is often different and always better in Shakespeare whether for sense or character or action. There is more historical detail in *The Troublesome Reign* not used by Shakespeare than vice versa. While there is some identity of language, only two lines are exactly identical. To quote these lines is to quote characteristic examples of the kind of language which these plays have in common. They are: 'Poictiers, and Anjou, these five provinces' (II. i. 528) and 'For that my grandsire was an Englishman' (V. iv. 42).

The belief that *The Troublesome Reign* is earlier than *King John* has recently been challenged, and the view argued that it is later and an endeavour to supply a makeshift play for a rival company (the Queen's players).[1] To this view there are two grave objections. If the author of the play knew Shakespeare's play so well that he could remember the plot and the sequence of the scenes and some of the words, if as some maintain he was a chronic imitator only differing from the magpie in that he pilfered without hoarding, how is it that he did not remember any of the language which we think of as characteristically Shakespearian, only colourless matter-of-fact words like those quoted above? One metaphor of the authentic stamp would suffice to convince us, or one collocation of two or three words ordinary enough by themselves yet startlingly effective in marriage, or one cadence that can come only from a man with a genius for musical phrasing. But it is not there. Another objection is that we make hay of Shakespearian chronology as generally accepted if we assign *King John* to so early a date as 1590. The play

---

[1] Notably by Professor Peter Alexander and by the editor of the New Arden edition of *King John*, E. A. J. Honigmann.

The English History Play

is indeed mixed in style and there are parts of it which might be early. Conceivably, *The Troublesome Reign* is based on an early play, perhaps an early Shakespearian play, which Shakespeare turned into our *King John* in 1594–5. But this is to lose oneself 'among the thorns and dangers' of a speculative world. No rewriting of single speeches, no mere process of touching-up, will account for the steady, subtle development of the character of the Bastard. Here is one who begins like a Richard III with an eye to 'commodity' and personal ambition and with something of the same bluff, hearty manner of speech; but here is one who sees the worst, seems to approve of it, and chooses the best. He brings humanity to a world of corrupt politics and marriage barters. And the ennoblement of character goes hand in hand with the ennoblement of speech which never falls into oratorical cliché and the verbal posturings of his betters, but even at its most authoritative and moving adheres to simple colloquial diction, whether in the ironical 'Your sword is bright, sir; put it up again' (IV. iii. 79), which is only comparable to Othello's 'Keep up your bright swords, for the dew will rust them', or in the words to Hubert after the discovery of Arthur's body (IV. iii. 125):

> if thou didst but consent
> To this most cruel act, do but despair;
> And if thou want'st a cord, the smallest thread
> That ever spider twisted from her womb
> Will serve to strangle thee; a rush will be a beam
> To hang thee on; or, wouldst thou drown thyself,
> Put but a little water in a spoon,
> And it shall be as all the ocean,
> Enough to stifle such a villain up.
> I do suspect thee very grievously.

The gentleman reader of *The Troublesome Reign*, part 1, is asked to entertain this play about a Christian as courteously as he received the Scythian Tamburlaine; it is a play, he is told, about a Christian (John) who set himself against 'the Man of Rome' (the Pope) till deceived by 'a damned wight' (the monk of Swinstead). To some extent this misrepresents the play, for while the anti-Catholic bias is strong and John is shown as the defender of the liberties civil and religious of the English people, he is also exposed —as not by Tyndale and Bale[1]—as morally corrupt. In Shakespeare there is little anti-Catholic bias and although the play leads up to the death of John, he is not cast as the champion of England or as a tragic hero. He is not spared the deep damnation of Arthur's death. The play's main preoccupations are not expressed through the personal tragedy of any one character, but what makes it a searching inquiry into the motives of kings and politicians is the presence of Faulconbridge; his presence changes the angle from which the play is to be seen as much as does the presence of Falstaff in *Henry IV*. To him is given the moral at the end, and it is spoken before the young Henry III and the now concordant nobles. It is a moral which the English people have been pleased to remember in times of crisis. In prose it had appeared more than once just before the Armada: 'our realme . . . was neuer conquered by any, so long as it was true within it selfe.'[2]

(v)

By its subject-matter *King John* stands apart from the first cycle of the Histories (*1–3 Henry VI, Richard III*) and from the second (*Richard II, 1, 2 Henry IV, Henry V*): by the maturity of its style and characterization it belongs to the second cycle rather than the first. In the interval between the writing of *Richard III* and *Richard II*, we may suppose Shakespeare had been writing comedy and his solitary early example of romantic tragedy, *Romeo and Juliet*. When he returned to history it was to a subject that like *Richard III* fell into the shape of a tragedy. In one respect he went out of his way to destroy the unity of theme academic theory demanded for tragedy. The life-blood of the main plot is concerned with the fortunes and misfortunes and the death of the king and does not circulate through the sub-plot of Aumerle's treachery to Bolingbroke; yet much of this, and especially the character of Aumerle's mother, is of his own invention. While the episode is often omitted from modern performances, the juxtaposition of two such markedly

---

[1] Bale's idealization of John was anticipated by Tyndale in his *Obedience of a Christian Man* (1528), and by the author of *A Proper Dialogue between a Gentleman and a Husbandman* (?Antwerp, 1530).

[2] G. D., *Brief Discovery* (1588), sig. R3ᵛ.

The English History Play

individual characters as York and his duchess pleading against and for the life of their son is dramatically exciting, and Bolingbroke, now Henry IV, acquires near the play's end (v. iii) a little of the credit of which he stands sorely in need.

Shakespeare's choice fell upon a king wholly dissimilar from Richard III but closely resembling Edward II. Marlowe's Edward and Shakespeare's Richard are fundamentally weak, characters not with a chink in their armour but with no armour at all. Both are like Lear who 'did ever but slenderly know himself', but unlike Lear they never arrive at self-knowledge. The gist of Richard's soliloquies is that man is the sport of Fortune and between conduct and fate there is no link. So in his farewell to his queen: 'I am sworn brother, sweet, To grim Necessity; and he and I Will keep a league till death' (v. i. 20). So he rails at Fortune, analyses and self-dramatizes his own sorrows, and remains oblivious of the causes of his sorrows. These causes lie in the play for all to find, but they are presented dramatically. No doubt Shakespeare believed less in Fortune than did his characters, but he makes no explicit judgement. To what a different world belongs the verdict of John Foxe on Richard!

It so fell, not by the blinde wheele of fortune, but by the secret hand of him which directeth all estates: that as he first began to foresake the maintaining of the Gospell of God, so the Lord beganne to foresake him.[1]

Shakespeare never writes a *drame à thèse*. On forms of government and on political theory he does not pronounce, but on the motives that inspire rulers and politicians he throws a searching light without doing so ostensibly. The belief that to oppose the Lord's anointed under any circumstances is impious is central to the play: indeed, the words 'anointed' and 'sacred' run through the play like a refrain. Yet Shakespeare, for the moment at any rate the disinterested artist, can balance two opposite and discordant views. 'Not all the water in the rough rude sea Can wash the balm off from an anointed king', says Richard (III. ii. 54), but he fails to profit from the counsel which the faithful Bishop of Carlisle gives him in the

---

[1] *Acts and Monuments* (1632 edn.), i. 669 a.

same scene—'The means that heaven yields must be embrac'd And not neglected', and again, 'My lord, wise men ne'er sit and wail their woes, But presently prevent the ways to wail.'

A belief in a divinely appointed hierarchy of society and in the wickedness of rebellion against a lawful sovereign, though most topical by reason of the fear of Spain and the uncertainty about the Queen's successor, had been firmly held by Tyndale and Bale, and the tenth homily on good order and obedience to rulers and magistrates was appointed to be read in churches from 1571. These beliefs had already appeared in Shakespeare, and the 'Tudor Myth' preached by Polydore Vergil and Edward Hall—that Henry IV's sin of usurpation and murder was only expiated by the accession of Henry VII—receives mention, if a rather muted mention, in *Richard III*. In *Richard II* the wickedness of destroying the Lord's anointed is a major theme. Is it lawful to make a choice between a king unfit to rule and a usurper fit to rule? Orthodoxy said no, and especially are those damned who resist tyrants, for tyrants come from God who sends them to punish the sins of the wicked.[1] Another dramatist might well have blackened the character of Bolingbroke. Shakespeare represents him as initially loyal, and not till Richard offers him the crown does he announce his intention of accepting it. Near the end he is shown as twice merciful—to Aumerle and to Carlisle. Put beside Northumberland he seems an angel of light. Upon his conscience, however, lies the prompting of Richard's murder. The point that obedience to God's deputy is due only so far as he acts as God's deputy is not put by Shakespeare, nor is it implicit in the play. Rather, the act of deposition, however necessary, brings a dreadful retribution, and in the courageous and eloquent prophecy of Carlisle (IV. i) spoken 'Lest child, child's children, cry against you woe', the evil consequences are seen passing from generation to generation. If in this play Bolingbroke is a confident and efficient man of action, in a later play we see him a broken and dying king conscious of the 'by-paths and indirect crook'd ways' by which he acquired his crown; and even the warrior-hero Henry V remembers in his prayer before Agincourt 'the fault My father made in compassing the crown'.

[1] Cf. Whetstone, *The English Mirror* (1586), p. 202.

Raleigh, writing in the reign of James I, not in the reign of Elizabeth, took the sin back to the cruelty of Edward III and forward to the cruelty of Henry VIII: he observed that all Henry's children died without increase and James I by waiting his time received the crown at God's hand! The belief in a divinely appointed order to which it was man's duty to submit was still in 1688 a cause for which many gave up fame and fortune.

Of all Shakespeare's plays this has the least trace of comedy. A touch of flippancy in the king's comments on Gaunt's approaching death is the nearest approach to laughter, and this is far from being laughter for its own sake. Nor is there any prose, not even in the form of stage property, such as a letter or proclamation: nothing like the Cade scenes in *2 Henry VI* or the murderers in *Richard III*. Even the conversation of the two gardeners with themselves and with the queen is serious and in verse. The scene is Shakespeare's own amplification of an ancient and popular parable or 'semblance' of which Erasmus's treatment (englished by Baldwin in 1547) is characteristic:

> Euen as a good Gardyner is very diligent about his gardeyn, waterynge the good and profitable herbes, and rootynge out the vnprofytable weedes: so shoulde a kyng attende to his common weale, cheryshyng his good and true subiectes, and punyshyng suche as are false, and vnprofitable.[1]

The scene was not suggested to Shakespeare by any one source but by many. Good examples of his inventiveness are the sympathetic study of Gaunt, which discredits most vividly the young king and his minions, and the characters of Isabel, historically only a child, and the groom, their devotion bringing to Richard's last hours a humanity so absent from Marlowe's play. The tragedy covers historically a brief two years (1398-1400) and Holinshed is the main source. The most interesting of other possible sources is Daniel's epic *Civil Wars*, entered in October 1594 and printed in 1595; the doubt is whether the debt is Shakespeare's or Daniel's.

In all the plays which we may suppose Shakespeare to have written at this time—*Richard II, Romeo and Juliet, A Midsummer*

---

[1] *A Treatise of Moral Philosophy* (1547), Q5.

Night's Dream, so many-sided was his genius—there is a strong lyrical element. The intimacy and seeming spontaneity of Richard's soliloquies reveal the poet, never neglectful of structure and character yet revelling in the fertility of his imagination and the unity of hand, heart, and head all working together for good. And with this lyrical grace goes a greater variation of cadence and very often the mellifluousness of rhyme. He continues to delight in elaborate figures of speech, taking still a virtuoso's pleasure in playing with words and word schemes to create delightful patterns. When he wrote *Love's Labour's Lost*, perhaps in 1594 just before *Richard II*, he laughed at these 'dulcet diseases', this 'spruce affectation', and seemed to be deriding his own excesses; but he had not worked them out of his system, and perhaps he never quite did. A particular favourite is the polyptoton or the repetition of words derived from the same root, well named by Puttenham 'the translacer'. "'Tis true 'tis pity; and pity 'tis 'tis true' said Polonius, and dismissed the figure as foolish. It was mainly responsible for the unsettling of Don Quixote's wits, and some commentators may have spared the knight a thought in their attempts to thread the labyrinth of Shakespeare's word-play. Not unrelated is the pun, and comic dialogue in Shakespeare's time and sometimes in ours is sustained by a series of verbal quibbles. 'How every fool can play upon the word!' But the rich ambiguities of the language were not used merely for fun. 'Gaunt am I for the grave, gaunt as a grave' says Gaunt, provoking Richard's 'Can sick men play so nicely with their names?' and Gaunt's answer, 'No, misery makes sport to mock itself.' To this use of language we can accommodate ourselves and can grant the truth of Coleridge's remark that a play upon words such as Gaunt's, or Lady Macbeth's play on 'gild' and 'guilt', is an 'effectual intensive of passion'. It is harder to adjust ourselves to passages of elaborate and (to us) frigid conceit. In *King John* the contrast between this style and the vigorous straightforward speech of Faulconbridge seems deliberate; an extreme example is the number of changes Cardinal Pandulphus rings upon the verb 'to swear' (III. i. 263 ff.) in an admirable speech of casuistry. Elsewhere it is used for passages meant to be most moving, as with the farewells of Richard and his queen:

The English History Play

Rich. . . . One kiss shall stop our mouths, and dumbly part;
Thus give I mine, and thus take I thy heart.
Queen. Give me mine own again; 'twere no good part
To take on me to keep and kill thy heart.
So, now I have mine own again, be gone,
That I may strive to kill it with a groan.
Rich. We make woe wanton with this fond delay.
Once more, adieu; the rest let sorrow say.

Some have conjectured that the mixture of styles is due to the mixture of scenes revised and unrevised, late work and early work, but there is no good evidence contradicting the view that every one of Shakespeare's plays, or almost every one, was written at one go.

In *1* and *2 Henry IV* we reach the peak of Shakespeare's achievement in the history play and this in spite of the fact that he has moved away from tragedy to the looser form of the chronicle play. Although the death of the king is reported in the last act of the second part, the canvas is too wide, the interests too dispersed, for us to think of tragedy. But dispersed as the interests are, they are interrelated and work upon each other: the nemesis which pursues the care-worn Henry IV until death releases him from the crown he once so ardently desired; the patriotic and political interest which Shakespeare's audience would take in the representation upon the stage of the evils of civil discord; power politics and their effect upon all involved in them; the clash between character and character, Shakespeare in defiance of history making Hotspur and Hal of an age for this purpose; the conflict not only between different temperaments (as with Hotspur and Glendower) but between different attitudes to life (as with Falstaff and the characters from history); the incidental satire on such 'poor abuses of the time' as cony-catching, highway robbery, the league between inns and robbers, eating flesh in Lent, bribery and corruption of recruiting officers and justices. Perhaps, wrote Johnson,

no author has ever in two plays afforded so much delight. The great events are interesting, for the fate of kingdoms depends upon them; the slighter occurrences are diverting, and, except one or two, sufficiently probable; the incidents are multiplied with wonderful fertility of invention, and the characters diversified with the utmost nicety of discernment, and the profoundest skill in the nature of man.

Coleridge suggested that Shakespeare's approval of characters may be judged by the 'truth and vivacity with which he describes them and enters into their feelings'; if so then Shakespeare identified himself in Part 1 with Hotspur and Falstaff and in *King John* with Faulconbridge. Perhaps when he created Faulconbridge his imagination was already trembling on the brink of Hotspur and Falstaff, and, as Middleton Murry put it, the Bastard may have divided by an imaginative fission 'into the cynical critic of honour and its idolator; his bluntness and bravery into Harry Percy, his wit and his humour into Jack Falstaff'. How disinterested is the art of a man who could identify himself so completely with two such contrasting characters! Few of his critics have tried to be so disinterested. Either they have taken sides against Prince Henry and found the rejection of Falstaff at the end of Part 2 brutal and offensive—remembering maybe the old rhyme 'Perhaps it was right to dissemble your love, But why did you kick me downstairs?' —or they have insisted that Falstaff gets his deserts and that we are carefully prepared for his fate by the Prince's soliloquy at the end of the short scene (Part 1, I. ii) in which he and Falstaff make their first appearance. To Bergson one of the characteristics of the comic character is that he slackens in the attention that is due to life and abandons social convention; and our impulse is, for a short time at any rate, to join in the game. Falstaff, as James Joyce observed, 'was not a family man'.[1] He gave no hostages to fortune. The black ox never trod upon *his* foot. To make his rogueries less attractive, as in some recent productions, by deliberately playing him down, lest we should enjoy him more than we should, is even more objectionable than to expend a sentimental pity over his suppression. Apart altogether from the Prince's soliloquy we are given sufficient warning that Falstaff is to be banished the new king's company. There should be no surprise and no shock.

'But Falstaff, unimitated, unimitable Falstaff, how shall I describe thee?' cries Johnson in perhaps the only exclamatory question in his

---

[1] *Ulysses* (Paris, 1922), p. 198.

commentary on Shakespeare; and he proceeds to ask why it is that a character loaded with faults which naturally produce contempt should make himself necessary to the prince and to draw the moral that 'no man is more dangerous than he that with a will to corrupt, hath the power to please'. Taking their cue perhaps from Hal's abusive reference to Falstaff as 'that reverend vice' some modern critics have compared Falstaff to the Vice of the morality play; but the term is so abusive because it is so untrue. He bears only the most superficial resemblance to the Vice, whether to the grimmer Vice of the earlier morality plays or to the merely mischievous and wholly comic Vice of the later. If he had been a Vice, or if he had resembled the prince's boon companions in *The Famous Victories of Henry the Fifth*, we could have parted with him much earlier than we do, and without a pang. As Maurice Morgann saw, his character is compounded of many paradoxes. He is old, yet ever pretending to be young. He is a coward, who never loses his presence of mind. His words of repentance are never translated into deeds, the sanctimoniousness of some of his sentiments being quickly counterbalanced by the hilarity of others, and whether sanctimonious or hilarious always surprising us by their wit and unexpectedness. A knight hob-nobbing with princes, he is also a cony-catcher living by his wits. Surrounded by men who would sacrifice their lives for ambition or honour, he cares for nothing but good fellows, sack, and sugar. The corpulence of his body is at odds with the dexterity of his mind, and in nothing is he more unlike his namesake in *The Merry Wives of Windsor* than in the skill with which he extricates himself from tight corners. He speaks not in the tumbling verse of the Vice, but in a colloquial prose that is fully expressive of all the quirks and poses of the character his maker endows him with.

Shakespeare's historical knowledge for *1* and *2 Henry IV* and *Henry V* is predominantly from Holinshed, but in comparison with what he invented his debt seems small. As slight is his debt to *The Famous Victories of Henry the Fifth*, printed in 1598. This edition may not be the first, for a play of the same title had been entered to the same printer-publisher (Thomas Creede) on 14 May 1594, the year in which the Queen's company who acted the play ceased to have a London career. Whether to this text, or to a fuller and better text now lost, Shakespeare owed something—little in *1 Henry IV*, more in *2 Henry IV*, most in *Henry V*. The older play is an extreme example of the biographical history play, beginning with the prince's riotous youth in company with Oldcastle (the original name of Shakespeare's Falstaff) and others as highway robbers at Gadshill and frequenters of the tavern in Eastcheap, the king's grief over his son's prodigality and the death-bed reconciliation, the coronation and repudiation of his old companions, Agincourt, and the wooing of 'sweet Kate'. But for the strong likelihood that the text of 1598 is a mere reprint of one of 1594, we might suppose that here and there the anonymous author or compiler pieced out his botched text with memories of Shakespeare's play—for example— 'God knowes my sonne, how hardly I came by it [the crown], and how hardly I haue maintained it'. But the differences between the plays are enormous and in nothing more striking than in Shakespeare's care to present a prince loose rather than corrupt.

Some have supposed that the old play in its original form was in two parts, and Professor Harold Jenkins has made and plausibly argued the suggestion that Shakespeare at first intended the two parts of *Henry IV* to be one.[1] Until the middle of Part 1 the doom of Falstaff, the doom of Hotspur, and the reformation of the prince are all in sight. The death of Henry IV and the new king's coronation might then have come hard after the battle of Shrewsbury, as they do in Daniel's *Civil Wars*, where also the prince and Hotspur are made of an age. But they come a play later. We are shown the quelling of a second rebellion, and the prince is permitted 'to go again through the cycle of riot and reform' and Falstaff once more to pursue his cony-catching way in town and country. Falstaff suffers a little by the postponement of his banishment. He can hardly be the same Falstaff because there is no Hotspur to balance him against. He even takes second place in some of the company he finds himself in—the Lord Chief Justice's or Shallow's.

The Shallow scenes are a remarkable example of Shakespeare's art *in minimis*, the art of making the seemingly trivial both comic and poignant. From high politics and a London tavern we are

---

[1] *The Structural Problem in Shakespeare's 'Henry IV'* (1956), Inaugural Lecture at Westfield College, 1955.

The English History Play   41

suddenly transported to a Cotswold house and a conversation between the slow-witted and slow-spoken Silence and the volatile Shallow, two men as incompetent in their office as justices of the peace as Dogberry in his. Yet these characters, their wits rusted by sixty and more summers and winters and soon to fall easy victims to the cony-catcher from Eastcheap, talk inconsequentially about country matters and convey, as is nowhere else conveyed unless it is here and there in Hardy, the feeling for mortality naturally present to the mind of a countryman observant of the passage of the seasons and the life-cycle of crops and animals, not excluding that animal called man. 'How a score of ewes now? . . . And is old Double dead?'

The epilogue to *2 Henry IV* promises to continue the story 'with Sir John in it, and make you merry with fair Katharine of France', but the sequel is not as promised, for Falstaff is dead, his heart 'fracted and corroborate'. Two or three years later Shakespeare revived Falstaff in *The Merry Wives*. If the late tradition (first recorded by Dennis in 1702) that the Queen commanded him to write the comedy is true, perhaps she did so because he broke his promise. In *Henry V* Shakespeare wrote a patriotic play if ever there was one; and if ever man intended a warrior-hero, he did—the only one in his ten plays on English history; and he could not have done so if he had preserved so large-sized an anti-hero as Falstaff. Henry is not to be seen through the eyes of an early-nineteenth-century republican like Hazlitt, or of early-twentieth-century poets like Yeats and Masefield, writing in a century that is hardly famed for patriotic poetry. Holinshed comes nearer to what Shakespeare intended than these do, though he leaves out all the shading the dramatist gives to his sketch:

a maiestie was he that both liued and died a paterne in princehood, a lode-starre in honour, and mirrour of magnificence: the more highlie exalted in his life, the more deepelie lamented at his death, and famous to the world alwaie.[1]

And so, Shakespeare, speaking as dramatist in his own Epilogue:

[1] Holinshed (1587), p. 583.

> In little room confining mighty men,
> Mangling by starts the full course of their glory.
> Small time, but, in that small, most greatly liv'd
> This star of England.

Here, in the prologue, and in four very spirited choruses Shakespeare shows himself conscious of the limitations of his stage (like other dramatists before him, and after him), conscious too that so epic a subject—the celebration of a national hero's exploits—is in some respects intractable to drama, and begs us to eke out the actors' performance with our minds. These speeches whip up the imagination of the spectators and supply gaps in the action. They make a virtue of necessity. Next to the king the chorus is the chief part in the play, and the actor of that part has the speaking of some of the best rhetoric Shakespeare ever wrote. We cannot doubt that as in each chorus he prepares his audience for the scenes that follow it, so he prepares them for the way in which he would have them interpret the characters and the action. It is open to a critic to maintain that Henry's virtues are all commonplace and to withhold respect from one who is so unfailingly successful in all that he undertakes, but not to hold that the 'little touch of Harry in the night' is ironical or that Shakespeare praised the virtues there shown—'cheerful semblance and sweet majesty' among them—with tongue in cheek.

We see Harry in isolation, as we see none of Shakespeare's other kings. There is no clash or contrast of character, for the Dauphin is no Hotspur and Nym no Falstaff. But if Henry's virtues are heroical, he is shown to us as a man among men, a man called to bear upon his shoulders an almost intolerable burden, the welfare of a kingdom. The poignancy of his situation is fully felt in the conversation with the three common soldiers before the battle. Their searching comments upon war and the cant of war are extraordinarily frank. This is how common soldiers at war will talk, in our time or any time.

The Scroop conspiracy, the French wars, Harfleur, Agincourt, the wooing and marriage of Henry and Katharine, the connection between these events is not necessary and inevitable; the unity is one of hero. Two subsidiary inventions fill in the play. The one

The English History Play 43

continues the tavern scenes of *Henry IV* at a lower level—certainly with no danger of distracting the attention from the main business, as there may be in *Henry IV*: Pistol, Bardolph, and Nym are given a longer lease of life. In the Folio list of characters in *2 Henry IV* these with Falstaff are bracketed together as 'Irregular humorists'. This and Nym's catchphrase 'That's the humour of it' may remind us that between *1* and *2 Henry IV* (1597-8) and *Henry V* (1599) was acted Jonson's first humour comedy *Every Man in his Humour* (1598), where all the 'humorists' are 'regular'. The other subsidiary invention is a good example of how Shakespeare may take a conventional theme and make out of it something new and vivid. For generations a common rhetorical exercise was to characterize the qualities of different nations. The number of set pieces in which these are stated —Spain for pride, Germany for drinking, the French for rashness, the Italians for subtlety, the English for gluttony—is countless and all are stereotype and tedious. In *Henry V* Shakespeare passed from rhetoric to drama when he created representatives of the four people of these islands. For the Scot and the Irishman, Jamy and Macmorris, there is no room for dramatic development; Gower the Englishman is a mere foil, though a solid one; but the Welshman Fluellen is one of the great minor figures of drama. 'Though it appear a little out of fashion, There is much care and valour in this Welshman'—Henry's remark is to the credit of both.

With this play Shakespeare ended the series of English history plays which had helped to keep him busy during the fifteen-nineties. He had given a conspectus of English history from the reign of Richard II till the accession of Henry VII. While each play is a dramatic unit, the plays taken collectively have an epic sweep, and we cannot but think of the varieties of kingship presented and of the links between play and play as the sins of the fathers are visited upon the children. The Bishop of Carlisle's curse goes echoing down the generations until it is removed by the establishment of the Tudor dynasty. These plays were a mirror for that age, but they are a mirror for any age, for both rulers and ruled.

The central and continuous image in these plays, [wrote Miss Una Ellis-Fermor in a fine study of Shakespeare's political plays] more specific than a mood, more comprehensive than a character, is, I believe, a composite figure—that of the statesman-king, the leader and public man... The portrait... is the result of a series of explorations, now the study of a failure, now of a partial success; a vast, closely articulated body of thought imaged always in terms of actual character, yet completely incorporated in no one character... It is this which gives coherence to the material of the history plays, which nevertheless remain individual works of art.[1]

To conceive of history in terms of kings was natural to men of that age, natural also to a dramatist who presents history not in terms of political doctrine but of human agents. It follows that the world of the history plays is a man's world, much more than the comedies, more even than the tragedies. The only full-scale character of a woman is that of Margaret, the wife of Henry VI, the only character to appear in all four plays of the first group. We meet her as a young bride in *1 Henry VI*, in *2* and *3 Henry VI* we follow her fortune as she fights the cause of her saintly but ineffective husband and of her son, and in *Richard III* she takes her farewell, an old embittered woman with curses on her lips.

If *Henry V* is Shakespeare's last play about English history—apart from *Henry VIII* which may be only partially his—it is not his last history play. There is good evidence for believing that *Julius Caesar* was his next play: both belong to 1599. The first of the three Roman plays, however, is better regarded as a tragedy than as a history, not because it is grouped as one in the Folio but because it has some of the characteristics of mature Shakespearian tragedy. In Shakespeare's development as a dramatist there is no more sudden and astonishing change. Of all his kings Henry V is the most remote from the tragic spirit. A successful man of action, he is never troubled with doubts or conflict of mind. As he is in public, so he is in private. In *Henry IV*, however, so much more complex in dramatic motive and character, so much richer in the figured texture of its verse, we may find a hint of what is to come, especially in the character of the king and the images that express his tormented mind:

> How many thousand of my poorest subjects
> Are at this hour asleep! O sleep, O gentle sleep,

[1] *The Frontiers of Drama* (1945), pp. 36–7.

> Nature's soft nurse, how have I frighted thee,
> That thou no more wilt weigh my eyelids down,
> And steep my senses in forgetfulness?

But Henry is not at the centre as are Shakespeare's tragic heroes. In *Julius Caesar* we find a tragic hero in the character of Brutus the foundations of whose soul are shaken and torn by dissension within himself as was England within herself during the Wars of the Roses. Now, when Shakespeare's powers are ripe for tragedy, he turns from the tragedy of disorder in the state to the tragedy of disorder in the soul; he turns from Holinshed to Plutarch.

A POSTSCRIPT

THE chronicle history play was in its heyday in the last decade of the century; then, while remaining popular for a time, it went out of fashion. The children's companies who for ten years (1599–1609) were serious rivals to the public stage avoided English chronicle plays. The best dramatists seem to have felt the vein had been exhausted. They turned to other kinds of drama or so transmogrified the history play that it became another kind. Except for *Henry VIII*, Shakespeare abandoned the form after *Henry V* (1599), and when he and Jonson turned to history for tragic material they turned to the ancient Roman world, Chapman to contemporary European history. But if the chronicle play was no longer the vogue, it still appealed to some dramatists writing for some public theatres. And the apologists for the drama continued to point to the beneficial effects of acting plays on English history before the populace. So Thomas Heywood, himself a writer of history plays before and after 1600. He claimed, in his *Apology for Actors* (1612), that history plays had instructed the illiterate in our English chronicles to such good effect that he was a man of weak capacity who could not talk of any notable events from William the Conqueror, nay, from the landing of Brute, to his own time. This sounds a gross exaggeration, yet the titles of plays recorded by Henslowe in his diary suggest many a lost play before and after 'William the conkerer'. More plausibly, he urged that these plays were written with this aim:

> to teach the subjects obedience to their King, to shew the people the vntimely ends of such as haue moued tumults, commotions, and

insurrections, to present them with the flourishing estate of such as liue in obedience, exhorting them to allegeance, dehorting them from all trayterous and fellonious stratagems.[1]

If we look at the extant plays written just before and just after the turn of the century, we find that they were written not for the Chamberlain–King's men but for companies, like the Admiral's– Prince Henry's men, more willing to make concessions to popular taste. Their relation to history is often tenuous, whether because they indulge in unhistorical amplifications or because they elaborate legendary rather than historical characters; they take violent liberties with chronology; and what comedy there is is the comedy of low life. Among the most serious is *Edmond Ironside*,[2] of obscure origin, one of the few that seriously present Anglo-Saxon history in dramatic form. The word 'seriously' is used advisedly. The earlier *A Knack to Know a Knave* (c. 1592) may go to Holinshed for particulars of King Edgar, but in so far as the play is not a morality play it is one of romantic love. Likewise Dekker's *Old Fortunatus* (1599) and his *Welsh Ambassador* (c. 1623) have but a nodding acquaintance with the reign of King Athelstan. It is a little remarkable that we have no play about King Alfred. While the chroniclers are mostly concerned with his battles, they also write of the vision vouchsafed to St. Cuthbert, of his visit to the Danish camp disguised as a minstrel, and of the burning of the cakes. In *Ironside* also there are many battles, so much so that at one point the dramatist throws in his hand and takes refuge in a chorus:

> The waye is longe and I am waxen faint.
> I fain would haue you vnderstand the truth,
> And see the battailes acted on the stage,
> But that theire length wilbe to tedious.
> Then in dumbe shewes I will explaine at large.

This sounds naïve, as naïve as the scene beginning 'Enter at one door the Archbishop of Canterbury, at the other the Archbishop of York' and ending with Canterbury's 'Ile follow thee with Curses and with Clubbes'. Crudeness of another sort is the mutilation of

---

[1] Sig. F3ᵛ.
[2] Preserved in the collection of plays in MS. Egerton 1994.

The English History Play 47

two hostages *coram populo*. Yet the play is not merely naïve and crude. The characters of Edmond and Canute are well defined, the scales are held pretty evenly between the Danes and the English, there is reflection on good government, and while the dramatist was not much of a poet many of his images, often from nature, are freshly observed. The chief character is the slippery ambidexter Edricus. A second part has not survived: it would have shown Edmond's death soon after the division of the kingdom and the punishment of Edricus, Canute fulfilling his promise 'I shall raise thy head above all the lords of England' by hanging him.

Pseudo-historical figures so legendary that invention could be given free reign were popular dramatic material, and among them none more popular, none more legendary, than Robin Hood, for centuries a favourite theme for drama of some kind at May games. Legend conferred a peerage upon him in the sixteenth century, and in *Look about You* (*c.* 1599, printed 1600) he appears as the Earl of Huntingdon, young ward of Prince Richard, not yet Richard I. But anyone who goes to the play for news of the outlaw will be disappointed. The main action is prompted by the enmity to Henry II of two of his sons (Henry and John) and his wife Eleanor (poisoner of fair Rosamond), and especially the enmity of all but Henry II and his son Richard to the good Robert Duke of Gloucester. Several low comedy servants join in a series of disguises so complicated that they become a *cheval de frise* between the reader and the play: nor would the action become much clearer if (as seems unlikely) it were ever given a modern production.

In two other plays, the *Downfall* and the *Death [of Robert Earl of Huntingdon]*, we come nearer, especially in the *Downfall*, to Robin Hood. These plays, as also *Look about You*, belonged to the Admiral's men, and payments to Munday for *1 Robin Hood* and to Chettle for Part 2 are recorded in Henslowe's diary in 1598. In the *Downfall* Richard is now king, but off crusading, and the treacherous John and contumelious Eleanor drive Robin to the woods till the king returns. Here are all Robin's merry men from Friar Tuck to Much the clown, though without many of the traditional gests and jests, and here is Maid Marian, otherwise Matilda, daughter of Lord Fitzwater. Here too are the wicked Sheriff of Nottingham, the more wicked Prior of York, and the most wicked 'Sir Doncaster'. A set-piece in which rural delights are praised above those of the court, written perhaps in the very year of *As You Like It*, was anthologized by Lamb, who missed very little that suited his purpose:

> For the soule-rauishing delicious sound
> Of instrumentall musique, we haue found
> The winged quiristers, with diuers notes,
> Sent from their quaint recording prettie throats,
> On euery braunch that compasseth our bower:
> Without commaund, contenting vs each hower.
> For Arras hangings, and rich Tapestrie,
> We haue sweete natures best imbrothery.
> For thy steele glasse, wherein thou wontst to looke,
> Thy Christall eyes, gaze in a Christall brooke.

Another set-piece is the description of Richard killing his lion in which the epithets 'fier-eyde', 'heart-amazing', 'iron toothed', 'death-threatning' appear in four successive lines. John quaked to hear it. But this sort of play is not to be examined too seriously. It and many another like it were designed not for the scrutiny of a distant posterity but for the amusement of a popular audience in Elizabethan London. A Shakespearian play is a work of art which it is a crime to dislocate, but the *Downfall* has the informality of a pantomime. The part of Friar Tuck is taken by Skelton, the supposed author, who sometimes forgets himself and speaks 'ribble-rabble rhymes Skeltonical'. Much begins a speech in verse but breaks off with, 'I'll speak in prose, I miss this verse vilely.' Of a higher strain is a speech by the plain-dealing Fitzwater (III. i) on the theme: 'The hearts of old gave hands; But our new heraldry is hands, not hearts.'

The second part has a misleading title, *The Death of Robert Earl of Huntingdon*, misleading because Robert is poisoned at the end of the first act, at which point a new play, introduced by three dumb shows, may be said to begin. The plot is the love of the infatuated King John for Matilda, a favourite theme with Michael Drayton and years later to be treated dramatically by Robert Davenport. The *Death* is 'roughhewen out by an vncunning hand: Being of the most materiall points compackt, That with the certainst state of truth doe stand'. So the Epilogue; but the dramatists are, as Drayton said of his epistle, 'much more Poeticall then Historicall', and the play may be dismissed as an inferior tragedy.

Of much the same date is *Edward IV* in two parts, both printed in 1600, both acted by the Earl of Derby's men, and both attributed in great part to Thomas Heywood. Part I in twenty-four loosely connected scenes is made up of three plots which provide variety without unity. Two of these, the rebellion of Thomas Nevill, a bastard son of Lord Falconbridge, and Edward's seduction of Mistress Shore, wife of a London citizen, are fully treated by Hall (and Holinshed). Both are London stories, and the dramatist took pleasure in providing bright authentic detail and in fanning the flames of local patriotism, as when the apprentices put on a bold front—'Although our chines be bare, Our hearts are good'—and after some stiff fighting the rebels are repelled from the city gates. Swashbuckling characters like Falconbridge and Stukeley who believed themselves ordained to glory and applauded such sentiments as 'So I have honour, let me swim in blood' sober citizens must have regarded with fascinated horror. To this plot the Jane Shore plot is precariously attached by the device of making Shore lead the citizens' vanguard: in refusing a knighthood he shows himself as class-proud as George a Green. All this is much in the vein of the trade novels Thomas Deloney was writing at that very time. So too is the third plot for the outline of which we turn not to Hall or Holinshed but to a ballad:

> In Sommer time when leaves grow greene
>   and blossoms bud on every tree,
> King Edward would a hunting ride
>   some pastime for to see.

It is the folk-tale of Edward IV masquerading as the king's butler and hob-nobbing with the honest free-spoken tanner of Tamworth. The dialogue is spirited; and so is the song they sing, for it is Drayton's *Ballad of Agincourt*.

The second part presents the same medley of high life and low life, and as before the high life is not really high. The stage-direction 'Jockie a comic servant is led to whipping over the stage, speaking some words, but of no importance' is too often applicable. The general tone, however, is much more serious than in Part I. The first six scenes relate to Edward's expedition to France and tell how his treaty with Louis XI double-crossed Burgundy who would have double-crossed them. A chorus prepares us for a change of subject. The story of Jane Shore is resumed at the point reached in Part I—her departure for Edward's court and her sorrowful husband's self-banishment. To the theme of her death and his all else is subordinated, the murder of Clarence and the two princes and the accession of Richard III. No opportunity is lost of underlining the miseries of Jane persecuted by the vindictive Richard; and all is due to her weakness in leaving her husband's safe protection instead of tending him and his shop. In this kind of domestic tragedy and in this sort of woman, not evil but weak and passively suffering a punishment in excess of her sin, Heywood delighted. But like Churchyard in his mournful and maudlin monologue of Jane Shore in *The Mirror for Magistrates*, Heywood detains the pathos so long that it becomes rancid. Here is unbridled sentiment intended to communicate a 'handkerchiefly' feeling nearly a century before Colley Cibber's *Love's Last Shift*. Heywood can no more present the woman who prefers death to dishonour than he can present the woman who makes a magnificence of her crime. A Vittoria Corombona was as much beyond his reach as a Duchess of Malfi.

So far as we know, neither Elizabeth nor her father, brother, or sister was represented on the public stage during her lifetime. The Elizabethan plays which present the tragedies of Sir Thomas More and Thomas Lord Cromwell carefully exclude from the dramatis personae the king who was responsible for their tragedies. But after the Queen's death it became possible to explore this reach of English history. One of the earliest dramatists to do so was Samuel Rowley in *When you See me, you Know me*, acted by the Admiral's–Prince Henry's men, perhaps in 1604 when the theatres reopened after the serious plague of 1603. To say that it was intended for those who had no brains to bring to the theatre or were content to leave them behind is hardly enough; for the play is stuffed with lively incident and was good for many a laugh. It is neither 'historical' nor 'poeti-

The English History Play

cal'. History is flouted to such an extent that Wolsey, who died in 1530, is one of the chief characters in a play that begins with the birth of Prince Edward and death of Jane Seymour in 1537 and ends with the charges of heresy brought against Catherine Parr by Gardiner and others in 1546. The King is the bluff monarch of tradition, terrible in rage, hearty and generous when in temper. He is the Harry of 'King Harry loves a man!' His favourite oath 'Mother of God' and his habit of crying 'Ha!' when roused come from tradition, as do some of the jests. Of folk-lore origin, though suggested by the chronicles and already treated in *Edward IV* and Dekker's *Shoemakers' Holiday*, is the motive of the disguised King mixing with his commoners. A nocturnal visit to London leads to a sword-and-buckler fight with Black Will and the arrest of both King and ruffian by a comic Watch who (like Dogberry of Messina) murder the king's English. Will Sommers (Summers), the King's all-licensed fool, as is only proper, is cleverer than Patch, the Cardinal's fool. Will exchanges bawdy jests with Emperor, King, and Queen: the manners are the manners of Billingsgate. We are given a pleasant glimpse of Prince Edward, his whipping-boy, his tutor (Cranmer), his music tutor (Christopher Tye); and every now and again comes some exposure of social wrong. Here in short is everything the public of those days wanted. The anti-papal bias is pervasive, Wolsey always angling for the papacy and he and his henchmen Gardiner and Bonner always bested by Queen Catherine (Parr) and Cranmer and Sommers. And while Edward's two sisters do not appear, it does appear that Elizabeth 'has his heart'.

Later examples of this sort of play are Dekker and Webster's *The Famous History of Sir Thomas Wyat. With the Coronation of Queen Mary, and the coming in of King Philip*, acted (probably) by Queen Anne's men c. 1604–5 and printed in a bad quarto in 1607, and Thomas Heywood's *If you Know not Me, you Know Nobody*, Part 1 printed in a bad text in 1605, Part 2 printed in 1606, and both parts acted by Queen Anne's men. The best thing in the *Wyat* play is not Wyat's rebellion and its suppression but the sad tale of Lady Jane Grey and her lover-husband Guildford. A genuine pathos, perhaps the work of Dekker, shines through the imperfections of the text. *If you Know not Me*, Part 1, begins where *Wyat* leaves off, but with the coronation of Mary promised in the title of that play not shown. (Both plays may be reworkings of *1* and *2 Lady Jane* financed by Henslowe in 1602.) It is surprisingly kind to Philip who shields Elizabeth from Mary's harsh treatment and joyfully reconciles the two sisters. Protestant fervour reaches its height in the dumb show in which two angels prevent the adherents of Rome from murdering the sleeping Elizabeth and place in her hand an English Bible which she protests on waking was given her 'by inspiration'. Part 2 has the merits and demerits noted in *Edward IV*. The ground covered in a pantomimic structure is the building of the Royal Exchange by Sir Thomas Gresham and the humours of Hobson a London haberdasher to whom alone the title applies, though it is extended to both parts. A chorus before the last two scenes begins 'From fifty-eight, the first yeare of her Raigne, We come to eighty-eight', and the play ends in a blaze of patriotism as Drake, Frobisher, and others, hot from the action, report to their Queen the victory over the Armada.

Such plays may remind us that even in the Elizabethan age masterpieces were not as plentiful as blackberries. On the whole masterpieces are not to be expected from the companies that acted these plays. We expect them from Shakespeare and the Lord Chamberlain–King's men and, for a few years after 1600, from the children's companies that so 'berattled the common stages' in comedy and satirical comedy. To conclude, we may mention two more plays that in their different ways are based on history. Dekker's *Whore of Babylon* is both new and old. It is old in that it is allegorical, and its one prose character Plain Dealing is just such a character as John the Commonwealth in *The Three Estates* or Honesty in *A Knack to Know a Knave*. And it is new in that the political allegory (unlike Lyly's) is daylight clear and often ceases to be allegory, as in the ship-by-ship description of the Armada. Dekker has a reputation for humanity, but it is not based on this virulent onslaught on Roman Catholics and their plots against Elizabeth. The style is bombastic and follows the fatal principle that big language is necessary for a big subject.

The play was printed in 1607 as acted by Prince Henry's men. Also printed in the same year was *The Travels of the three English*

Brothers with a dedication by John Day, William Rowley, and George Wilkins. The actors were Queen Anne's men. 'If this were play'd upon the stage now, I could condemn it as an improbable fiction' says Fabian in *Twelfth Night*. Yet the 'Scaene is mantled in the robe of truth', for these are the brothers Shirley, gentlemen of fortune in Persia and elsewhere, and all the dramatists claim to do is by the law of poetry 'To give our history ornament'. Such plays brought romance into the drab lives of London citizens. In a note to the reader of Heywood's prose pamphlet on Sir Richard Whittington and his cat the printer presumes that as the story is no vain conceit of poetical fiction it will serve to animate all people of whatsoever condition 'never to be dejected, though never so poor'. A play on this theme belonging to the Prince's men got as far as entry in the Stationers' Register in 1605, yet does not seem to have survived. Anyone who has read the plays last discussed will feel he knows exactly just what sort of a play it was.

2

Shakespeare's Comedies

WHEN Shakespeare began to practise the art of comedy, he could get little help from the theories of the learned. He had to manage without any substantial body of comic authority to aid him. Perhaps this was just as well. In the time of Rymer and Dennis the stage had a surfeit of authority. The only intelligent remarks made about comedy by an Englishman had been Sidney's in *The Defence of Poetry*, and he had adopted the neo-classical Renaissance conception with deference to the unities, to decorum in character, to consistency of tone, to comedy as a corrector of manners. For this he is not to be blamed. He was writing about comedy *in vacuo* without even a *Gorboduc* to fall back on. Shakespeare began to write for the stage ten years later, and they had been ten fruitful years. He must have been well aware that comedy acceptable to the public theatres was not the same as that acceptable to the learned. If he had not known it then, he would have had to know it a few years later when he met Jonson.[1] Here and there in his plays Shakespeare seems to show an amused awareness of learned controversy. His Polonius is ready for plays learned and popular, for tragedy and comedy as well as tragical-comical-historical-pastoral (like *Cymbeline*), for 'scene individable' (unity of place) as well as 'poem unlimited' (no unities at all). Again, Time, the Chorus in *The Winter's Tale*, explains that he slides over sixteen years

> since it is in my pow'r
> To o'erthrow law, and in one self-born hour
> To plant and o'erwhelm custom.

But we have laboriously to piece together Shakespeare's few

[1] The evidence for this is circumstantial, based as it is on a knowledge of Jonson's character and practice; but some kinds of indirect evidence are stronger than direct.

Shakespeare's Comedies 55

references to his craft. If he had written an *Arte Nuevo de hacer comedias en este tiempo*, would he have been as apologetic as Lope de Vega? Would he have explained that while not ignorant of the rules he had been forced against his will to write for the crowd? The crowd does not insist that characters and manners should be taken from common life but welcomes kings in comedy; it likes comedy in tragedy, prefers an action which tricks expectancy and keeps a man guessing till the last act, loves to have a scene end with a witty epigram and an elegant couplet, to help an actor off the stage, is prepared to see everything in two hours from Genesis to the Last Judgement. So Lope, trying to appear learned before a learned assembly. But Shakespeare could never have written thus. An untrammelled comedy was essential to his genius, to his art a matter of life and death. Not for him the clever epigrams about the difference between comedy and tragedy, about 'those who think' and 'those who feel'. When Hamlet describes the purpose of playing, and by implication of the playwright, he does so in words which are far from being doctrinaire: 'the end . . . was and is to hold, as 'twere, the mirror up to nature; to show virtue her own feature, scorn her own image, and the very age and body of the time his form and pressure.' It is all-embracing, for not only does it admit any kind of comedy, Jonson's as well as his own, but it does not insist on the separation of each kind. Many a comic dramatist of Shakespeare's time might have done better with more discipline and less liberty, but not Shakespeare, the tact and sequaciousness of whose genius is without any compare.

That Shakespearian tragedy has had its Bradley but not Shakespearian comedy has often been remarked. One reason is the scarcity of critics of Bradley's calibre in any age; another is that the four great tragedies to which he limited his scrutiny in his *Shakespearean Tragedy* were written at one period of Shakespeare's working life, so that while *Hamlet*, *Othello*, *King Lear*, and *Macbeth* differ widely from each other they share a certain homogeneity. *Romeo and Juliet* as immature, and *Titus Andronicus* as doubtfully authentic, he omitted; and *Julius Caesar* which preceded *Hamlet* and *Antony and Cleopatra* and *Coriolanus* which followed *Macbeth* were left out, together with *Richard II* and *Richard III*, as being tragic histories or historical tragedies. If a critic wished to achieve the same homogeneity in a book on Shakespearian comedy he would do well to confine himself to the run of comedies from *A Midsummer Night's Dream* and *Love's Labour's Lost* to *Twelfth Night*[1] if not to *All's Well*; but he would then need to exclude the three experimental comedies, *Measure for Measure*, and at the end the totally different art of comedy displayed in *The Winter's Tale* and *The Tempest*. A critic of Shakespeare with a rage for classification had better suppress it.

In his three earliest comedies, *The Comedy of Errors*, *The Taming of the Shrew*, *The Two Gentlemen of Verona*, all written before 1594, Shakespeare appears to be experimenting in the different kinds of comic material to be found on the stage *c.* 1591. Of all his comedies the two we could most easily dispense with are *The Merry Wives* and *The Comedy of Errors*. In the one Shakespeare may be working to order, the order of the Queen, in the other he is working to rule, the rule of Plautus. In *The Taming of the Shrew* his theme is as old as the hills, part of the paper war between the sexes which flourished in a bourgeois society during the later Middle Ages and the Renaissance, a war in which all the shots were fired by the male sex. This is the only comedy of Shakespeare's in which the hero outwits the heroine. One characteristic these three earliest comedies share: a main theme is the pangs of married love; and that is most uncharacteristic of Shakespearian comedy. So too is the strong element of farce in *The Comedy of Errors* and *The Taming of the Shrew*. These last hold the stage today better than *The Two Gentlemen of Verona*, but it is here that Shakespeare makes his first venture in the comedy of romantic love in which he was later to excel, a kind of comedy which Greene had recently introduced to the public stage under a flimsy historical disguise in his *James IV*.

The mistaken identity of twin brothers, Antipholus of Ephesus and Antipholus of Syracuse, the pangs of a jealous wife, Adriana, the courtesan who entertains an errant husband, the doctor called in to minister to a mind supposed diseased, these and other details of the plot of *The Comedy of Errors* Shakespeare took

---

[1] [Except that it includes the three experimental comedies, this is what this essay is confined to, since F. P. Wilson had not gone beyond 1600 in writing his Oxford History. H.G.]

from the *Menaechmi* of Plautus.[1] Something of the flavour of Roman comedy remains. Over the first scene and the last presides the Duke of Ephesus: otherwise the society is one of merchants and tradespeople, a usual setting for Plautine comedy, but in Shakespeare only to be matched in *The Merry Wives*. (True, Shakespeare's merchants carry swords which they do not hesitate to use to defend their honour (v. i), and in citizen comedy we might look in vain for anything so polite as 'Sir, I commend you to your own content.') The servants are often referred to as slaves and are much beaten or threatened. The relations of Antipholus of Ephesus with the courtesan are not those of a Shakespearian character in good repute, even if we allow his claim (in a play founded on improbabilities) to be innocent.

More interesting than the borrowings from Plautus are the departures. There is almost no convention an audience is not prepared to accept if it is well handled and promotes laughter. In this comedy we are called upon—in the expository first scene—to believe that in one self-same inn at the same hour a merchant's wife and a meaner woman both gave birth to male identical twins. The possibilities of mistaken identity are thereby doubled and the play prolonged to satisfy the two-hour traffic of the Elizabethan stage. Plays based on mistaken identity with or without deliberate disguise are characteristic of both learned and popular Italian comedy, and some like the originals of Gascoigne's *Supposes* and Munday's *Fedele and Fortunio* had been translated. (The 'supposes' or deceptions of Gascoigne are the equivalent of the 'errors' of Shakespeare.) Lyly's *Mother Bombie*, an original comedy of much more recent date, is founded on mistaken identity. Another departure from Plautus is the invention of Luciana, Adriana's sister, a respectable unmarried girl and so a type excluded altogether from Roman comedy. With her Antipholus of Syracuse falls suddenly in love, the only touch of romantic love we get. But stranger than that—indeed 'the strangest case that you ever heard: a man might make a Comedie of it', as a character in *Supposes* says of the reunion of a

[1] A translation by W. W. (William Warner?) was not printed till 1595, but may have circulated in manuscript: Shakespeare may have known it, or we may credit him with enough Latin to master the plot of this famous play.

father with a long-lost son—is the reunion of old Aegeon not only with his sons but with his wife and their mother.[1]

Perhaps the most significant departure from the *Menaechmi* is the comedy's occasional gravity. This must not be exaggerated, for the comedy is mainly for merriment, but here and there we fancy we hear a deeper note. It is characteristic of Shakespeare that this note is sounded by the women, above all in three set speeches of successful rhetoric: by Adriana suffering the pangs of a neglected wife (II. ii), by Luciana reading to the wrong Antipholus a lesson in the duties of a husband (III. ii), and by the Abbess (V. i) rebuking in Adriana 'The venom clamours of a jealous woman'. Here is a hint that to this dramatist comedy is to be not merely comedy of humours or manners, but profound comedy, and that women are to play as prominent a part in it as men.

That deeper note is not to be heard in *The Taming of the Shrew*, a comedy in which broad humour and complicated imbroglio are more important than character.[2] Plenty of analogues have been found to the Induction, in which a tinker disguised in drink is made to believe himself a lord, to the shrew-taming scenes, and to the wager scene. A characteristic fabliau is *A Merry Jest of a Shrewd and Curst Wife lapped in Morel's Skin*,[3] and the reading of it is good discipline if it shows how Shakespeare's play is saved from being total farce. Petruchio disproves the truth of the old proverb that any man can tame a shrew save he that has her, and does so in a battle of wits without a blow and with an elaborate courtesy. The elevation of the plot into high life also serves to distinguish it from fabliau as does the setting of the scene in Italy; and the high life and the setting are made more emphatic by the contrast with the presiding figure of Christopher Sly, a worthy descendant of the

---

[1] Shakespeare may already have known from 'old Gower' the story of Apollonius of Tyre (Pericles) whose wife also became abbess of a convent in Ephesus till reunited to husband and children after many years.

[2] Among the comedies written before 1598 it is exceptional in not being mentioned by Francis Meres, unless it be the still unidentified 'Love's Labour's Won'; but there is agreement that the play is early and of about the same time as *The Two Gentlemen of Verona*. Both have in common an Italian setting, a favourite location with Shakespeare and in 1590–3 an unusual choice for a comedy acted on the public stage.

[3] Printed by Hugh Jackson (?1580), but referred to in *Laneham's Letter* of 1575 as one of Captain Cox's books.

low life that 'came in with Richard the Conqueror'. The high life is in verse and the low in prose, but before her reformation Kate's language is much the same in either medium. Her 'To comb your noddle with a three-legg'd stool' remains to this day part of the folk-language of England. To the high life belongs the wooing of Kate's younger sister, Bianca. The disguises which two of her three suitors assume, and especially the disguise of the master (Lucentio) as his servant (Tranio) in order to outdo a rival and obtain access to his beloved, these owe something to Gascoigne's *Supposes*, and the debt is perhaps acknowledged in the line addressed to Bianca's father as he is being undeceived: 'counterfeit supposes blear'd thine eyne.'

The problem of the relationship of *The Taming of the Shrew*, published in the Folio of 1623, and *The Taming of A Shrew*, published in quarto in 1594, is still unsolved. The old view that the text of the quarto was Shakespeare's source play, or even Shakespeare's first draft, no longer holds the field, and most critics now believe that *A Shrew* is dependent either on *The Shrew* as we have it or on an earlier version of *The Shrew*. The text of 1594 bears many of the marks of a 'bad quarto'. Its imperfections are too serious to be accounted for by bad printing. Some passages are senseless as they stand and one or two jests effective in *The Shrew* have no point in *A Shrew*. Moreover, the quarto text is patched up with blatantly clumsy borrowings from *Tamburlaine* and *Doctor Faustus*, and a passage from Kate's last speech derives most surprisingly from *La Première Semaine* of Du Bartas.[1] While there are no radical differences between the two texts as regards the Induction and the main plot, verbal identity is rare—it is most common in two of the taming scenes (IV. i and iii) and in the wager scene (V. ii)—and the only characters that bear the same names are Sly and Kate. As Greg observed, the quarto may be regarded not so much as a reconstruction of an original as an imitation based on recollection of it. But it contains no recollection of the sub-plot. In *A Shrew* there are three sisters, each with their suitor; in *The Shrew* there are two, the younger (Bianca) having three rival suitors; and the debt in these scenes to *Supposes* is far greater. Perhaps then the redactor of the

[1] Printed in French in 1578, in English not until 1595 in a translation ascribed to Sylvester in *S.T.C.*, but probably not his.

quarto was recollecting an early (but Shakespearian) version of *The Shrew*, before the sub-plot of Bianca's wooers was revised. Those critics who fail to see Shakespeare's hand in this sub-plot will say that the revision was done by a collaborator.

In *The Shrew* Sly makes a comment on the action of the play at the end of the first scene, and then is heard no more. In *A Shrew* he speaks at three points in the action before he falls asleep, is removed to the place where he was found, awakens from 'the best dream that ever I had in my life', and goes home to tame his own shrew. There is every likelihood that similar passages once appeared in *The Shrew*, but we may not assume that any of Shakespeare's language has survived in the quarto. Almost the only two words in common in the two Inductions are Sly's 'Ile fese you.'

With *The Two Gentlemen of Verona* we are on the border of Shakespeare's characteristic comic world, but we certainly have not crossed it. In youth as in age desire sometimes outruns performance. Two famous types of friendship between man and man had already been put upon the stage, the lost *Titus and Gisippus* and Richard Edward's *Damon and Pithias*, both acted by children. The story of Titus and Gisippus gives us the better parallel because it hinges both on the love of man for man and of man for woman. The moral is that true friendship is more to be esteemed than the love of woman or kindred. Titus is the swooning lover dear to the writers of romance who falls in love with the betrothed of his dearest friend, his *alter ego*, Gisippus. Gisippus, to save his friend's life, relinquishes his claim: in Sir Thomas Elyot's version in *The Governor* (1531)[1] he does so in words that cannot fail to remind us of Valentine's notorious line, 'All that is mine in Silvia I give thee'; 'Here I renounce to you clearely all my title and interest that I nowe haue or mought haue in that faire mayden.' But in the story no Julia swoons. The friends exchange places on the wedding night, and while there are protests against the behaviour of Gisippus, they do not come from the wife. In the play, a few lines later than the lines just quoted, Valentine shows a proper anger at the pretensions of Thurio to Silvia's hand; but then, Thurio was not a friend.

[1] Book II, Chapter 12.

The source, direct or indirect, is the pastoral romance *Diana*, written in Spanish by Jorge de Montemayor, a translation of which was made by Bartholomew Yong *c.* 1582–3, though not printed till 1598. A lost play which the clerk of the Revels called *Felix and Philiomena* (for *Felismena*), the names of the two lovers who correspond to the Proteus and Julia of the play, had been acted at court by the Queen's company in January 1585. The resemblances to the Proteus–Julia story—Felismena's coy reception of the love-letter which her maid brings from Felix, how when his father sends him abroad she follows in man's clothing, how urged by the host of her inn she goes to hear music and discovers Felix serenading her rival, how she becomes his page and is employed to plead his love—these and other resemblances are too close to be accidental. And possibly the situation in which the disguised Felismena sent to woo for her master is wooed herself lay dormant in Shakespeare's mind until he created Olivia and Viola.

The story offered him just such a circle as was to give him most delight in comedy: a courtly setting in a foreign land, two pairs of lovers with servants and maids, heroines who are more severely tested than is usual in comedy, who face adversity with more courage, intelligence, and fidelity than their lovers, and who sometimes reveal these qualities by disguising themselves as boys. (How romantic this was is suggested by the fate of a woman found so disguised in London in 1604: she was sent to Newgate!)[1] Smaller matters used later in comedy and some in *Romeo and Juliet* are a convenient friar, the inventory and ridicule of suitors by heroine and maid, a rope-ladder, banishment and outlaws, a change of scene from court to country. A characteristic anticipation, in this instance of *As You Like it*, is the soliloquy of the banished Valentine, where the verse is more mellifluous and figured than is usual in this play:

> How use doth breed a habit in a man!
> This shadowy desert, unfrequented woods,
> I better brook than flourishing peopled towns.

[1] [*Dom. S. P.* 1604, p. 92, records the penalty meted out to Mary Worley and Henry Boucher. Mary Worley, dressed as a man, visited Boucher (a Fellow of All Souls) in his rooms. The assembled Heads of Houses sentenced them to public confession in St. Mary's, followed by matrimony. I can find no reference to any similar story for this year which would include mention of Newgate. H.G.]

> Here can I sit alone, unseen of any,
> And to the nightingale's complaining notes
> Tune my distresses and record my woes.
> O thou that dost inhabit in my breast,
> Leave not the mansion so long tenantless,
> Lest, growing ruinous, the building fall
> And leave no memory of what it was!
> Repair me with thy presence, Silvia;
> Thou gentle nymph, cherish thy forlorn swain.

But the play is among Shakespeare's *juvenilia*. The machinery creaks loudly, especially in the outlaw scenes, and however the critics may wriggle they cannot escape from the enormity of Valentine's line. The final resolutions of Shakespeare's comic plots do not always end with rose-water, and many who think they ought to have deplored the characters of Bassanio, of Bertram, and of Claudio. But these are angels of light beside Proteus. Never again did Shakespeare write a line so contrary to the run of the action as Valentine's. Never again did he create a 'hero' like Proteus. Launce sums him up in a word: 'my master is a kind of knave.'

The character of Launce is ripe as nothing else in the play is ripe, and it is worth asking how. Camden, while quoting Giraldus Cambrensis to the effect that the English and Welsh 'delighted much in licking the letter, and clapping together of Agnominations', felt that 'this merry playing with words' had been 'too much vsed by some',[1] and there will be few readers of Shakespeare, especially of his early comedy, who do not agree. He would not have been an Elizabethan if he had not delighted in verbal wit. The masters as well as the servants in the play indulge in it, and the first two acts provide examples in the dialogue of Valentine with Proteus or Thurio or Speed and between Proteus and Speed. But as in *Damon and Pithias* and as in Lyly the disease is most prevalent among the servants. Speed's dialogue is all verbal wit, and there is much in Launce's. When Speed says to Launce 'Your old vice still: mistake the word', he attacks one form of punning: Jonson twenty years later attacked the 'Stage-practice' of 'mistaking words'.[2]

---

[1] *Remains* (1605), p. 27.
[2] Induction to *Bartholomew Fair*.

What preserves Launce is humour. The contrast between Speed's verbal wit and Launce's mother-wit is to be remarked: the one perished almost as soon as it was born, and the other is, in its kind, imperishable. The tradition of this sort of clowning was already ancient and is in part preserved in the Vice of many a morality play and in the tales and legends about Tarlton. Shakespeare raised it into art and fixed it for every generation to admire. There is astonishing shrewdness with simplicity, the direct appeal to the audience ('look you') as the clown tells about his family, his milkmaid, and above all his dog, and there is the warm humanity of his sentiments. Launce takes no essential part in the action as does Dogberry, but his soliloquies are no mere music-hall turns. They throw a corrective light upon the goings-on of his superiors.

To have argued fifty years ago that *Love's Labour's Lost* was no immature comedy but a play which shows its author employing his full comic strength and revelling in it would have been startling. To many it seemed his earliest comedy, and except for an occasional performance as a curiosity it was not thought worthy of revival. Pater's tribute in *Appreciations* (1889) did nothing to change the attitude of critic or actor-manager, but from the nineteen-twenties many notable productions have revealed what a lively and gracious play it is. Here and in the contemporaneous *Midsummer Night's Dream*, as never in the earlier comedies or in *Henry VI* and *Richard III* or in *Titus Andronicus*, ideas and images crowd into Shakespeare's verse and prose from reserves that seem inexhaustible. To adapt the words of Holofernes, we are shown 'a spirit full of forms, figures, shapes, objects, ideas, apprehensions, motions, revolutions . . . the gift is good in those in whom it is acute, and *we* are thankful for it.'

An examination of Shakespeare's life and time may make it appear that the change was not so sudden as it might seem. Suppose, for example, that the three experimental comedies were completed by the summer of 1592. For many months in late 1592, in 1593, and in early 1594 plays were prohibited in London on account of the plague, and dramatic companies were forced to disband or to amalgamate and travel through a countryside that did not welcome them. Some notion of the hardships of players is given in letters which passed in the summer of 1593 between Philip Henslowe and his son-in-law Edward Alleyn. Alleyn was then travelling in the country as leader of the joint Admiral's–Strange's men and longing for his young wife and the London theatres. Pembroke's men were even worse off. Unable to pay their charges by travel and forced to pawn their players' apparel, they were obliged to return to London in August when the plague was at its height. By 1594, however, the embargo on plays was lifted, and for nine years the plague ceased to threaten the livelihood of players. In the same year Strange's men, after the death of their patron on 16 April, obtained a new patron in the Lord Chamberlain, Henry Carey, Lord Hunsdon, and in June, together with the Admiral's men, they were acting at Newington Butts *Andronicus*, *Hamlet* (not Shakespeare's), *The Taming of A* (probably *The*) *Shrew*, and other plays. At Christmas the Chamberlain's men appeared at court in two comedies, and the payees were William Kemp, William Shakespeare, and Richard Burbage. Kemp soon departed, but for the rest of his life Shakespeare was writing for a company in which he was a leading shareholder and for actors whom he valued and who valued him ('so worthy a Friend and Fellow'). And during the months of inactivity we are not obliged to suppose him a strolling player. In the spring of 1593 and 1594 respectively he published his *Venus and Adonis* and *Rape of Lucrece* and dedicated them to the Earl of Southampton with the confidence that his verses and his devotion were alike acceptable. To the same time belong many of his sonnets and the experiences they convey to us 'as in a glass darkly'. No wonder that when he returned to the stage in the propitious year 1594 his work gave signs of poetic and dramatic growth.

For evidence we need not look further than the opening lines of *Love's Labour's Lost*, in which the King of Navarre comments upon the 'little academe' into which he and three of his Lords (Berowne, Dumain, and Longaville) have formed themselves:

> Let fame, that all hunt after in their lives,
> Live register'd upon our brazen tombs,
> And then grace us in the disgrace of death;
> When, spite of cormorant devouring Time,

> Th'endeavour of this present breath may buy
> That honour which shall bate his scythe's keen edge,
> And make us heirs of all eternity.
> Therefore, brave conquerors—for so you are
> That war against your own affections
> And the huge army of the world's desires—
> Our late edict shall strongly stand in force:
> Navarre shall be the wonder of the world;
> Our court shall be a little Academe,
> Still and contemplative in living art.

Here all or almost all is old yet all is new. The figure in the third line 'And then grace us in the disgrace of death' was in vogue at the time, made fashionable by Sidney, especially in his *Arcadia*; it is both a figure of words and a figure of thought, both a play upon words and a paradox. More remarkable is the evidence that this poet is thinking in images. Some of these already had a long tradition behind them: 'devouring time'; Time's scythe; Fame registered upon brazen tombs. Yet even here all is new, though all is old. It is not merely Time's scythe but his 'scythe's keen edge'. It is not merely 'devouring time', but 'cormorant devouring time'. Add to all this the boldness of imagery and the swell of rhythm in the lines 'And make us heirs of all eternity' or 'And the huge army of the world's desires'. There is a resonance in the verse, an assured strength of diction and musical phrasing, far beyond the power of any earlier dramatist, far beyond, it would seem, the Shakespeare of *The Comedy of Errors* or *The Two Gentlemen of Verona*. No one before in English comedy had spoken with such authority and brilliance.

In the dramatist's mind and in ours is the knowledge that the plan which the King so seriously propounds is not level with life, will not work. The speech is serious as far as the character is concerned but to us fundamentally comic. Of all Shakespeare's comedies this most nearly approaches the special definition given to comedy by George Meredith. Here are four young men who shut themselves up in a little academe and resolve—Berowne most reluctantly—to abstain from feminine society for three years and to devote themselves to study. And Shakespeare examines what is 'affected, pretentious, bombastical, hypocritical, pedantic, fantastically delicate'. He shows his characters 'drifting into vanities, congregating in absurdities, planning shortsightedly, plotting dementedly'. And in the persons of the Princess and her three ladies life comes breaking in, and 'with vollies of silvery laughter' educates the men out of their follies and turns them once more into useful members of society.

Love's Labour's Lost is a comedy of affections, but it is never suggested that Rosaline and the other ladies are infected. They are the fixed point of reference, the desired norm from which to some degree all other characters depart. In the use of the Queen's English they set an example to the men—even to Berowne. Language, said one of the ancients, 'most shows a man; speak, that I may see thee'. Berowne, the character behind whom pulses the fullest dramatic life, beside whom the other courtiers are shadows and are meant to be shadows, is shown as not wholly free from affectations. There is a significant passage in the last scene when after successive humiliations Berowne owns himself beaten and throws himself on the mercy of Rosaline:

> Thus pour the stars down plagues for perjury.
> Can any face of brass hold longer out?
> Here stand I, lady—dart thy skill at me,
> Bruise me with scorn, confound me with a flout, . . .
> Taffeta phrases, silken terms precise,
> Three-pil'd hyperboles, spruce affectation,
> Figures pedantical—these summer-flies
> Have blown me full of maggot ostentation.
> I do forswear them; and I here protest,
> By this white glove—how white the hand, God knows!—
> Henceforth my wooing mind shall be express'd
> In russet yeas, and honest kersey noes.
> And to begin, wench—so God help me, law!—
> My love to thee is sound, sans crack or flaw.
> *Rosaline.* Sans 'sans', I pray you.
> *Berowne.*   Yet I have a trick
>   Of the old rage; bear with me, I am sick;
>   I'll leave it by degrees.

Pater and others have thought it not fanciful to take Rosaline's questioning of Berowne's 'sans' and Berowne's admission 'Yet I have a trick of the old rage' as a landmark in Shakespeare's development, as a sign that he was beginning to grow away from the affectation of language and the addiction to figures of sound which had fitted so well into the single-moulded verse of his earlier plays, or at least was able to engage in delicate raillery of his own chosen manner. A comparison of the verse in this play with that in his earliest historical plays shows that in words which W. B. Yeats applied to his own poems Shakespeare had 'begun to loosen rhythm as an escape from rhetoric'.

Not that he ever shook himself entirely free from what seem to us affectations of language. The very games with which Elizabethan gentlemen and gentlewomen whiled away their leisure hours encouraged verbal dexterity: decorums and absurdums, griefs and joys, yeas and noes, buts, and those exercises of the sub-standard fashionable world—posies for rings, riddles, substantives and adjectives, and the rest—which Jonson holds up to scorn in *Cynthia's Revels*. But henceforth Shakespeare, who had an instinct for what was permanent and central in the language, does not exceed. We cannot listen to a play of his with as quick an apprehension of the turns and twists of the dialogue as that which came without effort to an intelligent Elizabethan, yet so great is the vitality behind the lines no playgoer *need* be at the mercy of a commentator in order to be entertained and refreshed by *Love's Labour's Lost*.

The play is not merely conducted at court levels. In Shakespearian comedy the people will keep on breaking in. A great variety of low comedy is expressed through characters contrasting as much with each other as with the courtiers, and each with his own manner of speaking—or not speaking. We meet Dull and Costard, Moth and Armado early in the play. Dull the constable, so called because (like Dogberry) he has 'as much wit as a constable', is ill furnished with language. The clown Costard is blessed with common sense and knows that 'remuneration is Latin for three farthings'. Dull has no wit at all. Costard has mother-wit, but the young Moth is superabundantly witty, skilled in chop-logic, as full of puns as an egg of meat, and in a flash able to turn the meaning of any sentence inside out. 'My father's wit and my mother's tongue assist me!' he cries and he inherits both. Moth, Dull, and Costard are content with that station in life to which it hath pleased God to call them, but the other characters of this comic underworld are eaten up with affectation: Moth's master is the braggart, the fantastic Don Armado, the 'refined traveller of Spain',

> A man in all the world's new fashion planted,
> That hath a mint of phrases in his brain . . .
> A man of fire-new words, fashion's own knight,

one who breaks all the laws of decorum, for however low the matter he puts it all into high words. The last indignity he suffers is his infatuation with Jaquenetta, the country wench. She speaks only in catchwords. Every age has its supply of these, and they are the staple of conversation among those whose wits barely cross the threshold of intelligence.[1]

As if these five characters were not enough, another two are introduced as late as IV. ii—the pedantic schoolmaster Holofernes and his parasite, Sir Nathaniel the curate. Holofernes is not blown up with the ostentation of fashion like Armado but with the ostentation of learning. He is a kind of learned Bottom, with something of Bottom's gusto. He has that confidence in the rightness of his own opinion sometimes observable in those whose profession it is to teach the young. The interesting suggestion has been made that in the choice of these types of low comedy, though not of course in the treatment of them, Shakespeare took a hint from the stock characters in the *commedia dell'arte*: the Spanish braggart or *capitano* who was often married off to some ill-favoured female, the *pedante* and his parasite, the foolish magistrate.[2] But if we seek ancestors for Moth and Costard we had better look to Richard Edwards and John Lyly.

Some critics have found in the play satirical or gaily mocking allusions to men of the day. Shakespeare, they have held, an adherent of the Essex–Southampton faction at court, is ridiculing

---

[1] Cf. 'Shakespeare and the Diction of Common Life', p. 115 below.
[2] For a detailed discussion, see O. J. Campbell, '*Love's Labour's Lost* Re-studied', *Studies in Shakespeare, Milton and Donne* (University of Michigan, 1925).

Sir Walter Raleigh in Don Armado, Thomas Harriot (or John Florio) in Holofernes, Thomas Nashe as Moth. And they have seen in the King's reference to 'the School of Night' (IV. iii. 251) a supposed 'School' for the study of astronomy if not of 'atheism' of which Chapman, Harriot, Raleigh, and others are conjectured to have been members.[1] That a play built round contemporary affectations should conceal personal allusions seems likely enough; and the case for these identifications has been presented with great ingenuity. But the sceptic may still doubt the existence of any 'School of Night', and may withhold belief that English Raleigh, the flail of the Spaniards, a good poet, and a master of English prose should be concealed under so unlikely an exterior as Don Armado. As Johnson said, 'the sarcasms which, perhaps, in the author's time *set* the playhouse *in a roar*, are now lost among general reflections'. No one seems to have sought an original for the character of Boyet. If any man at court recognized it as a portrait of himself he cannot have been flattered. Boyet is the Lord-in-waiting on the Princess, her messenger and go-between. Had he been lower in the social scale he would have been a gentleman-usher, and in the whole range of Elizabethan drama no dramatist had a good word to say for such a man and such an office. Presumably players had suffered too many humiliations in their contact with these men at court and in the houses of the great. He is responsible for the miscarriage of the masque of the Muscovites, and Berowne's speech only becomes venomous when describing Boyet's profession and character. He endows him with all the characteristics of the gentleman-usher: a man who can carve and lisp, can show his teeth as white as whalebone, knows the trick to make my lady laugh, 'and, in ushering, Mend him who can' (v. ii. 315 ff.). Costard praises the obscenity of his wit: 'O! a most dainty man, To see him walk before a lady, and to bear her fan!'

The characters of the comic underworld live their own lives but are also firmly tied to the main action, the wooing of the Princess and her three ladies. Shakespeare has already learned how to bring into a unity many themes and many characters. His plot, such as it is, bears some resemblances to two embassies from France to the

[1] See Frances A. Yates, *A Study of Love's Labour's Lost*, 1934.

court of Navarre in 1578 and 1586, resemblances too close to be accidental; but the play is not historical. He needed some excuse for bringing a princess on an embassy to a king, and this served his purpose. The important thing was not *how* they should meet but that they *should* meet with their attendant lords and ladies, and that before they meet all of them should be fancy-free. What the play is about is the relation between the sexes, the cross-wooings on the level of king and princess being set off against those of lower levels of society.

Much of the action is based on the entertainments which Elizabeth was offered while on progress: pageants; hunting the deer—the Queen observing the hunt from a stand specially built for her; dramatic shows sometimes performed seriously by country people and organized by the local schoolmaster, sometimes a burlesquing of rural life and character and presented to the Queen out of doors in the park adjoining her host's house or castle; a masque or disguising ending in a dance and in song. Many of these are to be found in the most famous account of the most famous of all Elizabeth's progresses: Robert Laneham on the entertainment given to the Queen by the Earl of Leicester at Kenilworth in 1575.

The following of the events of a progress or royal entertainment accounts for the episodic structure of the play; and perhaps mistaken notions about the 'well-made' play helped to account for nineteenth-century neglect of it. The last scene is perhaps the longest that Shakespeare ever wrote—longer even than the yet greater scene in *The Winter's Tale* (IV. iv) which begins with the sheep-shearing. How much happens in v. ii! The ladies' mocking comments on their lovers; Boyet's report of the approach of the King and lords disguised as Muscovites; the humiliation of the masquers; their return and realization how they have been tricked; their submission and declarations of love; the pageant of the nine worthies; the new turn given to the plot by the news of the death of the Princess's father; the sentence on each of the lovers to a year's probation during the period of mourning; and to wind up the play the songs in praise of the cuckoo and the owl! Episodic yes, but each leading so naturally into the next and each with its own pace and its own vitality.

All eyes turn in some way to the court. The title-page of the 1598 quarto tells us the comedy was acted before the Queen. Some have doubted whether it could have been acceptable to a mixed audience at a public theatre. All Shakespeare's plays were written with one eye on the court, for the ambition of every company was to be invited to perform at court. Both the honour and the emoluments were welcome. But usually plays acted at court were tried out at the public theatres first. Whether *Love's Labour's Lost* was an exception we do not know. The play owes something to the court comedies of John Lyly. Critics have seen his influence in the witty dialogue, in the symmetry of the characters, in the use of song, in correspondences like those between Sir Thopas, Epiton, and Bagoa in *Endymion* and Don Armado, Moth, and Jaquenetta. And those who find in the comedy much topical allusion will say that Shakespeare resembles Lyly in that respect too. Certainly Lyly was the writer of comedy from whom Shakespeare could learn most. But, as certainly, by 1594 he had turned his back on the ladder by which he rose: he was no longer disciple to any man. He was on his own. Lyly was no dramatic poet, and Shakespeare was already a great one. There are four references to rhetoric in this play and only two in the rest of Shakespeare, but the rhetoric is already dramatic, sense in speech rhythms and wedded to music. In Berowne's splendid speech in praise of love (IV. iii) the formality of the verse is tempered by the constant change of image and pause, aiding and abetting the march of argument:

> Love's feeling is more soft and sensible
> Than are the tender horns of cockled snails;
> Love's tongue proves dainty Bacchus gross in taste.
> For valour, is not Love a Hercules,
> Still climbing trees in the Hesperides?
> Subtle as Sphinx; as sweet and musical,
> As bright Apollo's lute, strung with his hair.
> And when Love speaks, the voice of all the gods
> Make heaven drowsy with the harmony....
> From women's eyes this doctrine I derive.
> They sparkle still the right Promethean fire;
> They are the books, the arts, the academes,

> That show, contain, and nourish, all the world,
> Else none at all in aught proves excellent.

Here is something of what Shakespeare is going to give us in the comedies yet to be written, the quintessence of a gracious world of courtesy and of love not so refined as to exclude feeling and passion.

To say that Shakespeare discovered in *Love's Labour's Lost* the kind of comedy that most suited his genius during the next seven years (c. 1594–c. 1601) does not imply that he went on repeating himself. He never gives us the mixture as before. *A Midsummer Night's Dream*, for example, called by Croce the quintessence of the comedies as *Hamlet* is of the tragedies, is a dream, a fantasy, an illusion, and in that sense made of stuff more shadowy and less 'real' than later comedies. Yet some remarks may be made which are generally applicable to this comedy and the four that follow— *The Merchant of Venice* (1596–7), *Much Ado About Nothing* and *As You Like It* (1598–1600), and *Twelfth Night* (1600–2). They are not applicable to *The Merry Wives* (1597–1601), the only comedy of his with an English setting, or to *All's Well That Ends Well* (?1602–3), the stage history of which is far from being distinguished. The dates are inevitably approximate, yet sufficiently firm to provide a warning against dividing Shakespeare's work into such watertight compartments as Dowden's notorious classification of 1877—In the workshop, In the world, Out of the depths, On the heights: for on this dating *Twelfth Night* is later than *Julius Caesar*, possibly later than *Hamlet*.

One remarkable fact, unparalleled in the long history of English drama, is that this run of five comedies has kept its popularity upon the stage almost without a break from Shakespeare's day to ours. There have been times when the plays were perverted to droll or spectacle or opera, yet there has never been a time when a London audience could not acquaint itself with Oberon and Titania, Bottom and his crew, Shylock, Beatrice and Benedick, Viola and Malvolio.

The comedies are set in some foreign country not much more localized than by a general reference to Athens, Venice, Messina, Illyria. This universalizes Shakespeare's comedy: his court is and is not the English court; his characters are and are not English. If as patriots we seek for Englishness we may find it especially in the scenes of low comedy, though even here there is no such gross topicality as some of his contemporaries admit—Thomas Heywood, for example—even in his Roman plays. What *is* thoroughly English is the language, and he uses the whole gamut from high to low, just as he uses the whole available range of metre and rhythm, verse and prose, blank verse and rhymed, long line and short, song and doggerel.

What is also English is the scenery. The importance varies from play to play. Scenery is never introduced for its own sake. Its most important function is to transport the audience into a mood that chimes with the moral emotion. In *A Midsummer Night's Dream* the presence or absence of the moon is vital to the conduct of the piece: it is a major character that does not get into the dramatis personae. The whole play seems to move 'With the moon's beauty and the moon's soft pace'. Again, the dialogue between Lorenzo and Jessica (v. i) beginning 'The moon shines bright. In such a night as this . . .'—which Hazlitt unaccountably dismisses as a 'collection of classical elegancies'—brings a tranquil beauty after the passionate excitements of the trial scene: and Shakespeare takes care to dissolve the dialogue in humour before it is in danger of becoming tedious. Sometimes the poet is appealing from the bare boards of his theatre to the eye of the imagination, and without benefit of lighting and painted scenery he illuminates the scene by word of actor's mouth. It is so when Beatrice hides herself in a 'pleached bower, Where honeysuckles ripen'd by the sun, Forbid the sun to enter' or runs to a 'woodbine coverture' like a lapwing close by the ground. This may or may not be the scenery of Messina: it is certainly the scenery of Warwickshire. Neither in comedy nor tragedy does this popular dramatist hesitate to change the remote for the familiar, the unknown for the known. Pastoral is an exotic form, and perhaps this accounts for the presence in *As You Like It* of the green and gilded snake and the lioness and the sheep-cote fenced about with olive trees; but except for the artificial narration of the artificial Oliver (IV. iii. 74–131) the forest we are in is Arden. With the countryman Shakespeare the court is never far from the country. How different is the urban comedy of Jonson, who often banishes both court and country!

If there is satire it is a kindly satire directed at the foibles of men and women. 'Perhaps too good-natured for comedy,' said Hazlitt of *Twelfth Night*, 'it has little satire and no spleen.' But comedy is not necessarily a vent for spleen or an instrument of correction. In these comedies Shakespeare is too good-natured for Jonson's kind of comedy, but not for Chaucer's. The setting is usually a court, and the characters can leave the necessity of earning a living to their servants. In *A Midsummer Night's Dream* the only characters who work for their living (apart from Duke Theseus and his Master of the Revels) are those whom Puck airily dismisses as 'A crew of patches, rude mechanicals, That work for bread upon Athenian stalls'. *The Merchant of Venice* would appear to be an exception, but Antonio is a merchant prince, no 'petty trafficker'. Shylock, it is true, is an usurer, which blackened his character in Elizabethan eyes much more than his being a Jew, but usury had been a fair target for dramatists since the heyday of the morality play. Shakespeare is the last dramatist we think of turning to for light on contemporary manners or abuses. Sly satirical hits of an incidental nature there are, as to the mimicry of foreign fashions or the league between usurers and brokers to the undoing of many a rash gallant, both abuses abused in the morality plays; but we look in vain in his comedy for sustained reflections on the structure of society, though never in vain for inspired comment upon human conduct and feeling, comment suffused by poetry and presented in an ideal light. In all these comedies there is a reference from Venice to Belmont.

The confusion of the apparent and the real is an important ingredient of the drama and always has been. Is it Amphitryon or is it Jupiter? Is it a vice disguising himself as a virtue? Is it the 'supposes' of Italian comedy and of Gascoigne and Lyly and Munday? Shakespeare is as fond as any comic dramatist of complicating his plots with mistaken identities—the learned Balthazar and his little scrubbed clerk, Ganymede and Aliena, Cesario. The plot of *Much Ado About Nothing* hinges upon a 'suppose', the 'suppose' that Hero is her waiting gentlewoman Margaret. And the error may lead to laughter or sorrow. Shakespeare makes no attempt to deceive his audience. We share with him a knowledge of all that is happening. Not until the end of the play do the characters share this knowledge, and some never do. In *A Midsummer Night's Dream* the two pairs of lovers never know what has happened to them, and neither does Theseus, though he thinks he does with his 'More strange than true'. A brilliant example of the handsome dividends Shakespeare gets from taking us into his confidence is the business of the rings, introduced immediately after the disappearance of Shylock. Until it is resolved in the last act we share with the women a secret denied to the men. In comedy as in tragedy Shakespeare gives us all motives, all clues, 'not surprise but expectation' as Coleridge said, and so the satisfaction of perfect knowledge.

All five are romantic comedies, comedies of young love as *Romeo and Juliet* is a tragedy of young love. In his early thirties Shakespeare confined himself to this theme in comedy and tragedy. In the society of his day the first question to be asked about a girl was what she was worth.[1] It is Shakespeare's question too, but he does not answer in pounds, shillings, and pence. Parents who believe that being so much older and therefore wiser than their children the choice of a son-in-law or daughter-in-law should rest with them get no encouragement from Shakespearian comedy. His heroines choose for themselves, and because they are the kind of girl his heroines are they cannot choose wrong. Meredith maintained that high comedy was impossible where there did not exist some degree of social equality of the sexes, and declared 'the higher the Comedy, the more prominent the part women enjoy in it'.

Where women have no social freedom, Comedy is absent: where they are household drudges, the form of Comedy is primitive: where they are tolerably independent, but uncultivated, exciting melodrama takes its place and a sentimental version of them.... But where women are on the road to an equal footing with men, in attainments and in liberty—in what they have won for themselves, and what has been

---

[1] See Thomas Coppin to Vincent Denne, 6 April 1631: 'You know the manner of this age is first to know what shee is worth' (*Oxinden Letters*, ed. Dorothy Gardiner, 1933, p. 63).

granted them by a fair civilization—there, and only waiting to be transplanted from life to the stage, or the novel, or the poem, pure Comedy flourishes.

In Shakespeare's comedy the women are as prominent as the men and on an equal footing. We are made free of a world in which the love between man and woman does not abase but sharpens the wit, so that in both sexes the mind and the senses are fully exercised. If the balance of the sexes is upset it is because the women are superior to the men: Rosaline to Berowne as surely as Portia to Bassanio, Beatrice to Benedick, Rosalind to Orlando. In wit-combats they outdo the men at every turn. Their wits have 'the razor's edge'. The men, to use Fuller's metaphor, seem *Spanish Great Galleons* and the women *English Men-of-War*, 'lesser in *bulk*, but lighter in *sailing*'.[1] And how self-reliant Shakespeare's women are! The mortality among the parents of the major heroines seems excessive: Rosaline, Portia, Beatrice, Viola, Helena are all orphans, and Rosalind as good as orphaned. All manage their affairs most successfully without benefit of father or mother, though Portia is perhaps an exception being bound by her father's testamentary arrangements. Mothers-in-law and stepmothers, stock-in-trade of so much modern low comedy and knock-about farce, do not appear at all. Poor Hero has a father and at a pinch he is of no use. Shakespeare makes it very clear that Beatrice is fatherless:

> *Antonio* [*To Hero*]. Well, niece, I trust you will be rul'd by your father.
> *Beatrice.* Yes, faith; it is my cousin's duty to make curtsy, and say 'Father, as it please you'. But yet for all that, cousin, let him be a handsome fellow, or else make another curtsy and say 'Father, as it please me'.

Add that the satisfaction of mind and sense given to us in verse and prose which it is a pleasure to speak or hear or read radiates an extraordinary happiness. Only twice in these comedies are characters introduced who may be thought to spoil the harmony of this comic

---

[1] See Fuller, *Worthies*, 1662, 'Warwickshire', p. 126, on the 'wit-combates' between Shakespeare and Jonson: Jonson *'Solid*, but *Slow* in his performances. *Shake-spear* . . . could turn with all tides, tack about and take advantage of all winds, by the quickness of his Wit and Invention.'

world; but the effect of a Shylock and a Don John is to enhance the courage and fidelity the women show when wind and weather do their worst.

At this date it should not be necessary to defend the morality of Shakespeare's comic heroines. Robert Bridges, in an essay on the 'Influence of the Audience on Shakespeare's Drama' (1907) condemned his obscenities and went so far as to say that his women were 'tainted', blaming these blemishes on his desire to please the most vulgar stratum of his audience. That his women have every intention of getting husbands, of enjoying the rites of marriage, and of begetting children is true enough, and they express or imply this with the freedom of the fifteen-nineties or the nineteen-sixties. But the major heroines in these comedies, frank and outspoken as they are, are remarkably free from obscenities, and appear the more so if we compare them with the heroines of Shakespeare's contemporaries or successors, or with his own women of a lower social class. The conversation of those two vulgarians Nerissa and Gratiano is not free from bold bawdry, but the speech of Portia is. In *Much Ado About Nothing* Margaret supplies the bawdry, not Beatrice, not Hero. The difference is pointed in Margaret's answer to Hero's 'my heart is exceeding heavy'—''Twill be heavier soon, by the weight of a man'—in Hero's rebuke, and in Margaret's defence of her answer. The distinction becomes a subtle instrument of characterization, one of those many touches which give his characters so much body and incidentally show his sense of the differences in the social scale. The ladies in *Love's Labour's Lost* are an apparent exception, for some will say that they talk 'greasily' in IV. i. But the Princess is guiltless, and one or two of her ladies exceed only in conversation with Boyet, another bad mark against that character. However he earns the applause of Costard: 'most incony vulgar wit! When it comes so smoothly off, so obscenely, as it were, so fit.'

It is likely that *A Midsummer Night's Dream* belongs to the year 1594 or 1595 when Shakespeare was also writing the most lyrical of his tragedies, *Romeo and Juliet*. And indeed the plays resemble each other not only in their lyricism but in the dramatic ideas lying behind them. 'Lord! what fools these mortals be', says Puck, and leads the mortals up and down the wood like puppets on a string. The immortals are not immune from human tantrums and jealousies, and they make mistakes, Puck confusing one Athenian with another; but the result is a *comedy* of errors. The lovers in *Romeo and Juliet* are overruled as are Lysander and Hermia, Demetrius and Helena; they are 'star-crossed lovers', the prey of Fortune. But the directing intelligence of Oberon is absent, and only death shakes off the yoke of inauspicious stars. Chance or Fortune or Circumstance brings these blameless lovers to their end, as it restores to happiness and marriage the Athenian lovers.

Because these lovers are the sport of the immortals we shall not expect them to be endowed with much individuality. In this respect (but in no other) the play resembles the old comedy of *Love and Fortune*.[1] The troubles of Shakespeare's lovers as of Titania are as 'the fierce vexation of a dream'. The labels the heroines are given are useful to distinguish them on the stage—Hermia short, dark, and shrewish, Helena tall, fair, and timid—but it is unnecessary for Shakespeare's purpose to distinguish further. For one thing, this is a midsummer night's dream, and for another, we can only spare to the lovers one quarter of our attention. The play mingles theme after theme in what (not to speak extravagantly) is a miracle of construction. The marriage of Theseus and Hippolyta, the reconciliation of the four lovers, the fairies, Bottom and his crew—these are brought into a unity by an imagination and a constructive skill that never falters.

Of the many qualities dramatic and poetic that work together to make possible this unity the most easily analysable is the constructive skill, what a recent critic calls the engineering. In this gift Shakespeare surpasses his contemporaries as he does in all others. The complicated plot evolves with unhurried pace, and the play deserves Hamlet's praise: it is well digested into scenes. Theseus opens and (for the mortals) closes the play and appears in the important hunting scene (IV. i). His power and authority are felt throughout. One father, Hermia's, Helena's being a mere name, suffices to set the affairs of the lovers in train. After a short scene

---

[1] Printed in 1589 and identified with 'A Historie of Love and Fortune' acted before the Queen at Windsor on 30 December 1582 by the Earl of Derby's players.

introducing the tradesmen (I. ii) we move (II. i) to the wood near Athens where we remain (except for the brief IV. ii) until the last act. The moon has risen, Oberon and Titania and Oberon's servant Puck are introduced, the four lovers are in the wood, and, by III. i, so are the mechanicals, Bottom being translated before the rehearsal is over. The long III. ii is wholly devoted to the perturbations of the young lovers. In IV. i dawn is breaking, Oberon is reconciled to Titania, the lovers are disentangled, Theseus succeeds Oberon as master of their fate, and Bottom is himself again. In IV. ii he rejoins his mates in Athens. The sequence seems inevitable, and the effect is that all is clear for the last scene (V. i). What a contrast with the last scene of *Cymbeline*!

A Shakespearian comedy is often a matter of strains and tensions which, exercising their strength in different directions, create a delicate but assured balance. If in his tragedies they are concentrated in one character, in comedy they are distributed among several characters or attitudes. So in *A Midsummer Night's Dream* almost all the variations which he plays in his comedies upon the theme of love are indicated: the romantic convention which has been his main theme in *The Two Gentlemen*, now happily subordinated in the quarrels and confusions of the two young couples; the fairy love of Oberon and Titania; Titania's burlesque wooing of Bottom; and the mature affection for Hippolyta of Theseus, the man of the world, which alone defies the vagaries of the moon. To take Theseus as the *point de repère*, the standard against which the aberrant passions of the other lovers are to be weighed, is perhaps to take him too seriously. When he is urging Hermia to 'take time to pause' and to look at life with her father's judgement—to 'fit her fancies to her father's will'—his position is not central but on the extreme right. It is a doctrine against which Robin Goodfellow had argued with some passion in *Tell-Troth's New-Year's Gift* (1593). And again, in his remarks on 'The lunatic, the lover, and the poet' the restrictive sense which he gives to poetry can hardly be Shakespeare's—that it gives 'to airy nothing A local habitation and a name. Such tricks hath strong imagination.' His later reflection on the drama—'The best in this kind are but shadows'—is as restrictive. Marprelate's enemy Dr. John Bridges had said that

'*Fortis imaginatio* in a man's owne brayne may worke wonders',[1] and had said it scornfully of adversaries who followed the devices of their own brains without reference to the truth. Theseus might almost have been speaking for Burghley, a grave and responsible statesman who might have been more favourable to poets if he could have conceived that they showed 'the very age and body of the time his form and pressure'. Yet to maintain that Shakespeare is expressing through Theseus sentiments not his own is not to doubt the importance of this character. We need to hear the balancing voice of 'cool reason' before and after a midsummer night under a midsummer moon.

In this play as in Peele's *The Old Wife's Tale* poetry and prose, romance and satire, folk-lore, fantasy and realism, sense and nonsense exist together and enrich each other. The prose is for the mechanicals only, verse for the rest, except in the last scene where the mechanicals infect their betters. The lyricism of the piece has often been remarked, as of *Romeo and Juliet* and *Richard II*, all written about the same time. It is the lyricism of a young poet who has mastered the technique of dramatic poetry and revels in the command he now has over his medium. The play has more of the sweetness of rhyme than any other except *Love's Labour's Lost*, but whether rhymed or unrhymed the verse has a simple and seemingly spontaneous grace and a variation of rhythm that banishes monotony. The last sixty or seventy lines are in short measure with a beat predominantly trochaic, a measure for fairy song and dance. Till break of day the benign immortals bless 'with sweet peace' the three couples and all that live in the palace. Then without change of measure Puck speaks his epilogue, and if this play was originally written for the wedding of some nobleman surely he did not withhold his plaudits.

The question of probability and improbability does not arise here. From start to finish we are under a spell. But in *The Merchant of Venice* some have found troublesome the clash between probable characters and improbable situations, and at times (as never in Shakespeare's tragedy) there is a suspicion that the characters are bent to suit the situation. Johnson held the story to be so wildly

---

[1] *A Defence of the Government of the Church of England* (1587), p. 83.

improbable and the changes of scene so frequent and capricious that 'the probability of action does not deserve much care'. Yet Shakespeare took every care to give the spectators a willing suspension of disbelief. Moreover, the themes which he blended would be acceptable because they were traditional and familiar. For example, apart from the assurance which the text gave them (I. ii. 27–32), his audience knew from many a moralist that no one can guess the jewel by the casket,[1] would accept the scene as a reasonable way of choosing a suitor, and would be confident that Bassanio would pass his moral test triumphantly.

The story of the Jew and the pound of flesh had been known to generations of Englishmen. In a translation of Alexandre Sylvain's *Épitomes de cent histoires tragiques*,[2] also published in 1596, a Jew pleads his case before the judge who had sentenced him to death if he cut more or less than his pound of flesh and is answered by the Christian. But the whole story, including a newly married woman's impersonation of the lawyer unknown to her husband and the jest of the ring (but without a Nerissa), is in Ser Giovanni Fiorentino's *Il Pecorone* (1558), a tale of which no English translation has survived. If this was indeed the source, the character of Portia becomes a striking example of Shakespeare's way of leaving things better than he found them. The praise given to the comedy of *The Jew* by the moralist Stephen Gosson in 1579, with a plot representing 'the greedinesse of worldly chusers, and bloody mindes of Usurers',[3] has suggested to some that the themes of a Jew and his bond and of the caskets had already coalesced. For a Jew's daughter who turns Christian Shakespeare needed to look no further than Marlowe's *Jew of Malta*. Like Barabas Shylock divides his allegiance between three ruling passions, himself, his gold, and his daughter. Both have good reason to resent their treatment at the hands of the Christians,

---

[1] The sentiment 'A precious stone may be set in ledde' (J. Case, *Praise of Music*, 1586, p. 29) was becoming proverbial, and in the year the play had its first production another moralist was linking this theme with another of much greater Shakespearian interest: '*Critius* sometimes wil choose a gilden boxe full of bones, before a leaden one ful of pretious gems, for men iudge onely by the outward appearance and protestations of men, and so . . . beleeue subtil *Rodeyan* because she can tell the smoother tale before simple *Cordeill*' (M. B., *The Trial of True Friendship*, 1596, C2).

[2] Paris, 1581, 237ᵛ–41; translated by L. P. (presumably Lazarus Piot who signed the dedication) under the title *The Orator: handling a hundred seuerall discourses*.

[3] *The School of Abuse* (1579), ed. Arber (1868), p. 40.

and in both hatred turns to a violent passion for revenge. But after the second act Marlowe's Jew becomes a monster, and Shakespeare's is never less nor more than a man. There is little verbal correspondence in the two plays if we discount as proverbial 'The devil can cite Scripture for his purpose' and 'Sufferance breeds no ease'; but Shakespeare never needed and seldom cared to borrow another man's words.

'Shylock . . . wrapped in the mystery of a thousand interpretations', wrote a dramatic critic of the nineteen-twenties. The advertisement on the title-page of the first quarto (1600) may stand for an Elizabethan interpretation: 'With the extreame crueltie of *Shylocke* the Iewe towards the sayd Merchant, in cutting a iust pound of his flesh'; and there is nothing in the text that runs contrary to this view of the character. It is unlikely that any Elizabethan actor could have presented Shylock sympathetically at the expense of the Christians or would have wished to do so; but since the time of Macklin and Charles Kean many an actor has done so. And many a critic. Shylock deserves our sympathy, the argument may go, as one notoriously abused. Despised and spat upon by Christians, and passionately resenting the theft of his ducats and his daughter, he thirsts for revenge and takes the only chance his circumstances permit. The balance of the comedy is upset thereby and brought perilously near to tragedy, but then Shakespeare was carried away by his own invention. You cannot put into a character's mouth words like

> I am a Jew. Hath not a Jew eyes? . . . If a Jew wrong a Christian, what is his humility? Revenge. If a Christian wrong a Jew, what should his sufferance be by Christian example? Why, revenge. The villainy you teach me I will execute; and it shall go hard but I will better the instruction.

or like

> *Tubal.* One of them showed me a ring that he had of your daughter for a monkey.
>
> *Shylock.* Out upon her! Thou torturest me, Tubal. It was my turquoise; I had it of Leah when I was a bachelor; I would not have given it for a wilderness of monkeys.

and expect us to withhold our compassion.

Yet compassion is tempered by repulsion. If in his sorrows Shylock attracts sympathy—'no revenge; nor no ill luck stirring but what lights o' my shoulders; no sighs but o' my breathing; no tears but o' my shedding!'—he repels it by his delight in Antonio's losses and his usurious greed: 'I will have the heart of him, if he forfeit; for, were he out of Venice, I can make what merchandise I will.' And in the trial scene he is for Justice without Mercy and the whole gist of the scene is for Justice seasoned by Mercy, a cause pleaded in noble speech by a character presented as essentially noble.

One way of playing Shylock up is to play Bassanio down. If we apply naturalistic and twentieth-century tests we can easily arrive at Quiller-Couch's conclusion that every one of Antonio's friends is 'either a "waster" or a "rotter" or both, and cold-hearted at that'.[1] Have we lost our way and strayed into Jonsonian comedy? The conclusion is as inappropriate as Masefield's scorn for Henry V who passes 'a sponge over his past and fights like a wild cat for the right of not having to work for a living'.[2] This is not Shakespeare's manner in comedy. If Justice and Mercy is one of his themes, Friendship and Love is another, as certainly as in *The Two Gentlemen* and so much more successfully. He never allows us to forget the genuineness of the love between Antonio and Bassanio. They are bosom-lovers, as Portia says. A contemporary proverb maintained that when love put in friendship was gone, but we might think that the reverse was true from Bassanio's lavish pronouncement in the trial-scene that he would sacrifice wife and all the world to save Antonio. The protest from the young doctor of Rome for a moment relaxes the tension with laughter, and goes to show that Friendship and Love are compatible. In the last act this is the dominant theme.

Producers who are dissatisfied with the terse stage direction supplied by quarto and folio ('Exit') have continued the story of Shylock beyond the point at which Shakespeare leaves him. Some mercy has already been shown to him. The Duke pardons his life, and though the text is not very explicit he is allowed at least half his estate, provided he leaves all of which he dies possessed to his

---

[1] *Shakespeare's Workmanship* (1918), p. 98.
[2] *William Shakespeare* (1911), p. 113. This remark is not to be found in the revised and much altered second edition of 1954.

daughter and her husband and becomes a Christian. To Portia's enquiry he answers 'I am content' and is given leave to go. 'Exit', and we are at once absorbed in the business of the rings. One producer may give Shylock the escort of a guard or a gaoler, another will show him leaving the court broken and lonely save for the company of the faithful Tubal, and a third may give him the company of a priest, indicating that the mercy of Mother Church is ready to receive him. Is it merely modern prejudice that finds the third way repulsive? In his pamphlet on *Certain Reasons why Catholics refuse to go to church*,[1] Father Robert Parsons, S.J., while he was convinced that those Catholics who for fear or favour attended another church against their conscience were already dead and damned in hell, went on to consider the case of those who compelled them to act thus:

> Surely, as I am now minded I wold not for ten thowsand worldes, compell a Jewe, to sweare that theire weare a blessed Trinity. For albeit the thing be never so trew, yet should he be damned for swearinge against his conscience, and I, for compelling him to commit so heynous and greevous a sinne.

Parsons's Protestant opponent, William Fulke, observed that he did well to say 'as I am now minded', for were he and his fellow papists to have the law on their side they would act far otherwise. Yet insincere or schismatical as Parsons may have been, what he says may induce us to believe that Shylock had better be left as Shakespeare seems to have intended us to leave him.

The Merchant of Venice is the latest of the plays to be mentioned in Francis Meres's list of 1598: for later plays we have to do without his help. But there is pretty general agreement that *Much Ado About Nothing* and *As You Like It* may be dated between 1598 and 1600. *The Merry Wives* (1597–1602) and *All's Well that Ends Well* (1600–3) cannot be dated so precisely.

The main plot of *Much Ado About Nothing* is the theme of a *novella* by Bandello also extant in Belleforest's French but not available in English; it is also the theme of cantos V and VI of *Orlando Furioso*. A *Panecia* acted at court in 1574 may be an error for

---

[1] Douai, 1580, f. 5ᵛ.

Fenicia, Bandello's name for his heroine, and another lost play, based on Ariosto's version,[1] *Ariodante and Ginevra* was acted by Mulcaster's boys in 1583. Ariosto lays the scene in Scotland, and we may be grateful that Shakespeare did not follow him as Robert Greene might have done: he borrowed from Bandello the setting in Messina and the names of Pedro of Arragon and Leonato. In another respect he did not follow Bandello. There the lover of Fenicia is betrayed by his friend, and when the friend confesses his guilt the lover reproaches him for not telling him of his love, so giving him the opportunity of preferring friendship to desire. Shakespeare was not falling a second time into this trap. In Ariosto the maid greets the lover at the chamber window and is an innocent accomplice; in Bandello there is no maid. Elsewhere Bandello is much closer. He suggests the feigned death of Fenicia, the penitence of her lover, the marriage to a sister, the discovery—in the *novella* after marriage, in Shakespeare before. Of this ancient story of deceit and injured innocence there are many other versions. Eighteen sixteenth-century ones have been counted before Shakespeare, no two of them alike. Here as so often he chose a plot he knew to be popular and shaped it to his desire, giving it and the characters just so much scope as suited him and no more. What above all made his treatment different from any other was the invention of two of his greatest characters. No one else had given the slandered maid a friend; no one else could have given her such a friend.

The title refers to the Hero–Claudio scenes, but Charles I wrote against the play in his copy of the Second Folio the words 'Benedick and Beatrice', as he wrote against *Twelfth Night* 'Malvolio'. So too Leonard Digges in his commendatory verses to the *Poems* (1640):

> let but *Beatrice*
> And *Benedicke* be seene, loe in a trice
> The Cockpit, Galleries, Boxes, all are full
> To heare *Maluoglio* that crosse garter'd Gull.

So too the Treasurer of the Chamber or his clerk when declaring

---

[1] Peter Beverley's rendering into English verse, the first of any part of Ariosto (*Orlando Furioso*, V) had appeared in 1566.

a payment to the King's players for performing 'Benedicte and Betteris' at court in 1613. The *Oxford English Dictionary* gives as its earliest example of 'character' in the sense of a personality created by a dramatist or a 'part' assumed by an actor a quotation from *Tom Jones* (1749). The usage goes back more than a century earlier, though in the early seventeenth century it was more usual to refer to the 'persons'. But, persons or characters, there has never been a time when playgoers and readers did not take their chief delight in Shakespeare's characters and high among these are Beatrice and Benedick.

Of all the comedies (except the uncharacteristic *Merry Wives*) this has the most prose. The distinction is no longer, as it was in *The Taming of the Shrew*, that the high life is in verse and the low in prose. The Hero–Claudio scenes, which rise to an emotional pitch above the level of comedy, are naturally in verse, but Benedick and Beatrice speak habitually in prose. The first occasion on which Benedick speaks verse is immediately after he has learnt that Beatrice is in love with him; when she enters with the discouraging 'Against my will I am sent to bid you come in to dinner', than which nothing can be more prosaic, he sighs out the adoration of a lover with 'Fair Beatrice, I thank you for your pains'. Except for some dozen lines scattered over the verse-contexts in the church scene and the last scene, this is the sum total of his verse. And the first and almost the last occasion on which Beatrice speaks verse is immediately after she has learnt that Benedick is in love with her; and her soliloquy is not merely in verse but in rhyme and not merely in rhyme but in an elaborate ten-line stanza—two quatrains with alternate rhymes and a couplet—a curiously stiff and formal speech which some have thought a relic from an earlier play. Yet if they speak in prose, no one thinks of them as prose characters, a tribute to the quality of Shakespeare's prose. More than any characters in high comedy they rise above verbal wit and pit mind against mind in dialogue that surprises in sense, image, and cadence, giving to character both body and beauty; 'She speaks poniards, and every word stabs'; 'You have a merry heart'—'Yea, my lord; I thank it, poor fool, it keeps on the windy side of care'; 'You were born in a merry hour'—'No, sure, my lord, my mother cried; but then there was a star danc'd, and under that was I born.' Without the Hero–Claudio scenes, and this is perhaps their chief justification, Beatrice and Benedick would not engage our feelings as they do. Her 'Kill Claudio' comes more suddenly in prose than it might have done in verse, and sometimes puzzles into laughter an audience slow in the uptake; but it has the splendour of verse.

Stopford Brooke maintained that not only is the play set in Italy but that it is Italianate 'in sentiment, in morals, in evil and good passions, in its high honour and villainy, in its scenery, pageantry, and love of war'. But these are not distinguishing marks. The English were as fond of fighting and fine shows 'as any man in Messina'. The scenery is not alien to us. Much Italian sentiment had been taken from Italy by English writers and translators and transformed in the taking: at this very time an Englishman was engaged in fashioning 'a gentleman or noble person in vertuous and gentle discipline'. To repudiate any responsibility for the villainy seems a little highhanded. Don John is a brief study in laconic villainy; he is malign even if his malignity is not motiveless. But his wings are clipped by his creator and the limits of his mischief strictly defined. The 'brave punishments' he has so richly deserved are left at the end to Benedick's invention, seemingly to add to the gaiety of the wedding festivities. The spirit of comedy prevails, and the punishments can hardly be more serious than those suffered by Mr. Thornhill in *The Vicar of Wakefield* whose time was pretty much taken up in keeping a relation in spirits and in learning to blow the French horn.

Dogberry and his companions are undeniably English: no shirking the responsibility for them. What of Benedick and Beatrice? Their witty war has reminded some critics of the wit-combats between Lord Gasparo Pallavicino and the Lady Emilia Pia in *The Courtier*, and who shall say that the young Shakespeare did not learn from this gracious work? But are these characters Italian in nature rather than English, as Brooke maintained? An answer is suggested by these lines from the fine poem on Shakespeare by the unidentified 'I.M.S.' in the Second Folio (1632):

> Not the ayre,
> Nor clouds nor thunder, but were living drawne,
> Not out of common Tiffany or Lawne,

> But fine materialls, which the Muses know
> And onely know the countries where they grow.

Suppose we are not satisfied with this and ask where in England Shakespeare might have listened to such talk. Wordsworth said that he did not see much difficulty in writing like Shakespeare, if he had a mind to try it, to which Lamb replied, 'It is clear then nothing is wanting but the mind.' So we may say that at Elizabeth's court intelligent men and women of good breeding might have talked like Benedick and Beatrice 'if they had had a mind'.

The *Merry Wives of Windsor*, the most English of Shakespeare's comedies and the least worthy, is also indebted to Italy. Its main theme—the deception of a lover who attempts the seduction of two women and is twice or thrice humiliated by them—is of a *novella* type and resembles a tale in Ser Giovanni Fiorentino's *Il Pecorone* (I. ii), a collection which Shakespeare may have used for *The Merchant of Venice*. On this central theme is grafted the wooing of Anne Page with the double deception of father and mother, another theme for which there is no certain source but several analogues, among them the *Casina* of Plautus. Add two topical references which in the texts that have survived have very little effect.[1] The date of first performance is uncertain, and various dates from 1597 to 1602 have been suggested, 1602 being the year of the very bad reported text fortunately replaced in 1623 by a better one.[2] It must surely

---

[1] The one is Shallow's reference to the dozen white luces (louses in the Welsh parson's English) in his cousin Slender's coat of arms, always taken to be a satirical reference to Sir Thomas Lucy, who (according to tradition) had punished young Shakespeare for deer-stealing in his park, until Dr. Leslie Hotson put forward as his candidate William Gardiner, an unscrupulous Justice of the Peace in Southwark, who also had luces in his arms and was in a feud with Shakespeare in 1596. There is also a veiled reference, singularly ineffective as topical allusions tend to become, to a Count of Mompelgart who visited England in 1592, importuned the Queen for the Garter, and was elected to the Order on 23 April 1597, though not invested till 1603. But there is no need to make him responsible for the three Germans who cozened the host of the Garter Inn of three horses.

[2] Dr. Hotson has argued that the play was specially written for performance at a Garter Feast held at Whitehall on St. George's Day, 23 April 1597. There is, however, no record of payment to the Chamberlain's men after Shrovetide (6 and 8 February) in the declared accounts of the Treasurer of the Chamber nor record of payment to the Office of Works for the erection of a stage at Whitehall after Shrovetide; and it would be uncharacteristic of the Queen to meet these expenses out of her privy purse. It must be added that if we accept Dr. Hotson's dating then we must re-date *1* and *2 Henry IV* before April 1597.

be later than *2 Henry IV*, and is perhaps (though not necessarily) later than *Henry V* of 1599; in the one Shallow and Pistol make their first appearance and in the other (if *Henry V* is earlier than *The Merry Wives*) Nym. But to dispute how the events of this play relate chronologically with those in *2 Henry IV* and *Henry V* is a task better suited to the Baker Street Irregulars.

To the comic scenes in *Henry IV* the play is neither a sequel nor a complement. We may be tempted to attribute some of the réclame of the *Henry IV* characters to their namesakes in *The Merry Wives*, but these suffer sadly in comparison. 'Falstaff could not love, but by ceasing to be Falstaff', said Johnson. He loses stature even in the Doll Tearsheet scenes, and it goes worse with him when he is consistently humiliated by two citizens' wives. The cause of deterioration goes deeper. A man is known by the company he keeps and so is a character in a play: in *Henry IV* he is a foil to his betters, in *The Merry Wives* a mere creature of farce. Shallow too has none of the old splendour, and in the text we have is overlooked in the winding-up. His young kinsman Slender and Anne Page are, however, happy inventions. Even more than old Silence Slender exhibits an almost total nullity of mind. 'Sweet Anne Page' belongs to a different station in life from Shakespeare's other heroines, and she has a father and a mother; but she has much the same sentiments about choosing a husband:

> This is my father's choice.
> O, what a world of vile ill-favour'd faults
> Looks handsome in three hundred pounds a year!

Of Falstaff's train Pistol and Bardolph survive but barely survive. To these humour characters are added three more—the ebullient Host of the Garter Inn and the two foreigners who make fritters of the Queen's English—Sir Hugh Evans a Welsh schoolmaster-parson and Doctor Caius a French physician. Ford also may be thought a humour character, the Jealous Man. About this time (1598) Ben Jonson wrote his humour comedies, and the word was much in the air; but Jonson would have disowned *The Merry Wives*, and the play is as uncharacteristic of him as it is of Shakespeare. In the last years of the century there was a vogue for comedies with an English setting in an English town among people of a middle station in life.[1] The only gentleman is 'Master' Fenton who once 'kept company with the wild prince and Poins'.

A living dramatist has been heard to say that he would not sign his name to this play. There is much to be said for the view that it was composed in a hurry—in fourteen days at the command of the Queen according to a tradition reported by Dennis in 1702. It is even possible that to expedite the composition Shakespeare rewrote an old play of which traces still remain. What Falstaff was doing at Windsor is never made clear, or in what circumstances Mistress Quickly became a servant to Doctor Caius in the same town. What is more surprising is that when these two old acquaintances meet (II. ii) they meet as strangers. Seldom can we accuse Shakespeare of making his persons speak out of character, but in the last scene the breaches of decorum are flagrant. The fairies speak in verse, as we should expect, though apart from the speeches of Anne and Fenton there is very little verse in the play. What we do not expect is that the verse should be inferior and sometimes out of character. The speeches of Mistress Quickly, especially her compliment to the Order of the Garter.—

> Th'expressure that it bears, green let it be,
> More fertile-fresh than all the field to see;
> And *Honi soit qui mal y pense* write
> In em'rald tufts, flow'rs purple, blue, and white;—

seem to have been designed for another character or for some court entertainment.

With *As You Like It* and *Twelfth Night* we return to the purest strain of Shakespearian comedy. Here are no Shylocks or Don Johns to disturb the harmony. True, there is an Oliver and a usurping Duke, but Shakespeare takes an even stronger line with them than he had taken with Don John. With tongue in cheek (it would seem) he makes Orlando his brother's rescuer in circumstances we should call improbable if they were not pastoral. The conversion of the usurping Duke is even more obviously the work of a *deus ex machina*,

---
[1] e.g. *The Merry Devil of Edmonton* and Henry Porter's *Two Angry Women of Abingdon*.

and what is in its abruptness already comic is made more comic by Johnson's regret that the dramatist 'suppressed the dialogue between the usurper and the hermit, and lost an opportunity of exhibiting a moral lesson in which he might have found matter worthy of his highest powers'.

For few of the comedies so far considered has it been possible to point to a source. Analogues there have been in plenty, showing that Shakespeare coveted rather than avoided a familiar tale, but of sources in the sense that Thomas Lodge's prose romance *Rosalynde* (1590) was the source of *As You Like It* there have been hardly any. Lodge too had a source, the fourteenth-century *Tale of Gamelyn*. This he transformed from a boisterous lay in rough couplets to a Renaissance pastoral in elegant prose. Here is no homely version of the Robin Hood legend but a romance set in court and forest and much more congenial to Shakespeare's comic purposes; and whereas woman does not enter the world of *Gamelyn* except for a perfunctory reference to 'a wife both good and fair', Lodge provided Shakespeare with the originals of Rosalind and Orlando, Celia and Oliver, Phoebe and Silvius. We may therefore examine under favourable conditions what the dramatist took over or altered or discarded and may ask ourselves why. In Lodge the two Dukes are not related so that Alinda (Celia) and Rosalynde are not cousins. Alinda is banished by her father whereas Celia is a voluntary exile who braves hardship and danger for love of Rosalind. Moreover, Rosalynde is page to Alinda not her brother and protector. Saladyne (Oliver) repents before he leaves for the forest. Ruffians in the forest steal Alinda away and give him the chance of rescuing her: in Lodge there is no cause for the surprised Orlando's 'Is it possible on so little acquaintance... you should love her?... and wooing she should grant?' Nor is there cause for the sudden conversion of the usurping Duke, for he is slain in battle. The romance can afford to be harsher and more eventful than the play.

The greatest change is made by the invention of Jacques and Touchstone. The last play into which Shakespeare had introduced pastoral—if we except *The Merry Wives* as doubtful in date and suspect in pastoral—was *A Midsummer Night's Dream*, and there the mechanicals from Athens had preserved it from pastoralism.

Pastoralism is the indulgence of a coterie living in courts and cities and depends upon conventions of treatment and style acceptable to the select society that breeds it. Outside the Phoebe-Silvius plot and Orlando's miraculous rescue of his brother there are few traces of it in the play, for humour and the language of life keep it at bay. And Touchstone is a powerful anti-pastoralist. As his name suggests, he is the touchstone by which we estimate the other characters, a commonsense chorus commenting by word and action upon the artificiality of a courtier's life in the Forest of Arden, the self-indulgent melancholy of Jacques, the sentimental love-rhymes of Orlando; while his wooing and mating with Audrey is an anti-masque to the marriages of the three pairs of romantic lovers. Touchstone himself is not invulnerable, no one who kept company with Rosalind and Celia could expect to be. When (striking an attitude) he refers to the decrees of destiny Celia deflates him with 'Well said: that was laid on with a trowel.'

Jacques is a sharper satirist, but he is both satirist and satirized. His character has been taken as a sign of the times—we are now at the turn of the century—and as the prologue to the yet more sharply satirical Jacobean age. A shrewd observer of some abuses in society, he is yet a figure to be laughed at, and this makes Shakespeare's first employment of some of the devices of the recently inaugurated satiric drama far milder than Jonson's or Marston's. Jacques does not destroy, he enhances by contrast, the happiness of the world of which he prefers to remain a disdainful spectator.

The varieties of love between men and women shown in the play are many. One kind of loving, the merely sensual, is omitted. Jacobean comedy is full of it, but not Shakespearian. Another kind is important to the play, as important as in the neighbouring *Much Ado*. That play depends on Beatrice's unshakeable faith in Hero, and the action of *As You Like It* hinges on the friendship between Rosalind and Celia. There are other loyalties, as that of Adam to Orlando. And when Touchstone strives to relieve with his jests the miseries of Ganymede and Aliena, he dimly foreshadows a later fool who laboured to out-jest his master's heart-struck injuries. One effect of Shakespeare's comedies is to make us think better of mankind.

Several critics have remarked on the absence of action once the lovers have moved to the forest. The bravura pieces like 'All the world's a stage', the Duke on the pleasures of life in the forest, Jacques' brooding over the death of a stag, the brilliant invention of Touchstone's speech on the degrees of the lie, these stand out the more. There is room also for comment—comment on Nature and Fortune, on self-knowledge, on court life and country life; and more room too for Jacques moralizing the spectacle and for Touchstone the jester free as air, free to marry (not too irreparably) his Audrey, free to use his folly as a stalking-horse and under the presentation of that to shoot his wit. Much of the comment comes from him directly or indirectly, indirectly when Jacques is reporter of some of his wit, Shakespeare hitting two targets, as it were, with one speech, or rather more than two targets; for apart from character we have the constant exercise of setting one comment against another. For example, 'To fleet the time carelessly, as they did in the golden world' is one aspect of life in the forest, but so is 'And so, from hour to hour, we ripe and ripe, And then, from hour to hour, we rot and rot.' The truth is that the characters form and reform so engagingly and the dialogue is so sparkling that they make up for the dearth of theatrical scenes. We miss—and if it be not heretical to say so, we are glad to miss—a character like Dogberry, for of that sort of clowning Shakespeare had already given his audience enough. (William is a bucolic version, but gets short shrift from Touchstone and Shakespeare.) William Kempe, who acted Dogberry, sold his share in the company and left it soon after the lease of the Globe was signed in February 1599, and if the only condition of his remaining was the provision of more clowning of this kind we should rejoice at his departure.

Much Ado About Nothing, *As You Like It*, *Twelfth Night or What You Will*, these off-hand titles are indicative of the mood of gaiety sustained in these comedies. If we follow one of Shakespeare's successors and divide plays into plays pleasant and plays unpleasant then these are among the most delightful of his 'pleasant' comedies. And *Twelfth Night* is the last of them. Perhaps we should not regret that this is so. *Julius Caesar* was already behind him, and he was standing on the threshold of *Hamlet* and *Troilus and Cressida* and

Measure for Measure. And before he enters a darker world, he pauses and recapitulates the mood of his comic mastery. So we may imagine; but dates of composition are most uncertain.[1] Yet whenever written, whether in 1599, 1600, or 1601, *Twelfth Night* is the culmination of the kind of comedy in which Shakespeare had worked so happily since 1594. And as a work of art it is the most harmonious of them all with the exception of *A Midsummer Night's Dream*, than which nothing can be more harmonious. The plot is not more improbable than romantic comedy permits, especially as the characters who carry it are so presented that we never doubt their probability; the low comedy is sufficiently related to the plot, adds to the variety of the piece, and never gets out of hand (unless a bad producer allows it to); the high comedy is tinged now and then with pathos; and the resolution of the plot is accomplished without any violence to the moral integrity of the characters.

The play may be called a culmination in the sense that many an ingredient tried out in earlier comedies reappears in new combinations and is perfected. As usual there are plenty of analogues and no certain source. The analogue that comes nearest is a tale of *novella* type by Barnabe Riche (*Farewell to Military Profession*, 1581). A duke's daughter in love with a duke runs away from home to enter his service disguised as a servingman, is shipwrecked on the journey, is employed by him to court a rich widow of noble rank, and is preferred by the widow to her master. A brother who has pursued her in the belief that she has run away with a family servant is mistaken for his sister by the amorous widow, and he gets her with child. The sister is imprisoned when the duke believes that she (he) has stolen away the widow's affections, but all ends happily and the sister marries the duke and the brother the widow. One compensation we may get from reading such stuff is

---

[1] Dr. Hotson will have it that *Twelfth Night* was written for performance at court on Twelfth Night 1601, and if he is right it may be later than *Hamlet*, now supposed to belong to 1600. But he has not proved his case, nor is proof possible on present evidence. Not only do the accounts of the Treasurer of the Chamber neglect as usual to mention the titles of plays but they record payments to no fewer than three companies for performances before the Queen on Twelfth Night 1601 at night—the Chamberlain's, Admiral's and Derby's men; they also record payment to the Chapel children for 'a showe with musycke and speciall songes prepared for that purpose on Twelfth day at nighte'. See *Malone Society Collections*, vi. 31-2.

to be reminded, if we need reminding, of the moral tact which Shakespeare always observes in anything relating to his heroines.

But the best analogues to *Twelfth Night* are to be found in Shakespeare. In scene, in phrase, in character, he repeats his past successes yet always as with a difference. When John Manningham saw the play at the Middle Temple feast on 2 February (Candlemas) 1602 it reminded him of *The Comedy of Errors*, the *Menaechmi* of Plautus and the Italian *Inganni*, by which he may have meant the *Inganni* of Nicolo Secchi or the earlier *Ingannati*.[1] The only resemblance to *The Comedy of Errors* rests in the confusions caused by identical twins, in the earlier play brothers and brothers and in the later the more exciting and more improbable identity of brother and sister. Manningham might also have been reminded of *The Two Gentlemen of Verona*, if he had known that play, for like Julia (like Lelia in the *Ingannati*) Viola finds herself under the necessity of acting as a go-between for the man she loves. But the irony of the situation is now handled by a master-poet. Of that power of poetry which strikes in a few words to the heart of a situation Viola is possessed. Her words wring tributes from Olivia ('You might do much') and from Orsino ('Thou dost speak masterly'). Not many dramatists can venture without fear of ridicule to make one of their characters so refer to speeches they have invented for another. But Shakespeare must have known that Viola's answer to Orsino's 'How dost thou like this tune?'—

> It gives a very echo to the seat
> Where Love is thron'd—

is masterly.

Viola is clearly a sister of the earlier heroines, though she has fewer opportunities of displaying her wit and none of exercising that wit upon the man she loves. Like her sisters she has courage but not more physical courage than becomes a woman. If Julia

---

[1] Acted at Siena in 1531 and put into French prose by Charles Estienne (*Le Sacrifice*, later *Les Abusez*) as early as 1543. A version in Latin verse, *Laelia*, the manuscript of which survives, certainly based on Estienne, was acted at Queens' College, Cambridge, in 1595. The play is grounded, like *Twelfth Night*, on crosswooings and mistaken identity, the heroine, Lelia, disguised in male attire being confused with her lost brother Fabrizio.

swoons when in danger of losing Proteus, if Rosalind faints at sight of her lover's blood, Viola is properly reluctant to fight Sir Andrew Aguecheek. Sir Andrew is obviously by the same hand as Slender, and Sir Toby Belch may suggest a Falstaff sadly fallen away.

Malvolio has been styled the most Jonsonian of Shakespeare's characters. In several plays of this date—in the 'irregular Humorists' who surround Falstaff, in Jacques the man of melancholy, in the French doctor of *The Merry Wives*—we may be reminded of Jonson and his comedy of humours, the earliest example of which (*Every Man In His Humour*) was staged at the Globe in 1598. The difference is often striking. Jonson's town and country gulls in that play are there to be corrected, but we have no wish to see Slender or Aguecheek corrected: we are invited to delight in the folly of their simplicity. Steeped in the Shakespearian ethos some of them take on a greater complexity than Jonson's two-dimensional characters. Malvolio is a suitable target for the comic muse. He suffers both from self-conceit and self-deceit. An admirable steward perhaps, but not in Illyria. But Shakespeare's humanising power is such that this character is not merely a laughing-stock for Maria, Belch, Aguecheek, and Fabian, and the treatment they give him seems too harsh. He has indeed been 'notoriously abused'. In Jonson a humour character is often ridiculed out of his humour, but not Malvolio. His creator leaves him angry and revengeful and as much in love with himself as ever. Did even Shakespeare have a blind spot in his vision? And did it include among dogs spaniels, and among men chamberlains, stewards, and gentlemen ushers? Two other major characters *are* educable, Orsino and Olivia. What Fletcher might have made of a woman in Olivia's position we may shudder to think: Shakespeare's tact is consummate. As she cossets her grief, so Orsino cossets his love:

> If music be the food of love, play on,
> Give me excess of it, that, surfeiting
> The appetite may sicken and so die.

These are the opening lines and with them the dramatist plunges *in medias res*. Both characters are gently treated, and both are cured.

Left to themselves they might have died, like the young lady buried in Dorchester Abbey, of excessive sensibility.

A word might be said about a very minor figure. In several plays Shakespeare keeps a holy father waiting in the wings ready to marry a couple at a moment's notice, willing to conceal the marriage if desired, and if things go wrong fertile in plans for putting them right. (Sir Oliver Martext, the hedge-priest in *As You Like It* who would have married Touchstone and Audrey but for the intervention of Jacques, is quite a different kettle of fish.) The priest who marries Olivia and Sebastian in a neighbouring chantry is the most shadowy of them all; nameless and speechless, he is yet a 'holy' man who does all that is asked of him. Macaulay, arguing that unlike Jonson Shakespeare has not left us a single caricature, illustrates his point from Jane Austen and four of her clergymen, all in a sense commonplace, such as we meet every day, and all different. 'Harpagon is not more unlike to Jourdain, Joseph Surface is not more unlike to Sir Lucius O'Trigger, than every one of Miss Austen's young divines to all his reverend brethren.'[1] Theobald long ago maintained that Shakespeare's clowns 'come all of a different House', and 'are no farther allied to one another than as Man to Man, Members of the same Species'.[2] This cannot be argued of his friars, for though they are not caricatures they are not sufficiently important to his plots to justify a nice discrimination. We hear much of friars in *Measure for Measure*, for not counting the Duke in his disguise as a friar, there are Friar Thomas, the holy father who supplies the Duke with his habit, and Friar Peter who marries Angelo to Mariana. The admirable Friar Francis in *Much Ado* has a much more important function than to marry Hero to Claudio, for it is he next to Beatrice who speaks up for the innocence of Hero and refuses to be browbeaten by her father. And it is he in the longest verse speech in the play who suggests the plan of announcing Hero's death and prophesies the good consequences to follow. Some two years earlier Shakespeare had invented another friar with a yet greater part to play. Friar Lawrence also

---

[1] 'Madame d'Arblay', *Edinburgh Review*, Jan. 1843.
[2] *Eighteenth-Century Essays on Shakespeare*, ed. D. Nichol Smith, 2nd edn. (1963), p. 60.

suggests a feigned death, but with ill success. A family feud and inauspicious stars drive two innocent young lovers to their death. What a strange whirligig of taste that Chaucer who was surrounded by friars could not find a good word to say for them, and Shakespeare presents them in the most favourable light though he may never have set eyes on one.

Feste is the last of Shakespeare's great jesters, for the clowns in *All's Well That Ends Well* and *Measure for Measure* and *Othello* are very inferior; if it were not for the names of the persons in the First Folio we should hardly guess that Trinculo was technically a Jester: and Lear's fool is there to make his master's tragedy more poignant. Feste is no Jonsonian character, for high life is excluded from the comedy of humours, and Jonson never gets nearer to the court than the fringe, the hangers-on. Olivia's fool follows the same trade as Touchstone and performs much the same function. His function as chorus is well analysed by Viola:

> This fellow is wise enough to play the fool;
> And to do that well craves a kind of wit.
> He must observe their mood on whom he jests,
> The quality of persons, and the time;
> And, like the haggard, check at every feather
> That comes before his eye.

The paradox that those who think they have wit often prove fools whereas the fool who knows he lacks wit may pass for a wise man (I. v) occurs to Feste. It had occurred to Touchstone too as he commented on the all-in wrestling of Charles as a suitable spectacle for ladies. And in *King Lear* the paradox recurs to us again and again. In two respects Feste differs from Touchstone. Touchstone is the court jester at his ease, on holiday, whereas Feste has to work hard at his profession and gives the impression that he is feeling the strain. And unlike Touchstone Feste is a singing fool. The reason for the difference may be a practical one—the departure of Kempe from the Chamberlain's company and the arrival of Robert Armin, but whatever the reason we think differently of Feste because he takes pleasure in singing 'Come away, come away, Death' and 'O Mistress Mine'. He sings also the verses which begin 'When that I was and a little tiny boy', verses which seem more a part of the play than an epilogue outside the play. They are nonsense verses, like many a rhyme spoken by earlier clowns, but they are this only in part, for a rather sad sense peeps out of every other line. Serious enough is the survey of man's life from childhood to old age supported by the burden 'For the rain it raineth every day'. They are fitting verses to put at the end of the comedies. 'To-morrow to fresh Woods, and Pastures new'; but it was a sterner world than the world of pastoral to which Shakespeare was to turn.

3

Shakespeare and the Diction of Common Life[1]

WE have heard much in recent years of the necessity of making ourselves Shakespeare's contemporaries. We shall understand him better, it is said, be in less danger of misunderstanding him, if we know as much as we can of the stage for which he wrote, of the actors who performed his plays, of the audience which saw them acted, of the psychological theories of the age, of its economic, political, and social life, of its taste in rhetoric, in language, and in criticism; in short, if we make ourselves good Elizabethans, if possible intelligent Elizabethans. I shall not quarrel with this ideal. It is one to which every scholar aspires, and most of this paper is taken up with some of the difficulties. But while it is impossible to exaggerate the difficulties, it is sometimes possible to exaggerate the results. It has been said that nothing but a whole heart and a free mind are needed to understand Shakespeare, and if we interpret this to mean a robust heart and an acute and sensitive mind that is true, and true in an important sense. How little Keats knew of Shakespearian scholarship may be a cooling card for the scholar's fancy. He read Shakespeare not in Malone's edition, but in plain texts without commentary, yet he understood Shakespeare 'to his depths'. If ever man made Shakespeare a part of his life, that man was Keats. He is the great Shakespearian humanist. And if we are ever tempted to forget, his example is a perpetual reminder that while we strive to make ourselves Shakespeare's contemporaries, it is even more important to make Shakespeare our contemporary, to keep him level with life and with our lives.

The title of this lecture was suggested by a man who believed in

[1] [The Annual Shakespeare Lecture of the British Academy for 1941, corrected and expanded.]

keeping literature level with life. In the Preface to his *Dictionary* Johnson observes:

> From the authours which rose in the time of *Elizabeth*, a speech might be formed adequate to all the purposes of use and elegance. If the language of theology were extracted from *Hooker* and the translation of the Bible; the terms of natural knowledge from *Bacon*; the phrases of policy, war, and navigation from *Raleigh*; the dialect of poetry and fiction from *Spenser* and *Sidney*; and the diction of common life from *Shakespeare*, few ideas would be lost to mankind, for want of *English* words, in which they might be expressed.

Johnson does not say that a lexicographer could find in Shakespeare the diction of common life and nothing else. Shakespeare may have had 'small Latin and less Greek', but Johnson himself always said, 'Shakspeare had Latin enough to grammaticise his English',[1] and he had enough also to use English words from that language with confidence. 'With cadent tears fret channels in her cheeks', 'My operant powers their functions leave to do', 'The multitudinous seas incarnadine', these and many other lines contain words or senses of words not yet found earlier than Shakespeare. Within fifteen lines of a speech of Agamemnon's there are four such words.[2] But while he realized the value to his cadence and meaning of the learned word beside the familiar, he was never in danger of becoming an inkhornist. He may use the word 'remuneration' comically in *Love's Labour's Lost* and seriously in *Troilus and Cressida*, or 'festinately' comically in *Love's Labour's Lost* and 'festinate' seriously in *King Lear*, but at no time could the creator of Holofernes have admired the sixteenth-century poet who asked his mistress what thing was 'equipollent . . . to her formositie'.[3] And although he profits from them all, he cannot be attached to any one of the various schemes for enriching the English vocabulary recommended by sixteenth-century grammarians and rhetoricians —whether with inkhorn terms, outlandish terms, archaic words, or dialect. What a Greek writer said of Homer is very true of Spenser but is not in the least true of Shakespeare: 'he did not stop

---

[1] Boswell, *Life of Johnson*, ed. G. B. Hill, revd. L. F. Powell (1934–50), iv. 18.
[2] *Troilus and Cressida*, I. iii. 7–21: conflux, tortive, protractive, persistive.
[3] T. C., *A Pleasant and Delightful History of Galesus, Cymon, and Iphigenia* (1560?), A6. (T. C. is translating from Boccaccio.)

at his own generation, but went back to ancestors; had a word dropped out, he was sure to pick it up, like an old coin out of an unclaimed treasure-house, all for love of words; and again many barbarian terms, sparing no single word which seemed to have in it enjoyment or intensity.'[1] The conditions of Shakespeare's art as a dramatist did not permit him to stray far from popular idiom, but even if they had his mind was of a cast that would still have found the material upon which it worked mainly in the diction of common life. The best of the Sonnets are evidence of that and all the familiar images in his plays which, as his art matures, flow more and more freely from the less conscious levels of his mind. At the same time his instinct for what was permanent in the colloquial language of his day is stronger than that of any contemporary dramatist. No other Jacobean would have displayed 'a Rogue' with so little use of canting or 'pedlar's French' as does Shakespeare in Autolycus. In the words of Coleridge, his language is that which belongs 'to human nature as *human*, independent of associations and habits from any particular rank of life or mode of employment.... It is (to play on Dante's words) in truth the NOBILE *volgare eloquenza*.'[2]

His retentive mind received its stores from books, more still from speech and his own penny of observation. 'It is probable', wrote J. M. Synge, 'that when the Elizabethan dramatist took his inkhorn and sat down to his work he used many phrases that he had just heard, as he sat at dinner, from his mother or his children.'[3] Shakespeare may often have cried 'My tables—meet it is I set it down', as Shaw represents him doing in *The Dark Lady of the Sonnets*. When we find in earlier writers that as in *Love's Labour's Lost* a hat or veil comes over a face 'like a pent-house',[4] that as in *Hamlet* this world is 'a sea of troubles',[5] or even that a man's

---

[1] Dion Chrysostom, translated by A. O. Prickard (*Longinus on the Sublime*, 1906, pp. 93–4).
[2] *Coleridge's Shakespearean Criticism*, ed. T. M. Raysor (1930), i. 149–50.
[3] *Works* (1910), ii. 3–4.
[4] *Love's Labour's Lost*, III. i. 15, Sir T. Elyot, *Pasquil the Plain* (1540), A3: 'The tirfe of the cappe tourned downe afore like a pentise'; and L. Wager, *Mary Magdalene* (1566), C4ᵛ (l. 585).
[5] *Hamlet*, III. i. 59, Painter's *Palace of Pleasure* (1566), ed. Jacobs, i. 202, Sir R. Barckley, *Of the Felicity of Man* (1598), pp. 147, 275, and F. *Q.*, VI. ix. 31. 'Mare malorum' is proverbial (Erasmus, *Adagia*, I. iii. 28).

Shakespeare and the Diction of Common Life

humour is 'tickle of the sear',[1] we may be in doubt whether these are phrases which Shakespeare had read or overheard, but we cannot doubt that in their boldness and concreteness they are characteristic of what he might have read or heard and of the climate in which his own image-making flourished. So, too, when Sir Thomas Egerton, Lord Keeper, urges the Parliament of 1597 to thank God 'upon the knees of our hearts',[2] we are not surprised at the bold extravagance of the metaphor. Egerton is not clipping the Queen's English: this was the current coinage of the realm and a commonplace.[3] He and his contemporaries did not suffer from 'the Danger of thinking without Images'.[4]

We could not know what wealth Shakespeare had to draw upon or how much by his own invention he added to that wealth until the completion of the great *Oxford Dictionary*, and we shall know more fully if the University of Michigan publishes its Early Modern English Dictionary. Perhaps it is not much of an exaggeration to say that a mere recital of the number of ways in which the Elizabethans could and did refer to their besetting vice of drunkenness would take up the greater part of this hour. Their dictionaries, especially Florio's and Cotgrave's, give us some indication of the wealth of synonym and of the delight these lexicographers took in assembling it. They practised 'copy' (*copia verborum*) even in their dictionaries. Florio calls his second edition 'A New World of Words': it is his voyage of discovery into the land of diction. Watch him exploring the possibilities of two Italian words. Under *tinca*: 'a fish called a Tench. Used also for a fresh-water soldier, or unexpert Captain that will have thirty men with him be it but to dig up a Turnip'; and under *squassapennacchio*: 'a tisty-tosty, a wag-feather, a tosse-plume, a swashebuckler'. Shakespeare does not use one of these four words, yet every one is rounded to an actor's palate, every one a moving picture.

[1] *Hamlet*, II. ii. 321, and *O.E.D.*, s.v. sear, *sb.*[1] I b.
[2] Townshend, *Historical Collections* (1680), p. 80.
[3] See G. Babington, *Exposition of the Commandments* (1583), p. 507, the speech of the Clerk Deputy at Edinburgh to King James in 1617 (Nichols, iii. 319), and the last scene of Heywood's *A Woman Killed with Kindness*. The original of the metaphor is the apocryphal 'Prayer of Manasses' (see *Oxford Dictionary of the Christian Church*): 'et nunc flecto genua cordis mei'. The expression is frequent in the Fathers.
[4] *Unpublished Letters of S. T. Coleridge*, ed. E. L. Griggs (1932), i. 163.

Unlike J. M. Synge, Shakespeare needed no 'chink in the floor' to enable him to overhear what was being said in the country-kitchen; he was free of it by birth; but he eavesdropped in the City and at Court and found there talk as fully flavoured. Landor has said that the best language in all countries is that which is spoken by intelligent women, of too high rank for petty affectation, and of too much request in society for deep study.[1] That is the language of Rosaline, of Beatrice, of Rosalind. If Shakespeare ever had a weakness for court affectations, he worked it out of his system in *Love's Labour's Lost*. We hear much of these affectations of speech in Elizabethan literature, of 'Arcadian and Euphuized gentlewomen', but as we should expect there were few affectations in the speech of those who were closest to the Queen. In *Cynthia's Revels* it is not Crites or Arete who drink of the fountain of self-love; and it is not Cynthia. However picked and patterned may be the language of Elizabeth's formal writings, there was no trace of affectation in her private speech or public utterances. Her very oaths identified her with all classes of her people except those who swore by 'yea and nay' or 'indeed la'. In a pious and spirited book which formed half the dowry of Bunyan's wife, Arthur Dent wrote of men who swore less vigorously than his Queen that 'Hell gapeth for them';[2] but fortunately for him his Plain Man's Pathway did not lead him into the Presence. And when she spoke to her people, then, as her great scholar Camden would have wished, she did not follow 'the minion refiners of English'; she spoke not State English, not Court English, not Secretary English, but plain English.[3]

Though *God* hath raised Me high; yet This I count the Glory of my Crown, That I have Reigned with your Loves. This makes me so that I do not so much rejoyce, That *God* hath made Me to be a *Queen*, as, To be a *Queen* over so Thankful a People. . . . There will never *Queen* sit in my Seat, with more Zeal to my Country, Care for my Subjects and that sooner with willingness will venture her Life for your Good and Safety, than My Self. For it is not my desire to Live nor Reign longer, than my Life and Reign shall be for your

[1] *Imaginary Conversations*, 'Samuel Johnson and John Horne Tooke' (*Works*, ed. T. Earle Welby, 1927, v. 5).
[2] *The Plain Man's Pathway to Heaven* (1601), p. 165.
[3] *Remains* (1605), p. 28.

Good. And though you have had, and may have many Princes, more Mighty and Wise, sitting in this State; yet you never had, or shall have, any that will be more Careful and Loving.[1]

As we read these strong and straightforward sentences we may flatter ourselves that we can read Elizabeth and Shakespeare as good Elizabethans, yet apart altogether from changes in pronunciation the words cannot mean to us what they meant to contemporaries. The words we most value rise from a well of associations fed by a thousand memories, and we cannot rid ourselves of these associations. But we can make an approximation, and in making it the greatest difficulty does not come from obsolete expressions and obscure allusions. When we meet with 'miching mallecho' either we look up a commentary or we pass on. There is a possibility of ignorance here, but not of misunderstanding, unless indeed the commentators mislead us. Nor in some contexts is the danger very great from words which have survived into modern English with very different meanings. Only a very stupid reader would misunderstand when it is said that in the Scotland of Macbeth 'violent sorrow seems A modern ecstasy'. The real danger comes with words to which it is possible to attach the modern meaning and make a sense. But the sense is not Shakespeare's. Sometimes the difference is so slight that the modern meaning does little or no harm. It matters little, to take an example of Henry Bradley's,[2] whether we understand Polonius's 'Still harping on my daughter' to mean 'Now as heretofore harping on my daughter' or, as Shakespeare meant, 'Always harping on my daughter'. It matters more if we forget how the dilatoriness of man has deprived of its urgency such a word as 'presently'.[3] How many a word has lost its vigour by continual usage may be illustrated from a famous passage in *Othello*:

> When you shall these unlucky deeds relate,
> Speak of me as I am; nothing extenuate,

[1] Townshend, pp. 263 and 266.
[2] *Shakespeare's England*, ii. 559.
[3] 'By and by' and 'anon' could still mean 'at once', and they sometimes bear their older meaning in the Bible of 1611; but in Shakespeare they can be given the modern meaning of 'soon'. In the 'anon, anon, sir' of the drawer the promise seems to bear the older meaning and the performance the modern.

> Nor set down aught in malice. Then must you speak
> Of one that lov'd not wisely, but too well;
> Of one not easily jealous, but, being wrought,
> Perplexed in the extreme.

'These unlucky deeds', 'perplexed in the extreme'. What colourless words, we are tempted to say, and good critics have seen here the irony of understatement. But in Elizabethan English 'unlucky' means or can mean ill-omened, disastrous; and 'perplexed' means or can mean grieved, tortured, the mind on the rack.[1] There is no hyperbole here, but neither is there understatement. In the noble and simple magnificence of Othello's speech, the emotion is fully and exactly stated.

Editors have not given us enough help here—Professor Dover Wilson in the later volumes of the New Cambridge Shakespeare is a notable exception—yet since Dr. Onions's *Shakespeare Glossary* of 1911 and the completion of the *Oxford Dictionary* in 1928 much of the evidence has been available. Even with this expert assistance the difficulty of choosing between the many possible meanings of some of the commonest words is often great. It may be important to remember that in addition to bearing its modern meanings the noun 'will' often signifies lust, the carnal passions in control of the reason. It is the last word in the longest speech in which Hamlet rebukes his mother, and it is a climax to the mood of disgust and revulsion which has almost unseated his reason:

> Rebellious hell,
> If thou canst mutine in a matron's bones,
> To flaming youth let virtue be as wax
> And melt in her own fire; proclaim no shame
> When the compulsive ardour gives the charge,
> Since frost itself as actively doth burn,
> And reason pandars will.

---

[1] [Mr. J. C. Maxwell has supplied (privately) a good example of 'perplexed' in Othello's sense from Fairfax's Tasso, ii. 26. 7, where the Italian is 'commosso'; and Mrs. Wilson adds that Palsgrave, *L'Eclaircissement de la langue française* (1530), lists under the English word 'Distresse' the French 'Perplexe', and Minsheu, *Guide to the Tongues* (1626 edn.) under 'Perplexed' says 'Greatly troubled or grieved. G. (= Gallica) Perpléx.' H.G.]

Shakespeare and the Diction of Common Life 107

And as we should expect, the word is prominent in the plays in which Shakespeare is above all at grips with the sin of lust. 'Redeem thy brother', cries Angelo, 'By yielding up thy body to my will'; of Antony it is said that he 'would make his will Lord of his reason'; Edgar, on reading Goneril's letter to Edmund, exclaims 'O indistinguished space of woman's will', and to Troilus eyes and ears are

> Two traded pilots 'twixt the dangerous shores
> Of will and judgment.

So far I have been considering the words apart as if in a dictionary, but let me no longer proceed by way of 'crumbling a text into small parts' but draw my observations 'out of the whole text, as it lies entire, and unbroken'[1] in Shakespeare himself. For more than a century critics have observed how his line became animated, and his paragraph interanimated, by the rhythms of speech. They have noticed, too, his growing mastery of dramatic prose, and how while never relinquishing its colloquial base it could become upon the lips of Falstaff and Hamlet as quick and forgetive as poetry. And all the time he was slowly working himself free from the overelaborate use of schemes and tropes inherited by him from his age and by his age from scholastic rhetoric. 'That wonderful poet, who has so much besides rhetoric, is also the greatest poetical rhetorician since Euripides'—these words of Matthew Arnold's[2] remain true of Shakespeare to the end, but there is as much difference between the rhetoric of *Richard III* and *King Lear* as between the verse. An Elizabethan schoolmaster might have set his boys many a speech in Shakespeare's early plays as an exercise in the identification of schemes and tropes, and to name the figure in (say) the soliloquy of Henry VI which begins 'This battle fares like to the morning's war', with its elaborate examples of anaphora with and without climax, would have been well within the capacity of the meanest scholar in Mulcaster's school,[3] although perhaps he would not have

---

[1] Cf. George Herbert, *A Priest to the Temple*, chap. 7.
[2] *Merope* (1858), p. xlv.
[3] The Elizabethan equivalent of 'every schoolboy knows'. Cf. F. Hering, *A Modest Defence* (1604), p. 27: 'a meane scholler of *Mulcasters* schoole will easily tell him that . . .' Burton has another equivalent: 'Every schoolboy hath . . . at his fingers ends', *Anatomy*, 3. 1. 1. 1.

observed how the speech is redeemed by the lyricism which cuts across the formalism of the rhetoric. But if the boy had been confronted with *Hamlet* or *King Lear* his task would have been more difficult. There is a development in Shakespeare similar to that which Professor Manly noticed in Chaucer: 'a process of gradual release from the astonishingly artificial and sophisticated art with which he began and the gradual replacement of formal rhetorical devices by methods of composition based upon close observation of life and the exercise of the creative imagination.'[1] Even in Shakespeare's earliest manner, as in Chaucer's, the natural is ever present with the artificial, but by the turn of the century Shakespeare has forged verse, prose, and rhetoric into the subtlest instrument of dramatic speech the world has known. How this dramatic speech is dependent upon language familiar to all his audience, upon the language of common life, may be illustrated by examining his use of three figures, paronomasia, the image, and the proverb. Paronomasia and the proverb were more valued in his age than in later ages, but command of the image,[2] especially metaphor, has seemed since Aristotle the greatest thing by far for a poet to have.

Johnson recognized that every age has its modes of speech and its cast of thought, but Shakespeare's use of agnomination or paronomasia, or more simply quibbling with words, he could not condone. Camden, too, while quoting Giraldus Cambrensis to the effect that the English and the Welsh 'delighted much in licking the letter, and clapping together of Agnominations', felt that 'this merry playing with words' had been 'too much used by some'.[3] There will be few readers of Shakespeare's comic scenes who do not at times agree. The contrast between Speed's verbal wit and Launce's mother-wit is to be remarked: the one perished almost as soon as it was born, and the other is, in its kind, imperishable. Shakespeare inherited a ripe tradition of clowning—it was Tarleton's legacy to the English stage—and in ripe clowning, in 'merry fooling', there is little to choose between his early work and his late. As his art matures, he may bring everything more and more into a unity—

---

[1] 'Chaucer and the Rhetoricians', *Proceedings of the British Academy* (1926), p. 97.
[2] See Note A, p. 124.
[3] *Remains* (1605), p. 27.

Shakespeare and the Diction of Common Life

Dogberry and Stephano are essential to the action, while Launce is a music-hall turn—but the humour of Launce's talk with his dog is already ripe, as nothing else in that play is ripe. But if being a good Elizabethan means enjoying word-spinning on the level of Speed, few of us can be good Elizabethans. It is some consolation to have Camden on our side, and Camden's greatest pupil who attacked the 'Stage-practice' of 'mistaking words' in *Bartholomew Fair*. Fortunately Shakespeare grew out of the abuse of the practice, and the fool in *Othello* is the last of his characters of whom it can be said: 'How every fool can play upon the word.'

Ben Jonson was inclined to attack all 'Paranomasie or Agnomination'—it is significant that he puts the words into the mouth of his Poetaster—but like most Elizabethans Shakespeare was never willing to relinquish it altogether. The figure played a chief part in their jests and riddles and in the many word-games of which they were so fond. If we wish to see to what good purpose Shakespeare puts the pun we cannot do better than turn to Beatrice and Falstaff. About the time that Shakespeare was creating them, Jonson's friend John Hoskins was blaming 'the dotage of the time upon this small ornament',[1] but there was no longer any question of Shakespeare doting upon it. While the quibble is Speed's only weapon it is one of many in the crammed arsenal of Beatrice's wit and Falstaff's. Beatrice's 'civil count, civil as an orange, and something of that jealous complexion' is gay and stimulating, one of many touches in Shakespeare's greatest exemplar of a love between man and woman that does not abase but sharpens the wits, so that in both sexes the mind and the senses are fully exercised. Falstaff's puns, too, do not merely spin upon themselves. The quibbles in 'thou camest not of the blood royal, if thou darest not stand for ten shillings' are quibbles with sense and are intimately concerned with the action. In this lively lordship over words he shows the agility of his mind. A contemporary proverb said that he who sought for a fine wit in a fat belly lost his labour.[2] That is only

---

[1] *Directions for Speech and Style*, ed. H. H. Hudson (1935), p. 16.
[2] Holyband, *The French Littelton* (1576), F1ᵛ. Cf. *Love's Labour's Lost*, I. i. 26: 'Fat paunches have lean pates'. On the other hand Falstaff well exemplifies another proverb: 'A red nose and a great panch is no sign of repentance', Howell, *Paroimiographia* (1659), Fr. Eng. 11.

one of the many incongruities that are reconciled in this character. A cony-catcher, he hob-nobs with princes of the realm. A coward, he never shows fear or loses presence of mind in the heat of battle. Surrounded by men who would sacrifice their lives for ambition or honour, he believes only in good fellows, sack, and sugar. An old man, he would persuade himself that he is for ever young. Shaken and diseased by his excesses, he is so exuberant with life that he seems to stand for the indestructibility of matter. No wonder he exacted from Dr. Johnson what is perhaps the only apostrophe in his edition of Shakespeare: 'But Falstaff unimitated, unimitable Falstaff, how shall I describe thee?'

To an Elizabethan the play upon words was not merely an elegance of style and a display of wit; it was also a means of emphasis and an instrument of persuasion. An argument might be conducted from step to step—and in the pamphleteers it often is—by a series of puns. The genius of the language encouraged them. 'Soe significant are our wordes', writes Richard Carew, 'that amongst them sundry single ones serve to expresse divers thinges; as by *Bill* are ment a weapon, a scroll, and a birde's beake; by *Grave*, sober, a tombe, and to carve.'[1] And we remember Mercutio's dying jest—which is so much more than a jest—'Ask for me tomorrow, and you shall find me a grave man.' The rich ambiguities of the language were used not merely for fun. Falstaff can jest: 'I would my means were greater, and my waist slenderer'; while in the additions to *The Spanish Tragedy* Hieronimo, in great agony of mind, can implore 'infective night' to 'Gird in my waste of grief with thy large darkness'. So in the famous lines of Lady Macbeth

> If he do bleed,
> I'll gild the faces of the grooms withal,
> For it must seem their guilt

the play upon words is no jest put in to enhance the horror of the scene, nor does it suggest hysteria, for at this point in the play Lady Macbeth is mistress of herself and of the situation. It under-

---

[1] *Elizabethan Critical Essays*, ed. G. Gregory Smith (1904), ii. 288. Cf. George Herbert's praise of our language's neatness in giving 'one onely name' to two things in 'The Sonne' (*Works*, ed. F. E. Hutchinson, 1941, p. 167).

lines her determination, it is in Coleridge's words an 'effectual intensive of passion',[1] and it gives to her departure from the stage something of the emphasis and finality of a rhyming couplet.

I have said that the Elizabethans sometimes conducted an argument from step to step by a series of verbal quibbles. In Shakespeare the progression is often indirect and involuntary. This was noticed by Walter Whiter, a friend of Porson's, in his *Specimen of a Commentary on Shakspeare Containing I. Notes on As You Like It. II. An attempt to Explain and Illustrate Various Passages, on a New Principle of Criticism derived from Mr Locke's Doctrine of the Association of Ideas* (1794), a book which anticipates in a most interesting way much modern work on Shakespeare's imagery. Whiter showed among other things how the images in which Shakespeare's train of thought is clothed may be suggested to his unconscious mind sometimes by similarities of sound, sometimes by words with an equivocal meaning, 'though the signification, in which they are really applied, has never any reference and often no similitude to that, which caused their association'. Whiter's most elaborate researches were made upon the words and images which came to Shakespeare's mind, often involuntarily, from association with the theatre and with masques and pageantry. What is perhaps his most interesting discovery relates to the nexus of images which in varying combinations recurs in play after play to express disgust at false flattery and fawning obsequiousness, a nexus represented by Antony's

>   The hearts
> *That spaniel'd me at heels*, to whom I gave
> Their wishes, do *discandy*, melt their *sweets*
> On blossoming Caesar.

But the passage which started Whiter on his inquiries was from the speech in which Apemantus upbraids Timon 'with the contrast between his past and present condition':

>   What, think'st
> That the bleak air, thy boisterous *chamberlain*,
> Will put thy *shirt* on *warm*? Will these *moist* trees,
> That have outliv'd the eagle, page thy heels
> And skip when thou point'st out?

---

[1] *Shakespearean Criticism*, ed. T. M. Raysor (1930), i. 150.

Hanmer in 1744 had read 'moss'd trees', remembering perhaps the description of the oak in *As You Like It* 'whose boughs were moss'd with age'; and in this reading he has been followed not indeed by the *Oxford Dictionary*[1] but by most, if not all, editors. To make a participial adjective of the past participle 'moss'd', where the metre did not accommodate itself to 'mossy', was not beyond the capacity of any Elizabethan, particularly of Shakespeare, yet there is no evidence that any writer did this before Hanmer did it for the purpose of his emendation. But the seventh canon of criticism for an editor of Shakespeare is, according to Thomas Edwards, that 'he may find out obsolete words, or coin new ones; and put them in the place of such as he does not like or does not understand'. By changing 'moist' to 'moss'd' the editors have given the passage a meaning the very opposite to that which Shakespeare intended. The emphasis in *Timon* is not on aged trees. The bleak air, Apemantus means, the trees whose strength is such that they have withstood the harshness of nature longer than the long-lived eagle, the cold brook, the naked creatures of nature, these will not flatter Timon. Whiter did not see that 'moist' in this passage bears the meaning 'full of sap', 'pithy'; but he did see that by an unconscious association of ideas the image of the chamberlain putting his master's shirt on 'warm' or 'aired' impressed the opposite word 'moist' or 'unaired' upon the imagination of the poet, and that while 'moss'd' may be the more elegant epithet, what Shakespeare wrote and intended was 'moist'.[2]

'In the fictions, the thoughts, and the language of the poet,' Whiter writes, 'you may ever mark the deep and unequivocal traces of the age in which he lived, of the employments in which he was engaged, and of the various objects which excited his passions or arrested his attention.' Later and more systematic inquirers have proved, what the researches of Whiter suggest, that the great bulk of Shakespeare's images is taken from every-day things, from the goings-on of familiar life, images as familiar as the chamberlain

---

[1] See under 'mossed', *ppl. a.*, and 'moist', *adj.* 2.
[2] Whiter, pp. 70, 73, 81–2, 138–40. See Note B, p. 124. [References here and in Note B are to the original edition of 1794. A second edition, incorporating Whiter's revisions, appeared in 1967, edited by Alan Over and Mary Bell. H.G.]

putting his master's shirt on warm, or that image of heaven peeping 'through the blanket of the dark' which excited Johnson's risibility but does not excite ours.[1] Remoter images there are, for example the simile—to Pope 'an unnatural excursion'—in which Othello likens his determination for revenge to the Pontic sea

> Whose icy current and compulsive course
> Ne'er feels retiring ebb, but keeps due on
> To the Propontic and the Hellespont.

But usually the images are images from sights and sounds and experiences of a kind that came home immediately to the senses of his audience, and even in Othello's simile the emphasis is not on the remote geographical names, as it might have been in Marlowe, but on a natural phenomenon readily grasped by a people that used sea and river as the Elizabethans did. Owing to Shakespeare's instinct for what was permanent and central, his images are perhaps less often obscure than those of some of his contemporaries, but it must sometimes happen that what was obvious to the groundlings of the Globe Theatre because they had seen it with their own eyes or heard it with their own ears becomes apparent to us only after painful research. I take an example from a puzzling passage in *Love's Labour's Lost*. Berowne and the King of Navarre have broken their oaths to renounce love, and when the third perjurer Longaville is unmasked, Berowne observes:

> Thou makest the triumviry, the corner-cap of society,
> The shape of Love's Tyburn that hangs up simplicity.

What image did 'corner-cap' call up in the minds of Shakespeare's audience and by what association of ideas did he proceed from 'corner-cap' to Tyburn? Corner-caps were worn in Shakespeare's time in the universities, in the church, and by the judges of the land, but by an injunction of 1559 these caps were always square, nor do I know of one scrap of evidence that Shakespeare could have seen in England the three-cornered cap which his image so clearly demands. But we may be very sure that a Catholic scholar, Dr. John Story, 'a Romish Canonical Doctor', wore 'a three-cornered

---

[1] *Macbeth*, I. v. 50; *Rambler*, no. 168. It is a judgement on Johnson that in this essay he should give Lady Macbeth's speech to Macbeth.

cap'. Story was martyred at Tyburn on 1 June 1571, and the execution was recorded in the usual way by ballad, broadside, dying confession, and by pamphlets both official and unofficial. What impressed itself upon the memory of the people was the use in this execution of 'a newe payre of Gallowes made in triangle maner',[1] and for many a year Tyburn or the gallows was known as 'Dr. Story's corner-cap' or his 'triangle', or simply as his 'cap'. It is not likely that Shakespeare was thinking of Story or of his 'simplicity' or folly; it was sufficient that 'corner-cap' could be associated without difficulty with a triumviry and with Tyburn. Longaville, as the third member of the company or 'society', has made up the triumviry and so recalls the shape of the gallows upon which Love hangs these foolish men who have tried to escape from her in their little academe. To an archaeologist 350 years is a short span, but the historian of manners may find all in doubt after the passage of a generation.

I have mentioned paronomasia, and I have mentioned the image. Let me mention another figure in rhetoric much valued by the Elizabethans. It can best be introduced by quoting a speech made in the Parliament of 1601. After the member for Southwark had begun to speak, had shaken for very fear, stood still a while, and at length sat down, the member for Hereford made this speech on a bill to avoid double payments of debts:

> It is now my chance to Speake something, and that without Humming or Hawing. I think this Law is a good Law; Even Reckoning makes long Friends; As far goes the *Penny*, as the *Penny*'s Master. *Vigilantibus non dormientibus jura subveniunt.* Pay the Reckoning over Night, and you shall not be troubled in the Morning. If ready Money be *Mensura Publica*, let every Man cut his Coat according to his Cloth. When his old Suit is in the Wain, let him stay till that his Money bring a new Suit in the Increase. Therefore, I think the Law to be good, and I wish it a good Passage.

If this were played upon a stage now—those of us who do not read Hansard will say—we could condemn it as an improbable fiction, and indeed Thomas Jones's speech, with its clusters of homely proverbs, is paralleled by many a speech put by the

[1] *A Declaration of the Life and Death of John Story, late a Romish Canonical Doctor by Profession* (1571), C2. See Note C, p. 127.

dramatists into the mouths of downright or simple characters; Downright in *Every Man in his Humour*, Basket Hilts in Jonson's only play of rustic humours, *A Tale of a Tub*, and the goldsmith Touchstone in the citizenly *Eastward Ho* are as full of proverbs as an egg of meat. Shakespeare seldom uses proverbs in this way. He does, however, in two of his earliest plays, use the catch-phrase as a pointer to character or the lack of it, and the Elizabethans made no sharp distinction between catch-phrases and proverbs. Every age has its own catch-phrases, and in every age they are the staple of conversation among those whose wits barely cross the threshold of intelligence. Luce in *The Comedy of Errors* and Jaquenetta in *Love's Labour's Lost* have no conversation outside such pert, ready-made phrases as 'Lord! how wise you are!', 'When? can you tell?', 'With that face?', 'Fair weather after you'. There is a similar dialogue in Lyly's *Mother Bombie* which Shakespeare may be imitating. Lyly calls them 'all the odde blinde phrases that helpe them that knowe not howe to discourse'. Some of them have survived to this day with little change: 'The better for your asking', 'You are such another', 'And therewithal you waked', 'Yea, in my other hose', and 'quoth you'. Some dramatists exploited the elementary humour which comes from the repetition of a catch-phrase, but in the first quarto of *Hamlet*—the doctrine is Shakespeare's if not the words—the clown is condemned who keeps one suit of jests, like 'You owe me a quarters wages' or 'Your beere is sowre'. The laugh it raised was too easy for Shakespeare, the label it attached to character too superficial, the character to which the label could be attached too shallow. Falstaff has no catch-phrases. His sentiments are a perpetual surprise.

There must still be many a proverb in Shakespeare which his audience recognized as proverbial and which we do not.

'The nature of his work', says Johnson, 'required the use of the common colloquial language, and consequently admitted many phrases allusive, elliptical, and proverbial, such as we speak and hear every hour without observing them; and of which, being now familiar, we do not suspect that they can ever grow uncouth, or that, being now obvious, they can ever seem remote.'[1]

---

[1] *Proposals* (1756), p. 5.

When Lovell in *Henry VIII* speaks of 'fool and feather', and the Princess in *Love's Labour's Lost* asks 'What plume of feathers is he that indited this letter?', the collocation was already so well established as to have become proverbial, and for many generations 'he has a feather in his cap' was a periphrasis for a fool. Again, when Falstaff says that if Bardolph were any way given to virtue he would swear by his face and his oath would be 'By this fire, that's God's angel', it has been supposed that Shakespeare was borrowing from Chapman in whose *Blind Beggar of Alexandria* a similar expression is to be found. But he was drawing upon the proverbial stock of oaths—the saying is at least as old as 1570[1]—and his audience received that peculiar delight which comes from the apt application of an old saying to a modern instance, Bardolph's nose.

Sometimes we are left in doubt whether Shakespeare was using a proverb or inventing one. Was Portia's 'a light wife doth make a heavy husband'[2] proverbial or is it Shakespeare's punning variation of 'Light gains make heavy purses', or a reversal of 'A good wife makes a good husband'? And when Dekker and Webster use the same sentiment in *Westward Ho*,[3] were they borrowing from Shakespeare or making use of proverbial stock?

Then there are many 'sentences' in Shakespeare which are commonplaces of his age yet were never crystallized into a set proverbial form. Hamlet's 'there is nothing either good or bad, but thinking makes it so' is an example. Spenser's 'It is the mind that maketh good or ill' has been cited in evidence, and a closer parallel is found in *Politeuphuia, Wit's Commonwealth*, an anthology of 'sententiae' published in 1597: 'There is nothing grievous if the thought make it not.'[4] Whether Shakespeare kept a commonplace book like Jonson, Bacon, Webster, and most of his contemporaries, is not known. Long before the evidence was discovered by Charles Crawford, J. A. Symonds hinted that Webster kept one.[5] But in

---

[1] *Misogonus*, III. i. 240: 'By this fier that bournez thats gods aungell.' The source may be Ps. 104: 4: 'Who maketh his angels spirits and his ministers a flame of fire', quoted in Heb. i. 7.
[2] *Merchant of Venice*, v. i. 130.   [3] v. iii.
[4] p. 59b. For further parallels, see 'Shakespeare's Reading', p. 140 below.
[5] 'Vittoria Accoramboni', *Italian Byways* (1883), p. 179: 'The sentences, which seem at first sight copied from a commonplace book, are found to be appropriate'; C. Crawford, *Collectanea*, First (1906) and Second (1907) Series.

Shakespeare and the Diction of Common Life

Shakespeare there are no ill-fitting joins which betray the borrower. He brings everything into a unity. In the anthology just mentioned we find 'Our good name ought to be more dear unto us than our life',[1] and the sentiment may be as old as civilized man;[2] it is no temporary opinion; but when Iago says to Othello

> Good name in man and woman, dear my lord,
> Is the immediate jewel of their souls

the commonplace takes on a new meaning. The maxim is embedded in the evil in the play: it has become an essential part of a great design.

It is a little difficult to adjust ourselves to the seriousness with which the Elizabethans treated the proverb. Soon after Shakespeare's death it began to lose favour. The decline of the native and homely proverb is suggested by the preference of George Herbert for 'outlandish proverbs', which, in comparison, have 'too much Feather, and too little Point',[3] or by Glanvill's attack on preachers who use 'vulgar Proverbs, and homely similitudes';[4] and before Swift made the graveyard of proverbs and catch-phrases which he called *Polite Conversation* proverbs had almost disappeared from polite literature. This change in taste happened long before Lord Chesterfield called them 'the flowers of the rhetoric of a vulgar man' and said that 'a man of fashion never has recourse to proverbs and vulgar aphorisms'.[5] But to an Elizabethan the proverb was not merely or mainly of use for clouting a hob-nailed discourse; it still retained its place as an important figure in rhetorical training, and the many sixteenth-century collectors and writers who acclimatized foreign proverbs to the English soil were hailed as benefactors who enriched the 'copy' of their native tongue. Proverbs were invaluable for amplifying a discourse, or they added grace and variety to wit-combats.

---

[1] p. 106b.
[2] Cf. Prov. 22 : 1: 'A good name is rather to be chosen than great riches'; and Eccles. 7 : 1: 'A good name is better than precious ointment.'
[3] *Baconiana* (1679), ed. T. Tenison, Introduction, p. 93: 'the *Jacula Prudentum*, in Mr. *Herbert*; which latter some have been bold to accuse as having too much Feather, and too little Point.' So Fuller may have thought, but not Jeremy Taylor, who adds Italian proverbs to the margins of *Holy Living*.
[4] *An Essay Concerning Preaching* (1678), p. 77.
[5] Letter to his son, 27 Sept. 1749.

Sometimes they are hardly distinguishable in kind or function from the 'sentence' and the 'example': as Richard Carew said, they prescribed 'under the circuite of a few syllables . . . soundry avayleable caveats'.[1] Preachers, orators, wits, dramatists, found them excellent persuasion. They could strengthen an argument, for they contained in themselves the authority of experience—'it must needs be true what every one says'; they were vivid and epigrammatic so that they stuck in the mind when abstract precepts were forgotten; and the use of a homely proverb might put preacher and congregation, orator or dramatist and audience, upon a friendly and familiar footing, one with each other.

Of the great English poets only Chaucer makes so good use of proverbs as Shakespeare. The contrast between Shakespeare and Jonson is striking. On the title-page of his best and most popular comedy, *The Alchemist*, Jonson put the words:

>   —Neque, me ut miretur turba, laboro;
>   Contentus paucis lectoribus.

As he despised the 'green and soggy multitude', so he despised their collective wisdom. Ancient proverbs, he said, might illuminate 'A Coopers wit, or some such busie Sparke',[2] and they have their place in his comedies, but they could serve no serious function in the work of this robust and independent writer. In *Volpone* one proverb, and only one, stands out by reason of its position and the new turn which Jonson gives it. It is the last line of the scene in which the Fox departs in disguise to gloat over the discomfiture of his victims. 'Sir, you must look for curses', says Mosca, to which Volpone replies in one of Jonson's magnificent exits:

>   Till they burst;
>   The *Foxe* fares ever best, when he is curst.[3]

If we turn to *Sejanus* and *Catiline* we shall not be surprised to find a dearth of proverbs or even proverbial phrases.[4] Gnomic passages there are in plenty, and in the first quarto of *Sejanus* the reader's attention is directed to the tragedy's 'fulnesse and frequencie of

[1] Op. cit. ii. 288.
[2] *A Tale of Tub*, Prologue.
[3] V. iii. 118–19.
[4] See Note D, p. 128.

sentence' by inverted commas. But English proverbs he rigorously excluded from the dignity of tragedy. His practice is of a piece with that fundamental contempt for the people which gives to his art so much of its bent and bias. Of all ancient proverbs, he would most strenuously have repudiated that which maintained that the voice of the people was the voice of God. And when in his tragedies his verses 'break out strong and deep in the mouth',[1] as they often do, they owe little or nothing of their strength to colloquial English idiom.

In Shakespeare proverbs are used as rhetorical ornaments, as moral *sententiae*, and occasionally as a means of building up character. From Richard's dissimulations in *Henry VI, Part 3*, until he achieves his throne in *Richard III*, old saws like 'I hear, yet say not much, but think the more' come pat to his purpose, especially in sardonic aside. He clothes his 'naked villainy' with 'odd old ends'. In Faulconbridge, a character that sees the worst, seems to approve of it, and follows the best, bluntness and good humour are strongly marked in the first scene by the proverbs that pour from his mouth, but as his character is tested and proved by events his speech, while remaining direct and vigorous, becomes less proverbial. Richard seeks popularity for his own ends, Faulconbridge has a native disposition to it, while Coriolanus despises it. To him the 'vulgar wisdoms' of the people are contemptible.

> They said they were an-hungry; sigh'd forth proverbs—
> That hunger broke stone walls, that dogs must eat,
> That meat was made for mouths, that the gods sent not
> Corn for the rich men only. With these shreds
> They vented their complainings.

It is a little ironical that when Aufidius prophesies the doom of Coriolanus he does so with a couple of proverbs: 'One fire drives out one fire; one nail, one nail.'

What the proverb meant to Shakespeare is best shown not by the number and variety which he uses, although those so far identified are indeed many, but by his use of them in the gravest and greatest passages in his plays. Proverbs are mingled with folk-tale

---

[1] *News from the New World* (1640), ii. 42.

and ballad in the snatches, half sense and half nothing, spoken by the mad Ophelia: 'They say the owl was a baker's daughter, Lord, we know what we are, but know not what we may be.' In *King Lear* Shakespeare puts into the mouth of the Fool the silliest catch-phrase—'Cry you mercy, I took you for a joint-stool' —with poignant effect, and the Fool's last speech is a reference to the homely, ironical proverb: 'You would make me go to bed at noon.'[1] Most touchingly, it is with a proverb, 'Forget and forgive', that the 'old and foolish' Lear closes the scene of his reunion with Cordelia. Perhaps the most famous proverb in the whole of Shakespeare is that of the cat who would eat fish but would not wet her feet, to which Lady Macbeth refers in pluming up her husband's faltering will; but there are others in this play as striking and powerful in their operation. Keats has said that 'nothing ever becomes real till it is experienced—Even a Proverb is no proverb to you till your Life has illustrated it.'[2] Macbeth has indeed tested the truth of the line, 'It will have blood: they say, blood will have blood', and with what potency is the proverb charged. As moving is the 'what's done is done' of Lady Macbeth. It is one of the many thoughts and deeds which recur to her broken mind in the sleepwalking scene—'What's done cannot be undone: to bed, to bed, to bed.' They give to her prose the concentration and associative force of poetry.

I have mentioned Jonson's care to exclude popular proverbs from his tragedies, and the reason lies not only in his conception of tragedy as something 'high and aloofe'[3] but also in his strict sense of decorum. Shakespeare interprets the Renaissance doctrine of decorum more liberally. His decorum is dramatic, not historical. His tact in translating the manners of the ancient world to the modern stage is superb. He concentrates on what is permanent in spiritual and human values, and if clocks strike and doublets go unbraced, there is no offence, for he never sacrifices the dignity of his theme by introducing the trivialities of the present or the

---

[1] Notice how covert Shakespeare's reference is. He could rely on his audience recognizing the proverb.
[2] *Letters*, ed. M. Buxton Forman (1935), p. 318.
[3] *The Poetaster*, 'To the Reader', l. 238, and again in the 'Ode to Himself' in *Underwoods*.

pedantries of the past. He is as far from the revolting anachronisms of Heywood's *Rape of Lucrece, a true Roman Tragedy*, in which a Roman senator sings a ditty

> Shall I wooe the lovely Molly,
> Shee's so faire, so fat, so jolly, . . .

as from Jonson's attempts at exact reconstruction of the manners and sentiments of the old Roman world. As the translators of the Bible did not hesitate, when necessary, to change the remote for the familiar, the unknown for the known—the musical instruments of Israel for the cornets, flutes, harps, and sackbuts of Elizabethan England, or the vanities of the attire of Israelitish women for the mufflers, the bonnets, the mantles, the wimples, the crisping pins of the sixteenth century—so Shakespeare writes of the entry of Coriolanus into Rome in words which are also applicable to the triumphal entry of James into the City of London:

> the kitchen malkin pins
> Her richest lockram 'bout her reechy neck,
> Clamb'ring the walls to eye him: stalls, bulks, windows,
> Are smother'd up, leads fill'd and ridges hors'd
> With variable complexions, all agreeing
> In earnestness to see him.

Unlike Jonson, Shakespeare thinks nothing unclean that can deepen and widen his tragic art. He works not by exclusion but by bringing all aspects of life into a sense of order. Other men of his day, Webster or Middleton, tried to be as all-embracing, but the Shakespearian unity is incomparably more sensitive and more closely articulated. The poet's power reveals itself, says Coleridge, in the balance or reconciliation of opposite or discordant qualities. Only the disinterested artist who has no cause to serve (for the moment) except his art can bring himself to balance or reconcile such discordant and opposite qualities as are revealed, for example, in *Antony and Cleopatra*. In this many-sided play he seems to balance nobility and self-indulgence, renunciation and vanity, the glory and the corruption of the flesh, the greatness and the pettiness of the world. In the scene on Pompey's galley, where if anywhere in

Shakespeare we find the diction and conduct of common life, the famous triumvirate, 'These three world-sharers, these competitors', drown their schemings and enmities in drink until Lepidus, the weak member of the axis, is carried drunk away, and the first and second parts of the world sing the refrain 'Cup us, till the world go round'. Is this a play then about a set of fools and rogues struggling for power in a world which does not signify? It is, and it would be less rich if it were not. But we remember how these baser elements are balanced by others, and as the play ends it is all 'fire and air'.

I have tried to suggest a few of the ways in which Shakespeare's drama is continually irrigated by the diction of common life. But it does not remain the diction of common life. It is transmuted, and with what nobility let us remind ourselves from his greatest play. When the tempests in Lear's mind and in nature have spent themselves, when 'the great rage . . . is kill'd in him', there is a simplicity in his speech which persists to the end. It is no mannered simplicity such as we sometimes find in Webster when he is trying to write like Shakespeare; but it is as if the fire of genius had reduced language to its elements. The monosyllabic base which some of his contemporaries thought the misfortune of our language he turns into glory.

> Pray, do not mock me:
> I am a very foolish fond old man,
> Fourscore and upward, not an hour more nor less;
> And, to deal plainly,
> I fear I am not in my perfect mind.
> Methinks I should know you, and know this man;
> Yet I am doubtful; for I am mainly ignorant
> What place this is; and all the skill I have
> Remembers not these garments; nor I know not
> Where I did lodge last night. Do not laugh at me;
> For, as I am a man, I think this lady
> To be my child Cordelia.

In these sentences there is no gap between the inspiration and the expression, between the mind and the hand, and without wastage they gather up together all the love, terror, and pity that have gone before. These are among the words and rhythms in which

Shakespeare expresses his vision of good and evil. It is no system of morality which remains in the mind. The play provides symbols for the experience which it gives us—a wheel of fire, or incense of the gods upon such sacrifices—but there are no words to express our experience, or only Shakespeare's words.

NOTES
A (p. 108)

Image in its rhetorical sense is now understood to include metaphor and simile, and I use it so here; but in the sixteenth century the sense was much narrower. Quintilian (v. xi. 24) in discussing 'similitudo' refers to the kind of comparison called by the Greeks εἰκών, which expresses the appearance of things and persons, and advised a more sparing use of it in oratory than of those comparisons or similes which help to prove a point. Something of this survives by what is no doubt a long and devious route in Richard Sherry's *Treatise of Schemes and Tropes* (*c.* 1550), sig. F6:

'*Icon*, called of the latines *Imago*, an Image in Englyshe, is muche lyke to a similitude, and if you declare it is a similitude: as if you saye: As an Asse wyll not be driuen from her meat, no not with a club, vntyl she be full: no more wil a warriour reste from murther vntyll he hath fylled his mynd with it. This is a similitude: but if you saye that a man flewe vpon his enemies like a dragon, or lyke a lyon, it is an Image. Howbeit an Image serueth rather to euidence or grauitie, or iocunditie, then to a profe. There is also a general comparacion, speciallye in the kynde demonstratiue, person wyth person, and one thing with an other, for praise or dispraise.'

As in Quintilian the examples of 'similitudo' are usually in the elaborate 'ut... ita [*sic*]' form, so in Sherry and usually in Francis Meres's anthology of similes, *Palladis Tamia* (1598), they are expanded into the 'As ... so' form. This is perhaps what Sherry means by 'if you declare', i.e. 'set out your comparison in full'. In his *Treatise of Schemes and Tropes* and also in his *Treatise of the Figures of Grammar and Rhetoric* (1555), ff. 53 and verso, Sherry's discussion of the image follows his discussion of the example, which he calls comparison with an act done, and his discussion of the similitude or 'comparation', which he calls comparison with something that is dumb or lifeless. His treatment and instances of these figures correspond in part to those found in the *Epitome Troporum ac Schematum* of Johannes Susenbrotus. The instances of the rhetorical use of image, resemblance, and icon given above are earlier than those in the *O.E.D.*, where the earliest instance of image is dated 1676 and of icon and resemblance 1589: the rhetorical sense of comparation is not given, although comparison in the sense of simile goes back to Wyclif.

B (p. 112)

As he acknowledged on his title-page, Whiter based his work on the doctrine of association of ideas in Locke's *Essay concerning Human Understanding*, especially the passage quoted on p. 64: 'Ideas, that in themselves are not at all of kin, come to be so united in some men's minds, that it is very hard to separate them; they always *keep in company*, and the one no sooner at any time comes into the understanding, but its *associate* appears with it; and if they are more than two which are thus united, *the whole gang* always inseparable shew themselves together.' By this involuntary association of ideas the poet is supplied with words and ideas suggested to the mind by a principle of union unperceived by himself and independent of the subject to which they are applied (p. 68). Whiter saw and illustrated the value of the principle for the establishment of Shakespeare's text, for the interpretation of his meaning, for deciding upon works of disputed authorship, and for the light it might throw on 'the employments in which he was engaged, and . . . the various objects which excited his passions or arrested his attention' (p. 73). He even hinted at the presence of recurrent imagery: 'There is scarcely a play of our Author, where we do not find some favourite vein of metaphor or allusion by which it is distinguished' (pp. 124-5). The whole tendency of his work, both in the commentary on certain passages in *As You Like It* and in the more general and more important essay which follows, was to support the readings of the original texts against the emendations of the editors. Many of the readings in *As You Like It* which he defended have been restored by modern editors, though seldom for the same reasons. Whiter is not uniformly happy in his arguments. He had in his nature 'much labour and shrewdness, with a considerable share of credulity' (Francis Jeffrey in a review of Whiter's *Etymologicon Magnum* in the *Monthly Review*, June and July, 1802, cited in the *D.N.B.*), and it is unfortunate that he should have chosen to illustrate the importance of his principle in deciding upon works of disputed authorship by attempting to prove that the Rowley poems, apart from some impurities introduced by the transcriber, are the genuine progeny of a medieval poet. 'Is he a sound man?' is the question asked of Whiter the philologist in *Lavengro* (ch. 24), and the answer is: 'Why, as to that, I scarcely know what to say: he has got queer notions in his head . . . upon the whole, I should not call him altogether a sound man.'

In his *Etymologicon Magnum* (1800, p. 300) Whiter referred to himself *sine nomine* as 'an obscure writer, who, in "A Specimen of a Commentary on Shakspeare" has laboured to enlarge the boundaries of Criticism, by applying a metaphysical principle to the elucidation of Poetic imagery, and figurative description'. He was disappointed with the reception of his book.[1] From an extract from his Journal inserted in his interleaved copy of the *Specimen*, now in the Cambridge University Library, it appears that even his friends were indifferent, an indifference which proceeded perhaps more from 'want of

---

[1] It was, however, favourably noticed in the *Monthly Review*, April 1798, in a review by Geddes which ends: 'He is, in our opinion, rather prodigal of his quotations, dogmatical in his remarks, and diffuse in his style: but the volume merits the attention of future commentators on Shakspeare. We are sorry, therefore, that it has lain unnoticed on our shelves during nearly *four years*: illness, and various causes, have contributed to this delay: but we were unwilling to let Mr. W.'s labours pass altogether unrecorded in our work' (from Dr. Ian Jack).

thought than want of feeling. But what is *feeling* but thought?' One of them, however, Raine, a lawyer, considered the book 'as able to form an æra in the style of our language, by which the strength of expression and the grace of composition are preserved without the apparent and perpetually occurring artifice of Johnson and Gibbon'. His diffuse style is overpraised here, as his learning is overpraised in W. B. Donne's statement that he was 'equal to Steevens in acuteness, in black-letter learning to Malone, and immeasurably superior to them both in his perception of the meaning and his sensibility to the metre of Shakspeare' (*British and Foreign Review*, 1844, xvii. 231).[1]

Coleridge and the critics of his generation ignored Whiter as they ignored Maurice Morgann, although both writers anticipated the romantic criticism of Shakespeare if only by their insistence upon the importance of the less conscious workings of the mind. Later editors and critics would not have left Whiter so severely alone if his work had been more often quoted in the Boswell-Malone Variorum edition of 1821. Four of his remarks are quoted or referred to in the commentary on *As You Like It*, but his work left no mark upon the text of that edition. We look in vain for any reference to his criticism of Hanmer's 'moss'd trees'; perhaps Malone would have agreed with the reviewer who wrote: 'From such associations good Lord deliver us! . . . We wish Mr. Whiter would learn to separate his ideas, instead of associating them' (*The Critical Review*, 1795, xiii. 100).

The first editor to make use of Whiter was Furness in the New Variorum edition of *As You Like It* (1890). He lists Whiter among his authorities and has a long note on his work at II. vii. 44: Jacques, 'It is my only suite' (pp. 109–10). Again, in the New Variorum edition of *The Tempest* (1892), commenting on the word 'racke', he refers to Whiter 'whose volume has never, I think, received its full meed of attention' (p. 213), and ends a long comment with 'Staunton's excellent note', which as Staunton owned was derived from Whiter. R. W. Babcock was, so far as we know, the first modern critic to call attention to Whiter's work on Shakespeare (*The Genesis of Shakespeare Idolatry*, 1931), although he hardly does justice to Whiter's genuine merits. The rediscovery of Whiter has taken place at the moment when the main preoccupation of critics is with Shakespeare's language and imagery, as the rediscovery of Morgann took place when criticism was still mainly preoccupied with Shakespeare's characters. J. Isaacs noticed Whiter's interest in the recurrent association of candy and fawning dogs in his contribution to *A Companion to Shakespeare Studies* (1934), pp. 312–13. For modern discussions of this nexus of images by writers who did not know that Whiter had to some extent anticipated them, see E. E. Kellett, *Suggestions* (1923), pp. 72–3; G. H. W. Rylands, *Words and Poetry* (1928), pp. 176–8; Caroline F. E. Spurgeon, *Shakespeare's Iterative Imagery* (1931), pp. 13–17, and *Shakespeare's Imagery* (1935), pp. 194–9.

[1] Donne also wrote on Whiter in a review of Watson's *Life of Porson, Edinburgh Review* (1861), No. 231, pp. 134–6.

Shakespeare and the Diction of Common Life 127

C (p. 114)

In the Arden edition of *Love's Labour's Lost* (1906) H. C. Hart called attention to the expression 'Dr. Story's cap' for Tyburn, and asked the question whether three-cornered caps were worn in Elizabethan England. But he did not notice that a special triangular gallows was used for the first time at Tyburn at Story's execution. Some recollection of this was in the mind of John Healey, translator of Hall's *Mundus Alter et Idem*, when to the words 'hee is forthwith condemned to commence at *Doctor Stories* cappe' he adds in the margin: 'Tiborne was built for him, as some say' (*The Discovery of a New World*, c. 1609, p. 225).

The history of the square cap is discussed by N. F. Robinson, 'The *Pileus Quadratus*' in the *Transactions of the St. Paul's Ecclesiological Society*, v (1905), pp. 1-16, and by E. C. Clark, 'College Caps and Doctors' Hats' in the *Archaeological Journal*, lxi (1904), pp. 33-73. Much is heard of the square cap as a relic of Popish apparel, both in the Vestiarian controversy of the early years of Elizabeth's reign and in the Marprelate controversy. Martin Marprelate often writes contemptuously of 'cater-caps'. And to take a later example Edmund Bolton, in a passage very like some speeches of Candido's in Dekker's *Honest Whore*, part 2, I. iii, and derived perhaps from a common source, observes that 'the square capp is retained not onely in the *Vniuersities*, but also abroad among vs, as well by Ecclesiasticall persons in high places, as by Iudges of the land' (*The City's Advocate*, 1629, p. 41). Philip Stubbes refers to the symbolism which was by some attached to the *pileus quadratus* of the Catholic Church in these words: 'The cornered cappe, say these misterious fellows [the Papists], doth signifie, and represent the whole monarchy of the world, East, West, North, and South, the gouernment whereof standeth vpon them, as the cappe doth vppon their heades.' (*Anatomy of Abuses*, 1583, part 2, ed. Furnivall, p. 115.); and William Turner, in *The Hunting of the Romish Wolf*, c. 1554, E 2, sarcastically provides a symbolism of his own: 'The messemongers of Englande go in shepes clothing, that is, they shewe great holiness in their outwarde apparel, they have iiij cornered cappes, to signifie that they go Est, West, North, and South to preache Gods worde (howbeit their foure corners maye as well signifie that they have destroyed the iiij Evangelistes and in the stede of them set up their owne traditions).' Sir Stephen Powle, clerk to the Crown, in his commonplace book (MS. Tanner 168, f. 206) has among other legal 'Problems', 'why do Judges weare square capps', and answers because they should possess the four Cardinal virtues, and because their sentences should be valid in the four corners of the world.

In another place (part I, p. 69) Stubbes compares women's 'Lattice cappes with three hornes, three corners I should say' to 'the forked cappes of Popishe Priestes', and just possibly the reference may be to the Italian three-horned biretta, a post-Reformation variation of the four-horned or four-cornered cap (Robinson, 6, and Clark, 36). The new triangular gallows might well have been named after Story even if he had worn a square cap, but if as a 'Romish Canonical Doctor' he was known to wear a three-cornered cap, the coincidence between the shape of the strange cap and the strange gallows would make the invention of Tyburn's new name irresistible. An expression of a similar kind—'Tyburn tippet' for a hangman's rope—is at least as old as Latimer (1549); the phrase appears in the margin of John Cornet's *Admonition of Doctor Story* (1571), a broadside in verse.

The earliest use I have met with of 'cornered' or 'corner' cap is in Gascoigne's *Supposes* (acted 1566), V. iv. 24: 'we will teach maister Doctor to weare a cornered cappe of a new fashion', where the jest is the usual one of cuckoldry. Lyly, in his *Pap with an Hatchet* of 1589 (Bond, iii. 401. 31), provides the earliest example yet found of the association of Tyburn with a cornercap: 'Theres one with a lame wit, which will not weare a foure cornered cap, then let him put on Tiburne, that hath but three corners.' I have not met with the expression 'Dr. Story's cap' before 1592,[1] but it may well have got into print earlier. A late example is in *The Wandering Jew*[2] (1640), where Tyburn is said to wear 'a Three Cornered Cappe' and the criminal to 'ride Westward, at the Sheriffs charges, on Doctor Stories wooden horse of *Troy*'.

Professor Dover Wilson explains 'the corner-cap of society' as a reference to the 'black cap' of the judge. The difficulties are: (1) A corner-cap was the wear of the learned professions, don, divine, as well as judge, and there is nothing in the context to indicate a reference to the corner-cap of a judge. (2) I know of no passage in which corner-cap is used in the sense of the sentence-cap. (*O.E.D.*'s earliest example of 'black cap' is from *Oliver Twist*; it does not give 'sentence-cap'.) According to Robinson (p. 7), in the sixteenth and seventeenth centuries judges wore their corner-caps in the courts at Westminster and during circuit sat in church in them: the wearing of them was not reserved to the sole occasion of pronouncing the death-sentence. (3) The judge's cap was square, and Shakespeare's image requires a three-cornered cap; there are not 'four woodcocks in a dish' until Dumaine has joined the triumvirate.

D (p. 118)

In the whole of *Sejanus* and *Catiline* I find only three homely, familiar proverbs—'laugh and lie down' (*Catiline*, iii. 697), and in oblique reference 'a woman's reason—because it is so' (*Catiline*, ii. 57–8) and 'Still waters run deep' (*Catiline*, iii. 571–2). The first two are to be found in those scenes of scornful comedy between Fulvia, Galla, and Sempronia which Dryden's Lisideius thought 'admirable of their kind, but of an ill mingle with the rest'. In addition there are two proverbs of a more sententious kind. 'He threatens many, that hath iniur'd one' (*Sejanus*, ii, 476) gets into Apperson's *English*

---

[1] 'Cuthbert Cony-Catcher', *The Defence of Cony-Catching*, ed. G. B. Harrison (1924), p. 6.

[2] By 'Gad Ben-Arod'.

Proverbs from Gabriel Harvey's *Marginalia* (ed. G. C. Moore Smith, 1913, p. 101), where it is found in the form 'He threatenith many, That hurtith any'. Harvey took it from the lost *Flowers of Philosophy* (1572) of Sir Hugh Platt, who could have found it in Publilius Syrus. A 'sentence' more often met with is 'Great honors are great burdens' (*Catiline*, iii. 1), of which examples are given in Latin (e.g. *Onus est honos*) and English in Tilley's *Elizabethan Proverb Lore* (1926), no. 346. 'Sentences' adapted from Latin proverbs or near-proverbs are 'The voice of Rome is the consent of heaven' (*Catiline*, iii. 61), and 'It is a madnesse Wherwith heaven blinds 'hem, when it would confound 'hem' (*Catiline*, iii. 392). I suppose that none of the English writers who observed 'watch the watcher' (*Catiline*, iii. 108) or exclaimed 'O age and manners' (*Catiline*, iv. 190) did so without remembering the originals. Of proverbial phrases—to limit these conveniently if mechanically to those mentioned by Apperson or in the *Oxford Dictionary of Proverbs*—I notice only 'to fear no colours' (*Sejanus*, i. 285), 'to have in the wind' (*Sejanus*, ii. 406), and, doubtfully, an oblique reference to 'take counsel of one's pillow' (*Catiline*, ii. 319).

4

Shakespeare's Reading[1]

JOHN SELDEN is reported to have said: 'No man is the wiser for his Learning, it may Administer matter to work in, or Objects to work upon, but Wit and Wisdom are born with a Man.' For two and a half centuries we have been asking how far learning administered matter for Shakespeare's wit and wisdom to work in or objects for them to work upon. If a friend had put to Shakespeare the Second Outlaw's question 'Have you the tongues?', would he have answered, with Valentine, 'My youthful travel therein made me happy'?

Soon after his death two poets wrote about Shakespeare in terms that suggest that his learning, that is, his knowledge of Greek and Latin, was scanty. One of them said that he had 'small Latin, and less Greek': the other praised him as Fancy's child, warbling 'his native wood-notes wild'. But Jonson and Milton are among the most learned scholar-poets this country has produced: and if we test Shakespeare, as perhaps they were testing him, by their own severe standards of scholarship, then indeed we must say he had not even the 'edging or trimming of a scholar'.

In the eighteenth century two extreme points of view were expressed. On the one hand, critics like John Upton and Zachary Grey, bent on making Shakespeare 'polite', found him learned in both the tongues and traced to classical originals many a passage of natural description and many a moral sentiment. On the other hand, Richard Farmer, a man deeply read in Elizabethan literature, traced to many a forgotten English book the learning which the dramatist was supposed to have taken direct from the classics and went so far as to state that he 'remembered perhaps enough of his

[1] [Reprinted, with minor corrections and additions, from *Shakespeare Survey*, No. 3, 1950. A paper read at the Fourth Annual Shakespeare Conference, Stratford-upon-Avon, on 12 August 1949.]

school-boy learning to put the *Hig, hag, hog*, into the mouth of Sir Hugh Evans; and might pick up in the Writers of the time, or the course of his conversation a familiar phrase or two of *French* or *Italian*: but his *Studies* were most demonstratively confined to Nature and *his own Language*'.[1]

Today, our estimate of Shakespeare's learning will not be pitched so high as Upton's, yet neither will it be pitched so low as Farmer's. We shall say he had 'small Latin and *no* Greek'; but that his Latin, small indeed in comparison with Jonson's, was yet sufficient to make him not wholly dependent upon translation. We shall say with the actor Will Beeston that he 'understood Latine pretty well' and mean by that much what Jonson meant by 'small Latin'. That he read Ovid as well as Golding's Ovid, some Seneca and Virgil as well as English Seneca and Virgil is, I think, proved. Nor is it in the least unlikely. He lived in an age that respected learning, an age that built its educational system upon the belief that in the classics alone, the sacred writings excepted, was to be found 'the best that is known and thought in the world'. Consequently some knowledge of Latin was possessed by all who had had a grammar-school education. To find a writer wholly ignorant of Latin we have to descend as low in the literary hierarchy as John Taylor, the Water Poet, who acknowledged that his 'scholarship' was but 'scullership' and that in Latin he proceeded only from 'possum' to 'posset'. So far as his attainments in learning go, Shakespeare may be likened to another popular dramatist. No university wit and schooled we do not know where, Thomas Dekker could yet read Latin with some facility. He could and did translate sentences from the Church Fathers from that popular and long-lived anthology *Flores Doctorum* assembled by a thirteenth-century Irishman, Thomas Hibernicus; and he could describe the terrors of hell in words borrowed from Sebastian Barradas's vast commentary on the four Gospels, a work which has not been translated into English, and (it seems safe to say) never will be. Shakespeare could have done as much, if he had cared.

On these matters there is general agreement. Few who have read through T. W. Baldwin's treatise on *William Shakspere's Small Latine & Lesse Greeke* will have the strength to deny that Shakespeare

[1] *Essay on the Learning of Shakespeare*, second, revd. edn. (1767), pp. 93–4.

acquired the grammar-school training of his day in grammar, logic, and rhetoric; that he could and did read in the originals some Terence and Plautus, some Ovid and Virgil; that possessing a reading knowledge of Latin all those short-cuts to learning in florilegia and compendia were at his service if he cared to avail himself of them; and that he read Latin not in the spirit of a scholar but of a poet. But granted that Shakespeare could read Latin, is there any evidence that he had access to any modern tongue other than his own? Here, I think, there is no general agreement. The evidence that he read Italian depends solely upon the fact that no English versions are known of some of the tales from which he took his plots. For *Cymbeline* did he turn to the *Decameron*, for *Othello* to Cinthio, and for *Measure for Measure* to Cinthio's *novella* and play as well as to George Whetstone's rendering of Cinthio? That an Englishman who can read Latin can make out the sense of an Italian *novella* has been proved experimentally again and again, but that Shakespeare read at all easily and widely in Italian literature—in Petrarch, Ariosto, and Tasso as well as in the writers of *novelle*—has not, I think, been proved. And as doubtful is the extent of his reading in French literature.

Let me illustrate the difficulty of coming to a decision by examining Shakespeare's alleged debt to Boccaccio. We know that Chaucer took the story of patient Griselda not from the *Decameron* but from Petrarch's Latin version of the last tale in the *Decameron*; and we argue that he did not know the *Decameron*, or at any rate possess a manuscript of it, because if he had he would most surely have made use of it. The evidence that Shakespeare had read the *Decameron* rests upon the resemblance between the wager-plot in *Cymbeline* and Boccaccio's tale of the four Italian merchants. If he knew the *Decameron*, it might be argued, it is odd that he did not give more evidence of it. But are we so certain that he knew even this one tale of Boccaccio's? That it could not have been his sole source has been proved. The stage-direction to the wager-scene in *Cymbeline* is sufficient to show this: '*Enter Philario, Iachimo, a Frenchman, a Dutchman, and a Spaniard.*' When Posthumus Leonatus joins them, representatives of five nations are upon the stage. To characterize the qualities of different nations was a common rhetorical device. Thomas Wilson recommends it in his *Art of Rhetoric* under 'Descriptio', and gives as an example: 'The Englishman for feeding and chaunging for apparell. The Dutchman for drinking. The Frenchman for pride & inconstance. The Spanyard for nimblenes of body, and much disdaine: the Italian for great wit and policie: the Scots for boldnesse, and the Boeme for stubbornnesse.'[1] Shakespeare followed this example in more than one passing reference in his plays, and in *Cymbeline* itself the 'wit and policy' of the Italian (in the bad senses of those words) are referred to by Imogen and Iachimo. In *Henry V* Shakespeare passed from rhetoric to drama when he created representatives of the four peoples of these islands, with the Welshman Fluellen so greatly outshining the rest. A Jacobean audience, then, identifying upon the stage (as perhaps they could from the appearance and costume of the actors) an Italian (Iachimo), a Frenchman, a Dutchman, and a Spaniard, might well expect some sharp satirical observations on national character. They were given nothing of the kind. The Italian and the Frenchman are necessary to the action, but the Dutchman and the Spaniard are mutes and hang loose upon the play as unnecessary encumbrances.

What has happened? It is not often that an examination of Shakespeare's sources convicts him of taking over recalcitrant material which he does not bend to his dramatic intention. Some critics, it is true, have argued that *Hamlet* provides an example. Those who find that Bradley's *Hamlet* is better than Shakespeare's 'in the sense that... it hangs together with a more irresistible logic', or those who believe that *Hamlet* is 'full of some stuff that the writer could not drag to light, contemplate, or manipulate into art' will speak of Shakespeare's failure, or partial failure, to modify or transmute the old traditional story which he knew from the lost play of *Hamlet* and other sources;[2] and some see in Hamlet's comments over the body of Polonius incongruous relics of that Amleth who dismembered the body of the courtier he had slain and threw it to the pigs. That Shakespeare in *Hamlet* found his materials

[1] Edited G. H. Mair (1909), p. 179.
[2] Cf. A. J. A. Waldock, *Hamlet* (1931), p. 49; T. S. Eliot, *The Sacred Wood* (1920), p. 91.

intractable and failed to impose upon them the subtle meanings of a new design will not be universally agreed; but here in *Cymbeline*, in these fossil characters of the Dutchman and the Spaniard, are clear vestiges of some unassimilated source. That source could not have been Boccaccio, for there the company is all Italian. There was, however, another treatment of this widely popular wager-theme, translated into English from the Dutch early in the sixteenth century and popular enough to go through at least three editions by 1560; and there sure enough, in *Frederick of Jennen*,[1] the company is said to come from 'divers countries', Spain, France, Florence and Genoa. *Frederick of Jennen* is a crude thing to put beside the choice Italian of Boccaccio, but in this detail and in a few others it is closer to *Cymbeline*; and editors have no longer the right to say that Shakespeare's sole source in this play was Boccaccio.[2]

Did Shakespeare then turn both to Boccaccio and to *Frederick of Jennen* or some similar analogue? Or was there some one work, now lost, in which he could have found all that he borrowed? It is here that conjecture raises its head, and with it rises the ghost of a lost play. I confess to feeling some impatience with those critics who, at a loss for a Shakespearian source, invent a hypothetical play. As Hamlet found, it is so difficult to test the honesty of a ghost. Belief upon belief is false heraldry, and false scholarship too. Yet I am not sure I am right to be impatient. That many printed books of that age have been lost I do not believe, but that many plays have been lost is certain. So serious are the losses that the historian of Elizabethan drama—especially of our drama in the sixteenth century, before the habit of reading plays had become popular—must often feel himself to be in the position of a man fitting together a jigsaw, most of the pieces of which are missing. Some sort of picture emerges, but is it the true picture? For example, how much of our dramatic history would need to be rewritten if those 'two prose Books' were to turn up which were acted at the Bel Savage Inn in London before 1579? They were acted some years before Lyly turned dramatist, yet Stephen Gosson could not have chosen apter

---

[1] Apparently an error for *Jenuen*, Genoa. The tale has been edited by J. Raith, *Aus Schrifttum und Sprache der Angelsachsen*, Band 4 (1936).

[2] Cf. H. R. D. Anders, *Shakespeare's Books* (1904), p. 63, and especially W. F. Thrall, '*Cymbeline*, Boccaccio, and the Wager Story in England', *S.P.* xxviii, (1931), pp. 639-51.

words if he had been describing the prose comedies of Lyly, 'where you shall find never a word without wit, never a line without pith, never a letter placed in vain'.[1] If by some happy chance the account-books of Shakespeare's company were to come to light, how many titles of lost plays might they reveal? We may argue that our losses are not so severe as for the companies which Philip Henslowe financed, because the Chamberlain–King's company was more stable and its plays worthier the reading. Yet we have lost much, and many a play which Shakespeare saw upon the stage, and perhaps acted in, has gone beyond recovery. What honey did he extract from that hive of activity, the Elizabethan stage, especially in his early years when he was finding himself? Here is a part of his reading and seeing and hearing where we cannot follow him, or can follow only imperfectly. Yet if I am told that his imagination may have taken impetus from some quite inferior play on a theme which he was contemplating, a play so inferior to his own as *The True Chronicle History of King Leir*, I cannot think that I am being told anything that is improbable.

But when all has been said of Shakespeare's knowledge and use of the tongues, the fact remains that what he read he read for the most part in English. Dryden said that 'he needed not the spectacles of books to read Nature; he looked inwards and found her there'. We shall do well to remember the context in which these words are placed. Dryden, himself a scholar-poet, was answering those critics who accused Shakespeare of wanting learning, that is, a knowledge of the classics, and was praising Shakespeare on the ground that they were not necessary to him.[2] He is not saying that Shakespeare was indifferent to the world of books. I find it impossible to believe in a Shakespeare who was not at some time in his life an avid reader. Did he never put his head into the shop of his fellow townsman Richard Field except to sell him *Venus and Adonis* or maybe to correct the proofs of that poem

[1] *The School of Abuse*, ed. Arber (1868), p. 40.
[2] Cf. the Prologue to Dryden's *Troilus and Cressida*, 'Spoken by Mr. Betterton, Representing the Ghost of *Shakespear*':
        And, if I drain'd no *Greek* or *Latin* store,
        'Twas, that my own abundance gave me more.
        On foreign trade I needed not rely
        Like fruitfull *Britain*, rich without supply.

and *Lucrece*? As he walked through Paul's Churchyard, did he avert his eyes from the advertisements of new books plastered on every post? To read some critics we might suppose so. It has been pointed out that while a whole library of Jonson's books has survived with his name and motto inscribed upon them, of Shakespeare's books there survive only a few more or less doubtful specimens. What does this prove? That Shakespeare was a modest man, perhaps, who did not write his name in books. Or that he read not for scholarship and erudition but to keep himself level with life. He too was *tanquam explorator*, though not in the same books and not in the same way.

Certainly he was no plodding reader. If Shakespeare is to be identified with any character in *Love's Labour's Lost* it is with Berowne, and Berowne says:

> Small have continual plodders ever won,
> Save base authority from others' books.

But the King of Navarre's answer will do for Shakespeare and Berowne: 'How well he's read, to reason against reading!' One supposes him to have been a rapid reader who could tear the heart out of a book as quickly as any man. It is to be observed how little use he made in his plays of some of the books that he looked at. We catch him dipping into that spirited piece of anti-Catholic propaganda, Samuel Harsnett's *Declaration of egregious Popish Impostures*, and coming up with the names of Edgar's fiends—Flibbertigibbet and the rest—and a few phrases. He perhaps remembers from Sir William Segar's *Book of Honour and Arms* the first and second causes for a trial of arms and builds them into the character of Don Armado.[1] When *The Tempest* was kindling in his mind, he remembered from Richard Eden's *History of Travel* the great devil of the Patagonian giants, and made him Setebos, the god of Caliban's dam; remembered also, so Malone suggested, some names for his characters, Alonso, Gonzalo, Ferdinand, and others.

---

[1] But see T. W. Baldwin, *Shakspere's Five-act Structure* (Urbana, 1947), p. 627, who points out that the 'first and second cause' had been stated in print an appreciable number of years before 1590 when Segar's book was printed, and adds 'For instance, the reader will find these causes stated more times than one in Sir John Ferne's *Blazon of Gentrie* (1586).'

Shakespeare's Reading

These were books to be tasted, and we know such books were among Shakespeare's books (when we know it at all) only from the 'orts' and fragments that he used. But there are 'some few to be chewed and digested'. So a contemporary of Shakespeare's with whom he is sometimes confused. There was the Bible, and North's Plutarch, and Hall and Holinshed. The evidence suggests that when a theme took possession of his mind, especially a theme with a long tradition behind it, he read widely—not laboriously, but with a darting intelligence, which quickened his invention. When the theme of Macbeth took possession of him, he read Holinshed on Macbeth, but turned back also, twenty folio pages earlier, to the reign of King Duff, and there read the story of Donwald in whom the King had a 'speciall trust', of the King's visit to Donwald's castle, of how Donwald 'though he abhorred the act greatly in his harte, yet through instigation of his wife' contrived the King's death, of his pangs of conscience, his dreadful end, and the monstrous sights observed in nature after this monstrous deed, horses eating their own flesh, the sun continually covered with clouds, 'a Sparhauke also strangled by an Owle'. Three pages later he read how a brave husbandman and his two sons defended a walled lane against the Danes with such bravery that they turned defeat into victory, stored it away in his retentive memory, and with careful husbandry made use of it in *Cymbeline*. If we may believe Wilfrid Perrett, who published in 1904 the best account that we have of the story of King Lear from Geoffrey of Monmouth to Shakespeare, Shakespeare consulted not only Holinshed on Lear, and Spenser, and the old play, but also *The Mirror for Magistrates* and Camden's *Remains* and even the original version in Geoffrey of Monmouth's Latin. And we have to add that at some moment of time, as he was meditating on these materials, they coalesced with Sidney's story in the *Arcadia* of the Paphlagonian unkind king.

Are these the speculations of scholars creating Shakespeare in their own image? They sound very like it. Yet recent critics make even more startling claims for one of his plays. Not indeed for all. Shakespeare knew when to stop, even if his critics do not. North's Plutarch was sufficient for his Roman plays, Lodge's *Rosalynde* for *As You Like It*, Hall and Holinshed for *Richard III*. But the historical background for *Richard II*, they tell us, did not come merely from Hall and Holinshed. The play depends also for incident and interpretation of character upon Froissart, two versions of a French chronicle on the death of Richard, a metrical history also in French, an anonymous play *Thomas of Woodstock*, and Daniel's *Civil Wars*. It sounds incredible, so incredible that J. Dover Wilson falls back upon the hypothesis of a lost play written by a historical scholar which would have given Shakespeare just those episodes and hints which he could not have found in the English books. But another able writer on the sources of *Richard II*, M. W. Black, observes with courageous logic that copies of the French works could have been borrowed in London from John Stow and John Dee —Holinshed tells us that—and argues that for a rapid reader, gifted in the art of skipping, the preparatory reading was not so formidable after all. And if Shakespeare prepared himself more thoroughly for this play than for any other play in the canon, he did so, says Black, 'because he was enthralled with the story and because he was laying the foundation for a great cycle of history plays'.[1]

So far, I have spoken almost exclusively of those works which gave him hints for plot and character. But what of the reflection in his plays of the political and moral beliefs of his time? What of that concern with order and disorder in the state, in society and in the mind of man, which Shakespeare shared with all thinking contemporaries and which is present in his plays more constantly and more powerfully than in those of any other dramatist? Was he, like Corin in *As You Like It*, a 'natural philosopher'? Did he absorb the culture of his age merely from the circumambient air? True it is that he was one who observed men and manners in court and city, town and country, church and tavern, and no man who writes on Shakespeare's reading should forget that the 'ample sovereignty of eye and ear' gave him more than books can give nature. Yet when we remember that he was profoundly concerned with the problem of good and evil, that most of the books published in his England were concerned with religion and morality, can we resist the conclusion that he was a reader of some of these? But which? The Bible, of course, which he knew as few men know it today, which he knew

[1] See *Joseph Quincy Adams: Memorial Studies* (1948), pp. 199–216.

as intimately and naturally as if his knowledge of it had come to him by instinct. But which other books? When we ask this question of his contemporaries we can usually give a certain answer. We can track Jonson and Chapman, Marston and Webster everywhere in the snow of the moralists. Long before Charles Crawford provided the evidence John Addington Symonds guessed that Webster kept a commonplace-book.[1] The contents of this commonplace-book he wove laboriously, though often skilfully, into the texture of his dialogue, and the verbal resemblances are so close that we cannot be in doubt.[2] But when Shakespeare is giving new life to some old commonplace we can never be sure in whose snow we are to track him. It is the rarest thing to find him borrowing from a book that is not his immediate source in words so close that they will convince a sceptic. When I have mentioned the opening of Prospero's speech, 'Ye elves of hills, brooks, standing lakes, and groves', which comes from Golding's Ovid, and Gonzalo's description of an imaginary commonwealth, which comes from Montaigne's essay on 'Cannibals' as translated by Florio, I have mentioned two strikingly exceptional examples. How remarkable it is that the question whether Shakespeare owed much or anything to Montaigne or to Florio's translation is still unsettled. Some say that he owed much; others hold that the parallels which have been adduced could have come to Shakespeare from other writers, or are the commonplaces of all time, or are opinions which seem to us singular but were then widespread. The great Montaigne scholar, Pierre Villey, came to the conclusion that if Montaigne had never written his essays, nothing warrants us in supposing that except for one brief passage in *The Tempest* a single word would have been changed in the plays of Shakespeare.[3] Does

---

[1] See J. A. Symonds, *Italian Byways* (1883), p. 179, and Charles Crawford, *Collectanea*, Ser. i (1906), pp. 20–46; Ser. ii (1907), pp. 1–63.

[2] To cite an example which escaped F. L. Lucas's notice, the Cardinal's speech (*The Duchess of Malfi*, V. v):
   When I look into the Fishponds, in my Garden,
   Methinks I see a thing, arm'd with a Rake
   That seems to strike at me
was suggested, as A. H. Bullen pointed out (*Gentleman's Magazine*, 1906, p. 78), by Julius Capitolinus, *Life of the Emperor Pertinax*. See also L. Lavater, *Of Ghosts*, ed. J. Dover Wilson and May Yardley (1929), p. 61.

[3] *Revue d'histoire littéraire de la France* (Paris, 1917), pp. 357–93.

this mean he was no reader? Or rather that his commonplace-book was his memory and he the very Midas of poets, transmuting all he touched?

Let me take as an example one thought and one image. And let the thought be Hamlet's 'there is nothing either good or bad, but thinking makes it so'. Had he been reading William Baldwin's *Treatise of Moral Philosophy* (1547) where it is attributed to Plato: 'Nothing unto a man is miserable, [but] if he so think it: for all Fortune is good to him, that constantly with patience suffereth it'?[1] Or Jerome Cardan's *De Consolatione*: 'A man is nothing but his mind: if the mind be discontented, the man is all disquiet though all the rest be well, and if the mind be contented though all the rest misdo it forceth little'?[2] Or had Shakespeare in mind Spenser's 'It is the mynd, that maketh good or ill'? Or, to come yet closer to *Hamlet* in wording and in date, had he been reading that anthology of *sententiae* published by Nicholas Ling in 1597, *Politeuphuia, Wit's Commonwealth*: 'There is nothing grievous if the thought make it not'?[3]

And let the image be that one which came to his mind more than once when he was writing of the chaos and anarchy which follow violation of 'degree'. It is in the famous speech on 'degree' in *Troilus and Cressida*, in a scene in *Sir Thomas More*, in *Coriolanus*, in this speech of Albany's when his eyes are at last opened to the cruelty of Goneril and Regan to their king and father:

> If that the heavens do not their visible spirits
> Send quickly down to tame these vile offences,
> It will come,
> Humanity must perforce prey on itself,
> Like monsters of the deep.

Go back a hundred years and more to the morality-play *Everyman*, and we find these words put into the mouth of God:

---

[1] Cited by T. W. Baldwin, *William Shakspere's Small Latine & Lesse Greeke* (Urbana, 1944), ii. 353, from the edn. of 1567. But the passage had already appeared in Sir Thomas Elyot's *Of the Knowledge which maketh a Wise Man* (1553), sig. M3ᵛ.

[2] Translated by T. Bedingfield (1573); cited by Hardin Craig, 'Hamlet's Book', *Huntington Library Bulletin*, vi. 29.

[3] p. 59*b*. Where Ling took it from, I do not know.

> For and I leave the people thus alone
> In their life and wicked tempests,
> Verily they will become much worse than beasts;
> For now one would by envy another up eat.

Go back nearly a hundred years again to *The Pride of Life*, where a bishop complains that men have ceased to fear God, truth has gone to ground, the rich are ruthless, and men

> farit as fiscis in a pol
> The gret eteit the smal.

But this proverbial image is much older than *The Pride of Life*. We can trace it back to the Fathers. But as John Poynet does this for us in a book which Shakespeare could have read, let me quote his words. In this passage from *A Short Treatise of Politic Power* (1556) Poynet is writing about the necessity of order and degree in the state and of what disasters follow when these are not observed:

> The Ethnikes ... sawe that without politike power and autoritie, mankynde could not be preserued, nor the worlde continued. The riche wold oppresse the poore, and the poore seke the destruction of the riche, to haue that he hade: the mightie wold destroye the weake, and as *Theodoretus* sayeth, the great fishe eate vp the small, and the weake seke reuenge on the mightie: and so one seking the others destruction, all at leynght should be vndone and come to destruction.

Shall we then say that this thought and this image were suggested by any one of the passages I have quoted? I would rather say they were suggested by none, yet were suggested by all. Somehow, like all thinking men in his day, he acquainted himself with that vast body of reflection upon the nature of man and man's place in society and in the universe which his age inherited in great part from the ancient and medieval worlds. And when the moment came, thought and image rose from the pool of his memory to receive their appropriate language and rhythm. We who are cut off for the most part from that great tradition in which Shakespeare was bred can realize only with difficulty how many thoughts and even images came to his audience with the pleasure not so much of discovery as of recognition, proverbial maxims and moral sentiments not newer than the familiar stories which he took over for his plots. And yet for his earliest audiences too, there was discovery, even when there was recognition; for what was old had become new. Always there was the power of 'dressing old words new'; always the power of bodying forth dramatic theme and idea in characters at once particular and general; always the power of bringing whatever concerns the needs, high and low, of the natural man into the order of a great design.

5

The Proverbial Wisdom of Shakespeare[1]

A PROVERB, so wrote James Howell in 1659, is 'a very slippery thing, and soon slides out of the Memory', and he recommends a reader 'to have his Leger-Book about him ... to Register therein such that Quadrat with his Conceit and Genius'. For some twenty-five years I have kept a ledger-book of proverbs whether they quadrated with my conceit or not. I cannot say that I have kept one very systematically, but at least I have kept one. At the moment one of my tasks is to prepare for press a revised and enlarged edition —it will be a third edition—of the *Oxford Dictionary of English Proverbs*. This is a historical dictionary of proverbs; that is, it aims at citing for each proverb the earliest literary reference, whether in manuscript or printed book, with a few examples from later centuries. It is not a period dictionary. It records proverbs from Anglo-Saxon times to our own. Therefore it has to be highly selective and to omit many hundreds of sayings which never had much circulation and are now obsolete. One Dictionary there is which attempts to give every English proverb within a certain period, the period from 1500 to 1700, and it does so with rich documentation. The editor was the late Morris Palmer Tilley, and his dictionary was published in 1950 by the University of Michigan. I shall often have occasion to refer to it. The University of Michigan Press has granted the Clarendon Press unrestricted use of Tilley's Dictionary, a sign that the generous brotherhood contracted among men of learning in all parts of the world, to which this Association is a living witness, extends also to learned presses.

A man with a hobby is apt to resent any aspersions cast upon the usefulness of his occupation. For him it suffices that the occupation

---

[1] [The Presidential Address of the Modern Humanities Research Association, 1961. The appendix is much expanded from that published in 1961.]

is innocent and keeps him busy and interested when he is too tired to do anything else. Let this be one excuse for my hobby of collecting proverbs; but I have others. Men have been attracted to the study of proverbs for a variety of reasons: for their value for philology, for psychology, for folk-lore, for the history of manners, or because they are said to illuminate the national character. My own interest is mainly literary. A knowledge of proverbs may help us to establish a text: it may help us to interpret its meaning; it may help us to discover with what tone a passage is to be read or spoken. The reader of eighteenth-century and nineteenth-century English literature is seldom at a loss to recognize a proverb and its meaning. Proverbs have remained a constant ingredient of popular literature, especially the novel; but by the late seventeenth century they had begun to disappear from poetry and polite literature and many became obsolete and are now unrecognizable without study. In the time of Shakespeare, however, the proverb was an important figure in rhetorical training, and the many collections of proverbs published in the sixteenth and seventeenth centuries provided material for dramatists and pamphleteers, politicians, orators, and preachers. No writer is richer in proverbs than Shakespeare. 'The nature of his work', wrote Johnson,

> required the use of the common colloquial language, and consequently admitted many phrases allusive, elliptical, and proverbial, such as we speak and hear every hour without observing them; and of which being now familiar, we do not suspect that they can ever grow uncouth, or that, being now obvious, they can ever seem remote.

The problem of definition I have discussed in a paper on 'English Proverbs and Dictionaries of Proverbs' contributed to *The Library* in June 1945, and more learned hands than mine, such as Professor Archer Taylor's, have written books about it. To the various early attempts at a definition objections may be raised. John Ward, who died vicar of Stratford-upon-Avon in 1681, required six things of a proverb: it had to be short, plain, common, figurative, ancient, true. But many proverbs are not figurative—'forget and forgive', for example, which Shakespeare puts to the noblest use near the end of *King Lear*: and while most proverbs are short, plain, common, ancient, true, so are the ten commandments. Indeed the commandments are much truer than the proverbs, which often contradict each other. Nicholas Breton could not have written a pamphlet called *The Crossing of Commandments*. Some have required that a proverb shall have the power of variant reference, and the best proverbs have that power; but some of the weather proverbs like 'September blow soft Till the fruit is in the loft' are restricted in their application. Some writers point to the fact that almost all proverbs are anonymous. In different countries and at different times they may seem to spring up by the process of polygenesis of which Professor Dámaso Alonso has spoken to us so persuasively; yet the most striking, we may plausibly conjecture, descend from one inventor, who must for ever remain nameless, as surely as the man who first sang in his head the original verses of *Sir Patrick Spens*. Popularity is another test which some apply. 'It is the Common-people alone', says Howell, 'that have the priviledge of making Proverbs.' A sixteenth-century writer, Thomas Bowes, said that the English make foreign words native by passing them to and fro upon the file of their teeth; and in this way the people 'make' proverbs as they 'make' ballads.[1]

The Oxford Dictionary's definition insists that a proverb must be popular: 'a short pithy saying in common and recognized use'. This applies well to the proverbs we assimilated in childhood, and it applies also to some newcomers of which the latest to come to my notice is 'Your head will never save your heels'. But the editor of an historical dictionary is forced to ask, 'In common use when, and in what circles, and how common?', questions it is not always easy to answer. The most famous reference to a proverb in the whole of Shakespeare is no doubt Lady Macbeth's

> Letting 'I dare not' wait upon 'I would',
> Like the poor cat i' th' adage;

and in his day the saying that 'the cat would eat fish yet dare not wet its feet' was in such common use that he could refer to it thus obliquely. But today perhaps only one in a thousand recognizes the

---

[1] Preface to his translation of *The French Academy* (1586), * 2ᵛ.

adage and how apt it is to the occasion. Here is the power of variant reference at its highest.

In the paper printed in *The Library* to which I have referred, I urged the lexicographer to include not only sentences but proverbial phrases and similes and to err on the side of inclusiveness, not exclusiveness. I was thinking of the generous nature of an Elizabethan's conception of a proverb, including as it did not only established similes, bywords or popular phrases which we might call catch-phrases, and mere tags and clichés, but also apophthegms and moral precepts of a sententious nature. Tilley was well aware that much that he included was not strictly proverbial in the modern sense, and a year before his death in 1947 he wrote to me to say how much he relied on what the sixteenth and seventeenth centuries understood as proverbial. 'Where no evidence from the collections turned up,' he went on, 'I have depended partly on the repetition of a thought and partly on "hunch". At times I have even admitted idiomatic phrases that seemed proverbial. I have erred decidedly on the side of inclusiveness.' If Tilley had excluded everything except gnomic sentences now or formerly in popular use, his dictionary would have been half as big and half as useful.

Shakespeare lived in the two great proverb-making centuries of the English tongue—the sixteenth and the seventeenth. They were centuries in which England exported almost nothing yet imported great riches without seeming to injure the balance of the language. I once attempted to draw up a list of the collections of English proverbs published between 1640 and 1670, that is, between the collection of 1640 known as George Herbert's and John Ray's of 1670. I found twenty-one and have since found two more. Consider how much has survived from the sixteenth century. Apart from the rich collections of proverbs mainly of native growth published by John Heywood in his *Dialogue of Proverbs* of 1546, enlarged *c.* 1549, consider the dictionaries and grammars and dialogues which give foreign proverbs and their English counterparts: the Latin-English ones done by Thomas Cooper, John Baret, and John Withals and such revisers of Withals as Abraham Fleming and William Clerk; or the Spanish by William Stepney and John Minsheu; or the Italian by James Sanford and John Florio—Florio in his dialogues but not

The Proverbial Wisdom of Shakespeare

in his dictionary; or the French by Palsgrave, Holyband, Delamothe, and (richest of all, but not until 1611) Cotgrave. Or consider the number of translations from that great disseminator of proverbs Erasmus: the *Dicta Sapientum* of *c.* 1526, Taverner in 1539, Nicholas Udall in 1542, William Baldwin in 1547, Robert Burrant's *Precepts of Cato* with the annotations of Erasmus, in 1545, and so on. One purpose these and other scholars had was to increase the 'copy' (*copia*, copiousness) of their native language, and they and their like put before the English public a vast quantity of proverbs, proverbial phrases and similes, wise saws, apophthegms, anecdotes, for the English people to file their teeth on, if they chose to. Often of course they did not choose to, but sometimes they did. The proverbial phrase 'To call a spade a spade' strikes one as being very English. And if a man wished to argue that a nation's proverbs throw light on a nation's character and wished at the same time to be patriotic, he might take the phrase as indicative of the honesty and forthrightness of the English character. In fact it came into English very early in the sixteenth century—my earliest example is from Rastell's *Four Elements*, printed *c.* 1526–7[1]—and from the Latin *ligonem ligonem vocare*, a phrase included of course in Erasmus's great thesaurus of proverbs.

What appears to be another importation is the proverb 'An empty sack can't stand upright'. The earliest English example that I can give is from Giovanni Torriano's *Select Italian Proverbs* of 1642 (p. 90): '*Sacco vuoto non può star in piedi* An emptie sack cannot stand upright.' It is still in popular use in England. In Cambridge in 1942 I heard it used with great effect by a sergeant in the Home Guard.

The translators were as bent on enriching the vernacular as the lexicographers. In some ways they are more interesting than the lexicographers, because when they translate a proverb they show the proverb in lively action not (as it were) as a stuffed specimen in a showcase. Sometimes I imagine—no doubt I fondly imagine, for the evidence can never be complete—I can observe the actual moment at which a proverb or proverbial phrase came into the language. Take as an example one of the earliest secular plays in English, *Calisto and Melibea*, printed by John Rastell about the year

[1] E7^v.

1529. Most of the play is adapted from *La Celestina*, and in the adaptation several Spanish proverbs are borrowed and make their first known appearance in English dress: 'Tomorrow is a new day' (*Mañana es otro día*), 'As soon goes the lambskin to market as the sheep's', 'The half knows what the whole means'. And to these we may add an expression without which it is difficult to see how a romantic lover could get on: *adoro la tierra que huellas*, 'I worship the ground you tread on'. In this way a language is enriched.

An interesting case is the weather proverb which has a seasonable airing every year in the English popular press: 'Cast ne'er a clout till May be out.' If there is one thing clear it is that May is the month, not the blossom of the hawthorn-tree. The evidence at present available to me suggests that it was imported in the early eighteenth century from the Spanish proverb 'Hasta Mayo (pasado Mayo) no te quites el sayo', a proverb which appears in the early-seventeenth-century *Vocabulario de refranes* of Gonzalo Correas Iñigo.[1] Captain John Stevens (s.v. Mayo) in his very useful *New Spanish and English Dictionary* of 1706 gives this translation: 'Do not leave off your Coat till *May* be past, that is, Leave off no Cloaths.' His dictionary is rich in proverbs, as indeed is the Spanish tongue, and it is his practice to give the idiomatic English equivalent whenever possible. The fact that he is here so literal suggests that the proverb was not yet familiar to him in an English dress. Not until 1732 do we find the rhyme: 'Leave not off a Clout, Till *May* be out', and then it is No. 6193 in that 'vast confus'd heap of unsorted Things, old and new', the collection of 6496 numbered proverbs collected by Thomas Fuller, M.D., under the title *Gnomologia*.

It is no part of my duty today to question the truth of this popular proverb, but I would point out that one Spanish version is more flexible: 'Hasta el cuarenta de mayo [June 10], no te quites el sayo; y si el tiempo es importuno, hasta el cuarenta y uno.' The English form makes no such concession to climatic conditions and is the same in Scotland as in England. If my history of the proverb is right—and any day a lucky discovery may prove it wrong—then the inhabitants of Great Britain should ask themselves whether the Spanish saying was adjusted to the meridian of Madrid or of Seville,

[1] See the edition by Miguel Mir (Madrid, 1906).

and at the same time should bear in mind that we borrowed it before we adopted the Gregorian calendar.

The borrowing has been most successful. Perhaps it is mainly responsible for such currency as the archaic or dialectal word 'clout' possesses in England today. Contrast the failure to take root of another proverb from the same language. Many a preacher, orator, or dramatist has valued the homely proverb for its power of putting him on a friendly and familiar footing with his audience, and so has many a traveller into foreign parts. Perhaps the traveller also values it because it persuades him if not his audience that his command of the language is greater than it is. I have found one of the many proverbs in *Don Quixote* of some service in these respects: 'Paciencia y barajar', 'patience and shuffle the cards' as the unlucky but persistent cardplayer may cry out to the dealer. Tilley gives the proverb under 'Patience and shuffle' and can quote only one example; and that is from Shelton's translation of *Don Quixote*!

Whether they came into the language early or late the proverbs used by Shakespeare were for the most part thoroughly English. Very occasionally he used what appears to be a foreign proverb or maxim, and I should like for a few minutes to examine two of these, for it is a puzzle how he came across them. The discovery of a pre-Shakespearian instance might give a clue to his reading, unless we suppose that he picked up these trifles, as undoubtedly he picked up more important matters, from hearsay.

One of these sayings is a proverb or maxim which Pistol repeats in slightly different form in *2 Henry IV*, II. iv. 171 and V. v. 97, both forms garbled by him or by Shakespeare or by the printer. Professor E. M. Wilson tells me that the original was probably Spanish, not Italian, and in choice Castilian would take the form 'Si Fortuna me atormenta, la esperanza me contenta', 'if Fortune torments me, Hope contents me'. Tilley treats it as proverbial but gives no example after Shakespeare before 1640. There is, by the way, a French saying very like it: 'Le désir nous tourmente, et l'espoir nous contente, Desire torments us and hope contents us.'[1] (The folio reading at II. iv. 171 is, perhaps by accident, half French: 'Si fortune me tormente, sperato me contente.') It is found with English

[1] Tilley, D212.

translation in 1592 in 'The Treasure of the French Tongue' added to *The French Alphabeth* by G. Delamothe, a Protestant refugee, one of the many foreign teachers resident in sixteenth-century and seventeenth-century London who tell us so much about the English language in the time of Shakespeare. Delamothe could have supplied the proverb which Shakespeare quotes in French at *2 Henry VI*, v. ii. 28—'La fin couronne l'œuvre', but obviously he cannot be the source of Shakespeare's Spanish saying.

Richard Farmer thought he had found the source, and in his classic *Essay on the Learning of Shakespeare* (1767), in which he sought to show that Shakespeare had little or no learning but took his knowledge of the classics and modern languages from English books, he pointed to two examples of this saying, one of them in a book called *Wits, Fits and Fancies* by Anthony Copley. In the enlarged second edition of the same year Farmer says that the book 'seems to have had many Editions', but only three are known, one in 1595 and two in 1614. (The copy in the Folger Library with the date 1596 is a mere variant of the edition of 1595.) Here is the passage:

> Hannibal *Gonsaga* being in the low Countries ouerthrowne from his horse by an English Captaine, and commanded to yeeld himselfe prisoner: kist his sword and gaue it to the English man saying: Si Fortuna me tormenta, Il speranza me contenta.

Some editors of Shakespeare refer the reader to the 1595 edition of Copley's work. Professor M. A. Shaaber in his New Variorum edition of *2 Henry IV* is an honourable exception: 'I have not succeeded in locating this passage in Copley's book.' It is, however, in the augmented editions of 1614[1]: but as *2 Henry IV* was written about 1597 and printed in 1600, Copley's book cannot be the source of Shakespeare's knowledge, unless indeed we assume (as we have no right to) that an augmented edition with this passage was published in time for Shakespeare to make use of it by 1597. Where Copley found the story I do not know. Many

---

[1] R. B. McKerrow observes how unlikely it is that two editions were needed in 1614 and suspects that one of them represents the using up of sheets of an earlier one (*The Library*, 4th Ser., x, 1930, p. 137). Capell quotes the passage from the 1614 edition in his *School of Shakespeare* [1779], p. 461.

of his jests and anecdotes he translates from the *Floresta Española* of Melchior de Santa Cruz de Dueñas, but not this.

The other example of the saying which Farmer refers to is in Sir Richard Hawkins's *Voyage into the South Sea. Anno Domini 1593*, p. 13. Hawkins had lost his pinnace in a storm off Plymouth Harbour, and writes:

> These losses and mischances troubled and grieved, but nothing daunted me; for common experience taught me, that all honourable Enterprises, are accompanied with difficulties and daungers; *Si fortuna me tormenta; Esperança me contenta*: Of hard beginnings, many times come prosperous and happie events.

But what Farmer does not say is that while Hawkins wrote an account of his voyage of 1593 he wrote it late in life and died while it was passing through the press in 1622. So we still do not know how the saying came to Shakespeare's hand.

The other foreign proverb I have in mind, again a proverb which never became English, Shakespeare puts to much more powerful use because he brings it into a much greater context. We are introduced to Iago in the first scene of *Othello* where he and Roderigo awaken Desdemona's father and Iago shouts at the old man the foul images of sex which spring to his mind. And one of these images is in the sentence: 'I am one, sir, that comes to tell you your daughter and the Moor are now making the beast with two backs.' Tilley gives 'the beast with two backs' as proverbial and cites *Othello* but no other example before 1650. One of his examples is from an English translation of Rabelais; in France the expression is much older than Rabelais. But in an English book it is found in 1611—in the French-English Dictionary made by Randle Cotgrave. Both under the word 'beste' and under 'dos' he gives the French form 'Faire la beste à deux dos ensemble', adding the gloss 'To leacher'. Still, Cotgrave belongs to the year 1611 and *Othello* to 1604, so Shakespeare could not have learnt it from Cotgrave. We noticed that 'Si Fortuna me tormenta' had a close parallel in French, and this is characteristic of the traffic of proverbs in the romance languages. 'The beast with two backs' is Italian as well as French, and Shakespeare could have found it in a book printed in London in 1591, 'Far la bestia a due dossi', one of the 6,150 proverbs John Florio printed in the *Giardino di Ricreatione* (p. 105), a companion volume to his *Second Fruits*. However the saying came to Shakespeare, it can hardly have been familiar to his audience; yet the meaning of these words on the lips of Iago no more needed a gloss then than they do today.

In what I have said and in what I am about to say I would not be thought to be decrying Tilley's *Dictionary*. If he had lived to see its publication he would at once have set about providing a supplement. It is to his praise that he has produced a firm foundation upon which a supplement may be based. But there are signs that demands are being made upon his work which it was not expected to meet. So too with the *Oxford English Dictionary*. We know it is so good that we are tempted to use it as a kind of lazy-tongs which will save us from the labour of making our own enquiries, a practice to which the editors of that Dictionary would have been the first to object. Tilley is now in danger of being maltreated in this way. In reviewing his dictionary[1] I said that in future it would seldom be necessary for an editor of Shakespeare or of any sixteenth-century or seventeenth-century author laboriously to collect his own set of proverbial parallels: a reference to Tilley would usually suffice. And this is true. But no dictionary of proverbs can ever be definitive, and the shortcomings of Tilley may be illustrated from his treatment of Shakespeare's proverbs, an excellent treatment immensely better than any we had before. He told me that his initial interest in proverbs began with Shakespeare's, especially in connection with the so-called borrowings by and from Shakespeare, which are not borrowings at all: and at the end of his dictionary he gave references to more than 2,000 proverbial or semi-proverbial quotations given in the dictionary from Shakespeare. This valuable work needs to be supplemented in three ways. First, earlier examples can be found of many of the proverbs for which Tilley's earliest is from Shakespeare. Secondly, Tilley failed to add Shakespearian examples to many of the proverbs which he cites. And thirdly, while he is remarkably inclusive, proverbs may be found in Shakespeare and other writers which do not appear in his dictionary. I will say a few words about each of these three ways.

[1] *R.E.S.*, N.S. iii (1952), pp. 192–5.

The Proverbial Wisdom of Shakespeare 153

I have been especially interested in discovering earlier examples of the proverbs for which Tilley's earliest is from Shakespeare. The only way of proving that a saying or phrase was absorbed by Shakespeare from the diction of common life and was not invented by him is to find an example in an earlier writer. That Shakespeare invented many a saying or phrase and gave it such currency that many a user forgets the original and assumes it to be proverbial, I do not doubt. Like some of the sayings of Sancho Panza they have become proverbs *since* he used them. But just as certainly many a saying and many a phrase which we take to be his invention came to his audience with the surprise not of discovery but of recognition. Doubtless he could have invented 'My dancing days are done' or 'Wit, whither wilt thou?' but as certainly he did not. Among other sayings for which earlier examples may be added to Tilley's Shakespearian ones are:

A coward dies many deaths, a brave man but once. You set an old man's head on a young man's shoulders. Sleep is the image of death. Youth and age will never agree. To be flesh and blood as others are. God stays long but strikes at last. Injuries are written in brass. Man's extremity is God's opportunity. There is nothing but is good for something. He may go hang himself in his own garters. Confess and be hanged. First thrive and then wive. It is better to wear out than rust out. Let well alone.

These and others will be found in the appendix to this paper as also such proverbial phrases as 'To come in with the Conqueror, To live within compass, To lick into shape' and such proverbial similes as 'As dry as a biscuit, As flattering as a spaniel, As honest a man as ever broke bread.'

A straightforward example is the line in *3 Henry VI* (v. iii. 13): 'For every cloud engenders not a storm.' Tilley's only quotation apart from Shakespeare is from Giovanni Torriano's great dictionary of Italian–English proverbs and proverbial phrases of 1666. If Shakespeare required a literary source for this not very profound reflection, he could have found one in Abraham Fleming's revision in 1584 of the highly popular English–Latin dictionary for children and beginners originally compiled by John Withals. Here it appears (on sig. A4) as the translation of a hexameter which I have not been able to trace: '*Non stillant omnes quas cernis in aëre nubes*, All the clowdes which thou seest in the ayre do not yeeld rayne.'

Not so straightforward is the repetition of a thought which either did not settle into a fixed form at all or settled late after Shakespeare's death. Tilley is usually alert for independent instances of the same thought in works of his period. The one I choose got into the dictionaries from 1616 and appears in Tilley in the form: 'Go forward and fall: go backward and mar all.' He quotes from *Macbeth*:

> I am in blood
> Stepp'd in so far that, should I wade no more,
> Returning were as tedious as go o'er.

But he might also have quoted from Anthony Munday's *Zelauto* of 1580: 'I am not so farre ouer shooes: but I may returne yet drie, nor I am not so far in, but I may easily escape out'; and from Minsheu in 1599: 'I had waded so farre in it, as without helpe I could not get ouer, nor without danger and shame returne backe.'

Under the same heading of examples of which Tilley's earliest is from Shakespeare I give a simile and a phrase. I cannot attach any significance to the fact that my earlier instances both come from the same dictionary, Richard Huloet's *Abcedarium* of 1552, another English–Latin dictionary. Tilley gives under one entry (F328) 'To swim like a fish (duck)'. For 'swim like a fish', which is not Shakespearian, he gives one example and that from Fletcher and Massinger's *Sea Voyage* of *c.* 1622; an earlier one is in Harington's *Orlando Furioso* of 1591: '*Orlando* nakt and light, swam like a fish'. Of 'swim like a duck' his only example is Trinculo's words in *The Tempest* (II. ii. 120). Huloet gives 'Swymme lyke a ducke. *Tetrinno. as*'. Huloet gets the meaning wrong, for I am assured that *Tetrinno* ought to mean 'I quack like a duck'. Nevertheless he gives the simile which Shakespeare was to use. In the same dictionary I find (under 'Trowell') '*thrullisco. as. ang.* to laye on wyth a trowell'. Here is a phrase which, as I have always thought, Shakespeare himself made proverbial. I still think so; for whereas Huloet is strictly literal, Shakespeare's Celia applies the expression ironically and metaphorically to Touchstone's fine language, so making it possible for us to apply it to any excess whether of style or manners.

The second way in which Tilley's dictionary needs to be supplemented is by adding to the proverbs which he gives the Shakespearian references which he neglects. In a recent reading of Shakespeare's early history plays I have noted five omissions in *Henry VI, Part 1*, in *Part 2* eight, in *Part 3* ten, and in *Richard III* eighteen. And while I am not anxious—now or at any time—to get involved in the problem of the authorship of *Henry VI, Part 1*, I venture to point out that the disparity between the use of proverbial or semi-proverbial language in that play as against the other three plays, a disparity already marked in the lists which Tilley supplies, becomes the more striking if we add the proverbs which he missed. One example of these omissions may be noted—from *3 Henry VI*, III. iii. 152: 'Having nothing, nothing can he lose.' This is Tilley's N331: 'They that have nothing need fear to lose nothing.' An example earlier than Shakespeare is in Roper's *Life of More* (1557, ed. Hitchcock, p. 7): 'He nothinge havinge, nothing could loose.' This command of the diction of common life is apparent in Shakespeare's earliest work as in his latest. No other English poet, not even Chaucer, held in his memory so many proverbial sayings.

Under this heading as under the first I take an example of a thought which did not crystallize into a set form in the time of Shakespeare. Tilley gives as proverbial 'You are a right Englishman, you cannot tell when a thing is well.' It appears more or less in this form in many seventeenth-century dictionaries of proverbs— in the 1616 edition of Withals, in Clarke (1639), in Howell (1659), in Ray (1670), and so on. Tilley's earliest is from Withals, but I think he would have added, if he had thought of it, Falstaff's 'It was alway yet the trick of our English nation, if they have a good thing, to make it too common.' Years earlier we find a pre-Shakespearian example. In 1545 Stephen Gardiner wrote to Sir William Paget: 'They saye that an Englishe man in al feates excellith, if he could leaue whenne it is wel, which they cal *tollere manum de tabula*.'[1] Gardiner, it will be noticed, puts up the proverbial signpost, 'They say'.

[1] *Letters*, ed. James Muller (1933), p. 180.

The third way in which Tilley may be supplemented is by the addition of proverbs which do not appear in his dictionary at all yet were used by Shakespeare. There must still remain sayings in Shakespeare which his audience recognized as proverbial and we do not. Among those omitted by Tilley are 'as good be an addled egg as an idle bird'; 'as like as a crab is like an apple', a variant of A291; 'as deep as a well'; 'wild horses'; 'to go like the crab backwards'; 'death is the end of all'; 'between asleep and awake'; 'when angry count a hundred'. This last is an example of a proverb which became fixed in shape and word very late. Other ways of allaying anger than counting a hundred were suggested. The popular Jacobean preacher Thomas Adams recommended the reciting of the Greek alphabet 'as a pause to coole the heate of choler' (1616, *Diseases of the Soul*, p. 16). The moral of *2 Henry VI* I. iii. 150–1 appears to be: when angry, walk once round the quadrangle. In *Richard III* (I. iv. 118) the second murderer about to murder the sleeping Clarence suffers some dregs of conscience and with grim irony observes: 'I hope this passionate humour of mine will change: it was wont to hold me but while one tells twenty.'

Another saying of a proverbial nature which Tilley missed altogether is 'Fair dovecots have most doves'. (His P588, 'Priests and pigeons (doves) make foul houses' is a different proverb.) In this form it appears in H. Peters's *Dying Father's Last Legacy* of 1660, while F. Hawkins in *Youth's Behaviour* of 1663 gives 'Doves flock to fair houses'. From these I move backwards (like the crab) to Greene's *Menaphon* of 1598 (Grosart, vi. 47: 'Doues delight not in foule cottages'); to B. Melbanke (*Philotimus*, 1583, A3: 'Doues vse no houses but that be goodly to the vewe'); and to one of the *Three Proper and Witty Familiar Letters* which passed between Gabriel Harvey and Edmund Spenser and were printed in 1580. Harvey quotes three of his brother John's variations in pseudo-quantitative verse on a theme in Ovid's *Tristia* (I. ix. 7, *Adspicis ut veniant ad candida tecta columbae*), the simplest and shortest of which is

See ye the Dooues? they breede, and feede in gorgeous Houses:
Scarce one Dooue doth loue to remaine in ruinous Houses.

Earlier still is this passage in Robert Burrant's *Precepts of Cato* of

1545 ('Seven Wise Men', C2): a comment on the proverb 'In time of prosperity friends will be plenty, in time of adversity not one among twenty.'

Ouid compareth suche flatterynge frendes vnto Piggions who as longe as the doufehouse is freshe and newe, they abyde and haunt there, but yf it begynne ones to wexe olde and rotten, they wyll flee [a]way from it to another.

Finally we come to Shakespeare or at least to *Henry VI, Part 1* (I. v. 21). The great Talbot comments on the defeat of the English soldiers by the witchcraft of Joan of Arc:

> A witch by fear, not force, like Hannibal,
> Drives back our troops and conquers as she lists.
> So bees with smoke and doves with noisome stench
> Are from their hives and houses driven away.

These homiletic similes drawn from nature—like 'Every cloud engenders not a storm' or 'Constant dropping will wear the stone' which Shakespeare used no less than eleven times—were stock ornaments when he began to write. As he reached maturity he tended to drop them or to transform them into metaphor, no longer hooking them on with an 'as' or a 'so', no longer making them serve as mere amplification. But in his early work, as in the early work of such a sententious poet as Drayton, proverbial and semi-proverbial expressions tend to come in clusters; as for example, in *Richard III*, II. iii. 32:

> When clouds are seen, wise men put on their cloaks;
> When great leaves fall, then winter is at hand;
> When the sun sets, who doth not look for night?
> Untimely storms make men expect a dearth.

Moreover, what is semi-proverbial assumes by association proverbial authority. By 1590 'Doves are driven from dovecotes by stench' might be considered proverbial, but not 'Bees are driven from their hives by smoke.' So in *2 Henry VI*, III. i. 53, Suffolk poisons the mind of Henry against Gloucester with 'Smooth runs the water where the brook is deep', a proverb known to medieval England, and continues: 'The fox barks not when he would steal the lamb', which then assumes all the authority of a proverb. So in *3 Henry VI*, II. ii. 17, 'The smallest worm will turn, being trodden on' is followed by 'And doves will peck in safeguard of their brood.'

To conclude. Shakespeare's mind received its stores from books, more still from speech. What he borrowed from books he so transmuted that only rarely can we trace with certainty where he had been reading. How much he took from speech we may surmise from his proverbs. He was an observer of men and manners in court and city, town and country, church and tavern. Whether he often cried 'My tables—meet it is I set it down', as Shaw represents him doing in *The Dark Lady of the Sonnets*, may be doubted. What he heard was stored away in his retentive memory. He could count on his proverbs being known to his audience, just as were his images, images as familiar as the chamberlain putting his master's shirt on warm, or that image of heaven peeping 'through the blanket of the dark' which excited Johnson's risibility but does not excite ours. While the learned word and the learned allusion are by no means absent from his work, yet basic to his style are these images drawn from the goings-on of ordinary life and these proverbs assimilated from the diction of common life. When the occasion demanded they were called from the 'vasty deep' of his memory, and they came at his call to receive their appropriate language and rhythm.

APPENDIX

(This appendix contains earlier examples of some of the proverbs for which Tilley's earliest examples are from Shakespeare. Letter followed by number refers to Tilley. I have followed Tilley in omitting medieval examples, even if a medieval example is the only one available before Shakespeare.)[1]

A32 As deaf as an ADDER[2]

    1590 Lodge, *Rosalynde*, ed. Greg, p. 45, All adder-like I stop mine ears. 1591 Greene, *Farewell to Folly*, ed. Grosart, ix. 273, The noble men plaide like the deafe Addar that heareth not the sorcerers charme.

---

[1] [As originally printed this appendix omitted forty-four examples printed in *The Review of English Studies*, N.S. iii (1952), pp. 195–8. These have been intercalated along with a few more noted by F. P. Wilson in an annotated offprint, and some earlier examples have been supplied by Mrs. Wilson. H.G.]

[2] Ps. 58 : 4.

The Proverbial Wisdom of Shakespeare

A42 ADVERSITY makes men wise
1579 Foxe, *Christ Jesus Triumphant*, tr. Day, 1607 edn., E3ᵛ, It was said of the Phrygians in a Greeke Prouerbe, that stripes strike wisdome into them.

A53 AFFLICTIONS are sent us by God for our good
1541 Bullinger, *Christ. State Matrimony*, tr. Coverdale, 1543 edn., L6, Affliccions tech to know god. 1579 Calvin, *Sermons*, tr. L. T., g3, Affliction is the triall of our faith.

A88 As free as the AIR (wind)
[1592] 1596 *Edward III*, II. i. 286, Religion is austere and bewty gentle; To strict a gardion for so faire a w[ar]d! O, that shee were, as is the aire, to mee!

A153 ALL is well and the man has his mare again
a1548 Copland, *Jyl of Brentford's Testament*, l. 62. The poore mare shall haue his man agayn.

A167 ALL that is alike is not the same
L288
1587 Bridges, *Defence*, p. 1387, It is an old and a true prouerbe, Nullum simile est idem, Nothing that is the like is the same. 1591 *Troublesome Reign K. John*, Pt. I, B1ᵛ, know you not, Omne simile non est idem.

A360 The ASS though laden with gold still eats thistles
[c1589] 1633 Marlowe, *Jew of Malta*, V. ii. 40, Liues like the Asse that Æsope speaketh of, That labours with a load of bread and wine, And leaues it off to snap on Thistle tops.

B99 The BASILISK's eye is fatal
1572 Pasquier, *Monophylo*, tr. Fenton, Y4ᵛ, The mortal sight of the basilicque, by whom we die but of one death onely.

B151 The BEAST with two backs
1591 Florio, *Giardino di Ricreatione*, p. 105, Far la bestia a due dossi.

B272 As sound as a BELL
1557 Edgeworth, *Sermons*, 2S4, If it [a mason's stone] rynge and sounde close like a Bell. 1576 Lemnius, *Touchstone of Complexions*, tr. Newton, f. 109ᵛ, They be people commonly healthy, and as sounde as a Bell.

B339 To run against the BIAS
c1580 Sidney, *Def. of Poesy*, ed. Feuillerat. iii. 40, we shall contrarily laugh sometimes to finde a matter quite mistaken, and goe downe the hill against the byas.

B365a A BIRD (egg) of the same nest
[See also under E81] 1553 Udall, *Ralph Roister Doister*, l. 192, 'of the same nest' say I, 'it is a birde.' 1588 Bulkeley, *An Answer*, p. 49, Master Harpsfield a bird of the same nest.

B404 As dry as a BISCUIT
[1599] 1600 Jonson, *Every Man out*, Ind. l. 165, And (now and then) breakes a drie bisket jest.

B567 Wide at the BOW HAND
1590–5 Munday *et al.*, *Sir T. More*, III. iii. 246, O good Master Wit, thou art now on the bow hand, And blindly in thine own opinion dost stand.

The Proverbial Wisdom of Shakespeare

B588 BRAG is a good dog but Holdfast is a better
   1583 Melbancke, *Philotimus*, F1, As to haue is good happ, so to hauld fast is a great vertue.

B692 As wild as a BUCK
   1530 Palsgrave, 1852 edn., p. 439*b*, He was as wylde as a bucke, but I have made him as attamed as a lambe.

B702 To nip in the BUD (blossom)
   1565 Osorius, *Pearl for a Prince*, tr. Shacklock, f. 31ᵛ, Princes doo vnwisely which doo not nyp wickednes in the hed, so sone as it doth begin. 1590 Lodge, *Rosalynde*, ed. Greg, p. 58, And now, through the decree of the unjust stars, to have all these good parts nipped in the blade.

B716 The town BULL is as much a bachelor as he
   1591 Harington, *Orlando Furioso*, xxxviii. Moral, Imagine some man so chast, (as Caesar was called) omnium mulierum vir, or to vse our homely English phrase (as the towne Bull of the Parish) so true of his word, as he that Heywood writs of that kept all the commandements, and namely that concerning false witnes.

C62 He may cast his CAP after him for ever overtaking him
   1592 Nashe, *Strange News*, ed. McKerrow, i. 318, *Pierce Pennilesse* may well cast his cappe after it for euer ouertaking it.

C83 CARE is no cure
   1588 Greene, *Pandosto*, ed. Thomas, p. 31, In sores past help salves do not heal but hurt, and in things past cure, care is a corrosive.

C499 As close as COCKLES
   [1601] 1616 Jonson, *Cynthia's Revels*, v. iv. 534. shee kisses as close as a cockle.

C519 As many COLOURS as there are in the rainbow
   1562 Legh, *Accidence of Armoury*, p. 171, He beareth Argent, a flower de luse Sable. Althoughe thys be of Coloure Sable, yet naturally it hath all the colours of a Raine bowe, which giueth vnto the beholder thereof a marueylous delight.

C520 To fear no COLOURS
   1592 Nashe, *Strange News*, ed. McKerrow, i. 280, Helter skelter, feare no colours, course him, trounce him.

C577 Live within COMPASS
   1579 Calvin, *Sermons*, tr. L. T., p. 133/1, Wee haue need of some order or bridle, to hold vs within our compasse. 1590–95 Munday *et al.*, *Sir T. More*, IV. iv. 25, For keeping still in compass ... we have sailed Beyond our course. 1595 Chettle, *Piers Plainness*, E1, My neede droue mee to liue without lawe, if I had said with an outlaw, I had kept within compasse.

C587 CONFESS and be hanged
   1589 *De Caede et Interitu Gallorum Regis*, A2ᵛ, Confesse and be hanged In English some saie. 1595 *A Pleasant Satire or Poesy* [*A satire Menippized*], p. 42, Confesse and be hanged, as they say. 1595 Copley, *Wits, Fits and Fancies*, p. 143.

C594 He came in with the CONQUEROR
   1593 B. R., *Greene's News*, C1ᵛ, My auncesters came in with the Conquest.

C609 A quiet CONSCIENCE sleeps in thunder
   1584 Withals, *Short Dictionary ... augmented by Fleming*, O4, The man whose conscience pricks him not, A quiet minde hath for his lot.

The Proverbial Wisdom of Shakespeare 161

C623 CONTENT (A mind content) is a kingdom (crown)
[c1560] 1578 Lupton, *All for Money*, C1, Contentation makes me as rich as a king.

C705 To be put out of COUNTENANCE
1544 Stalbridge [Bale], *Epistle Exhortatory*, D6, Yf ye thynke Wraghton thus ouerthrowne or yet dasshed out of countenance ye are sore deceyued. 1551 Wilson, *Rule of Reason*, P6ᵛ, Thei will saie, he speaketh too too babyshelye, and so dashe hym out of countenaunce, that he shall not well knowe what to saie.

C739 Call me COUSIN but cozen me not
c1552 Walker, *Manifest Detection of Dice Play*, C3, Bee they young, be they old, that fauleth into our laps, and be ignorant of our arte, we call them all by the name of a cosin, as men that wee make as much of, as if they were of our kinne. 1580 Lyly, *Euph. and his Eng.*, ed. Bond, ii. 21, Cassander ... determined with him-selfe to make a Cosinne of his young Neuew. c1592 *Thomas of Woodstock*, I. i. 8, God for thy mercy! Would our cousin king So cozen us, to poison us in our meat?

C774 A COWARD dies many deaths, a brave man but once
1596 Drayton, *Mortimeriados*, ed. Hebel, i. 386, every howre he dyes, which ever feares.

C938 Come CUT and longtail
1590 Harvey, *Plain Perceval*, A3ᵛ. [c1591] 1599 [Greene?], *George a Green*, F3, Call all your towne forth, cut, and longtaile. c1592 *Thomas of Woodstock*, III. i. 158, A widow's a hermaphrodite, both cut and longtail. 1594 Nashe, *Christ's Tears*, ed. McKerrow, ii. 186, Raile vpon me till your tongues rotte, short cut and long-taile, for groats a peece euery quarter.

D42 He is out at first DASH
[1525-40] 1557 Erasmus, *Colloquia*, ed. de Vocht, p. 57, Gyue you me a mocke at the first dash. 1579 Calvin, *Four Sermons*, tr. Field, p. 19, at the firste dashe. 1583 Stubbes, *Anat. of Abuses*, ed. Furnivall (1882), ii. 29, The poore man, if hee haue scraped any little thing togither, is forced to disburse it at the first dash. c1591 *1 Henry VI*, I. ii. 71,[1] She takes upon her bravely at first dash.

D57 As merry as the DAY is long
1566 Erasmus, *Diversoria*, tr. E. H[ake?], ed. de Vocht, l. 427, They liue as well as hearte canne thinke, or, as the day is broad and longe to.

D118 My dancing DAYS are done
1573 Gascoigne, *Hundreth Sundry Flowers*, ed. Cunliffe, i. 397-8, my dauncing dayes are almost done. 1582 Fetherstone, *Dial. agst. Dancing*, B1ᵛ, Howe many mens seruauntes being set to woorke, do after their dauncinge dayes lie snorting in hedges, because they are so weary that they cannot worke?

D125 To lament the DEAD avails not and revenge vents hatred
1591 Harington, *Orlando Furioso*, ix. 41, By teares no good the dead is done, And sharpe reuenge asswageth mallice cheefe.

D142 DEATH is common to all
1579 Calvin, *Four Sermons*, tr. Field, I4ᵛ, Death is common to all. 1579 Calvin, *Thirteen Sermons*, tr. Field, p. 135 (sure to all). 1591 *Troublesome Reign K. John*, Pt. II, D2, A man of death. ... Behold these scarres, ... Are harbingers from natures common foe.

[1] Omitted by Tilley.

D506 To be old DOG at it

1590 Nashe, *Almond for a Parrot*, ed. McKerrow, iii. 351, Oh, he is olde dogge at expounding, and deade sure at a Catechisme.

D509 To die like a DOG

1529 Rastell, *Pastime*, 1811 edn., p. 57, He ... lyued lyke a lyon, and dyed lyke a dodge [*sic*]. [1591] 1593 *Jack Straw*, F1, You ... must in strangling cords die like dogs. 1594 Nashe, *Unfort. Trav.*, ed. McKerrow, ii. 241, He dyde like a dogge, he was hangd and the halter paid for.

D592 He never DREAMED of it

[See *O.E.D.*, s.v. Dream, v². 5.] 1538 Starkey, *England*, E.E.T.S., I. ii. 36, Yf a man haue helth and ryches, [he] ys then of al men iugyd happy and fortunate ... though he neuer dreme of vertue. 1588 *Marprel. Epist.*, ed. Arber, p. 27, They see themselues assayled with such weapons, whereof they neuer once drempt.

D634 Give everyone his DUE

1583 Melbancke, *Philotimus*, B2ᵛ, Art thou such a louinge woorme to succourles creatures, to robb God of his due.

D637 To dine with DUKE HUMPHREY

1590–5 Munday *et al.*, *Sir T. More*, III. iii. 343, He may chance dine with Duke Humphrey to-morrow. 1591 Nashe, *A wonderful Prognostication*, ed. McKerrow, iii. 393, Sundry fellowes in their silkes shall be appointed to keep Duke Humfrye company in Poules, because they know not wher to get their dinner abroad.

E6 To have an EAGLE's eye

1583 Prime, *Fruitful and Brief Discourse*, p. 26, Eagles eyes haue we till we looke into the sunne.

E18 Lend me your EARS awhile

1581 R.S. in Thimelthorpe, *Short Inventory*, L1ᵛ, Come lend your Eares to hear a word or twayne. 1583 Stubbes, *Anat. of Abuses*, ed. Furnivall (1882), ii. 6, The sweeter the Syren singeth, the dangerouser is it to lend hir our eares.

E100 To rub (scratch) the ELBOW¹

1594 Nashe, *Unfort. Trav.*, ed. McKerrow, ii. 219, had you seene him how he stretcht out his lims, scratcht his scabd elbowes at this speach.

E112 The END justifies the means

1583 Babington, *Exposition of the Commandments*, p. 260, the ende good, doeth not by and by make the meanes good.

E255 EYES as red as a ferret's

1530 Palsgrave, 1852 edn., p. 457*b*, His eyes be so bleared with drinkying that they be as reed as a fyrret.

F33 No FAITH with heretics

1554 Proctor, *Hist. of Wyatt's Rebellion*, p. 56, They thinking no part of their worshyppe stained in breaking promise with a traitour. c1566 Curio, *Pasquin in a Trance*, tr. W.P., f. 68ᵛ, their [the Papists'] curssed lawes, which saye, that promise must not be kept with Heretiques. 1571 Bridges, *Sermon at Paul's Cross*, p. 153, shall I trust his [a Catholic's] false faithe? ... Example ... their generall rule, *Nulla fides haereticis est habenda*, No faith must be kepte with heretikes. 1587 Marlowe, *2 Tamburlaine*, II. i. 33–6. [c1589] 1633 Marlowe, *Jew of Malta*, II. iii. 310–12.

¹ The sense is the scratching of the elbow as a sign of pleasure, the itch of satisfaction. There is also the phrase (not in Tilley) 'to claw the elbow (i.e. another man's elbow)', with the meaning 'to flatter'.

The Proverbial Wisdom of Shakespeare   163

F213 To give one a FIG.
1565–6 Churchyard, *Churchyard's Farewell*, in *Ballads and Broadsides*, ed. Collmann, 1912, no. 30, Whose nature geves the courte a fygge when worldly hap is gon. 1585 Munday, *Fidele and Fortunio*, E4ᵛ, Giue her a Fico out of hande. c1589 *Theses Martinianae*, C3, Have you strangled him? haue you giuen him an Italian figge? 1594 Nashe, *Unfort. Trav.*, ed. McKerrow, ii. 299, So haue the *Italians* no such sport as to see poore English asses, how soberlie they swallow Spanish figges, deuoure anie hooke baited for them. c1594 *King John*, II. i. 162¹, It grandam will Give it a plum, a cherry, and a fig.

F239 Lay thy FINGERS on thy lips
1509 Barclay, *Ship of Fools*, 1874 edn., ii. 232, he dare no worde let slyp But layeth his fynger anone before his lyp.

F328 To swim like a FISH (duck)
1552 Huloet, *Abcedarium*, s.v. Swim, Swymme lyke a ducke. Tetrinno as. 1591 Harington *Orlando Furioso*, xxix. 47, Orlando nakt and light, swam like a fish.

F345 That is FLAT
1567 *Common Conditions*, C2, I can do it, this is plaine and flat. 1577 Beza, *Abraham's Sacrifice*, tr. Golding, A8, But yit you must, or else I tell you flat, That both of vs our labour lose togither. [c1587] 1592 Kyd, *Span. Trag.*, III. vi. 47, Hangman, now I spy your knauery, ile not change without boot, thats flat. Ibid., III. xii. 21, And heere Ile haue a fling at him thats flat. [c1587] 1599 Peele, *David and Bethsabe*, l. 569 I will not goe home sir, thats flat. [c1590] 1595 Peele, *Old Wives Tale*, l. 897, Content you sir, Ile serue you that is flat.

F367 To be FLESH and blood as others are
1541 Bullinger, *Christ. State Matrimony*, tr. Coverdale, 1543 edn., E3, Thou wilt saye: alas we are but flesh and bloud. I answere: were not our fore fathers flesh & bloud also? c 1564 *Bugbears*, I. i. 18, You are master, I am servant, but else of fleshe & bone I ame as well mad as you. 1584 Lyly, *Campaspe*, II. ii. 68, Though she haue heauenly giftes, vertue and bewtie, is she not of earthly mettall, flesh and bloud? [1599] 1600 Munday et al., *Oldcastle*, IV. i. 165, I confesse I am a frayle man, flesh and bloud as other are.

F496 Let him be begged for a FOOL
1587 Fenner, *Def. of Godly Ministers*, p. 51, Then would you haue proued vs asses, not begged vs ... for innocents.

F514 You have not a FOOL in hand
1567 *Common Conditions*, F1ᵛ, Thinke not you haue a foole in hand I waraunt yee.

F572 To thrust one's FOOT under another man's table.
1545 *Precepts of Cato*, tr. Burrant, O3, Alwaies to thrust his legges vnder another mans table. 1573 Carr, *Larum Bell for London*, D1ᵛ, [The beggared prodigal] gladde to set his feete vnder other mens tables. 1589 Wright, *Summons for Sleepers*, f. 2ᵛ, The prelacie which these new deuising church founders are now so desirous to haue established ... must liue popularly with their feete vnder other mens tables, and their tongues tyed to other mens purses.

F655 When the FOX has got in his head (nose) he will soon make the body follow
1578 White, *Sermon at Paul's Cross*, p. 29, If his [the serpent's] head be once in, he will shifte for himselfe, and soone winde in his whole body.

¹ Omitted by Tilley.

F762 Trencher FRIENDSHIP
1576 Lemnius, *Touchstone of Complexions*, tr. Newton, p. 101, Trencher frends and Coseners. 1590 Greene, *Francesco's Fortunes*, ed. Grosart, viii. 130, Flattering *Gnatos*, that only are time pleasers and trencher friends.

G42 He may go hang himself in his own GARTERS
1591 Harington, *Orlando Furioso*, x. 37, But burned might'st thou be, or cut in quarters, Or driuen to hang thy selfe in thine owne garters.

G132 His GLASS is run
1590 Lodge, *Rosalynde*, ed. Greg, p. 2, All men might perceive his glass was run.

G152 GO forward and fall, go backward and mar all
1580 Munday, *Zelauto*, P2, I am not so farre ouer shooes: but I may returne yet drie, nor I am not so far in, but I may easily escape out. 1599 Minsheu, *Span. Dict.* A2, I had waded so farre in it, as without helpe I could not get ouer, nor without danger and shame returne backe.

G224 GOD stays long but strikes at last
1591 Harington, *Orlando Furioso*, xxii. Moral [Latin verses by Sir Walter Mildmay englished by Harington], If God stay long ear he to strike beginne, Though long he stay, at last he striketh sure. Ibid., xxxvii. 89, The silent soule yet cryes for vengeaunce iust, Vnto the mightie God, and to his Saints, Who though they seeme in punishing but slow, Yet pay they home at last, with heaue and how.

G230 He is either a GOD or a painter, for he makes faces
1557 Edgeworth, *Sermons*, 3D2^v, Some [women] can not be contente with their heere as God made it, but dothe painte it and set it in an other hue, ... Ibid., 3D4, This adulteration and chaunging of gods handy-worke by painting womans heere to make it seme faire and yelow, or of their leers of their chekes to make them loke ruddy or of their forehed to hide the wrinkles and to make them loke smoth, is of the deuils inuention and neuer of gods teaching.

G349 Good GOOSE (BEAR), bite not
1571 *Life and Death of J. Story*, A3^v, A kyndly beare wyll bite by tyme. 1592 Nashe, *Strange News*, ed. McKerrow, i. 307, Good Beare, bite not. 1593 Harvey, *Pierce's Supererogation*, ed. Grosart, ii. 244, Good Beare bite not.

G393 The GRACE of God is gear enough[1]
1590 Spenser, *F.Q.*, I. x. 38, The grace of God he laid up still in store ... He had enough.

G437 The GREATER embraces (includes, hides) the less
1581 Merbury, *Brief Discourse*, *4^v, I haue burst out into these few rude lines, not to th'Ende I am able to purchasse praise vnto th'Author, (Because the lesse can not authorize the greater) but that I may gaine commendation to my selfe.

G453 Never GRIEVE for that you cannot help
c1592 *Two Gentlemen*, III. i. 241, Cease to lament for that thou canst not help.

H67 For one's HAND to be in
1586 Day, *Eng. Secretary I*, 1625 edn., p. 44, There was no rake-hell ... but his hand was in with him, and that he was a copesmate for him.

---

[1] 2 Cor. 12:9.

H73 He is his right HAND
[See *O.E.D.*, s.v. Right hand, I c.] c1528–37 Ld. J. Butler in Ellis, *Orig. Lett.*, Ser II, ii. 48, O Connor... who hath maried the erle of Kildare's doghter, is his right hand. 1581 Elliot [*title*] *A very true Report of the apprehension... of that arch-Papist Edmund Campion, the Pope his right hand.*

H147 As fearful as a HARE
[c1591] 1592 *Arden of Feversham*, III. v. 126, Thou hast... heard as quickly as the fearefull hare.

H246 He dares not show his HEAD (himself) for debt
[See *O.E.D.*, s.v. Head, sb. 54.] 1551 Wilson, *Rule of Reason*, 1580 edn., p. 49, This manne... durst not once for his life shewe his hedde, for feare his name should betray his whole nature.

H278 As many HEADS as Hydra
1575 Churchyard in Nichols, *Progresses*, 1823 edn., i. 400, She [Elizabeth] hateth Hidras heads, and lovs the harmles mind.

H300 It is worth the HEARING
1587 Bridges, *Defence*, p. 1302, The Decrees... are published to the open viewe of euery man, if our Bretheren as yet can burthen them with any grosse or palpable errour... at all,... it were worth the hearing. 1590–5 Munday *et al.*, *Sir T. More*, I. ii. 24. That's worth the hearing.

H309 He is HEART of oak
[1582] 1589 *Love and Fortune*, l. 1677, Why then my noble youths of Oke pluck vp your harts with me. 1591 Lyly, *Entertainments at Cowdray*, ed. Bond, i. 425, All heartes of Oke, then which nothing surer: nothing sounder.

H438 It is neither HERE nor there
1543 Cousin, *Office of Servants*, B7, Better... to do a thing neither here, ne there, then that through idlenes they shuid intend to worse occupations. 1581 Manutius, *Phrases Linguae Latinae*, p. 62, It is neither here nor there or I passe not what you thinke of me. 1594 Nashe, *Unfort. Trav.*, ed. McKerrow, ii. 210.

H457 As common as the HIGHWAY
1593 Foulface, *Bacchus' Bounty*, C4, As common... as cartway.

H566 He is least worthy of HONOUR that seeks it
1539 Vives, *Introd. to Wisdom*, C1, Honour commonly fastest flyeth from hym, that moste seketh it, and gothe to them, that lest regarde it. 1567 Painter, ed. Jacobs, ii. 289, Wel remembering of my Mayster Plutarch, that honour ought rather to bee deserued than procured.

I71 INJURIES are written in brass
c1513 More, *Rich. III*, 1821 edn., p. 86, Men vse if they haue an euil turne, to write it in marble: and whoso doth vs a good tourne, we write it in duste. 1591 Harington, *Orlando Furioso*, xxiii. 1, Men say it, and we see it come to passe, Good turns in sand, shrewd turns are writ in brasse.

J46 Leave JESTING while it pleases lest it turn to earnest
1591 Harington, *Orlando Furioso*, xii. Moral, We may see that things done in iest oft turne to ernest.

J55 None can guess the JEWEL by the casket (cabinet)
1586 Case, *Praise of Music*, p. 29, A precious stone may be set in ledde.

J64 JOHN-A-DREAMS (John-a-nods)
1600 Breton, *Pasquil's Pass*, ed. Grosart, i. 11a, When Iohn a Noddes will be a Gentleman Because his worship weares a velvet coate.

K129 More KNAVE than fool
[c1589] 1633 Marlowe, *Jew of Malta*, II. iii. 37, more knaue than foole.

K186 One KNOWS not where to have you
M288
a1576 Whythorne, ed. Osborn, p. 42, I kowld not yet assiur my self to be siur to know wher and how to hav her. 1576 Lemnius, *Touchstone of Complexions*, tr. Newton, p. 140, They ... aunsweare so doubtfullye and perplexedlye, that a man cannot tel wher to haue them. 1578 Garter, *Susanna*, l. 253, You know wher to haue me [i.e. find me].

L9 You lose your LABOUR
[c1515] c1530 Barclay, *Eclog II*, l. 1103, Should wise men suppose in court so to preuayle? Lost is their labour, their study and trauayle. 1549 Erasmus, *Praise of Folly*, tr. Chalenor, H4, An other, that dranke two sortes of poyson at ones, through the conflict of their contrarie operacions, beynge driuen into a laxe, founde them rather medicinable, than deadly, vnto him, full sore against his wiues will, who lost bothe hir labour and cost about it. c1566 Curio, *Pasquin in a Trance*, tr. W.P., p. 42, he might haue gone thither, and haue lost all his labour.

L92a To LAUGH and cry at once
1531 Elyot, *Governor*, ii. f. 152ᵛ, She all blussing with an eye halfe laughinge halfe mourninge. 1578 Yver, *Courtly Controversy*, tr. Wotton, 2M1, Who hathe viewed in the Spring time, raine and Sunneshine in one moment, might beholde the troubled countenaunce of the gentlewoman, after she had read, and ouerread the letters of hir Floradin wyth an eye, nowe smilyng, then bathed in teares. 1582 Whetstone, *Heptameron*, Z1ᵛ, Who so in the Spryngtime, in one Moment had seene rayne and Sunshine, might againe beholde the lyke chaunge in Pierias troubled countenaunce.

L191 How came you hither? On my LEGS
c1590 Munday, *John a Kent*, l. 325, But will they come?—They will, if you will goe.—But how?—why on their feet, I knowe no other way.

L206 A LEOPARD (panther) cannot change his spots[1]
1546 Bale, *Exam. of Anne Askewe*, Parker Soc., p. 177, Their old conditions will change when the blackamorian change his skin, and the cat a mountain her spots. 1578 Lyly, *Euphues*, ed. Bond, i. 191, Can the Aethiope chaunge or alter his skinne? or the Leoparde his hewe?

L281 There is LIGHTNING lightly before thunder
1545 *Precepts of Cato*, tr. Burrant, K2, As the lyghtnynge goeth before thunder. So ...

L395 Let the longer LIVER take all
Cf. c1565 Wager, *Enough is as good as a Feast*, B2, the longest liuer pay all.

L423 LONG LOOKED FOR comes at last
1548 Udall, *Paraphrase*, i. π5, The birth of your Maiestie was the more swete, because it was so long wished for, so long looked for, and so long craued ere it came.

---

[1] Jer. 13:23.

The Proverbial Wisdom of Shakespeare 167

L452 He wears a whole LORDSHIP on his back

1576 Gascoigne, *Steel Glass*, ed. Cunliffe, ii. 173, On their backs, they beare . . . Castles and Towres, revenewes and receits, Lordships, and manours, fines, yea fermes and al. 1580 Lyly, *Euph. and his Eng.*, ed. Bond, ii. 121, An other layeth all his lyuing vppon his backe. c1590 *2 Henry VI*, I. iii. 78,[1] She bears a duke's revenues on her back. [c1590] 1605 *King Leir*, II. iii. 27, Sheele lay her husbands Benefice on her back, Euen in one gowne, if she may haue her will. [1592] 1594 Marlowe, *Edward II*, I. iv. 406, He weares a lords reuenewe on his back.

L571 A true LOVER's knot

1565 Osorius, *Pearl for Princes*, tr. Shacklock, f. 43^v, The holye ordynaunces which Christ hath ordeined . . . with the which we haue fastened our selues vnto hym as it were with a true loue knott. 1583 Melbancke, *Philotimus*, D1^v, Frendships . . . knitt with a trueloues knot made of siluer copper. 1588 Churchyard in Nichols, *Progresses*, 1823 edn., ii. 589, Friendship is (without comparison) the only true-love-knot, that knits, in conjunction, thousands together.

M65 As a MAN must take a wife, for better or for worse

[See *O.E.D.*, s.v. Worse, sb. B 3a.] a1500 *Sarum Manuale*, Rouen, 1501, f. xlvii, I N. take the N. to my wedded wif to haue and to holde fro this day forward for better for wers for richere for pouerer. 1548 Hall, *Chron. Hen. VIII*, p. 59*b*, And so for better or worse, the Frencheman called the Englisheman knaue and went away with the stockdoues.

M68 As honest a MAN as ever broke bread

1583 Dent, *Sermon of Repentance*, B3^v, I haue knowen . . . men, whiche before their conuersion, and inward chaunge were counted as honest menne as euer brake breade.

M125 Every MAN is either a fool or a physician to himself

1592 Greene, *Quip*, cancelled passage, Physitian or a foole. 1594 O. B., *Questions*, G1, This olde prouerbe; Either a foole or a Phisition.

M184 An honest MAN is as good as his word

1577 Stanyhurst in Holinshed, *Chronicles of Ireland*, 1587 edn., i. 104*a*, Both the earls gaue him heartie interteinment for his true and honorable dealing, that to be as good as his word, would not seeme to shrinke from his freend in this his aduersitie. 1589 *Just Censure and Reproof*, *Marprelate Tracts*, ed. Pierce, p. 353, I thank you Master Monday, you are a good gentleman of your word. Ah, thou Judas, thou that hast already betrayed the Papists, I think meanest to betray us also. c1590 Munday, *John a Kent*, l. 1053, Ye seeme an honest man, and so faith, could ye be as good as your woord, there be that perhaps would come somewhat roundly to ye.

M219 A MAN can die but once

1549 Bullinger, *Treatise or Sermon*, tr. Lynne, A6^v, What thyng can a man reproue in warre? because men do dye whiche must dye once, wherbye peace may follow? 1563 Foxe, *Acts and Monuments*, ed. Hebel-Hudson-F. R. Johnson, p. 192, To the most miserable man in the world this one thing is granted, that he can die but once. c1591 Marlowe, *Edward II*, V. i. 153, death ends all, and I can die but once.

---

[1] Omitted by Tilley.

M428 A wise MAN may sometimes play the fool (He is not wise who cannot play the fool)
    c1500 *Proverbs of Wressell, Antiq. Rep.* iv (1809), 415, It is no wysdome allway to seme sage, but sumtyme as be pretens to shew foly ... Sumtyme to be unwise as in apparens, Amonge the wyse is called grete prudens. 1553 *Precepts of Cato,* tr. Burrant, G3, some time to plaie the foole, is a poincte of wit.

M458 An honest MAN's word is as good as his bond
    a1500 *Lancelot,* E.E.T.S., l. 1673, O kingis word shuld be a kingis bonde.

M471 MAN's extremity is God's opportunity
    1602 Warner, *Albion's Eng.,* bk. 13, ch. 76, p. 315, Thou sensuall Epicure, thy selfe gainsaiste it [a Godhead] not for shame: Yea, Atheist, in Extremeties, thou touchest on his Name.

M500 You set an old MAN's head on a young man's shoulders
    1591 Smith, *Preparative to Marriage,* pp. 14-15, It is not good grafting of an olde head vppon young shoulders.

M544 MEN are not angels
    1548 Hall, *Chron.,* 1809 edn., p. 783, we be men frayle of condicion and no Angels. 1583 Babington, *Exposition of the Commandments,* p. 401, wee are men, and no Angels, and as men in this worlde wee must walke our course.

M553 MEN (Women) may blush to hear what they were not ashamed to act (do)
    c1558 Wedlocke, *Image of Idleness,* E6ᵛ, The common prouerbe saith, that women loue better to haue it, then to heare speke of it.

M755 To mince the MATTER
    1533 More, *Debell. of Salem,* in *Wks.,* 1557, p. 99, Though them selfe ... fall not by suche bokes to the myncyng of suche maters, and dyspute howe farre they maye go forwarde in theym.

M837 She is MEAT for your master
    1592 Nashe, *Pierce Penniless,* ed. McKerrow, i. 195, As if they were no meate but for his Maisterships mouth.

M874 Either MEND or end
    1578 White, *Sermon at Paul's Cross,* p. 74, It [the plague] hathe mended, as manye as it hathe ended. 1592 Lodge, 'Deaf man's dialogue' in *Euphues' Shadow,* Hunt. Club edn., p. 87, Neyther may we mend it till God end it. 1599 Tasso, *Of Marr. and Wiving,* G3ᵛ, I pray ... God ... for his great mercies sake, either (soone) to mend them [women], or quickly to end them.

M895 He shall find MERCY that merciful is[1]
    1513 Bradshaw, *St. Werburge,* E.E.T.S., l. 2750, Who-so wyll haue mercy Must be mercyable as in prouerbe wryten is; Who is without mercy of mercy shall mys.

M967 He weeps MILLSTONES
    1587 Bridges, *Defence,* p. 3, All their cheifest mourning and lamentation is for this, if indeed they weepe and mourne at all, and that euery tear be not (as they say) as big as a milstone.

---

[1] Matt. 5 : 7.

The Proverbial Wisdom of Shakespeare 169

M985 New out of the MINT

 1593 Nashe, *Christ's Tears*, ed. McKerrow, ii. 15, Newe mynt my minde to the likenes of thy lowlines.

M999a One must not bemoan (wail) a MISCHIEF but find out a remedy for it

 1578 Yver, *Courtly Controversy*, tr. Wotton, O3ᵛ, Seing there was no remedie in an act committed, but that according to the wise mans saying, a myschief must be prudently preuented, and being once happened, patiently supported.

M1105 MONMOUTH Caps

 1598 Rankins, *Seven Satires*, C1ᵛ, Vpon his head a Monmouth cap he wore, With a greene parrats feather brought before.

M1189 He is a MOTE in their eyes

 1546 Bale, *Exam. of Anne Askewe*, Parker Soc., f. 21ᵛ, Johan Frith is a great moate in their eyes.

M1243 MICE (rats) quit a falling house (sinking ship)

 1579 Lupton, *Thousand Notable Things*, bk. ii., no. 87, Rats and Dormyse, wyll forsake olde and ruinous houses, three monethes before they fall. 1586 Whetstone, *English Mirror*, p. 176, You may learne instructions of safetie of Mise, which runne from houses which are readie to fall.

M1265 What is sweet in the MOUTH is often sour (bitter) in the maw (stomach)[1]

 1592 Delamothe, *French Alphabet*, M5ᵛ, What is sweet in the mouth, is often bitter at the hart.

M1287 MUCH would have more

 1509 Barclay, *Ship of Fools*, 1874 edn., i. 101, Though he haue all yet wolde he haue more.

N36–7 To take one NAPPING

 1569–70 *Stationers' Register*, ed. Arber, i. 417 [Ballad title].

N183 To sit (sing) like a NIGHTINGALE, with a thorn against one's breast

 c1510 B.M. Royal Appen. (MS. Adds. 31922), printed *Anglia*, xii. 264, She syngeth in the thyke And under hur brest a prike To kepe her fro slepe. 1563 Hall, *Poesy in Form of a Vision*, A3, For as they fayne the thorne so sharpe dyd serue to touch hyr [Philomel's] breast. 1576 Gascoigne, *Steel Glass*, ed. Cunliffe, ii. 146, And thus I sing, with pricke against my brest, Like Philomene. [c1587] 1592 Kyd, *Span. Trag.*, l. 806, The gentle Nightingale... singing with the prickle at her breast. [1589] 1594 Greene, *Friar Bacon*, l. 1623, Ile play with you as the Nightingale with the Slow-worme, Ile set a pricke against my breast.

N184 NIGHTWORK

 1594 Plat, *Jewel-House*, p. 67, My purpose is onely to put some in minde of their grosse night-woorkes.

N327 There is NOTHING but is good for something

 a1500 *A fifteenth Century School Book*, ed. Nelson, p. 61, There is nothynge but it wyll serve for sumwhat, be it never so course.

---

[1] Rev. 10: 9–10.

N363 It is NUTS to him
1578 Whetstone, *Promos and Cassandra*, B2ᵛ, As iumpe as Apes, in vewe of Nuttes to daunce.

O9 To drink the OCEAN dry
1550 Gribaldi, *A notable & marvellous Epistle*, C2, as possyble as too take the whoole waater of the Sea, in one spoone, and to drynke it vp at a draught.

O29 There is OIL (no oil) left in the lamp
1573 Gascoigne, *Dan B. of Bath*, ed. Cunliffe, i. 127, Who hath seene a Lampe begyn to fade, Which lacketh oyle to feede his lyngring light.

O81 To heap OSSA upon Pelion
1561 Seneca, *Herc. Furens*, tr. Heywood, K1, Let Chiron vnder Ossa see his Pelion mowntayne grette. 1584 Scot, *Disc. of Witchcraft*, p. 559, they imitate the old giants ... piling vp *Pelion* vpon *Ossa*, and them both vpon *Olympus*. 1580 H. I. in C. Carlile, *Discourse of Peter's Life*, P4ᵛ, *Ephialtes* with *Othus* ... Who heaped hils on mountaines high, *Ossa* on Pindus backe, And placed *Pelion* on them the starrie skie to sacke.

P57 Like a PARISH top
[c1580] 1590 Sidney, *Arcadia*, ed. Feuillerat, i. 227, Even like a toppe which nought but whipping moves. 1601 W. I., *Whipping of the Satire*, D6ᵛ, As boyes scourge tops for sport on Lenten day; So scourges he the great towne-top of sin.

P153 To make PEACE with a sword in his hand
1594 Lipsius, *Six Books of Politics*, tr. Jones, 2A3, Let not the olde prouerbe deceive thee, It is best treating of peace, with weapons in ones hand.

P465 Standing POOLS gather filth
1579 Gosson, *Sch. Abuse*, ed. Arber, p. 52, Standing streames geather filth; flowing riuers, are euer sweet.

R33 The croaking RAVEN bodes misfortune (death)
1578 T. W[hite]., *Sermon at Paul's Cross*, p. 77, It was a greate faulte in this people [the Jews] ... to obserue dreames, singyng of byrdes, and the lyke paltrie as many doe nowe, ... the crying of Rauens, the flying of Owles, a sorte of ... olde wyues fables, whereby the Diuell deludeth manye, and weakeneth their faythe. 1584 Lyly, *Sappho and Phao*, III. iii. 60, I mistruste her not: for that the owle hath not shrikte at the window, or the night Rauen croked, both being fatall.

R93 Saving your REVERENCE
1528 Roy and Barlow, *Rede me and be not wroth*, ed. Arber, p. 41, Nowe for all his hye magnificence They counte him savynge reuerence Not moche better than a knave. 1562 *Jack Juggler*, l. 816, Ney then were I a knaue misteris, sauing your reuirence. 1564 Bullein, *Dial. agst. the Fever Pestilence*, ff. 58ᵛ–9, the worlde and please your maisship, and my mistres honestie, & sur reuerence of myne owne manhoode, is full of verletrie. c1566 Curio, *Pasquin in a Trance*, tr. W.P., f. 50ᵛ, Cardinals ... by force, & not by loue, haue they gotten to them selues authority, and reuerence, or as we may say, sauing your reuerence also. [In margin] This worde sauing your reuerence is vsed of vs when we speake of some thing that is vnclenly or filthie, for men vse some time to saye sauing your reuerence he is a knaue, or a Cardinal, and so the Author meaneth that this word reuerence belongeth to ther riches and highe estate, and this worde sauing your reuerence to their vile and filthy life. 1581 Rich, *Rich his Farewell*, B1ᵛ, I haue gathered together this small volume of Histories, all treatying (sir reuerence of you) of loue.

The Proverbial Wisdom of Shakespeare

R156 To kiss the ROD
1528 Tyndale, *Obed. Christ. Man*, Parker Soc., p. 196, If he knowledge his fault and take the corrective meekly, and even kiss the rod. 1580 Munday, *Zelauto*, O4ᵛ, The childe . . . willing to kisse the rod, and so to pacifie the yre of his Parents. [c1590] 1605 *King Leir*, l. 611, I do willingly imbrace the rod.

R196, B569 There is the RUB
1577–8 Stanyhurst in Holinshed, *Hist of Ireland*, p. 100b, howe daungerous it is to be a rubbe, when a King is disposed to sweepe an Alley.

S28 Enough to make a SAINT swear
1567 Pickering, *Horestes*, l. 97, Would it not anger a saynt at the hart.

S117 No sooner SAID than done (so said so done)
1566 Beverley, *Ariodanto and Jenevra*, ed. Prouty in *Sources of 'Much Ado'*, p. 98, So thought, so don. 1577 FitJohn, *Diamond most Precious*, H2ᵛ, So sayd, and so done, is a thread well spone.

S284 To lick into SHAPE
1562 Broke, *Romeus and Juliet*, ¶4, The mountaine beare Bringes forth unformd . . . her young . . . her often lycking tong geves them . . . shape. 1576 Caius, *Of English Dogs*, tr. Fleming, in *Social England*, ed. Lang, p. 44, I hope, having, like the bear, licked over my young, I have waded in this work to your contentation.

S337 He is put to his SHIFTS
1542 Borde, *Dietary of Health*, E.E.T.S., p. 240, Thus a man shall lese his thryfte, and be put to a shefte. 1581 Manutius, *Phrases Linguae Latinae*, p. 29, ech thing is so deare, that euery man is driuen to his shiftes.

S408 More SHOW than substance
1594 Nashe, *Terrors of the Night*, ed. McKerrow, i. 353, The spirits of aire . . . are in truth all show and no substance.

S443 Ecce SIGNUM
1583 Elizabeth to Burghley, in Wright, *Eliz. and her Times*, 1838, ii. 201, I have of late seen an *ecce signum* that if an asse kicke you, you feele it too soone. c1592 *Thomas of Woodstock*, III. iii. 16, Though I cannot write, I have set my mark: ecce signum.

S527 SLEEP is the image of death
1534 Lupset, *Treat. of Dying Well*, ed. Gee, p. 275, Nowe than what shall we saye of dethe? the whiche by hym selfe is not vnlyke to an endles slepe of the bodye. 1577 Bishop, *Beautiful Blossoms*, 2A2ᵛ, sleepe is an Image of death.

S577 I will SMOKE you
c1552 Walker, *Manifest Detection of Dice Play*, C3, beware that we cause him not to smoke, least that hauing any fele or sauor of gyle intendid agaynste hym, he slyppe the collor . . . & shake vs of for euer. Ibid., D5, when the money is lost, the cosin begins to smoke. [1598] 1601 Jonson, *Every Man In*, V. i. 35, I haue smokt you yet at last.

S647 SORE upon sore is not a salve
1572 Pasquier, *Monophylo*, tr. Fenton, Pt. II, f. 3ᵛ, A pinching sore cannot abide a smarting playster. 1592 Delamothe, *French Alphabet*, O5ᵛ, sore vpon sore is not a salue.

S704 As flattering (fawning) as a SPANIEL
1585 Greene, *Planetomachia*, ed. Grosart, v. 103, Like Spanyels flattering with their tayles.

S715 As lustful as SPARROWS
[c1580] 1590 Sidney, *Arcadia*, ed. Feuillerat, i. 134, The Sparrow, lust to playe. 1594 Nashe, *Unfort. Trav.*, ed. McKerrow, ii. 225, The sparrow for his lechery liueth but a yeare.

S742 What we SPENT we had, what we gave we have, what we lent we lost
1579 Spenser, *Shep. Cal.*, May, Gloss, Much like the Epitaph of a good olde Erle of Deuonshire, . . . The rymes be these. Ho, Ho, who lies here? I the good Erle of Deuonshere, And Maulde my wife, . . . That we spent, we had: That we gaue we haue: That we lefte, we lost.

S794 Untimeous SPURRING spills the steed
1581 Guazzo, *Civil Conv.*, tr. Pettie, Tudor Trans. edn., i. 134, By too much spurring, the horse is made dull.

S914 It is no more STRANGE than true
a1534 Heywood, *Love*, A3, The case as ye put it I thynke more straunge Then true. 1575 Laneham, *Letter*, ed. Furnivall, p. 46, A thing, master Martin, very rare and straunge; and yet no more straunge then tru. 1590–5 Munday *et al.*, *Sir T. More*, v. iii. 50, It's very strange.—It will be found as true.

S987 To get the SUN of one
1548 Hall, *Chron.*, 1809 edn., p. 418, Betwene both armies ther was a great marrysse which therle of Richemond left on his right hand, for this entent that it should be on that syde a defence for his part, and in so doyng he had the sonne at his backe and in the faces of his enemies. 1581 Averell, *Charles and Julia*, H4^v, By tracing ground, they got of them, bothe winde and shining Sun. Sir Phoebus blerde the Rebels eyes, his glistering beames so shinde.

T88 When? Can you TELL?
[1590] 1592 *Soliman and Perseda*, II. ii. 3, I must betraie my maister? I, but when, can you tell? c1590 Munday, *John a Kent*, l. 62, But can ye tell me when?

T89 So you TOLD me
[1497] c1512–16 Medwall, *Fulgens and Lucres*, l. 1088, Ye, so I harde you say.

T128 Give a THING and take a thing, that is the devil's gold ring

T129 (*or* and you shall ride in hell's wain)
1571 Bridges, *Sermon at Paul's Cross*, p. 29, Shal we make God to say the worde, and eate his worde? to giue a thing, and take a thing, little children say, This is the diuels goldring, not Gods gifte.

T219 First THINK and then speak
1557 Edgeworth, *Sermons*, B6, Thinke well and thou shalt speake wel.

T228 He that sows THISTLES shall reap thorns (prickles)
1583 Prime, *Fruitful and Brief Discourse*, p. 33, As the mother sinne is, so are the daughters of sinne. Of a thistle a prick, of a bramble commeth a bryer.

T240 As swift as THOUGHT
[1589] 1592 Lyly, *Midas*, IV. i. 172, Report flies as swift as thoghts.

The Proverbial Wisdom of Shakespeare 173

T259 To stumble at the THRESHOLD
1579 Spenser, *Shep. Cal.*, May, l. 229, Tho went the pensife Damme out of dore, And chaunst to stomble at the threshold flore: Her stombling steppe some what her amazed, (For such, as signes of ill luck bene dispraised).

T264 First THRIVE and then wive
1577 Breton, *Works of a Young Wit*, in *Poems*, ed. Robertson, p. 65, And now I thinke thou seest, how I beginne to thryue, And thryuing now you may suspecte, that I would seeke to wyue.

T325 TIME cures every disease
1539 Taverner, *Proverbs*, f. 38, Tyme taketh away greuaunce. 1578 Yver, *Courtly Controversy*, tr. Wotton, 2N2, The oyle of Tyme is a soueraigne salue for euery sore. 1591 Harington, *Orlando Furioso*, vi. 2, Thus making worse the thing before was nought, He hurt the wound which time perhaps had healed.

T402 To keep a good TONGUE in one's head
1542 Erasmus, *Apophthegms*, tr. Udall, p. 258, Augustus sent hym a gentle warnyng to kepe a better toung in his hedde, and to vse it more sobrely.

T515 A good TRENCHERMAN
1590 Greene, *Francesco's Fortunes*, ed. Grosart, viii. 199, Mullidor tried himselfe so tall a trencher man, that his mother perceiued by his drift he would not die for loue.

T555 TRUST is the mother of deceit
a1536 Hill, *Commonplace Book*, ed. Dyboski, E.E.T.S., p. 130, In whom I trust most, sonnest me deseyvith.

T583 TRUTH loves (fears no) trial
1581 Howell, *Devices*, L4^v, Truth feareth no tryall.

T591 TRUTH will come to light (break out)
1539 Taverner, Publius, B1, The thyng that good is (as trouth and iustice) thoughe it be suppressed and kepte and vnder for a tyme, yet is it not quenched vtterly, but at length wyll breake out agayne. c1588 *Wealth and Health*, l. 934, Truth wyll appeare. 1559 *Mirror for Magistrates*, ed. Campbell, p. 220, Truth wil out, though all the world say no.

T609 To turn TURK
[c1590] 1592 *Soliman and Perseda*, III. v. 7, What say these prisoners? will they turne Turke, or no? 1592 Nashe, *Strange News*, ed. McKerrow, i. 291, Is it not a sinfull thing for a Scholler and a Christian to turne Tully? a Turke would neuer do it.

V18 VARIETY takes away satiety
1579 Lyly, *Euph.*, ed. Bond, i. 272, It is varietie that moueth the minde of all men. [1589] 1592 Lyly, *Midas*, II. i. 1, Of gold there is sacietie... in loue there is varietie. 1592 Delamothe, *French Alphabet*, p. 37, Nature hath pleasure in diuersitie. 1599 Minsheu, *Span. Dial.*, p. 10, Varietie breedes delight.

V52 It is a great VICTORY that comes without blood
1591 Harington, *Orlando Furioso*, xv. Moral, It cannot be denied but bloudie conquests are no praise to the conqueror. a1593 Ovid, *Amores*, tr. Marlowe, II. xii. 5, That victory doth chiefely triumph merit, Which without bloud-shed doth the pray inherit.

W130 Shallow WATERS make the greatest sound
c1578 Sidney, *Lady of May*, ed. Feuillerat, ii. 333, The highest note comes oft from basest mind, As shallow brookes do yeeld the greatest sound, c1580 Sidney, *Arcadia*, ed. Feuillerat, iv. 54, Shallow brookes murmur moste, Depe sylent slyde away.

W135 As pliable as WAX
c1549 Erasmus, *Two Dial.*, tr. Berke, ed. de Vocht, f. 14ᵛ, Take hede ... that thou, when christ shall laye his myghty hande vpon the be as tendre as waxe, that accordynge to his eternall wyll he maye frame and fashyon the with his hande. 1576 Lemnius, *Touchstone of Complexions*, tr. Newton, f. 98ᵛ translating Horace *Ars Poet.*, l. 163 To vyce he pliant is as waxe. 1590 Lodge, *Rosalynde*, ed. Greg, p. 109, Cupid hath drugs to make them more pliable than wax.

W152 The WAY to be safe is never to be secure (He that is secure is not safe)
1585 Prime, *Sermon in St. Mary's Oxford*, B7, Security maketh fooles.

W204 To beat one at his own WEAPON
1591 R. W., *Martin Mar-Sixtus*, E1, Who would not breake out and laugh, to see how hee beateth himselfe with his owne weapon. c1600 *Tarlton's Jests*, 1611 edn., ed. Halliwell, p. 8, You have beene beaten at your owne weapon.

W209 It is better to WEAR out than rust out
1557 Edgeworth, *Sermons*, A1ᵛ, Better it is to shine with laboure, then to rouste for idlenes. Ibid., 2X2ᵛ, The fleshe ... had leuer rust for slouthe and idlenes, then to shyne fayre and bright wyth labour.

W258 WELCOME is the best cheer
c1550 Heywood in Redford, *Wit and Science*, ed. Halliwell, p. 112, Wellcum is the best dyshe. 1584 Wilson, *Three Ladies of London*, ed. Hazlitt, vi. 290, I haue bread and beer, one joint of meat, and welcome, thy best fare.

W260 Let WELL alone
[c1565–6] 1626 *Merry Jests of Scoggin*, *Shakespeare Jest-Books*, ed. Hazlitt, ii. 143, When it was well, you could not let it alone. 1577 Holinshed, *Chron.*, 1587 edn., i. 162*b*, Ye iudged well once, but ye may not change well againe.

W432 To go down the WIND
1600 Breton, *Pasquil's Pass*, ed. Grosart, i. 11, Want and vertue must go downe the wind.

W570 WIT, whither wilt thou
1539 Vives, *Intro. to Wisdom*, I8ᵛ, How fowle, howe peryllous, a thynge is, Lingua quo vadis? Tunge whether goest thou? 1575 Higgins in Udall, *Flowers for Latin Speaking*, Z6ᵛ, Wisdome, you speake in vaine, wyt whither wilt thou.

W638 Trust not a WOMAN when she weeps
1597 [Bodenham], *Wit's Commonwealth*, p. 27, Trust not a woman when she weepeth.

W776 While the WORD is in your mouth it is your own, when it is once spoken it is another's
1509 Barclay, *Ship of Fools*, 1874 edn., i. 110, Whan a worde is nat sayd, the byrde is in the cage ... whan thy worde is spokyn ... Thou arte nat mayster, but he that hath it harde. 1547 Baldwin, *Treatise Moral Philosophy*, K7ᵛ, A man hath power ouer his wordes til they be spoken, but after they be vttered they haue power ouer hym.

W924 The WORTH of a thing is best known by the want
 1586 Whetstone, *The English Mirror*, p. 110, the goodnesse of a thing is knowne by the depriuement thereof.

Y43 YOUTH and age will never agree
 1550 Heywood, *Two Hundred Epigrams . . . with a Third Hundred newly added*, no. 33, age and youth together can seeld agree.

6

The Elizabethan Theatre[1]

THE title 'The Elizabethan Theatre' is perhaps indefensible. There were two main kinds of theatre, public and private. Between each kind of theatre there was great difference: between theatres of the same kind, some difference. Moreover, if the meaning of the word 'theatre' is extended to include any building in which plays were acted in Elizabethan times—for example, a chamber or hall at court—it becomes even clearer that we must speak not of the Elizabethan theatre but of Elizabethan theatres. In this lecture I begin with an account of some of these theatres, their kinds and their location; then I consider some problems of Elizabethan staging; and I end with some notes on audiences and acting.

I. THE THEATRES

The only Elizabethan building which could and did call itself the Theatre was that which James Burbage built in Shoreditch in 1576, the first public theatre in England specially built for the production of plays. In 1577 the Curtain was put up nearby, and during the next thirty years many a rival public theatre appeared, whether to the north of London like the Fortune in Golding Lane (1600) and the Red Bull in Clerkenwell (*c.* 1605) or on the Bankside to the south of the Thames like the Rose (1587), the Swan (1595), and the Globe (1599). To these add inns like the Bell Savage on Ludgate Hill and the Bull in Bishopsgate Street which were used as theatres before 1576 and for many years after.

These were all public theatres used by professional adult actors, and except for the inns they were all carefully placed outside the jurisdiction of the hostile City of London. It is very clear that if the court had not been addicted to drama, or had been powerless to

[1] [Text of a lecture delivered on the Allard Pierson Foundation, University of Amsterdam, published in *Neophilologus*, 1955.]

The Elizabethan Theatre

protect the players, there would have been no Elizabethan drama. In the year Burbage built his theatre the supremacy of the adult actors was still in doubt. A better record of performances at court was held by children's companies from the choir-schools especially of the Chapel Royal and St. Paul's. These children were carefully chosen and trained by their masters, who were given an authority to recruit almost as drastic as that of a press-gang. Late in the same year 1576, Richard Farrant, Master of the Children of Windsor Chapel and deputy to the Master of the Children of the Chapel Royal, inspired perhaps by the example set by Burbage, established the first of the so-called private theatres by converting the frater in the old Priory buildings of the Black Friars into 'a continual house for plays', so providing in the eighth and last year of this theatre's existence a stage for the art of John Lyly. The excuse was the necessity of a private hall for the rehearsal of plays to be performed at court, but the opportunity was taken to charge for admission. From their beginnings the private theatres like the public were commercial ventures.

This first Blackfriars theatre is overshadowed in importance by the second, constructed in 1596 in some other rooms in the same buildings. The proprietor and converter was James Burbage himself. What a debt did the Elizabethan drama and theatre owe to him and to his sons Cuthbert and Richard! Many years later Cuthbert claimed that the success of the Globe and the Blackfriars was 'purchased by the infinite cost and paynes of the family of the Burbages, and the great desert of Richard Burbage for his quality of playing'.[1] James's attempt to introduce a common theatre into the fashionable precinct of the Blackfriars met with powerful opposition; he died in 1597, and in 1600 Richard let the theatre to the proprietor of a children's company. He did so to the great enrichment of our drama. Under successive managements the genius of Jonson, Chapman, and others found here a congenial setting for plays some of which could not have flourished in the robust air of the public theatres. By 1608 the heyday of the child actors was over. In

[1] J. O. Halliwell-Phillipps, *Outlines of Shakespeare* (1887 edn.), i. 319. I have not added references to documents which may be easily traced in such standard works on the theatre as those by Sir Edmund K. Chambers, J. Q. Adams, and G. E. Bentley.

that year Richard Burbage, Shakespeare, and their fellows at last entered into possession and began to use the Blackfriars as their winter home while still using the Globe during the summer months: they were the first company of adult actors to act regularly in a private theatre. That what had proved impossible in 1596 had become possible by 1608 is a pointer to the increased power of the company, now the darlings of the court. And they were strongly entrenched by 1619 when the inhabitants of the Blackfriars made a fruitless attempt to eject them.[1]

The ambition of public and private theatres alike was to have as large a proportion of their repertory as possible chosen by the Lord Chamberlain and his deputy the Master of the Revels for performance before the court. The profit of acting at court was an important source of revenue, and the prestige an incalculable stimulus to standards of acting and production. At the accession of James I in 1603 the London companies were taken under royal patronage, and the Lord Chamberlain's company of Shakespeare and Burbage became His Majesty's players. Under Elizabeth plays had been acted at her favourite palaces of Greenwich, Hampton Court, Windsor, Richmond. During Christmas and Shrovetide, however, Whitehall was especially favoured, and we hear of productions in the Great Hall and in the Great Chamber. Under James *Othello* was produced in the Elizabethan Banqueting House on 1 November 1604, and famous is the use for masques and plays of the 1607 Banqueting House and for masques of Inigo Jones's great Renaissance building of 1622 which still survives for our delight.

The public and private theatres and the court—these were the centres of dramatic activity when Marlowe and Shakespeare came to town in the fifteen-eighties; and as we have seen, permanent public and private theatres had only recently been established. How recent and how important was the establishment of these theatres let me illustrate from one small detail: not until 1584, when the Queen's reign was more than half over and seven to eight years after the opening of the Theatre, the Curtain, and the Blackfriars, do non-academic plays begin to announce on their title-pages the theatres or companies which had produced them. In that year Lyly's

[1] *Malone Society Collections*, I. i (1907), pp. 90-4.

Sappho and Phao was published as played before the Queen by the children of the Chapel and the boys of Paul's, and Peele's *Arraignment of Paris* as presented before the Queen by the children of the Chapel. These two plays are chiefly important because they announce, for the first time and at long last, that art and poetry have come to the drama and that the golden age has arrived. But for our present purposes they are important because the publishers have tied them so clearly to their environment—the environment of the court and the private theatres. A third play published in 1584 is certainly no herald of a new age. For one thing Robert Wilson's *Three Ladies of London* is morality drama, and for another it is written in tumbling or doggerel verse, a verse as hostile to poetry as the monotony of strict syllabic verse which begins to afflict the drama from about the year 1560. But yet observe that Wilson's play, old-fashioned as it is in other respects, is new-fashioned in this: it is published 'as it hath been publiquely played'. And so in the advertisements of these three plays we are given a short view of the great nurseries of Elizabethan drama, the court and the public and private theatres.

That dramatists when they wrote their plays had in mind the particular theatre for which they were writing is more than a probable conjecture. As much is said in 1620 by the printer of that inferior play *The Two Merry Milkmaids*: 'Every Writer must gouerne his Penne according to the Capacitie of the Stage he writes too, both in the Actor and the Auditor.'[1] How far a writer governed his pen to suit the capacity of particular actors I must not stay to inquire,[2] but that he was influenced by the kind of theatre he was writing for, whether private or public, is certain. This is the theme of Professor Alfred Harbage's recent book, *Shakespeare and the Rival Traditions* (1952). Shakespeare stands alone among the major dramatists of his age in that he never wrote for a children's company acting at a private theatre. Even when his company acquired the Blackfriars in 1608, he continued to write for a public theatre, for his last plays had to please both at the Globe and at the Blackfriars. But the plays of his contemporaries may show marked differences

---

[1] Edmond Malone wrote in his copy of this play: 'The most stupid stuff I ever read'; and he was extremely well read.

[2] See, however, T. W. Baldwin's *The Organization and Personnel of the Shakespearean Company* (1927).

according to which 'rival tradition' they were written for. In the public theatre, unroofed and holding perhaps some 2,000 persons,[1] the actors had to amuse an audience drawn from all classes of society: courtiers, inns of court men, university men, gentlemen and their wives—many of them up from the country and seeing the sights—citizens and their wives, soldiers, journeymen, apprentices, thieves, and women of the town. The task of feeding so wide a range of interests cannot have been easy. Contrast the private theatres, roofed over and lit by candles and torches, playing to a select and wholly seated audience paying higher prices, a coterie audience more in touch with courtiers than with citizens and eager for wit and satire. No doubt the difference may be exaggerated; but it exists.

We ought to speak, then, not of the Elizabethan theatre but of the Elizabethan theatres, and this is important in considering the methods of production on Elizabethan stages. At one extreme we have the elaborate performance of an accredited company at court and at the other the performance in the country of a strolling company stalking 'vpon boords, and barrell heads, to an old crackt trumpet'[2]!

But to narrow the range a little. Consider under what astonishingly diverse conditions the plays of Shakespeare may have been produced. Players were often engaged to act in private houses, as when in 1600 the patron of Shakespeare's company, Lord Chamberlain Hunsdon, entertained the Flemish ambassador to a banquet and a performance of *Henry IV*. Even Lord Mayors entertained distinguished guests to plays, sometimes in the halls of their City companies; for example, Merchant Taylors' Hall in 1614 and Drapers' Hall in 1616.[3] We should not expect the city companies to look upon the drama with favour, and after it had ceased to be religious they spent no money on the employment of professional companies. Quite exceptional was the action of the Goldsmiths'

---

[1] Estimates differ. A Dutchman (Johannes de Witt) estimated the capacity of the Swan in 1596 at 3,000 (cf. *Shakespeare Survey*, i, 1948, p. 24), and a Spaniard guessed that the Fortune in 1624 held 3,000 and more (E. M. Wilson and O. Turner in *M.L.R.*, xliv, 1949, pp. 478 and 482). For a modern estimate see A. Harbage, *Shakespeare's Audience* (1941), ch. 2.
[2] *The Poetaster*, III. iv. 169.
[3] *Letters of John Chamberlain*, ed. N. McClure (1939), i. 499 and ii. 35.

Company in 1609 in lending their garden-house to Sir Lewis Lewknor when he wished to entertain his friends to a play.[1] Much kinder to the players were the inns of court, 'the noblest nourseries of humanity, and liberty, in the kingdome', as Jonson called them, and it is sufficient to recall the performances of *The Comedy of Errors* at Gray's Inn in 1594 and of *Twelfth Night* at the Middle Temple in 1602. Occasionally a private performance took place in an inn or tavern. On St. George's Day 1618 Buckingham gave his forty gentlemen and ten yeomen £100 to make them a supper and a play the next night at the Mitre in Fleet Street.[2] As at that date they could have hired the best company in town for £10, they had money left over for the supper. In the summer and early autumn players went 'strolling' in the country, and there accommodation might be primitive. Robert Armin, who succeeded William Kempe as the leading comedian in Shakespeare's company, writes of players and 'the Players boy... in his Ladyes gowne' dressing in the kitchen of a gentleman's house in the country, and entering through the entry into the hall.[3] In 1610 the king's players visited Oxford. They took with them the brand-new *Alchemist,* and a strict observer was shocked at the behaviour of the *theologi* of the University who flocked *avidissime* to see a play which made so profane a use of scriptural language. But he admitted that the players acted tragedy *decore, et apte* and that the death of Desdemona brought tears to the eyes. He also observed that they acted before full houses *cum applausu maximo.*[4]

What a varied scene it is that we must contemplate! A play of Shakespeare's, primarily designed for the Globe but acted whenever possible at court, and after 1608 at the Blackfriars, may also have been performed in the hall of an inn of court or city company, in the private house of a lord or gentleman or city magnate, in a garden-house, privately in an inn or tavern, and in the country on many a

[1] Lewknor was Master of Ceremonies at court, and no easy man to refuse. For the reference see the *Malone Society Collections* iii, 'Calendar of Dramatic Records in the Books of the Livery Companies of London 1485–1640', edited by Jean Robertson and D. J. Gordon, p. 175.
[2] John Chamberlain, ed. cit., ii. 159. Cf. T. Middleton, *A Mad World my Masters* (1608), v. i. 78: 'This will be a True feast, a right Miter supper, a play and all.'
[3] Armin's *Fool upon Fool* (1605), in Works, ed. A. B. Grosart (1880), p. 26.
[4] G. Tillotson, *Essays in Criticism and Research* (1942), pp. 41–8.

makeshift stage. That a company exiled from its proper stage sometimes had to dispense with elaborate scenic arrangements is suggested by the direction at the end of *Alphonsus King of Aragon* (1599): 'Exit *Venus*. Or if you can conueniently, let a chaire come downe from the top of the stage, and draw her vp'; and that with some companies there may have been rough moments during a performance acted in strange and cramped surroundings is suggested by a direction in William Percy's *Aphrodysial*:[1] 'Here went furth the whole Chorus in a shuffle as after a Play in a Lords howse.' But I take leave to doubt if Burbage and his fellows were so dependent upon circumstances for a good performance. We are speaking not of men who used the stage as a hobby but of men who devoted their lives to it, and the best actors in the country. When Mr. Tyrone Guthrie took *Hamlet* to Elsinore in 1937, with Laurence Olivier as Hamlet, the intention was to produce the play in the courtyard of the castle, but at the opening performance rain and tempest made an open-air performance impossible and all there was time to do was to move to a neighbouring hotel and there mark out a stage in the hotel ballroom.[2] The players were surrounded by spectators, and without rehearsal made their entrances and exits through the aisles of the audience; yet they gave what they felt to be one of the most successful and enjoyable performances of their lives. Actors have always been an adaptable race. And when I am told that because a play was produced one way at the Globe it was necessarily produced in the same way at the Blackfriars and at court, I do not believe it.

2. STAGING

I approach the second part of my lecture with some anxiety, partly because I have no practical knowledge of the theatre, partly because nowadays controversy rages so furiously about the question of Elizabethan staging that the remarks of the most innocent bystander may give offence. A man cannot even sit upon the fence without finding it charged with electricity.

I begin with some remarks on the public stages, but in the time at my disposal I must make the most drastic omissions. Was the

[1] Cited by G. F. Reynolds, 'William Percy and his Plays', *Modern Philology*, xii (1914–15), p. 258.
[2] F. Baxter, *The Oliviers* (1953), p. 129.

Globe on the south or on the north side of Maiden Lane in Southwark? The proof by Mr. W. W. Braines and others that it was on the south side is an admirable example of historical method, but does not concern me here.[1] I cannot myself get excited about whether the Globe was round or polygonal in shape, the position of the entrances to the theatre or of the stairways behind the scenic wall leading down to the cellarage and up to the balcony and higher still to the turret, whether the platform stood 6 or 8 feet above yard level or only 4 or 5 feet, so necessitating excavation to provide room for the Ghost. I do not care, though if I were attempting a model of the Globe—like Dr. J. Q. Adams or Professor Lüdeke or Mr. Richard Southern—I should have to care. But what I should like to know more about are the nature of the stage and the methods of production.

At this point I must remind you of two famous documents long familiar to historians of the theatre, the contract for the building of the Fortune Theatre and the drawing of the Swan Theatre. The contract was agreed in 1600 between Philip Henslowe and the actor Edward Alleyn on the one part and on the other by Peter Street who a few months earlier had built the Globe Theatre. Measurements are given of the frame of the theatre, exterior and interior, 80 feet each way and 55 feet each way, and of the three galleries which ran round the house and rose to a height of 32 feet. Within this frame was erected a tiring-house, in front of which was a stage 43 feet wide and extending as far as the middle of the yard. Paled in below with strong oak boards, it was covered in part by a shadow or covering so tilted that a gutter of lead carried the rainwater backwards. In all respects but one the builder was instructed to follow the model of the Globe: the Fortune was square, not round or polygonal. One other early contract has survived—that for the Beargarden or Hope Theatre of 1613. Here the model was the Swan. But as the Hope had to serve as bearbaiting arena as well as theatre, its stage stood upon trestles and was removable, and the 'Heavens' (as in this contract the shadow is called) covered the

---

[1] W. W. Braines, *The Site of the Globe Playhouse Southwark* (2nd edn., 1924); I. A. Shapiro in *Shakespeare Survey*, i (1948), pp. 28–9, 36; *London County Council Survey of London*, xxii (1950), 'Bankside', pp. 75, 133.

whole stage and was not supported by posts resting upon the stage.

Nothing is said about decoration in either of these contracts, except that at the Fortune the main posts of frame and stage were to be square pilasters with carved satyrs at the top. From other sources we know that the posts or columns at the Swan were painted to look like marble so cunningly as to deceive the 'noseyest' persons (*nasutissimos*), that arras was hung on the back wall of the stage, and that when a tragedy was to be performed the stage was hung with black. Peter Street was specially exempted from the charge of painting the Fortune, but that does not mean that there was not much expenditure of paint. Perhaps we do not go far wrong if we think of an Elizabethan theatre in terms of the gay haywains and canal barges of our youth before these vehicles became severely functional.

The Fortune contract tells us nothing about the tiring-house wall at the back of the stage except that it was to be modelled on the Globe. The only authentic evidence of the interior of a public theatre in Shakespeare's time is a contemporary copy of a drawing made by a Dutchman John de Witt, who visited the Swan Theatre in 1596.[1] The copy is now in the library of the University of Utrecht. There is much that will be familiar in it if we bear in mind the Fortune contract and the light that throws upon the Globe: the round amphitheatrical shape with three galleries running up to the scenic wall, the platform projecting from the wall as far as the middle of the yard, the shadow protecting a part of the platform and supported by two pilasters. So far so good, but we get into serious trouble when we examine the scenic wall. This plain flat wall, behind which lies the 'mimorum aedes' or tiring-house, is broken at ground level only by two substantial double doors on either side of its centre. At an upper level a balcony runs along the whole length of the wall. In the very front of the platform a comic scene is in progress. A lady sits on a bench, behind her stands a maid who appears from the position of her arms to be expressing some amazement, and before them stalks with affected gait a man with well

[1] Often reproduced. The best reproduction is in *Shakespeare Survey*, i (1948), plate III.

developed beard and moustaches, grasping in his left hand, as a steward or other officer might do, a rod or wand. If the drawing had been five years later and of the Globe, everyone would say 'Malvolio walking cross-gartered before the Lady Olivia and Maria', and some have not scrupled to say that in spite of the place and date. The only property is the bench on which the lady sits; but de Witt paid only one visit to the theatre, and we may not assume that the Swan stage was always so empty. This scene is being played before an empty yard and empty galleries, but in the balcony are eight figures. What do they represent? If spectators, why should de Witt have put them in there and not elsewhere? If musicians, where are their instruments? If actors, like the three figures on the stage, what sort of play was that which required as many as eight eavesdroppers or commentators?

Two views have been taken of this drawing. A few have said that this is the only contemporary evidence of the kind that we have, we must make the best of it, and we must not depart from it without very good reasons. Others have held that it is a clumsy copy of a clumsy drawing, that the original was based on a single visit and may have been drawn from memory, and that even if it be true of the Swan in 1596 it cannot be true of the Globe of 1599. Those who abide by the drawing and those who do not are agreed that a third entrance or exit (not necessarily a door) is essential in addition to the two shown in the drawing. The point about which controversy rages most furiously is whether there was or was not at the Swan of 1596 and at the Globe of 1599 an alcove or inner stage beneath the balcony and forming a permanent part of the structure of the scenic wall. We are shown such a curtained space beneath a balcony in the engraved title-pages of two later plays. One of them—William Alabaster's *Roxana* (1632)—is academic (Trinity College, Cambridge); and the other—Nathaniel Richards's *The Tragedy of Messalina* (1640)—was acted at Salisbury Court, a private theatre opened in 1629.[1] Neither illustration affords good evidence for the Swan or the Globe, though both show the low rails which ran round the stage in theatres both public and private.

---

[1] In the *Messalina* view the curtained space appears to be a projection, not an alcove.

Among those who have been most discontented with the de Witt drawing is Dr. J. Q. Adams. His book on *The Globe Playhouse. Its Design and Equipment* (1942) shows a practical knowledge of building construction rare indeed among scholars. With much learning and ingenuity he explores every nook and cranny of the Globe from cellarage to turret and from public entrance to stage door. We are left with a beautifully tidy and reasonable view of the first Globe and of the theatre which replaced it after the fire of 1613. He demands an inner stage beneath the balcony. When not in use it was screened by curtains behind which variable realistic scenery might be set for a later scene. The necessary third entrance was through the curtains or through the back wall of the alcove. The tendency of this inner stage, he argues, was to expand with the increasing popularity of interior scenes, until it became coextensive with the whole of the scenic wall at ground level. The two side doors were then placed in flanking bays of the wall, facing each other obliquely across the stage, so that opposing armies entering at these doors no longer needed to wheel to right or to left before engaging each other. Above these side doors were windows or boxes. Let it be admitted at once that these arrangements agree much better than the Swan drawing with modern conceptions of what an Elizabethan theatre ought to have been like.

Two years before Dr. Adams's book, but too late for him to take notice of it, appeared a work from the effects of which we are still reeling. Though the theme of Professor G. F. Reynolds's book was *The Staging of Elizabethan Plays at the Red Bull Theatre 1605–1625*, it prompted the remark: 'The Globe has gone up in smoke once more.' Starting from the premiss that the Swan drawing may not lightly be set aside, that at that theatre at any rate there was no permanent inner stage and no doors obliquely facing each other, he went on to accuse earlier writers—including himself—of failing to allow for the strange mixture of realism and imagination in Elizabethan stage methods. While the audience of those days liked to see represented what could be represented, while if blood was shed they wanted to see the colour of it, they were also ready to accept imaginative descriptions in a manner which may seem naïve to one bred solely on modern naturalistic conventions. All lighting in their open-air theatres and daylight performances was imaginative, except for the token use of tapers, candles or torches. As the late John Palmer neatly if unfairly put it,[1] where a modern stage-manager calls for two reds, back stage, on the O.P. side, Shakespeare gave his audience:

> But look, the morn, with russet mantle clad,
> Walks o'er the dew of yon high eastward hill.

There was no visible dawn, no visible hill. Reynolds, refusing to draw information from allusions in the dialogue to settings and properties which may have been purely imaginative, and arguing that allusions in stage directions are sometimes as imaginative as in the dialogue itself, examines with a careful scepticism and a strict discrimination the repertory of the Red Bull Theatre and comes to the conclusion that the plays could have been presented on a stage structurally like that of the Swan with the addition of a third entrance. He is too cautious to say that there *was* no permanent inner stage at the Red Bull. There may have been. But he concludes that all the scenes supposed to have been played there could have been played in temporary structures placed in front of the scenic wall and easily brought in and removed.

That properties and sometimes large properties were used is not in dispute. In the inventory of the properties of the Admiral's men in 1599 we find a rock, a cage, a tomb, a hell-mouth, a bedstead, two steeples and a chime of bells, a wooden canopy, an altar, two mossbanks; and elsewhere in the Henslowe papers at Dulwich a tent placed upon the stage and revealing Henry VI asleep in it. In Shakespeare's *Richard III* soldiers set up upon the stage, while the play is in action, the tents of first Richard and then Richmond, and they are tents into which the audience can look and see the sleeping warriors. And at the Red Bull Reynolds finds evidence of the use of formal seats (like that in the Swan drawing), tents, shops, a tomb, a bank, an altar, a scaffold, barriers, and lists.

We have to consider not merely the use of properties which could be removed when the action of a play has ceased to need them, but also the presence of structures which remained upon the stage from

---

[1] *The Future of the Theatre* (1913), p. 64.

beginning to end of a play. The practice of simultaneous or multiple staging survived from the middle ages into the sixteenth century in several countries in western Europe. In England, a stage map for the early-fifteenth-century morality play *The Castle of Perseverance* shows a central castle surrounded by five scaffolds, each structure becoming non-existent to the audience as its attention shifted to another in accordance with the action of the play. In the unusually detailed records of the Revels Office for performances at court in the fifteen-sixties, seventies, and eighties these structures are called 'apte howses of paynted Canvas'.[1] On this principle, as W. J. Lawrence showed in 1912,[2] were staged some of the comedies of John Lyly, his *Alexander and Campaspe* requiring three houses or 'mansions': Alexander's palace, Apelles' shop, and the tub of Diogenes. Sir Edmund Chambers allowed that two late-sixteenth-century plays originally written for the public theatres were probably produced in this way—*The Comedy of Errors* and Peele's *Old Wives Tale*. But Chambers, while agreeing that simultaneous staging continued to be used at court and at the private theatres when the action of a play demanded it, denied that it was used in the public theatres in the seventeenth century. This view Reynolds challenged. Simultaneous staging *was* sometimes used at the Red Bull, and the indications are, he maintained, that most of his conclusions are as true of the plays of Shakespeare at the Globe as of Thomas Heywood's at the Red Bull.

I seem to detect Reynolds's influence in Dr. Leslie Hotson's lively essay 'Shakespeare's Arena'[3] and in Mr. C. Walter Hodges's *The Globe Restored*, both published in 1953. Reynolds had argued that in view of the Swan drawing we are not entitled to assume the existence of a permanent rear stage at all public theatres and had suggested that when a play demanded it a curtained framework which could be easily put up and removed might have been placed in front of the scenic wall. This suggestion Mr. Hodges welcomes.

---
[1] *Documents relating to the Office of the Revels*, ed. A. Feuillerat (W. Bang's *Materialien*, 1908), xxi. 116 (1563–5), 129 (1571), 145 (1571–2), 391 (1587–9), etc.
[2] *The Elizabethan Playhouse*, i. 237–43. G. Kernodle, *From Art to Theatre* (1944), gives the European background.
[3] *The Sewanee Review*, July 1953: reprinted in *The Atlantic Monthly*, vol. 193, February 1954. [The reader should remember that F.P.W. when he gave this lecture had not seen Dr. Hotson's *The First Night of 'Twelfth Night'*, 1954. H.G.]

It has the obvious attraction of bringing nearer to the audience the interior scenes usually placed on the inner stage: Desdemona's bedchamber, Romeo in the Capulet tomb, the bedroom of Hamlet's mother. Dr. Adams assures us that there is no cause for alarm, that the distance from the back wall of the alcove and 'the spectator at farthest remove in the top gallery was not more than 85 feet', that the inner stage was well lit by the daylight which flooded the open yard. The fact remains that the distance between the scenic wall and the front of the platform was $27\frac{1}{2}$ feet at the Fortune and much the same at the Globe. Granville-Barker, a believer in a permanent rear stage, was uneasy about this empty space and admitted that the scene of Iachimo in Imogen's bedchamber, if played at the Globe and the Blackfriars wholly on a rear stage, would be doubly effective at the Blackfriars, where the stage was not more than 10 or 12 feet in depth.[1]

Hotson is dogmatic where Reynolds is sceptical. He seems to believe what Reynolds, with the authority of Granville-Barker behind him,[2] counsels us not to believe: that the Elizabethan theatre was consistent in its usages. He is sure that there was no permanent inner stage at a public theatre, sure that the only system of staging was that of multiple scenes, of 'transpicuous' curtained structures dispersed about the stage. His argument depends on his view that simultaneous settings were always used at court and that 'it stands to reason that the means employed... were sufficiently similar to permit the same actors to produce the same play both at the Globe and on a temporary stage in an indoor hall without radical change of method.'

Before the construction of Jones's Cockpit-in-Court in 1630 there was no permanent theatre at Whitehall, and at those festive seasons of the year when plays were to be acted special stages had to be built. Many records of expenditure have survived, and they are particularly detailed in the Revels documents of the fifteen-sixties, seventies, and eighties. So detailed were they in that period that once, in 1574-5, the Clerk of the Revels lost patience, and ended a long itemization of the money owing to a deceased property-maker

[1] *Prefaces to Shakespeare*, ii (1930), p. 252.
[2] *R.E.S.*, i (1925), pp. 60 ff.

with the words '... Nayles hoopes horstailes dishes for devells eyes heaven hell and the devell and all the devell I should saie but not all'.[1] Yet in spite of all this detail how exasperatingly little precise information do we have about the methods of production at court. The references in these Revels records to the 'apte howses of paynted Canvas' belong mainly to the period 1560–90. Exceptional at a later date is the mention in the accounts of the Master of the Revels for the year 1614–15 of 'Canvas for the Boothes and other necessaries for a play called Bartholmewe ffaire xli.^{s} vi.$^{d'}$.[2] This is poor evidence from which to generalize about a consistent use of multiple settings at court, for Jonson's play cries out for them. Indeed it is difficult to imagine how the life of the fair could properly have been staged, whether at court or at the play's first performance at the Hope on 31 October 1614, without multiple settings.

Some of the documents in the Public Record Office that throw light on staging at court in late Elizabethan and early Stuart times have yet to be printed; in particular, the evidence supplied by the declared accounts of the paymasters of the Queen's (King's) Works have escaped the attention of historians of the theatre. From this source Hotson quotes evidence for the years 1601–2 and 1603–4 of a stage being built in the middle of the Great Hall at Whitehall, a hall about 40 feet wide and 70 feet long.[3] The purpose in 1603–4 and probably in 1601–2 was to bring the players nearer to the 'State' or Chair of State. On the strength of this evidence Hotson challenges the view that the State was placed at the upper end of a hall and the stage at the lower end before the 'screens', asserts that stages at court were always located in the centre, and maintains that actors were always surrounded on all sides by spectators. Of the obvious convenience for ingress and egress of placing the stage near the doors in the 'screens' he says nothing; and apparently he makes no allowance for differences in size and shape in the many chambers or

[1] Feuillerat, ed. cit., xxi. 241.
[2] Public Record Office, E 351/2805 *sub anno* 1614–15: cited in Chambers, *The Elizabethan Stage* (1923), iv. 183. Here and elsewhere I have expanded contractions.
[3] In *Jonson*, x (1950), Dr. Percy Simpson quotes from these accounts evidence relating to the performance of Jonson's masques: see pp. 445, 457, 494, 519, 635–7, etc. The two references to a stage being built in the middle of the Great Hall at Whitehall were first printed in the London County Council *Survey of London*, xiii (1930), 'The Parish of St. Margaret, Westminster', pp. 25 and 50.

halls in which plays were acted at court. Here again he is presuming a consistency of usage for which I see no justification. Apart from the two documents which he quotes I find no other information about stages in the middle of a hall in the declared accounts of some 50 years and I have a suspicion that in these two years the situation of the stage may have been mentioned because it was exceptional.

We may pause for a while to examine some of these records, most of them, so far as I know, unpublished. Often they are too brief to be of much use, as is the record of expenditure at Hampton Court in 1603–4—'making of the stage and setting vp degrees and particions for the playe in the hall, . . . making of the stage newe in the hall against Candlemas day'—and at St. James's in 1621–2—'makinge ready the Councell chamber with degrees and boordinge them for playes'.[1] They tell us much more about masques than about plays, as is only natural, for the expenditure upon masques was many times greater. In the accounts for 1621–2 under Whitehall we find:

> framinge and settinge vpp eleven bayes of degrees on bothe sides of the banquettinge house every bay conteining xvi^{en} foote longe beinge twoe panes in every of them; fitting the hall and greate Chamber for playes; . . . makinge ready the banquetting house for the maske; . . . .
>
> To Ralphe Brice Carpenter for frameinge and setting vpp xi^{en} baies of degrees on both sides of the banquettinge house every bay conteyninge xvi^{en} foote longe, beinge twoe panes in every of them; the degrees belowe beinge seven rowes in heighte; and two boordes nayled vpon every brackett the degrees in the midle gallery beinge fower rowes in heigthe and twoe boordes nailed vpon brackettes also with a raile belowe and another raile in the midle gallery being crosse laticed vnder the same; working framinge and settinge vpp of vpright postes wroughte with eighte cantes to beare the same woorke; the kinge findinge all maner of materialls and he woorkmanshipp onely at xxx^s the baye the some of xvi^{li}. x^s.[2]

The masque was Jonson's *Masque of Augurs*, the first masque to be performed in Inigo Jones's Banqueting House (6 January 1622). As the seating arrangements were clearly for the masque rather than the plays, we may not use this document in evidence against

---

[1] Public Record Office, E 351/3239 (1603–4) and E 351/3255 (1621–2).
[2] E 351/3255.

192   *The Elizabethan Theatre*

Hotson's views. Certainly, at the sumptuous masques performed at James's court and Charles's, there was no room and no view for spectators behind the stage.

Nor were there seats for spectators behind the actors at Inigo Jones's Cockpit-in-Court of 1630. The documents which I have been citing tell us much about the construction and ornamentation of this theatre and something about the lighting and the machinery.[1] They establish the authenticity of the well-known plan of the Cockpit in many particulars.[2] There is mention of the columns, ten great with Corinthian capitals and ten smaller with Composite capitals, on each of the two storeys of the classic semicircular façade, of the five doors of the lower storey and the 'one open dore and iiij^{er} neeches' of the upper storey, of the statues, and of the freeze painted by John de Critz and others. There is provision for 'degrees' in the galleries. And there is payment to de Critz and other painters for 'directinge the Carvers and Carpenters to followe the Designes and Draughtes given by the Surveyor', i.e. by Jones. So much do we now know about this theatre that a modern builder could construct to scale a building which was substantially a replica. It is the only English theatre before 1642 of which this can be said.[3]

Two more documents may be cited, one relating to a Cambridge play acted at Royston in March 1616 (possibly *Susenbrotus*)[4] and the other to Barten Holyday's *Technogamia* acted (unsuccessfully) before King James at Woodstock in August 1621:

fytting and setting vp a stage with particions on the sides, for schollers of Cambridge to acte a Comedy in the Chamber of presence, and taking the same downe agayne[5]

---

[1] Especially E 351/3263 (1629–30), E 351/3264 (1630–1) and E 351/3265 (1631–2). Some of these documents are published in the excellent survey of the parish of St. Margaret's Westminster in the London County Council's *Survey of London*, xiv (1931). [These and other documents of dramatic interest in these accounts have now been published in the *Malone Society Collections*, vi (1962). H.G.]

[2] Often reproduced. See, for example, the reduced facsimile in E. K. Chambers's *The Elizabethan Stage*, iv, frontispiece.

[3] Incidentally, the accounts go far to confirm G. E. Bentley's conjecture that the new theatre opened on 5 November 1630 (not in 1632) with a performance by the King's company of 'An Induction for the House': *The Jacobean and Caroline Stage* (1941), i. 28.

[4] Cf. G. C. Moore Smith, *College Plays Performed in the University of Cambridge* (1923), p. 101; E. K. Chambers, *The Elizabethan Stage* (1923), iv. 130, 378.

[5] E 351/3250 (1615–16).

The Elizabethan Theatre

fitting and putting vp twoe particions in the Hall all the length of it on either side one, being cxviii foote long a peece and xii foote high to keepe the people from pressing into the middle Isle of the Hall the Schollers of Oxford being to acte a Playe before the King fitting and making of Seates there making of Stage with Boords and Ioysts xxiiii foote long and xvi foote wide.[1]

I do not pretend that these documents confute Dr. Hotson's contentions. I quote them in order to plead for a suspension of judgement until the records of performances at court have been more thoroughly examined. Even then there may be no room for dogmatism.

But I am dwelling too long on matters of disagreement. All are agreed that at the public theatres a stage that thrust itself out into the auditory and was surrounded or almost surrounded by its audience, was a stage for emotional acting, a stage which established great intimacy between actor and audience. The worst sort of theatre in which to act Shakespeare is one in which the audience is cut off from the stage by a proscenium arch. Shakespeare survives that handicap, as he survives worse handicaps, but it *is* a handicap. When the semi-oval platform of the sixteen-nineties had shrunk by 1740 by another four feet, Colley Cibber looked back regretfully to the days of his youth when the actors were in possession of that forwarder space to advance upon. 'The Voice', he says, and what he says of *his* theatre is *a fortiori* true of the Globe,

> The Voice was then more in the Centre of the House, so that the most distant Ear had scarce the least Doubt, or Difficulty in hearing what fell from the weakest Utterance: All Objects were thus drawn nearer to the Sense; . . . A Voice scarce rais'd above the Tone of a Whisper, either in Tenderness, Resignation, innocent Distress, or Jealousy, suppress'd, often have [*sic*] as much concern with the Heart, as the most clamorous Passions; and when on any of these Occasions, such affecting Speeches are plainly heard, or lost, how wide is the Difference, from the great or little Satisfaction received from them.[2]

Perhaps we are better instructed nowadays than we were fifty years ago, and do not need to turn for evidence to the eighteenth

---

[1] E 351/3254 (1620–1).   [2] *Apology for his Life* (1740), p. 241.

century. If the theatre at Stratford were burnt down to-morrow—this is no incitement to arson—it would not be rebuilt in its present form. It is ironical that the theatre at Stratford, Ontario, is a better place for the acting of Shakespeare than that at Stratford, Warwickshire. For Mr. Guthrie's production of *All's Well* in August 1953 at Stratford, Ontario, with Mr. Alec Guinness as the King and Miss Irene Worth as Helena, no attempt was made to reconstruct a hypothetical Globe. A hillside sloping down to the Avon supplied an auditorium, the audience sat in semicircular tiers rising up the hillside, in the centre of the semicircle's diameter was a projecting pavilion of columns supporting a roof which supplied a second level, and a few steps from the pavilion led down to a platform. The audience of some 1500 persons were on three sides of the actors, could hear and see perfectly, and were absorbed with ease into the play. True, we were better off than the Globe spectators in several respects. We were all seated, and we were protected from the weather by a canvas roof, whereas what happened sometimes at the Globe is suggested by the mock-prophecy: 'If... about the houres of foure and fiue, it waxe cloudy, and then raine downe-right, they shall sit dryer in the Galleries, then those who are vnderstanding men in the yard.'[1] Again, we had more room. I suppose a modern audience can hardly be expected to submit to the conditions which an Elizabethan audience tolerated, especially 'the vnderstanding men', who were only so called because they stood under the stage. Mr. Guthrie maintains that playgoers can be too comfortable: put them as close together as may be without making them positively uncomfortable, and emotion can spread like a prairie fire. A happy mean was observed at Stratford, Ontario. The audience had dined well before the play—at the First Methodist Church—but while there were no plush arm-chairs into which they could sink, they were not positively uncomfortable.

3. AUDIENCE AND ACTING

Finally, a few notes on the audience and the acting. We hear of pamphlets and fruits in season being sold in the theatre, and of citizens and their 'squirrels' cracking nuts in the twopenny galleries. I know of no evidence for a theatre bar at the Globe, but bottle-ale

[1] 'Jack Daw', *Vox Graculi* (1623), sig. I2.

The Elizabethan Theatre

was sold: when unstopped, it gave out a hiss, a sound unpleasing to an actor's ear. The audience, if it were displeased, might become unruly. Not all spectators were as reasonable as Father Augustine Baker, O.S.B. As a young student at the inns of court *c.* 1596–9 he found recreation at the theatre; but he never went there, we are told, 'without a pocket book of the law, which he did read when the play or any sort of it pleased him not'.[1] Just before the turn of the century gallants began to sit upon the stage in theatres both public and private, and dramatists often complain of those who during the action of the play departed noisily and with a screwed and discontented face, so drawing attention to themselves and to their clothes.

> The Globe to morrow acts a pleasant play,
> In hearing it consume the irksome day.
> Goe take a pipe of Tobacco, the crowded stage
> Must needs be graced with you and your page.
> Sweare for a place with each controlling foole,
> And send your hackney seruant for a stoole.[2]

The small stage of a private theatre must indeed have been crowded. In the Prologue to *The Devil is an Ass* Jonson begs the 'Grandees' not to force the players to act 'in compasse of a cheese-trencher'.

Yet this sort of *genre* painting, based as it must necessarily be on the gibes of satirists, can be overdone. Shakespeare's plays 'stood out all appeals' at the Globe and the Blackfriars, and if he had any failures we do not hear of them. If the Globe audience hissed *Every Man out of His Humour* off the stage the blame was not theirs: Jonson should have sent it to the children at the Blackfriars. As a corrective to the bias of the satirists let us note the impression made on the chaplain to the Venetian ambassador when he visited the theatre in 1617–18. He knew no English, but he admired the costly dresses of the actors, the instrumental music and the dancing and the singing, the well-dressed audience listening so silently and so soberly. True, a pretty lady sat herself beside him, displayed her jewels, and asked for his address in French and in English, but this

---

[1] *Memorials of Father Augustine Baker*, Catholic Record Society (1933), p. 66.
[2] H. Hutton, *Folly's Anatomy* (1619), sig. B2ᵛ.

appears to have been a joke played upon the chaplain by the ambassador's secretary.¹

Silent and sober as the audience may have been, the players provided plenty of noise. It was one of Jonson's quarrels with the popular stage that they were too fond of 'the roll'd bullet and the tempestuous drum'. When elsewhere he objected to plays that 'were nothing but fights at sea, drum, trumpet and target', he had especially in mind the Red Bull plays of the actor-playwright Thomas Heywood, which overstrained in the crudest fashion the limited capacity of that theatre for scenic effects. There is no shirking the fact that in sixteenth- and seventeenth-century London playhouses were undesirable neighbours. In Clerkenwell or Shoreditch or on the Bankside all was well: those neighbourhoods could hardly be let down further. But, as we have seen, it was otherwise in the precinct of the Blackfriars where many noblemen and gentlemen of quality resided, and only with difficulty did the Burbages establish and maintain themselves there. An attempt to open another theatre in that neighbourhood in 1615 was thwarted by the Privy Council even though the speculators had been clever enough to secure a royal patent. An unpublished document presents the objections of the residents. Plays are evil in themselves, theatres attract tippling houses and idle and dissolute people, the streets would become so choked with traffic that gentlemen would be forced to abandon their coaches and walk to their houses. Above all, divine service at a neighbouring church would be grievously interrupted by 'the divers and variable noyses' which players 'commonlie vse'.²

Among these 'divers and variable noyses' was the voice of the turbulent actor. We hear much of the 'tear-mouths' and 'terrible tear-throats' of the stage, of the actors who in Hamlet's famous phrase tore a passion to tatters. 'Haue you neuer seen', writes Middleton in a private theatre play, 'a stalking-stamping Player, that will raise a tempest with his toung, and thunder with his

¹ *Calendar of State Papers Venetian*, xv (1617–19), p. 67. See also *The Quarterly Review*, cii. 398–438. The theatre was probably a private one, perhaps the Blackfriars. I do not know on what evidence Furnivall in his edition of Harrison's *Description of England* (Pt. ii, 1878, p. 55*) assigns the visit to the Fortune.

² Guildhall Record Office, *Remembrancia* for 1614–15, no. 45.

heeles?'[1] But this style could not have been encouraged at the Globe. Hamlet's advice to the players appears both in the good quarto and in the Folio, so presumably was part of the acting version. It would indeed be strange if Shakespeare was forcing Burbage to utter precepts at variance with his practice.[2] Therefore at the Globe a speech was not mouthed as if the town-crier spoke the lines, a player did not strut or bellow or saw the air too much with his hand: in the very whirlwind of his passion he was encouraged to acquire and beget a temperance—but not a tameness—that might give it smoothness.

In the character of 'An excellent Actor' probably written by John Webster with Richard Burbage as model, we are told that 'Whatsoever is commendable in the grave Orator, is most exquisitely perfect in him; for by a full and significant action of body, he charmes our attention.'[3] I believe with Dr. Bertram Joseph[4] that we have something to learn about Elizabethan acting at its best from the precepts on Pronunciation—i.e. the use of voice and gesture—in the books of rhetoric intended for the use of orators. The differences are, of course, important. For one thing, the orator spoke in his own person and unlike the actor had never to sustain a part, and often a part that departed widely from approved standards of speech and gesture. For another, he did not move about: indeed he was expressly told that he might 'stirre a step or two' only when the place was large and the auditors very many, and then seldom.[5] But in much that relates to voice and gesture, what was commendable in the grave orator was commendable in the great actor. It is true that when the books on rhetoric mention actors they do so only to attack them; but what they are really attacking is bad acting, and their attacks agree with the precepts of Hamlet. Oratory and rhetoric had in that age great practical value—for lawyers, preachers, and those who wished to rise in the service of the state and the great—and much time was devoted to it at school and university. It does not

[1] *The Puritan* (1607), III. v. 84. See also *Troilus and Cressida*, I. iii. 153–6.
[2] Cf. *Great Expectations*, chapter xxxi: 'When he recommended the player not to saw the air thus, the sulky man said, "And don't *you* do it, neither; you're a deal worse than *him*."'
[3] J. Webster, *Complete Works*, ed. F. L. Lucas (1927), iv. 42.
[4] *Elizabethan Acting* (1951).
[5] Cf. A. Fraunce, *The Arcadian Rhetoric*, ed. E. Seaton (1950), p. 129.

seem fanciful to say that many men in an Elizabethan audience, especially university and inns of court men, were better informed in these matters than their counterparts today. The advocates of play-acting at the schools and universities never suggest that there are differences between the highest standards of Pronunciation for the orator and those for the actor. Bacon considered stage-playing an essential part of a young man's education: it strengthened the memory, regulated the tone and effect of the voice, taught a decent carriage of the countenance and gesture, begat no small degree of confidence, and accustomed young men to bear being looked at.[1]

'Suit the action to the word,' says Hamlet, 'the word to the action; with this special observance, that you o'erstep not the modesty of nature.' No more difficult word to interpret than the word 'nature'. Whatever Shakespeare may mean he does not mean that acting should be naturalistic. He may mean that acting should give the impression of naturalness, but even so we are still baffled in our efforts to pry into the past; for what looks natural to one age may look mannered to another. The Elizabethans often set nature against art, as Miss Madeleine Doran has recently reminded us.[2] They said that nature surpassed art if their emphasis was on the necessity of natural gifts; they said that art surpassed nature if their emphasis was on the necessity of discipline; but they did not deny that both were necessary. And they are as necessary to an actor as to a poet. Conceivably, the young Burbage was as self-conscious in voice and gesture and movement as was the young Shakespeare in exornation. But both in their different ways had been granted the good gifts of nature, and in both art became in time a second nature.

The actor's reward as he infused into his hearers Sorrow, Rage, Joy, Passion, was great and immediate. If I interpret aright some lines of Michael Drayton's, the burst of applause in a thronged theatre might break out at the end of a well delivered speech:

> With Showts and Claps at ev'ry little pawse,
> When the proud Round on ev'ry side hath rung.[3]

Drayton as a dramatic poet did not forget that the applause was also due to the poet, and as I have neglected the poet to-day, I will

[1] *De Augmentis*, vi. 4. [2] *Endeavors of Art* (1954), p. 54.
[3] *Works* ed. J. W. Hebel, ii. 334.

add a tribute from another poet to the power of dramatic poetry. In his prologue to *If It Be Not Good* spoken at the Red Bull, Dekker speaks of 'the vast roomes' of that theatre standing empty after a bad play. But a good poet, he goes on,

> Can call the Banished Auditor home, And tye
> His Eare with golden chaines to his Melody:
> Can draw with Adamantine Pen euen creatures
> Forg'de out of th'Hammer, on tiptoe to Reach vp,
> And (from Rare silence) clap their Brawny hands,
> T'Applaud, what their charmed soule scarce vnderstands.

And so to all actors and playgoers this Jacobean toast:

A FAIRE DAY, A GOOD PLAY,
AND A GALLANT AUDIENCE.[1]

[1] 'Jack Daw', *Vox Graculi* (1623), sig. G3ᵛ–G4.

7

Two Shakespearians[1]

(1) EDMUND KERCHEVER CHAMBERS (1866-1954)

EDMUND KERCHEVER CHAMBERS was born at West Ilsley, Berkshire, on 16 March 1866. He was descended on both sides of his family from incumbents in the Church of England. His mother was the daughter of the Reverend Thomas Kerchever Arnold (1800-53), Fellow of Trinity College, Cambridge, the projector of *The Churchman's Quarterly Magazine*, and editor of many classical school-books. His father was the Reverend William Chambers, Fellow of Worcester College, Oxford (1851-65), Curate of West Ilsley from 1865, and from 1881 till 1907 Rector of St. Mary Blandford.

Educated at Marlborough under G. C. Bell, he went up to Corpus Christi College, Oxford, as a classical scholar in 1885, the year after another distinguished English scholar from Marlborough and Corpus, his life-long friend Oliver Elton, took his first in Greats. Like Elton, he came under the influence of a great teacher, Arthur Sidgwick, to whom Gilbert Murray has recently paid tribute. Nor was the debt merely intellectual. He writes of his walks on the ridge over North Hinksey and on the Cumnor hills, 'pursuing *lepidoptera* with Arthur Sidgwick of beloved memory'. He was placed in the First Class in both Honour Moderations and Greats, and in 1891 was awarded the Chancellor's English Essay Prize for an essay on 'The History and Motive of the Principal Literary Forgeries'. In this year *The Oxford Magazine* was complaining that the subjects set for this prize were too large for any man to do more than master superficially what had been written on them. Certainly, Chambers's essay (published by B. H. Blackwell) cannot be condemned for lack

---

[1] [Reprinted from *The Proceedings of the British Academy*, vol. xlii (1956), and vol. xlv (1959).]

of matter. With characteristic thoroughness he pursued his subject from the Orphic forgeries to the pseudo-Chaucer, from *Phalaris* to George Steevens and J. P. Collier. If he read this essay in later life he must have winced at the statement that *Pericles* was included in the First Folio of Shakespeare.

He did not go down after taking Greats in 1889, but remained in residence till 1892. Traces of his activities are found in *The Oxford Magazine* and in *The Pelican*—the earliest of the Oxford college magazines with a continuous history to this day. It was founded in 1891 through the enterprise of Arthur Sidgwick and owed much in its earliest years to three young co-editors who were all to become men of distinction—P. S. Allen, W. M. (now Lord) Hailey, and Chambers. For *The Pelican* he wrote verses over a number of years— some of which he collected in the privately printed *Carmina Argentea* (1918)—and also essays, skits, and reviews. One of these skits he was willing to reprint in *Shakespearean Gleanings* (1944): it betrays an intimate knowledge of the text of Shakespeare. We find him President of the Pelican Essay Club, joining in discussions on 'Some Problems in Elementary Education' and on Robert Proctor's paper on the successors of Caxton, himself reading a paper on 'The Arthur Saga'. Not so characteristic is his one recorded speech at the Union when he moved 'That the popularity of Mr. Rudyard Kipling is a sign of the incompetence of public taste.' He did some extension lecturing, and, recommended no doubt by Sidgwick, champion of women's education and other liberal causes, for four terms (1891–2) he lectured mainly on Elizabethan literature for the Association for the Education of Women in Oxford. To 1892 belongs his first work, an edition of *Richard II* in the Falcon Series. It was reviewed in *The Pelican* together with Elton's *King John*, the reviewer observing that the purchaser of Chambers got more than twice as much information for his money as the purchaser of Elton.

He had been encouraged by Sidgwick, Thomas Case, W. L. Courtney, one of his examiners in Greats, and Nettleship—'I think him a very good classical scholar'—to try for a fellowship, but he was to be disappointed. Perhaps it was as well, for his interests, like Elton's, had already turned from classical studies to English, and there was no English School at Oxford before 1894 and no university post there for the teaching of modern English literature before 1900 when Ernest de Selincourt became university lecturer. In 1892 there fell vacant a junior examinership in the Education Department, one of the few departments in which appointments were made direct and not by examination, and his application was successful. While he would undoubtedly have preferred a life of scholarship, he had already shown an interest in problems of education. In 1890 he had applied unsuccessfully for the Secretaryship of the National Home Reading Union, and a testimonial from Michael Sadler, then secretary to the Oxford Delegates for University Extension, testified to the great interest Chambers took 'in the attempts to popularise higher education for busy adults'. This was the same man who thirty years later was to earn the gratitude of Albert Mansbridge and the Workers' Educational Association. When he revisited his old rooms in Corpus in the Easter Vacation of 1893 his mood was not despondent. He remembered

hours spent in converse with dear friends, in the rifling of countless books. Now the place seemed given over to the dead, and I was tingling with life. I felt myself a stranger here, another personality from the boy that was then. A few months ago I had crept away from Oxford, a weary scholar, chagrined by defeat; now I came back renewed, strong in young hopes, refilled with the lust of living. . . . Ghosts of buried ideals and old ambitions, aspirations that I never realized and shall never want to realize, here where they were born and died, they stared at me reproachfully, relentlessly.[1]

The mood of exultation was not perhaps unconnected with the announcement of his marriage on 5 September 1893 to Miss Nora Bowman, younger daughter of J. D. Bowman of Newton House, Teddington, and late of the Exchequer and Audit Office, a marriage which brought him great happiness. To her 'unfailing sympathy, encouragement and patience' he owed much, and to her he dedicated all three of his major works.

When Chambers became a civil servant the best known of those who wrote 'on the by' (in a phrase of Ben Jonson's) were A. B. Walkley of the Post Office, also a Corpus man, and Austin Dobson

[1] Printed as 'Ghosts' in *The Pelican*, vol. ii (June 1893), and reprinted as 'Oxford Revisited' in *A Sheaf of Studies* (1942).

and Edmund Gosse of the Board of Trade, the two last made immortal by Max Beerbohm in the cartoon which shows them taken unawares by their President, Joseph Chamberlain, while composing a *ballade* in office hours. An article on the Home Civil Service in *The Pelican* of June 1903, which may or may not be by Chambers, pointed out that Gosse and Walkley occupied positions in their departments which were 'respectable without being exacting', and adds: 'but it may be doubted if they could do really onerous public work without a sacrifice of their literary reputations'. In early days, before he was engaged on 'really onerous public work', and when he could spend the greater part of each day at the British Museum, Chambers did much higher journalism and editing of texts. He contributed articles and reviews to such periodicals as *The Academy* and *The Athenaeum*, for a few months he was dramatic critic to *The Outlook* (1904–5) and *The Academy* (1905), and he edited many editions of the English classics, especially Shakespeare, for use in schools. In 1904 he undertook an edition of all Shakespeare's plays for the Red Letter Shakespeare (1904–8), the introductions to which he collected in *Shakespeare: A Survey* (1925). Mr. Kenneth Sisam once asked him how, with all the duties of a civil servant, he found time to do so many introductions: 'If one had the subject-matter in hand,' he answered, 'a long lunch-hour would see most of an introduction written.' In 1896 he published editions in the Muses' Library of the poems of Donne and Vaughan, but these were tasks which demanded more leisure than he could give them.

Of later date—and in mentioning these *opuscula* chronology may be disregarded—is the anthology of *Early English Lyrics* (1907) chosen by him and his friend Frank Sidgwick (son of Arthur Sidgwick), and published by another friend, A. H. Bullen. Many readers are grateful to this book for their introduction to the beauties of medieval English lyric. His essay 'Some Aspects of Mediaeval Lyric' is both learned and illuminating; while not neglecting detail it takes a wide sweep, and it admirably fulfils the function of helping the reader to a better reading of the poems. If in so many of his books he leant to erudition and historical scholarship, it was not because he lacked the critical sensibility to do otherwise. Another work which retains its value is his edition of Aurelian

Townshend's poems and masques (1912). Nor should the part he played in the foundation of the Malone Society (1906) go unrecorded. He was its first president, and he remained president till 1939. To the early volumes of its *Collections* he contributed valuable papers on dramatic records.

That 'Great things always begin small, never with a flourish of trumpets' was the rooted belief of his revered chief, R. L. Morant. Most men in office, if they sought any literary outlet for their energies at all, would be content, and more than content, with such miscellaneous labours as Chambers undertook before he resigned from the Board of Education in 1926. But almost, if not quite, from the time he left Oxford he was working at 'a little book about Shakespeare and the conditions, literary and dramatic, under which he wrote'. This little book grew into the two volumes on *The Mediaeval Stage* (1903), the four volumes on *The Elizabethan Stage* (1932), and—the coping-stone only placed in position in 1930—the two volumes on Shakespeare.

As Chambers is a man of two careers, a consideration of these three great works, by which he will be chiefly remembered, must be preceded by an account of his work at the Board of Education. This has been generously and fortunately supplied by Professor Dover Wilson:

Anonymity being the constitutional and salutary principle of the British civil service, it is generally very difficult to discover after an eminent official's death exactly what the nation owes to him, or even much about his personality. No one, of course, denies the importance of Robert Morant or challenges his claim to have been the chief architect of our system of state education; yet the true nature of the man remains an enigma which different persons interpret differently. And the writer of the following account of the departmental labours of Chambers, who was for sixteen years Morant's colleague, and helped to determine the decisions of the Board of Education for fifteen years after Morant left it, found when he came to the point that he had little to go upon save memories, many years old, memories of intermittent personal contacts, and of conversations with others now dead, whose work brought them into closer touch with him than he had enjoyed. That it is not still more unsatisfactory is due to three or four other officials past and present who supplied the table of dates below, and after reading the document in draft offered their comments and criticisms.

Chambers entered the department in 1892; Morant in 1895. Their duties, however, were at first very different: Morant, as assistant to Sadler, later Sir Michael, in the Office of Special Enquiries and Reports, being mainly concerned with foreign education and educationalists; Chambers as a 'junior examiner' dealing with the day-to-day correspondence relating for the most part to the board schools and voluntary schools which supplied the elementary education of England at that date. It is not therefore likely that they saw much of each other until the Acts of 1899 and 1902 transformed the whole system. By the first the Education Department was given greatly enlarged powers and became a Board, and by the second the control of elementary education was transferred from the School Boards to the county authorities, which were charged at the same time with the provision of secondary schools, technical schools, and other forms of higher education. And in 1903 Morant was appointed Permanent Secretary to this newly constituted Board, the chief function of which was the supervision of these newly constituted local education authorities, while it was during his brief tenure of office (1903–11) that the English system of state education, with its four main branches of elementary, secondary, technical, and universities and teacher-training, took the shape it now bears. The speedy and successful erection of this vast administrative structure could only have been carried through by a man of immense force of character, such as Morant possessed. But the task also demanded powers of imagination, of improvisation, and of strategic foresight comparable with those displayed by military genius. That Morant was in great measure gifted with these too cannot be doubted. But when he took command in 1903 he found in Chambers an able lieutenant who made himself responsible, I have always understood, for the creation of the requisite administrative machinery of the central office. The following table setting forth the bare facts of Chambers's official career lends support to this belief, since it shows him promoted shortly after Morant's appointment and then moving round from branch to branch and advancing steadily in rank as he did so, while it is legitimate to attach special significance in this connexion to the ten months in 1904 when he acted as Chief Clerk, a post now known as Director of Establishments. It is symptomatic also of a keen interest in bureaucratic machinery that in 1921 a staff committee of Principal Assistant Secretaries and

Chief Inspectors was set up, probably at Chambers's instigation, to co-ordinate the work of the Board. He was in the chair as Second Secretary, and the member of the committee to whom I owe this information was specially impressed by his zeal for neat classification.

Rank	Branch	Date
Temporary Examiner	Elementary	21.11.1892
Junior Examiner	,,	1.1.1893
Senior Examiner	,,	1.1.1903
Senior Examiner	Elementary (R)[1]	18.7.1903
Senior Examiner (and acting as Chief Clerk, Whitehall)	,,	1.1.1904
Assistant Secretary	,,	1.11.1904
Assistant Secretary	Secondary	1.2.1907
Assistant Secretary	Technical	14.6.1909
Principal Asst. Sec.	,,	1.4.1910
Principal Asst. Sec.	Day Continuation	9.1.1919
Second Secretary		1.1.1921
Resigned		16.3.1926

That Morant greatly appreciated his work is evident from the following extracts from letters to Chambers, and that Chambers greatly appreciated praise from his chief is shown by the fact that he preserved these letters. Clearly the two were on intimate terms officially.

(i) 1907. 'I must write you a line to say how I *delighted* in the perusal of your Notes for S men on P.T. matters. To have been able to produce such a comprehensive and thoroughly clear document on such complex regulations shows (if I may say so) not only a most welcome but rare appreciation of how our work should be and can be organised, but also the effective way in which you have evolved and worked the P.T. Regulations themselves since their inception. . . . Your Memorandum is a *model*: and also a proof of high qualifications, of effective zeal in having worked up the P.T. Division in E, and of coming success in doing great good in S in similar directions, but under vastly greater difficulties.'[2]

---

[1] Training of Teachers, Higher Elementary Schools.
[2] 'S men', officials dealing with Secondary Schools. 'P.T. Division in E', the division of the Elementary Branch concerning Pupil Teachers.

(ii) 1909. 'No one has so unquestionably merited every improved recognition that can possibly be obtained, as *you* have.'

(iii) 1911. 'You were one of those ... who *most* earnestly and effectively "did things" from 1903 onwards for which such an absurd amount of credit has been attributed to *me*. ... How deeply I wish I had you *now*,[1] I can't say.'

(iv) 1912. 'I shall *never* forget your steadfast persistence and hard work and loyal devotion and splendid brainwork. I wish we could have had it in my new work.'

There is affection here and a realization that the affection was reciprocated. Their attitude towards their duties is, I think, well expressed in a note by Chambers prompted by the death in 1917 of Hugh Sidgwick, friend and colleague. After speaking of 'the singular imperturbability with which he could dispatch a number of different matters at the same time without ever allowing himself to be rattled', it goes on: 'This was partly due to the spirit with which he entered into the great game of administration, although one was conscious that behind this there lay the perfectly serious intention to do everything as well as it could possibly be done and to high ends.'

I did not enter the service of the Board until a year after Morant left it, and though for eleven years a member of the same branch (Technical)[2] as Chambers, I was an inspector in the country, and thus very seldom brought into personal touch with one whose work lay wholly at Whitehall and who had by that date already attained the lofty grade of Principal Assistant Secretary, that is to say the head of a branch directly responsible to the Permanent Secretary himself. Moreover he was a painfully shy man; a shyness interpreted as Oxford hauteur by ruffled deputations from the provinces, and as sardonic cynicism by some of his colleagues. With others he was no doubt more at home, and one of them must have been Frank Pullinger, my own chief, a man scarcely less brusque than himself. For the two had been exact contemporaries at Corpus, there being but three days' difference between their ages. And they now presided together over the Technical Branch, Chambers as head in the office and Pullinger as chief inspector—not the only instance of a college friendship helping to make English history.

[1] On leaving the Board Morant became Chairman of the Insurance Commission for five years before being appointed the first permanent secretary to the Ministry of Health.
[2] A label which covered not only all types of technical instruction but all forms of instruction in the evening, including that given in evening continuation schools, W.E.A. classes, and university tutorial classes.

To most of his juniors, however, Chambers presented a different manner. His appearance of contempt may be illustrated from an incident in which I was involved. Shortly after being appointed, in 1924, a professor at King's College, London, I called at the office for one or two personal leave-takings, of Chambers among others. Seeing my head poking round his door, 'What do *you* want?' he wearily asked. 'I've come to say good-bye,' I said. 'Oh, where are you off to?' —'London University.'—'London University, umph; English, I suppose?'—'No,' I replied, hoping he would be pleased, 'Education.' At this he almost leapt from his chair, all lethargy vanished. 'Education,' he snorted, 'a *disgusting* subject!' He was then Second Secretary to the Board of Education.

This outburst was probably caused by dislike for what as Assistant Secretary (Elementary, R) he had discovered went on in some training colleges and university departments of education. I suspect, however, it may also have been partly due to the distaste of an exact scholar and a hard-boiled official for the somewhat nebulous ideas about education ventilated by Michael Sadler while in the department from 1895 to 1903, at which date he had resigned owing to differences with Morant. Sadler was a great man in his way, but it was a way which neither Morant nor Chambers could have much sympathy for.

I only once saw Chambers and Sadler together. But the meeting left no doubt in my mind that Chambers had been of Morant's party at the time of the split in 1903. The occasion was a dinner at Sheffield University following a conference concerning university tutorial classes, and the time was late in 1916, during the interval between the fall of Asquith's government and the announcement by Lloyd George of the names of his new ministry. Sadler, then Vice-Chancellor of Leeds University, sat at the foot of the table, with Chambers and myself on either side of him. Fisher, the host of the evening, presided at the other end, but moved down to join us after drinking the king's health. Who was to be the new President of the Board, was a question in the minds of all present. And Sadler, eager and charming as ever, began telling us what he would do if the choice fell upon him. 'What we need', the theme ran, 'is *research* in education. We ought to set aside some administrative county or county borough as our laboratory, and carry out there all sorts of experiments in teaching and organization. For only so can we hope to arrive at positive results.' Chambers's face as this went on was an interesting study. At last he could stand it no longer. 'What would the *parents* say?' he blurted out, and the question brought the topic to an end. Fisher kept silence, smiling his Chinese smile, and a few days later we read in the newspapers that it was he whom Lloyd George had chosen, as he knew as we sat there.

I tell these stories about Chambers the more readily as I received positive testimony from those who knew him better than I did that they reflect only one side of his character, that he could be geniality itself with juniors who succeeded in getting behind his shyness, and that the sardonic mask he habitually wore concealed a genuine enthusiasm for education and more liberal notions on the subject than those held by many other officials of the Board. Yet his forbidding manner with deputations from local education authorities and other bodies was perhaps one of the reasons why in 1925 he was not offered the post of Permanent Secretary.

One cause in which he took a particular interest was that of the Day Continuation School. Section 10 of Fisher's Education Act, an Act which the Commons passed while the Germans were breaking through the Western Front early in 1918, envisaged the provision of part-time schooling for all boys and girls between the ages of 14 and 18; and the Board put Chambers in charge of a special branch or department for dealing with the Day Continuation Schools that would accordingly be set up. It was a development in which I was myself much concerned, having been instructed to draw up a special memorandum about their curriculum.[1] But we won the war; and as one of Chambers's juniors bluntly put it, 'the Day Continuation Schools died under the stroke of the Geddes Axe'.[2] Hopes for them were not, however, given up in the Board until about 1921. And but for the untimely death at the end of 1920 of Frank Pullinger, a stout defender, and probably with Chambers the originator, of Section 10, they might have come into being. As it was, timidity triumphed and the nation lost a golden opportunity. For these schools would have kept a whole generation of the adolescent population under the public eye, including the eye of the doctors, and so saved us from some at least of our modern evils, much juvenile crime at any rate. And, perhaps of even greater permanent importance, they would have compelled industry and education to face each other for the first time, to the incalculable advantage of both. Chambers appreciated these

[1] This received the approval of Chambers and was printed under the title of *Humanism in the Continuation School* as Educational Pamphlet, no. 43 (Board of Education).
[2] Charles Douie, *Beyond the Sunset*.

issues, and the shipwreck of the scheme must have been a bitter disappointment to him as it was to others.

On 1 January 1921 a Principal Assistant Secretary for Day Continuation Schools being no longer required, he became Second Secretary of the Board. During his last five years of service he gave much attention to Adult Education, though indeed it had been one of his main interests since the early days of the Board, an interest he shared with Morant himself. I feel confident, for example, though I cannot now remember who told me, that he was the official whom Albert Mansbridge, founder of the W.E.A. in 1903, interviewed nine years later when he went to enlist the Board's support on behalf of the University Tutorial Classes into which that movement had begun blossoming in 1908. The upshot of this meeting was (i) the promise of a very substantial grant per class (provisionally endorsed by a corresponding promise from the Treasury which I understand Chambers secured on the spot, while Mansbridge waited, by just walking into the next street); (ii) the issue in June 1913 of a highly ingenious series of special regulations for the conduct of these classes, regulations which, embodying the best features of the classes already in being, established them as a standard for the future; and (iii) the appointment in 1912 of two special inspectors, Alfred Zimmern and the present writer, to see that the regulations were observed. Thus, though his Day Continuation Schools branch never came into being, Chambers's hand helped to shape one of the most important educational experiments of our age. Every university in England and Wales became committed to it and a large proportion of the lecturers in the Faculty of Arts took tutorial classes, while since 1908 tens of thousands of working men and women, the intelligentsia of the working-class it may be said, have passed through them. The University Tutorial Classes did not save the country from a social revolution; one was due and after a Second World War was seen to be inevitable. But it is certain that but for them the revolution would have been far more extreme, and perhaps violent. And Albert Mansbridge, prophet of Adult Education, might have been speaking for the nation as a whole when he wrote congratulating Chambers on his knighthood in 1925: 'You have earned it well. I, and many others, hold all you have done in never failing gratitude.'

J. D. W.

Testimonials written for young pupils do not always stand the test of time, but when in the very early nineties the senior members of his college wrote that he thought with definiteness and precision (T. Case), that he had the not very common merit of 'seeing the point' (T. Fowler), and that he gave every sign of a natural gift of organization (A. Sidgwick), they hit on three gifts, which—if we add to them great power of application, and exceptional quickness of mind and pen—go far to explain both the quantity and quality of his contributions to scholarship.

The Mediaeval Stage (1903) had taken shape in his head, and some of it on paper, by 1898, when it was accepted by the Clarendon Press. He was convinced that any history of drama which does not confine itself solely to the analysis of genius must start from a study of the social and economic facts upon which the drama rested; and his work is the first to provide these facts in so far as they affect the English stage. Only in the last and shortest of the four books into which the work is divided—the Interlude—was he traversing well-trodden ground. The third book on the religious drama from its beginning in the liturgy immensely improves on earlier histories of the kind, while the first two books on minstrelsy and folk drama, impressive in their wide sweep, are the first consecutive histories that we have. The book on the folk drama is nearly twice as long as the long third book. It is out of scale, and he knew it. But where is the fun of scholarship if a man is not permitted to develop a new interest that has taken hold of him? No doubt he would have had an answer to anyone who objects that he writes about religious drama and leaves out religion. And no doubt he had an answer for his friend Elton who wrote a laudatory review praising the clear and serried style and the occasional happy efflorescences (*The Pelican*, vii, 1903), and expressed the hope that when Chambers came to the stage of Marlowe and Jonson he 'would not bind himself against appreciating the plays as literature'. He was not to be diverted from the work that he was born to do.

More than fifty years old, the work is still required reading. Karl Young in 1933 greatly added to our knowledge of the liturgical drama (*The Drama of the Medieval Church*), and in 1955 Hardin Craig gave a new synthesis of the matter covered in the third and fourth books (*English Religious Drama in the Middle Ages*), but both acknowledge their debt. Young's tribute must have pleased him: '... that master of dramatic history... I cherish my memory of his courtesy, years ago, to a youthful investigator, and I take pleasure in pointing to my use of his *Mediaeval Stage* in most of the chapters that follow.'

In the preface Chambers wrote of his 'want of leisure and the spacious life' and drew a picture—which was perhaps romantic even in 1903—of Oxford scholars at liberty from morn to eve to 'class' their documents and 'try' their sources, 'disturbed in the pleasant ways of research only by the green flicker of leaves in the Exeter garden, or by the statutory inconvenience of a terminal lecture'. During the twenty years when he was writing *The Elizabethan Stage* (1923) his administrative duties became increasingly responsible, and he had more reason than ever to deplore his want of leisure. Night after night, after a heavy day at his office, he would retire to his study immediately after dinner in order to make a little progress. His library when it came to be sold was found to be not considerable. The work that he did at this time, when visits to the British Museum were infrequent, is an impressive tribute to the resources of the London Library.

A notice long pinned up in a cupboard in his house at Lansdowne Crescent read: 'Shakespeare and the Stage. Writing began 31 July 1904.' The first intention seems to have been to treat Shakespeare in the same work with his contemporaries, and this may explain why he chose to stop at 1616 instead of the more logical date of 1642. Later he had regrets, but by that time the decision not to push on to the closing of the theatres had long been irretrievable. Fortunately a worthy sequel has been supplied by another hand.

Chambers's achievement appears the more outstanding when compared with the only two extensive chronicles of the stage before his—Collier's and Fleay's. Their work had been supplemented or corrected in detail by scores of writers—Chambers himself so encrusted with marginalia a copy of Fleay's *Chronicle History* that he was forced to buy another—but what was wanted was one work which would order and estimate all existing knowledge and theory. His work is one of consolidation, not discovery. He was well aware that valuable information lay dormant in the Public Record Office and elsewhere, but for the most part he had to be dependent on secondary authorities. Consolidation was impossible, however, without interpretation, and he was as much a master in weighing evidence as in assembling and ordering it. Although the literature to be surveyed was vast, he missed little and the materials seemed almost to sort themselves into a logical form—whether he was writing on the Court (Book I), the control of the stage (II), the dramatic companies (III), the theatres (IV), or was supplying a dictionary of the playwrights (V). Detail he was used to in his daily occupations—one of Morant's sayings was that 'no detail is insignificant'—and the reader may suspect him sometimes of pursuing detail for its own sake: yet anyone who has had occasion to make frequent use of the Court Calendar in Appendix A tracing the movements of the Court from 1558 to 1616 must wonder at the patience and accuracy with which it is compiled from far-flung sources. 'The great qualities that stand out in it', wrote Sir Walter Greg in a review, 'are the grasp of all relevant evidence, the orderly planning, the almost unfailing lucidity of exposition, and last but not least a caution which may be described as monumental.'

Though no professional historian, though (as he deplored) Oxford maintained in his day no *École des Chartes*, he made himself a master of the many records he had to interpret. This appears not merely in the three great works but in the little book *Sources for a Biography of Shakespeare* (1946) which gives the substance of the lectures he delivered at Oxford (1929–38) to students working for the Bachelorship of Letters. For the history and function of the great medieval offices of state he could depend on Tout and others, but for Elizabethan times he had often to find his own way. It was a help to him that he was himself a government official. When he praises an Elizabethan for a capable summary, or sound administrative sense, it is praise indeed. Also he knew how to make allowances for departmental jealousies and disputes, and for the disinclination of government officials to make sweeping reforms. The Second Secretary of the Board of Education was not useless to the historian of the English stage.

Soon after his retirement he went to live at Eynsham near Oxford, where he resided until he moved to Beer in Devonshire in 1939. For ten years he became a frequent visitor to Bodley, especially while at work on the last stages of his *Shakespeare* (1930). Now at last he had the leisure he had often craved. *The Elizabethan Stage* was marred to some extent by inaccuracies and inconsistencies inevitable in a work written in odd snatches of time and over many years. The *Shakespeare* is carefully composed and designed to scale. It is 'a study of facts and problems'. All the material facts and problems are considered here, the poet's life, his life as a man of the theatre, the transmission of his text in manuscript and print, the canon, the chronology; and the whole of Volume II is taken up with *pièces justificatives*. Aesthetic judgements must enter into a discussion of authorship, chronology, and so on, but they are subordinated to the main purpose. While the book is brightened by flashes of sardonic wit, the style is not allowed to effloresce. The last paragraph of the biography begins 'Death took place on April 23' and ends 'There are no existing descendants of Shakespeare'.

His caution remained 'monumental'. He had to a high degree a faculty which Macaulay denied to Niebuhr, that 'by which a demonstrated truth is distinguished from a plausible supposition', and he made short work of the many implausible suppositions. ('One cannot be expected to argue whether Lord Buckhurst was or was not Sir Toby Belch.') His conservatism is shown in his opposition to those who would parcel out the plays among several dramatists and to those who detect in the plays strata belonging to different dates and find therein evidence that Shakespeare was revising old plays whether his own or another's. This was the theme of his Shakespeare Lecture to the British Academy, 'The Disintegration of Shakespeare' (1924). Because we come to regard him as the very pink of orthodoxy and paragon of caution we are the more startled on the very rare occasions when his caution seems to desert him, as when he accounts for the transition from the late tragedies to the late comedies by supposing a religious conversion following a nervous breakdown or an attack of the plague. No book on Shakespeare can be expected to last for ever, but after a quarter of a century this one remains invaluable.

He did not abandon Elizabethan studies after 1930, but wrote several papers which he collected, with older matter, in *Shakespearean Gleanings* (1944). Also he chose with admirable taste (though he left out Gavin Douglas) the *Oxford Book of Sixteenth Century Verse* (1932);

and in *The English Folk-Play* (1933) he presented the new evidence which had come to light since he wrote on the Mummers' Play in *The Mediaeval Stage*. And the essay which gives the title to *Sir Thomas Wyatt and Other Studies* (1933) is in his best manner. But he turned also to nineteenth-century poetry. His tastes in English poetry were for medieval lyric, Elizabethan and early seventeenth-century poetry, and the romantic poetry which persisted down to his own day and of which his own poems are late examples. He called himself 'an impenitent Victorian'. To more recent developments in English poetry he was not indifferent but hostile, and like Arnold he was blind to the merits of eighteenth-century poetry.

In answer to a letter praising his Warton Lecture on Arnold (1932) he wrote: 'It is rather pleasant to be getting back to critical work after so many years of indigestible erudition.' But the critical work which he got back to shows few signs of that critical sensibility which makes memorable his essay on medieval lyric. His paper on Coleridge's Annus Mirabilis, contributed to the English Association's *Essays and Studies* in 1934, 'will be a little dry', he confessed, 'to anyone less interested than I am in the balancing of complicated evidence', and while his book on Coleridge (1938), awarded the James Tait Memorial Prize for the best biography of the year, is a valuable study of the facts of his author's life and character, the poet and the critic are wholly neglected.

His gifts are shown in a better light in *Arthur of Britain* (1927). He had already published an essay on Sir Thomas Malory and his *Morte Darthur* (English Association, 1922), praised by Professor Eugène Vinaver as 'a valuable study of its genesis and structure', and now he turned to those *Arturi regis ambages pulcherrimae* on which he had written a paper in his Oxford days. Here if anywhere was a chance to balance complicated evidence. There was little or nothing of value in the vast literature which has collected round King Arthur which he had not read, and his book is a synthesis and reassessment solidly based on the available records.

But the flames which once burnt around the memory of Arthur have long ago sunk into grey ashes. He wakes no national passions now. He has been taken up, with Roland and with Hector, and with all who died fighting against odds, into the Otherworld of the heroic imagination. His deeds are the heritage of all peoples; not least of the English folk against whom he battled. To this outcome many men have worked; the good clerk Wace, Chrétien de Troyes, the unknown author of the *Lancelot* and the *Mort Artu*, our own Thomas Malory. But most of all are we bound to praise that learned and unscrupulous old canon of St George's in Oxford, Geoffrey of Monmouth. And withal we still do not know where is Arthur's grave.

Ubi nunc fidelis ossa Fabricii manent?

This peroration is a good example of how when moved by his subject he sometimes allowed his prose to rise from a good expository level to a controlled eloquence.

Less satisfactory is his *English Literature at the Close of the Middle Ages* (1945). The editors and publisher of the *Oxford History of English Literature* were willing to diverge from the general plan of the series in order to entice him to return to subjects which he had once adorned: medieval drama and lyric, the ballad and folk-poetry, Malory. He was working on the book when war broke out, and he put it aside, to find when he returned to it that it had gone cold on him. It is concise and erudite, or it would not be his, but it is dry.

It was characteristic of him that he could not live in a place without discovering all that could be discovered of its history and its legends. A learned article on the symbolism of the pelican is an early example (*The Pelican*, December 1891). A late one is his contribution to 'that characteristic Oxford quest', the site of the 'signal-elm' in 'Thyrsis': the quest was pursued during his Eynsham days when Arnold's line 'In the two Hinkseys nothing keeps the same' was already acquiring a sinister meaning. Also belonging to his Eynsham days are his elaborate study of *Sir Henry Lee* (1936), the Ranger of Woodstock, and his one work on medieval local history, *Eynsham under the Monks*, contributed to the Oxfordshire Record Society in the same year. But his interest in places was not merely antiquarian. He was strongly imbued with their sentiment. The one poem of his which has been much anthologized begins:

> I like to think how Shakespeare pruned his rose,
> And ate his pippin in his orchard close.

Nor did his enjoyment of natural beauties depend upon their human associations. He acquired in his schooldays a considerable acquaintance with Natural History, fostered by the many holidays spent at Helmside, Grasmere, the house of his grandmother, Mrs. Kerchever Arnold. The flower-garden and the English countryside were tastes which he shared with his wife. And they were great walkers.

> Then, of the memories poor Time may save,
> I know of three that most will visit me—
> The vale where Rotha rolls her waters brown
> To that still lake that laps by Wordsworth's grave,
> Green meadows and grey walls of Oxford town,
> And Cornwall sleeping by a halcyon sea.

Gardening and walking, these were almost the only recreations of his later years. The time he might have spent in play—and, for that matter, in church-going—he gave to scholarship. During his one visit to the United States—as a member of the Bodleian Library Commission in 1930—he was taken to see a baseball match. The difficulty of writing authentic history is shown by the report of one observer that he was visibly bored and of another that in the hotel the same night he was displaying to a disguised reporter a real enthusiasm for the game and that baseball was one of the few institutions in the United States of which he expressed appreciation. The only certain evidence of athletic prowess is that in a college match against Balliol on 23 January 1888 he scored a try.

Mr. Sisam contributes these valuable reminiscences:

I knew E.K.C. only in his years of retirement at Eynsham. In person he was tall and slim, with a scholar's stoop; his face alert and inquiring; his hair, even in age, a vigorous blue-black. He dressed carefully, favouring tweeds of a tint that would have pleased William Morris, and brightly coloured ties; and his buttonhole was seldom without a choice flower.

He had the reputation of being a formidable man, and sometimes played up to it. His humour, ranging from sub-acid to caustic, was quite impersonal, but none the less shattering to those whose bubbles he pricked. In purely personal relations I found him so gentle that it was hard to credit the depth of his wrath when some active form of stupidity aroused it.

When he was working one noticed first the extraordinary pace of his mind, which was more outstanding in a company of quick thinkers. He had besides the power of regular, sustained, and orderly work, so that he finished whatever he undertook. The information he needed seemed to drop easily into his hands. When he was writing his study of Coleridge, I chanced to say it was a pity that J. L. Lowes could not find a 'lost' Coleridge Diary that might have been enlightening. 'I have it in my pocket', said Chambers, and produced it: he had guessed who was likely to have inherited it, inquired, and had the Diary almost by return of post. When he visited the Chicago University Library with the Bodleian Library Commission, he was asked to tea in the English Department with Professors Baskervill and Manly, who had prepared a surprise problem for him. A few months before they had bought what is still the only known copy of an edition of Greene and Lodge's *Looking Glass for London and England*, but had made no progress towards explaining the circumstances in which some early marginalia had been added to it. Chambers turned the leaves slowly for perhaps two minutes, stopped at the name 'Reason', and then, with a trick he had of letting his spectacles slide down his nose so that he peered out over them unexpectedly: 'I recollect that an actor named Reason was a member of a company touring the provinces early in the seventeenth century. I expect you will find this was one of their prompt-books.'

He liked to have three learned works on hand at once, in different stages of preparation and preferably on unrelated subjects. He had no difficulty in keeping them in their separate compartments, and at lunch-time (which was the end of hard work in his years of retirement) they were all laid aside completely. He had the old civil servant's habit of leaving a clear desk. I remember that Karl Young, who made an afternoon call when the *Shakespeare* was far advanced, was astonished to see no sign, in paper or proof or displaced book, that any work was going on in Chambers's study.

His services to education and to scholarship earned him many honours: C.B. (1912), Hon. D.Litt. Durham (1922), F.B.A. (1924), K.B.E. (1925), Hon. D.Litt. Oxford (1939). He was also Foreign Member of the Royal Society of Letters of Lund (1928) and Corresponding Fellow of the Mediaeval Academy of America (1933). He was disappointed not to be elected to the Professorship of Poetry at Oxford in 1938. Election is by Convocation, a very large body, and in such an election energetic canvassing can produce unexpected results. He lost a three-cornered contest by a few votes. The distinction which gave him perhaps the greatest pleasure was his election to an Honorary Fellowship at Corpus (1934). This had been one of the ambitions of his later life, as the failure to secure an ordinary Fellowship had been one of the disappointments of his youth. In accepting the honour he wrote: 'The College has had a great part of my affection for just half a century now, and the new link encourages me to believe that I have done what I could to be faithful to its traditions.'

Old age struck first his active mind. In his eightieth year a serious illness affected his memory and the coherence which was so characteristic of him. But the habit of work persisted. His last book was on Arnold (1947), a poet to whom he was devoted. He liked to remember that 'Thyrsis' appeared in *Macmillan's Magazine* a fortnight after he was born and that in the week he came up to Corpus Arnold was staying there 'with Thomas Fowler of genial memory' and taking his last walk 'in the happy combes of Hinksey'. But after his illness he could only give the dry bones of a book. An anthology of Wordsworth's poems was not completed. He died at Beer on 21 January 1954.

[Bodley's Librarian has allowed me access to Chambers's papers in the Bodleian Library. For help and advice I am indebted to Professor Nichol Smith, Mr. Kenneth Sisam, and Professor Dover Wilson.]

(II) WALTER WILSON GREG
(1875–1959)

WALTER WILSON GREG was born on 9 July 1875, the only child of William Rathbone Greg by his second wife, Julia, second of the six daughters of the Right Hon. James Wilson.

Tradition connects my family with the clan Macgregor, but it can be traced no further than the village of Ochiltree in Ayrshire, whence a John Greg, born late in the seventeenth century, migrated to Ulster. My Grandfather, Samuel Greg, came from Belfast and built his cotton mill at Style, Cheshire, some years before the French Revolution. My father was born in 1802, the same year as Tennyson and Darwin.[1]

---

[1] I quote here and elsewhere from some 'Biographical Notes' which I persuaded Greg to make early in 1948. He foresaw that they might some day serve for a memoir,

Greg's surname and his Christian names recall memories of three eminent Victorians: his grandfather James Wilson who 'first evoked order out of the chaos of Indian finance' and who founded *The Economist* (1843) and in its early days wrote nearly all of it himself; Walter Bagehot its most distinguished editor, who had married Wilson's eldest daughter; and W. R. Greg. All three men appear in the *Dictionary of National Biography*, as do his uncles Robert Hyde Greg and Samuel Greg and his half-brother Percy Greg. Bagehot is a writer who can never drop out of sight, but the books of W. R. Greg, such as *Enigmas of Life* (18th ed., 1891, with a memoir by his wife) and the *Literary and Social Judgements* (4th ed., 1877) are now read only by historians of the Victorian scene. Yet for the son's sake we may note John Morley's verdict that no article of his ever showed a trace either of slipshod writing or of make-believe and perfunctory thinking, and Oliver Elton's that he could both write and think and that his English 'is better than easy, being efficient and well-trained'.[1] Wilson died in 1860, Bagehot in 1877, and W. R. Greg in 1881 at the age of seventy-two. Walter Greg had no recollections of Bagehot and few of his father. If these economists had lived to exercise their influence over him as a young man, the current of his life might well have been changed. He grew up knowing that *The Economist* was a family paper and that he was designed some day to be its editor.

He was born at Park Lodge on Wimbledon Common, a house bought by his father in 1857 as being within easy riding distance of town. His father's death left his mother in rather straitened circumstances, the house was let, and for seven years mother and son led a nomadic existence in the more picturesque parts of Europe, returning to England only for brief periods to stay at Langport with his aunt, Walter Bagehot's widow, or elsewhere. No doubt this sort of education is unorthodox, and no doubt it has its advantages; his Greek and Latin may have suffered, but he acquired a taste for

---

as indeed they do. A limited number of copies are being printed in the Bibliography Room of the Bodleian Library for distribution among his family, a few of his friends, and the chief libraries upon which he depended.

[1] See Morley's tribute 'W. R. Greg: A Sketch' in *Macmillan's Magazine*, xlviii (1883), reprinted in *Critical Miscellanies*, iii (1886); and Elton's *Survey 1830–1880*, i. 303.

Switzerland and the mountains of south-eastern France, of northern Italy, and of Austria which he was to indulge again and again in later life. Also he acquired French from a French governess and later in this *hegira* German. Wintering at Davos in 1883–4 mother and son saw much of John Addington Symonds and his wife and daughters. Of all men he had known, he would say, Alfred Marshall and Symonds were those who struck him as having most of the 'prophetic' character. In keeping with his later work was a visit to a passion play in one of the hill villages above the Worther See near Klagenfurt:

> It was in Windisch, the local Slovene dialect, and none of us could understand a word, but it was impressive in its rude simplicity, especially the procession of actors (all village folk) and audience alike from the open barn that served as stage along the hillside to Calvary.

This was in 1886 or 1887, and in the summer of 1888—very late in life, for he was thirteen—he was sent to a preparatory school at Wixenford near Wokingham kept by E. Arnold. As we might expect, he was not happy there, and he disliked Arnold. But there he met G. M. Trevelyan whom he was to follow to Harrow and Trinity. At Harrow in 1889 he entered the 'small' house of E. W. Howson, 'an estimable man whom I tolerated, and to whom I probably owed much'. Later he moved to the house of the headmaster, J. E. C. Welldon, 'whom I detested, but for whose housemaster Searle I came to have great affection'. Some of his school reports have survived. If the form-master was being just who accused him of insufficient attention to detail, then the child was no father to the man. On the other hand a letter from Howson to Greg's mother shows a profound understanding of her son's character already formed by the time of his eighteenth birthday. It had come to the headmaster's knowledge that the boy had been in London during the Eton and Harrow match without going to Lord's, so cutting himself off unnecessarily 'from the social feeling and life of the School'; and there was adverse comment in his school report. Howson begged the mother not to show it to her son:

> In Walter's case considering his natural bent, character, and interests I candidly but in confidence do not endorse such criticism. . . .

> He is of course a boy out of the common, and not cast in the usual mould. He takes his own line and his own views and except to a few intimate friends is rather reticent and inaccessible.... It would be foolish and even wicked to try and remould a marked character like his.

With a consideration of the strong and weak points in a character of this kind this Victorian schoolmaster concludes a letter that does honour to an honourable profession.

After a year in the lower school he was able to go on the 'modern side', where his knowledge of French and German and an aptitude for geometry—'in algebra I never really mastered the binomial theorem'—sent him rocketing up through the shells and the remove to find a comfortable place under an easy-going master in the lower fifth.

> I remained there the rest of my school life, so missing the stimulating but more exacting rule of E. E. Bowen. Games I hated: I had to play football, but cricket I successfully avoided, devoting the time to volunteering and rifle-shooting. Three years I went to Bisley in the school eight, but was never a dependable shot. I also fenced, sometimes with Winston Churchill.... The only school prize I ever won was for translation into German.

Volunteering he found so attractive that after leaving school he took a commission in the 2nd Volunteer Battalion of the East Kent Regiment, rising to be captain of the Lamberhurst company. But while he enjoyed the periods of training in camp, the duties interfered too much with other pursuits and he resigned in 1901.

He went up to Trinity in October 1894, managed to his surprise to pass the Little-Go, and at once started to read for the Modern and Medieval Languages Tripos, taking the sections of modern English and German. His career at Cambridge was not more distinguished than at Harrow. The freedom of university life went to his head, his work was 'sometimes intensive, more often superficial, and always desultory', and in 1897 the man who was one day to be elected into an Honorary Fellowship at Trinity failed to take Honours and was allowed only the pass degree. 'It probably did me good.' The failure to take Honours debarred him from reading the Moral Sciences Tripos, which included Political Economy, but it was decided that he should stay up another year to study economics. In this way he came to know and to value Alfred Marshall. To prepare himself for a career in financial journalism he even spent a summer as a bank clerk at Kirkby Lonsdale and Lancaster. But it was already clear to him if not to his family that his interests lay elsewhere. Instead of joining the staff of *The Economist* he gladly embraced the alternative of becoming a trustee in the family interest, and in later years the responsibility of getting rid of one editor and appointing two others was to fall chiefly upon him. He remained a trustee till the property was sold in 1928, and at the time of his death he was still the largest individual shareholder. He never lost interest in the paper and was an occasional contributor—for the last time on 10 May 1947 with a letter on the tobacco duty.

Inglorious as his performance in the Tripos was, there were those among his teachers (Skeat, Verrall, Breul) and among his contemporaries (G. M. Trevelyan) who recognized his quality. His mother's friend Sir Mountstuart Grant Duff, then staying with Sir George Trevelyan at Wallington, Northumberland, sent her a consolatory letter on 27 August 1897:

I am delighted to find that George Trevelyan the younger who is *most* remarkable speaks *very highly* indeed of Walter and says that his mischance was a pure accident resulting from the ill-organized condition of the School. The impression produced upon contemporaries and those a little older is of course the important thing. . . . I think that Walter's stumble will be a perfect blessing. He will now make Early English and all the rest of it a hobby and amusement—not the business of life.

But perhaps Grant Duff had never heard of Greg's undergraduate friend, R. B. McKerrow, for his future by far the most formative influence on his life. They had met on the rifle-range at Harrow but did not become intimate till Greg's second year at Trinity. Then they became inseparable and did much of their work together. That this duumvirate—with the accession of A. W. Pollard to become a triumvirate—were friends, 'a happy band of brothers', will not be a matter of indifference to the future historian of Shakespearian studies, as he passes to them after narrating the enmities of Pope and Theobald, Steevens and Malone, Collier and Dyce, Furnivall and

Halliwell-Phillipps.[1] McKerrow was two and a half years older and correspondingly more mature, and no doubt Greg profited not only from his scholarship but from his stability and sense of direction. Together they founded the Cambridge University English Society, and while it was shortlived it had some distinguished members. At the preliminary meeting in McKerrow's rooms on 29 May 1896 Skeat was elected President, Greg Secretary, and McKerrow one of the two committee men. Other members were Trevelyan, Gollancz, E. Magnússon, and 'that charming and wayward genius A. W. Verrall'. Among the visitors were G. E. Moore, F. M. Cornford, and the man who inspired many young bibliographers in those halcyon days before the First World War, Charles Sayle.[2] Seldom if ever has a literary society initiated by undergraduates laid such emphasis on scholarship, and perhaps by reason of the severity of its standards or because McKerrow left Cambridge in 1897 the Society's nineteenth meeting on 16 February 1898 was its last. Both McKerrow and Greg, however, had read papers which gave a foretaste of work they were to publish later, McKerrow on 'The so-called Classical Metres in Elizabethan Verse' and Greg on 'The Pastoral Drama on the Elizabethan Stage'.

Greg's paper was published in the *Cornhill* for August 1899, but his first appearance in print was in 1896—as poet in the *Spectator* (18 September) and as mountaineer in the *Alpine Journal* (November) with an account of the ascent of 'Piz Vadret by the N.W. Arête'. It is to be remarked that Greg and E. K. Chambers both wrote verses. *Verses by W. W. G.* was published at Cambridge by Macmillan and Bowes in 1900 [1901] in a small octavo pamphlet.[3]

Mountaineering was a taste which Greg indulged as long as he was able, and many vacations were spent in Switzerland and Italy,

---

[1] Cf. p. 76 of the work mentioned below at p. 233, note 1. In the same year, 1942, G. M. Trevelyan wrote to Greg: 'I cannot help feeling that Shakespeare scholarship gained greatly by the fact that you and McKerrow were such personal friends. I often think of you and him in the room of the Great Court here together in the old days.'

[2] The minute-book preserved with careful husbandry by the secretary became, when turned back to front, the minute-book of the Malone Society.

[3] On Chambers's verses see above, pp. 201, 216–17. The only verses of McKerrow I have seen are those on Joan of Arc (a set theme) for which he was awarded the Chancellor's Medal in 1895.

at first with his mother, then alone or with McKerrow, later with his wife, also a mountaineer. He was not deterred by a serious accident in 1893 climbing alone among the Coolins in Skye when he lay out for two nights before crawling back to shelter. He climbed also at Trinity. Geoffrey Winthrop Young, a friend and contemporary, who became one of the greatest English mountaineers of this century and wrote the classic *On High Hills*, also wrote *The Roof-Climbers Guide to Trinity. Containing a Practical Description of all Routes* (1899). Greg never climbed with the Trinity Alpine Club, but in a pencilled note in his copy of the last-named book he claims to have been 'one of the first to indulge in the sport, when I did the South side of Great Court, the Kitchen, Hall, and South side of Nevile's with H. A. Rose on the evening of the 1897 Jubilee'. Hugh Arthur Rose, fellow Harrovian and fellow roof-climber, whose presence at Trinity diverted Greg from Magdalen College, Oxford, was to become Chairman of the General Board of Control for Scotland.

While yet an undergraduate Greg was already discussing with McKerrow projects for editing Elizabethan drama and the textual methods to be used, and when he should have been writing essays on monetary theory he was collecting material for a bibliography of the drama. In 1898 he joined the Bibliographical Society, a momentous year for him and for the Society, and so began a forty years' friendship and association with its secretary, A. W. Pollard; and in the next year at the age of twenty-four he submitted to the Council a skeleton finding-list of English plays written before 1643 and published before 1700. It appeared in 1900, with the titles set out in full by another hand, and was followed by a list of masques and pageants in 1902. These were the Society's first important contributions to English studies. The lists were mere 'bibliography by enumeration', and they earned for the compiler a reputation for learning beyond his years. In the end he completed the descriptive bibliography of which these were the first-fruits. But he was 'sixty years on the job'.

In 1900 the lease of Park Lodge fell in and Greg and his mother returned after an absence of eighteen years. By this time
my mother had become reconciled to the idea that I was never to be a

figure in public life like her father, her husband, and brother-in-law, or like her friends Lord Avebury, Sir Mountstuart Grant Duff, and R. H. Hutton of the *Spectator* (consoling herself with *The Grammarian's Funeral*); and I had given up all thought of economics, extension lecturing, or teaching abroad, and had settled down to the only life and study that appealed to me.

Fortunately for him and English scholarship he was able to follow his bent without the distraction of earning a living. He was fortunate too in his place of residence. Pollard was at hand in the British Museum, McKerrow was a constant reader there, at lunch in the Vienna Café nearby Moore Smith was often to be found, and Furnivall held court (in his tweed cap) at a neighbouring ABC. The Museum became the best centre for Elizabethan studies in the world, especially during the summer migration from America. And for relaxation there were—for Greg, McKerrow, and Frank Sidgwick and from 1904 till 1907—the Vedrenne-Barker productions at the Court and later at the Savoy. (Granville-Barker, one of Greg's heroes, he was to meet by chance when serving with the Friends' Ambulance Unit in France.) In July 1900 at the suggestion of Moore Smith he became sub-editor of the *Modern Language Quarterly* under Frank Heath, whom he succeeded as editor in 1903. But when the task became burdensome he resigned, so precipitating a crisis which led in 1905 to the founding of *The Modern Language Review*.

Among the many men to be found in the British Museum or its purlieus was that breezy Elizabethan scholar A. H. Bullen, precariously running his publisher's business from 47 Great Russell Street. With Bullen Greg published, but at his own expense, his *Pastoral Poetry and Pastoral Drama* (1906), a theme which he had touched on in his paper to the Cambridge English Society and which led to his spending a summer at Courmayeur at the head of the Val d'Aosta improving his Italian. He thought poorly of this book and he learned from it, so he told me, that he had no gift for writing literary history. Yet the book has the merit of convincing the reader that he had sought for, read, and understood all the relevant texts, and that his conclusions were solidly based on the evidence. So far there is no better book about English Renaissance pastoral, both poetry and drama, in its relations to Italian and French pastoral. He would have been surprised, but I think gratified, to learn that an American publisher has reprinted it. But Bullen was to do Greg a greater service than publishing this book, and Bullen's encouragement was as important to McKerrow as to Greg. He it was who suggested to McKerrow an edition of Thomas Nashe, one of the best editions of any English author, completed while the editor was still under forty. About the same time (1902) he suggested to Greg an edition of *Henslowe's Diary*, and he published the text in 1904, the commentary in 1908, and miscellaneous papers from the Alleyn collection at Dulwich (*Henslowe Papers*) in 1907. It was Greg's first major work as the Nashe was McKerrow's, and in the commentary he began to skip about 'the Serbonian bog of Elizabethan theatrical history' with an agility and a surefootedness only rivalled by E. K. Chambers.

The work of preparing these was the foundation of what knowledge I have of Elizabethan palaeography and theatrical history. The one side brought me into touch with George Warner at the British Museum, whose ever ready help and cautious criticism were of inestimable value to a beginner; the other led to close association with E. K. Chambers.

In the opening years of this century, then, he was establishing himself as a palaeographer and as an authority on theatrical history, but also in many an article and review as the upholder, with Pollard and McKerrow, of new standards of accuracy and knowledge in the bibliographical analysis of Elizabethan texts. He was always a diligent and fearless reviewer, and in the two-hundred-odd reviews he wrote there are few that do not contribute to the subject in hand. As a reviewer he was just, though often severe. A good idea of his acuteness and of his standards while still a young man may be gathered from his reviews of the Clarendon Press's editions of Kyd, Lyly, and Greene and of the Cambridge University Press's Beaumont and Fletcher, all published between 1901 and 1906. Most severe of all is the review of Churton Collins's *Greene* in the *Modern Language Review* for April 1906. The Syndics of the Cambridge

University Press are said to have hesitated before venturing to publish it, and the publishers of *Greene* are said to have taken advice about improving the standards of their editors. 'It is high time', Greg observed in his review of the edition, 'that it should be understood that so long as we entrust our old authors to arm-chair editors who are content with second-hand knowledge of textual sources, so long will English scholarship in England afford undesirable amusement to the learned world.' But if he was often severe in blame, he was often generous in praise. We came to rely upon him for a just judgement of a book, and there is no one now who can speak with the same authority. An American scholar has recently paid him this tribute:

> One did not dare print work that was not one's very best, simply because one knew that Greg would read it, regardless of whether he would comment on it or not. In many unknown ways that doubtless would have amused him, he set for us all standards that as a matter of pride we had to try to meet. This is the kind of unconscious impress that a great man makes upon his world.[1]

Both he and McKerrow were contributors to the series of reprints of old plays launched by W. Bang of Louvain in 1904. Two years later the Malone Society was founded at the suggestion of A. W. Pollard, and of this Society Greg was general editor till 1939. For the last twenty years of his life he was president, and his successor as general editor can testify that he was almost as active after he changed office as before. Of the 108 volumes published between 1907 and 1957 there are few that did not profit in some way from his scrutiny and for many he was solely responsible. He has been rightly called the Atlas of the Society. My own friendship with him dates from 1919 when he asked me to collaborate with him in editing the first edition of *Every Man Out of his Humour*. 'Collaborate' is hardly the right word. It was he who identified for the first time the first edition and who drafted the introduction, and I remember how he overrode my protest that my name had no business to be mentioned on a level with his. His great gifts as a palaeographer

---

[1] Fredson Bowers in *The Library*, 5th Ser., xiv (1959), p. 173, a number which also contains tributes by J. C. T. Oates, J. Dover Wilson, Alice Walker, Muriel St. Clare Byrne, and F. C. Francis.

and as a textual critic found most scope in the editions of manuscript plays, and the most famous of these was that of *Sir Thomas More*, three pages of which are believed to be in Shakespeare's hand. His is the first accurate transcript and the first in which the seven hands in the manuscript are properly distinguished and described. One apparently small bit of work has always astonished me by its excellence. The rules for the guidance of editors of the Society's reprints which he printed in 1909 could only have been drawn up by a master, so acutely do they anticipate the problems which arise in printing diplomatic reproductions of Elizabethan texts.

He was no great keeper of letters, unless indeed there was substance in them, when his practice was to bind, paste or tuck them into an appropriate book; but he kept a letter of 22 January 1904 from Aldis Wright, Vice-Master, thanking him on behalf of the Council of Trinity for the 'admirable catalogue' of the Capell collection 'which you have compiled with such care'. (In 1909 he did the same service for Eton and its early editions of Shakespeare.) The Capell catalogue had important consequences, for he attributed to that and to his friendship with Wright his appointment in 1907 as Librarian of Trinity, his one salaried academic post. 'I know that Henry Jackson, my only other friend on the College Council, had misgivings about the appointment.' The conditions were not arduous—two hours a day four days a week during term, weekends at home, and rooms in Nevile's Court, one of two sets previously occupied by Lord Acton, in which he was succeeded by Eddington. Soon after returning to Cambridge he submitted his edition of Henslowe for the degree of Doctor in Letters and was presented by Jackson.

Pollard asked me whether the College expected its Librarian to be a doctor, or whether it was mere *hubris*. I replied that I wished to wipe out the disgrace of my first degree, so that it was perhaps as much *aidôs* as *hubris*; which I think pleased him.

While his work remained chiefly in the Elizabethan field, he found some outlet for the medieval interests which both he and McKerrow had acquired from attending Gollancz's lectures while undergraduates. It was a stimulus to be in charge of one of the great collections of early manuscripts, and he completed a detailed description of Trinity's English manuscripts before 1500 which would probably have been printed but for the war and still remains in the Library. In 1913 he published facsimiles of twelve of its Early English manuscripts in the hope that it might be of use to such students of his college as might wish to begin the study of earlier English literature: for, without familiarity with the original texts 'I do not believe that the study can be profitably pursued.' Had he not been committed to his dramatic bibliography and to the general editorship of the Malone Society he might have devoted his life, though he was no philologist, to a study of the manuscript sources of English medieval literature. He planned an ambitious series of volumes—'I was always fond of planning ambitious schemes'— which would have described the actual manuscripts (estimated at 5,000) with particular attention to their bibliographical make-up, dealt with the individual works with reference to the manuscripts in which they were preserved and the relation of the texts, offered extracts of not more than fifty lines of every important work or collection, and concluded with an atlas of at least a hundred plates from the most nearly datable manuscripts as a basis for the study of English palaeography. In 1906 another ambitious scheme was suggested by Walter Raleigh writing on behalf of the Clarendon Press, a press with which he was to establish the happiest relations. (This approach may be taken as evidence that the salutary shocks which Greg had given the Delegates and their Secretary were not without effect.)[1] The proposal was for a select corpus of early English drama in three fat volumes from the beginnings down to the appearance of the regular types in *Roister Doister* and *Gorboduc*.

The scheme never came to anything, but I did a lot of work on it, and some *parerga* saw the light. Towards the solution of certain problems I designed a series of studies to include editions of *The Assumption of the Virgin* from the so-called 'Ludus Coventriae', the *Antichrist* of the Chester cycle, *Christ and the Doctors* in parallel extracts from York, Chester, and Coventry, and an investigation of the very complex

[1] On 17 April 1906, fresh from reading Greg's review of *Greene*, Henry Bradley wrote to the Secretary (Charles Cannan): 'I do not know Greg, and have not even any notion who or what he is, but he seems to know his ground splendidly. The Press ought to get him to do an edition of something.' (Privately communicated.)

Vespasian manuscript. The first of these appeared in 1915, the second not for another twenty years; the third was included, also in 1935, in a collection of *Chester Play Studies* issued by the Malone Society; the fourth never was ... written, though it presents perhaps the most fascinating puzzle of the lot. The *Antichrist* involved problems of textual criticism the principles of which were far from clear to me, however they might appear to others, and what was designed as a section of the introduction eventually grew into a small book, printed in 1927 as *The Calculus of Variants*. Another *parergon* was the series of lectures on 'Bibliographical and Textual Problems of the English Miracle Cycles' that I delivered as Sandars Reader in Bibliography at Cambridge in 1913 and that appeared in *The Library* the following year.

Little notice has been taken of *The Calculus of Variants*,[1] an examination of how far in treating the descent and variation of manuscripts formal rules may be substituted for the continuous application of reason. He would have denied that as logician or mathematician he was anything but an amateur, but it is very remarkable that he was able to read and discuss with interest and understanding 'difficult books, written largely in symbols' like Whitehead and Russell's *Principia Mathematica*.[2] When I confessed that I had not read his book, he was rather cross with me for suggesting that a knowledge of symbolic logic was necessary to its understanding, and it is true that the look of (say) $(x)A^c(AB)(CD)(EF)$ is the most forbidding thing about it. In this attempt 'to define unambiguously the notions required in textual criticism, and by the more rigorous methods of symbolic treatment to obviate some of the errors into which critics appear to have fallen' the extraordinary quality and acuteness of his mind are as apparent as anywhere else in his work.

Meantime, while the Bibliography of the drama sometimes receded from sight, it was never wholly lost to sight, and some of

---

[1] It is discussed with other works, from a philosophical angle, by John Mackie in 'Scientific Treatment in Textual Criticism', *The Australasian Journal of Philosophy*, xxv (August 1947), pp. 53–80; and it is touched on in *Bulletin bibliographique de la Société internationale arthurienne*, no. 3 (1951), pp. 83–90. See also W. W. G. in *M.P.*, xxviii (1931), pp. 401–4 and V. A. Dearing's respectful treatment in *A Manual of Textual Analysis* (1959).

[2] J. C. T. Oates citing C. D. Broad in *The Library*, 5th. Ser., xiv (1959), p. 151.

the discoveries which he made during the course of this work brought him to the notice of a far larger public than did his work on Henslowe, because they affected the work of the editors of Shakespeare and the financial interests of the collectors of Shakespeare. As far back as 1903 he had written a damaging review of Sidney Lee's introduction to the Oxford collotype facsimile of the First Folio. Lee at that time held almost a monopoly of the Shakespeare market in popular esteem, but Greg was never reluctant to disturb accepted reputations or views, and he questioned Lee's sweeping assertions about the piracies of Elizabethan printers and the characteristics of prompt copies and private transcripts. (If Lee was more often right than Greg allowed at the time, it was for the wrong reasons!) Pollard had told him that he would print the review if it was polite; this he refused to be, Pollard's curiosity was piqued, and the review appeared in *The Library* for 1903.

Pollard's own bibliographical work had hitherto been mainly concerned with foreign printing and book illustration, but his experience as a bibliographer and editor was at the service of Greg and McKerrow, both of whom thought of him as their friend and master.[1] His insistence that the bibliographer must have continually in his mind's eye the actual material manuscript from which the compositor was working inspired and encouraged them in their desire to extract from the available evidence the utmost information. In 1906 Pollard's attention was turned to Shakespeare, and one of the consequences was the writing of his exciting *Shakespeare Folios and Quartos* (1909), a landmark in the bibliographical study of Shakespearian texts. At this time so close was the co-operation of Pollard and Greg, so frequent their consultations, that disentanglement of the work of one from that of the other is not easy. This is suggested by the charming inscription in Greg's copy of *Shakespeare Folios and Quartos*—'To W. W. Greg All here that's mine. A. W. P.'

What turned Pollard's attention to Shakespeare was the inspection of a volume, brought to him at the British Museum, of ten 'Shakespearian' quartos, two undated (the 'bad quartos' of 2 and 3

---

[1] So causing Pollard to write to Greg on 13 August 1926: 'The main reason of this letter is to express my abashment (*and* pleasure) at your calling me your friend and *master*. Of course it makes me laugh, as you and McKerrow both not only know more than I do, but know it much more accurately.'

Henry VI) and the rest dated 1600, 1608, and 1619, and purporting to be published or printed by four different men.[1] In 1902 he had been brought a similar volume containing the same plays, and he could not believe the coincidence to be accidental. The solution he proposed was one which would not too much disturb accepted views, but which did not explain the identity of type in the imprints and their unusual brevity or why typographical peculiarities pointed to the press of William Jaggard after 1610 or why all these quartos of whatever date were printed on the same mixed stock of paper. In two articles in *The Library* for April and October 1908 'On Certain False Dates in Shakespearian Quartos' Greg proved that all ten plays were printed by Jaggard in 1619. The publisher, Thomas Pavier, was in fact attempting a collection without the authority of the players, a scurvy attempt as compared with the authorized collection of 1623, for with two exceptions the texts are corrupt or apocryphal. The conclusions Greg reached were (as Coventry Patmore said of the critical sayings of Goethe and Coleridge) 'demonstrable and irreversible'; in future no one could hold, for example, that the 'Roberts' quarto of *The Merchant of Venice* (1600 = 1619) was earlier than the quarto printed by Thomas Hayes (1600). Here was a notable victory for the 'new bibliography' and for Greg. His mother, who died in 1911, lived long enough to realize that if her son was not to become a public figure, he was yet to achieve fame, if a narrower fame. McKerrow wrote to her on 6 May 1908:

> Everyone is delighted with Walter's article in the 'Library', really a most brilliant piece of work and one that must give him a permanent position among the foremost of Shakespearian scholars. I think Trinity should be proud of their librarian.

In 1913 he resigned his librarianship on his marriage to his cousin Elizabeth Gaskell, youngest daughter of his namesake Walter Greg of Lee Hall, Prestbury, Cheshire, a marriage which brought him great happiness. After a long honeymoon they settled at Park Lodge, and he resumed work seriously on his Bibliography.

[1] I have told this story more fully in a chapter on 'Shakespeare and the "New Bibliography"' in *The Bibliographical Society 1892–1942: Studies in Retrospect* (1945), pp. 78–80, a chapter written in 1942.

But not for long. When war broke out his first job was to drive a car for Scotland Yard, where his friend Frank Elliott was an assistant commissioner; then (1915) he served for a few months as a chauffeur with the Friends' Ambulance Unit in France; and finally he joined the staff of the War Trade Intelligence Department, being at first concerned with a publication called *Who's Who in War Trade* and later with a series of 'Peace Books' intended for use at the peace conference, of which he wrote the portion on the geography and communications of Tibet! During his convalescence from an attack of influenza and pleurisy early in 1917 he wrote the first of several articles on Hamlet's Ghost with its highly ingenious but subversive plea that the Ghost is a figment of Hamlet's brain. It led to a spirited controversy with Dover Wilson in which neither party changed his mind but both settled into a lasting friendship.

The war over, he turned once more to the Bibliography. The Cambridge libraries he had exhausted during his residence there, and now he worked systematically through the collections in the British Museum, at South Kensington, and at Eton, and paid two long visits to Oxford. 'But I could not keep other irons out of the fire.' So many irons did he have in the fire that the surprising thing is not that the Bibliography was not completed till 1959 but that it was completed at all. The lists of his writings published in *The Library* for June 1945 and for March 1960 show the extraordinary activity of his mind and pen.[1] 'Pen' is to be taken literally, for he never used a typewriter, but sent all his manuscripts to the press in his own clear and beautiful script. Like his friend E. K. Chambers he was a fast drafter because he knew before he wrote exactly what he wanted to say and was not forced (like lesser mortals) to make the discovery during the process of writing. His 'foul papers' often looked like fair copies. The 'Biographical Notes' which I am so often using in thirty-three quarto pages hardly contain a single erasure. What was not impeccable—and this may be a comfort to some—was his spelling of modern English.

To attempt in this place any detailed account of this vast output which continued without diminution of quality or quantity to the

---

[1] Because of these lists I have been sparing in giving detailed references to his work.

end of his long life and all of which has not yet been published is impossible. But we may consider some aspects of his work which have profoundly influenced current theory and practice. On the function of bibliography he had much to say. Before the early years of the century its importance was hardly recognized. Pollard was one of the pioneers, and McKerrow exercised great influence through a *Library* article (1913) and above all through his *Introduction to Bibliography* (1927).[1] Greg's first thoughts are in a paper entitled 'What is Bibliography?' (1912), and he also considered the subject in his two presidential addresses to the Bibliographical Society (1930, 1932) and in the Society's *Studies in Retrospect* (1945). But perhaps the finest statement of his views on the relations of bibliography and textual criticism is in the lecture on 'The Function of Bibliography in Literary Criticism illustrated in a Study of the Text of *King Lear*' delivered at Amsterdam in 1933. 'I think', Pollard wrote to him, 'that for weight of argument, conciseness, and the pleasure with which it can be read the lecture is your masterpiece. May you produce many more!'

He took a less conservative view than McKerrow. Like McKerrow he maintained that bibliography is the study of books as material objects irrespective of their contents with the purpose of ascertaining the exact circumstances and conditions in which they were produced, and that as in the case of the false-dated quartos or of the two issues of the quarto of *Troilus and Cressida* it could establish complete certainty where a non-bibliographical approach would fail. But he went on to extend its boundaries by insisting that manuscripts and the investigation of textual transmission fall within its province. That it was the duty of the critic to establish the genealogy of family relationships between all the extant manuscripts of a book with a view to arriving at the text of the original was a discovery of the nineteenth century; but that the same duty devolved upon the editor of a printed text not merely in establishing the relationships between the different editions of a work but in attempting to discover what sort of copy the printer had before him when he was setting up the type—this doctrine Greg had very much at heart. If the boundary between bibliography and textual

---

[1] See Greg's obituary notice of him in *Proceedings*, xxvi (1940).

criticism became a little uncertain at times, no harm was done: it was sufficient that there was a bridge, and a substantial bridge, between the two. It came to be recognized that analytical bibliography was an essential preliminary to textual criticism, and he was delighted to know that at Oxford Herbert Davis, the Reader in Textual Criticism, presided over the Bibliography Room in the New Bodleian, 'welcome evidence, to me, of the recognition of the kinship of the two studies'.

Of the important part which he took in making it possible for us to know, as we did not know at the beginning of the century, the exact circumstances and conditions in which a particular book was produced, something must now be said. And we may begin with his work on printers and publishers. Of typography he knew more than most men, but he was no great expert, and when a printer needed to be identified or an ornament to be dated he was content to rely (as who is not?) upon the learning and generosity of F. S. Ferguson. Of the interpretation of typographical evidence the study of *The Variants in the First Quarto of 'King Lear'* (1940) shows him to have been a master. The most recent advances, however, especially the advances which concern the method of casting off and the distinctions between different compositors, these came from younger scholars like Fredson Bowers, Charlton Hinman, Alice Walker, all admirers of his who kept in touch with 'the master'; and although these advances invalidated here and there some of his latest work he welcomed them, and the more so because they were bibliographical advances of which a textual critic had often to take heed. The sound of younger generations knocking at the door was to him a pleasant and a cheerful noise.

In his later years he turned more and more to the history of publishing between 1557, when the Stationers' Company received its charter, and 1640, in fact during the period covered by Edward Arber's *Transcript* of the Stationers' Registers. In 1930 he edited with Miss Eleanore Boswell (Lady Murrie) the records of the Company's Court (1576–1602) from Register B, records which Arber for some reason had not been allowed to print. These and the later records (1602–40) edited by W. A. Jackson in 1957 tell us much about that underworld of stationers concerned with the 'baggage literature' of the age. Greg was never content merely to print records; he had always to interpret them. Some scraps of evidence from these records which had been printed by William Herbert in 1785–90 and which throw a lurid light on the publishers of *The Spanish Tragedy* and *Arden of Feversham* and their internecine warfare he interpreted in '*The Spanish Tragedy*—A Leading Case?' (1925) and was to interpret more fully later (1949). During the Second World War, when rare books became inaccessible and the Bibliography was stored away, he returned to these studies in earnest. In an open letter to me before his *Some Aspects and Problems of London Publishing between 1550 and 1650* (1956), the Lyell Lectures in Bibliography delivered at Oxford in Trinity Term 1955, he maintained that some chance remarks of mine, throwing doubts on the significance of what the Stationers' Registers record, set him off on a detailed study of the Registers themselves and such associated documents as were in print. However that may be, he spent two months in 1943 entering in the margins of Arber the Short-Title Catalogue numbers of the books identified in that work and considered that he had never spent time to better purpose. 'At the end of a couple of years or so I had accumulated material that filled close on a thousand pages of the appropriate foolscap.'[1] These he digested and made use of in a paper on 'Entrance, Licence, and Publication' (1944) but above all in his Lyell Lectures, in which he considers the decrees and ordinances affecting the book trade, the stationers' records, licensing for the press, entrance and copyright, the interpretation of imprints, and so on. These topics, with much else, he also discussed in his book on *The Shakespeare First Folio: Its Bibliographical and Textual History*, an admirably clear and authoritative exposition of the existing state of knowledge and opinion in 1955. In 1903 he had said, in the review of Sidney Lee, that 'it must be frankly confessed that we know very little about the old copyright regulations'. If this is now not true, we owe it to him as much as to any man. One mystery, indeed, has not been solved: why it is that so many works, often highly respectable, were never entered for copyright. His last thought on this problem was that we do not know.[2]

---

[1] *Some Aspects*, p. v. [2] *Bibliography of the English Drama*, iv (1959), p. clxv.

But this account of his work on early publishing conditions is not yet complete. The evening before he died he was at work on what he called *A Companion to Arber*,[1] his manuscript of which is in eleven portfolios. Within the period covered by Arber's *Transcript* he gave transcripts, with interpretations, of documents not printed by Arber; a calendar both of the documents printed by Arber and those not printed; an account of all concerned with the licensing of books; an analysis under appropriate headings of such occasional notes in the Register as throw light on the organization, rules, and customs, of the printing and publishing business; and an index to the miscellaneous information in Arber. In a draft preface he wrote that this sort of work was perhaps the only activity he was then capable of, but there is no sign of failing powers, and when the work is printed it will be found not unworthy of him; for it both advances and consolidates knowledge. It should be mentioned that without a generous grant for the purchase of books and photographs in the United States, offered to him in 1946 by the Rockefeller Foundation who wrote to ask him if it could in any way further his work, much of his later writing could not have been done.

Turn next to the consequences of his insistence that the bibliographer must establish relationships between the different editions of a work and attempt to discover the sort of copy which lay behind the original edition. Of his skill in the former task one early example (1905) may be cited. Which is the earlier of two editions of *The Elder Brother*, both dated 1637? The Cambridge editors of Beaumont and Fletcher could not tell, but Greg found the proof in one reading. In Q1 an improperly adjusted space-lead had produced a mark before the word *young* which the compositor of Q2 mistook for an apostrophe, *'young*. The economy of the proof shows the workman's confidence in his tools. In his *Bibliography*, of course, the ordering of the editions and the distinctions between editions, issues, and variants receive constant attention.

In these matters proof is usually attainable. But what of the attempt to estimate the nature of the manuscript handed to the printer? A few non-dramatic manuscripts used by a printer have

---

[1] [Published in 1967, revised and prepared for press by C. P. Blagden and I. G. Philip. H.G.]

survived, of which the most interesting is Harington's autograph of his *Orlando Furioso*, xiv–xlvi, from which the first edition was printed in 1591. Greg gave an all-too-brief study of it in 1925, in which he inquired how far the printer departed from the spellings and punctuation of the author. But all dramatic manuscripts used by a printer have perished, and speculations on the nature of original dramatic copy are necessarily based on circumstantial evidence. Greg saw that if we were ever to get beyond Lee's glib statements about prompt copies and private transcripts, we must study the extant remains. We must not only examine the printed texts themselves for the evidence they may yield in stage-directions, textual corruption, mislineations, etc., but we must ask ourselves what sorts of printed texts the extant dramatic manuscripts would have supplied if they had been put into print. And side by side with this work we must explore the nature of Elizabethan handwriting in general and in particular the hands of authors and playhouse scriveners. So he set about the task of making the evidence available to all with characteristic pains and skill. Two types of theatrical manuscript he had printed and discussed in his *Henslowe Papers*—players' parts and theatrical 'plots' or skeleton outlines marking exits and entrances and properties scene by scene for use behind the stage. For the Malone Society he began to edit or inspire a series of editions of manuscript plays, whether prompt copies like *The Second Maiden's Tragedy* (1901) or the anomalous *Sir Thomas More* (1911) which may never have reached the stage or 'foul papers' as in *Bonduca* (1951) or private transcripts as in *The Witch* (1950). A major work is the substantial *Dramatic Documents*[1] *from the Elizabethan Playhouses* (1931) giving full descriptive accounts, with facsimiles, of the scanty remains of 'plots' and actors' parts, and of the more plentiful prompt copies and manuscripts of similar kinds. Another is *English Literary Autographs 1550 to 1650* (1925–32) with facsimiles, transcriptions, and comment on the hands of dramatists, poets, prosewriters, scholars, and archaeologists, done in collaboration with McKerrow, Pollard, J. P. Gilson, and Hilary Jenkinson. Thanks in part to these works, attempts to identify the hands of dramatists and playhouse scriveners have met with striking successes.

[1] He maintained that it should have been called *Theatrical Documents*.

He saw that where print and manuscript might be brought together for purposes of comparison and control the amount of speculation necessary would be reduced. With this in mind he made his comparison of the *Orlando* manuscript with the printed edition, and with this in mind he analysed the corrections which Massinger had written in copies of some of his plays (1923, 1924). His most elaborate contribution of the sort was his *Two Elizabethan Stage Abridgements: 'The Battle of Alcazar' and 'Orlando Furioso'* (1922),[1] written at a time when speculation was rife about the nature of what Pollard had called 'bad quartos', that is, texts marred by memorial transmission. For both quartos there is manuscript control, for the *Battle* a 'plot' and for *Orlando* the player's part of Orlando. Greg showed that not all 'bad quartos' have the same origin or history, for while both these texts are shortened versions Peele's play is a simple case of abridgement done no doubt for a provincial tour, whereas Greene's is marred by dictation from the imperfect memories of the actors. He emphasized too the necessity of examining the non-Shakespearian 'bad quartos' if the Shakespearian ones were to be seen in their proper light.

Many pages of his Clark lectures on *The Editorial Problem in Shakespeare* (1942; 3rd edition, 1954) and of his book on the First Folio are devoted to attempts to identify the nature of the manuscripts which served as copy for Shakespeare's plays. It must be confessed that so far these attempts have not always met with the success hoped for. McKerrow was sceptical of reaching any conclusions about the play manuscripts used in printing that could be more than *probably* correct at best, and in his last years Greg, I think, came near to sharing the same opinion. The elaboration of hypotheses concerning the nature of the copy from which some of Dekker's plays were printed forced him to ask the question: 'Is it that our hopes of being able to infer from the features of a printed text the nature of the manuscript that served as copy are fated to vanish like a dream?'[2] Here is the power of turning upon oneself which Arnold admired in Burke and took to be a sign of greatness.

---

[1] He presented this work to members of the Malone Society.
[2] See the review, published posthumously, in *R.E.S.*, x (1959), p. 415.

Walter Wilson Greg

Yet he would not have absolved the bibliographer and textual critic from the duty of *trying* to identify the nature and history of the printer's copy. One of the leading principles of the 'new bibliography' was, as he put it in his 'Principles of Emendation in Shakespeare' delivered before this Academy in 1928, that 'no emendation can or ought to be considered *in vacuo*, but criticism must always proceed in relation to what we know, or what we may surmise, respecting the history of the text'. A critic who proposes several emendations in a text should be sure that they do not involve contradictory theories of its origin. He may not treat textual variants as 'literary counters in a guessing game, quite apart from the sources whence they are derived'.

At the same time he was far from supposing that textual criticism could be reduced to a set of mechanical rules. He quarrelled with a principle which McKerrow had stated in his edition of Nashe and thirty-five years later in his *Prolegomena for the Oxford Shakespeare* (1939), that where an editor is satisfied that a later edition contains variants some of which are likely to be the work of the author then *all* those variants must be accepted, saving obvious blunders and misprints. This principle Greg attacked again and again, first in his obituary notice of McKerrow in our *Proceedings* (1940), and last (at my request) in a note on the text of *The Unfortunate Traveller* in a supplement to the 1958 reprint of *Nashe*. McKerrow was actuated by a desire to avoid the eclecticism of nineteenth-century editors, but in reacting against their aberrations was led to formulate a doctrine that evaded the responsibility of individual judgement. Greg loved adventure in textual criticism as in mountaineering, though in both he liked to be sure of what hazards he was running, and to leave as little as possible to chance and as much as possible to knowledge, experience, skill, and (if the metaphor may be pushed so far) illumination. To see him at his most daring we may consult his reconstruction of Jonson's *Masque of Gipsies*, published by the Academy in 1952. Many an editor might prefer to run away from a masque that was performed in three different versions and preserved in five independent texts; but not Greg. His edition is a manifesto to conservative editors. Not for nothing did he hail as master A. W. Pollard, 'that master of the art of concealing incendiary ideas under a cloak of respectable conservatism'.[1] The difference was that he cared nothing for respectable conservatism.

In this survey of a great man's work I have left till last the mention of his two finest works, his *Doctor Faustus* and the Bibliography so often referred to. Although he profoundly altered editorial procedure he never himself edited a play of Shakespeare with introduction, established text, and commentary. True, he published a text of the 'bad quarto' of *The Merry Wives* (1910) and even tested the theory of memorial transmission by seeing how much he could remember of *John Bull's Other Island* after four visits. Also he wrote introductions to the twelve *Shakespeare Quarto Facsimiles* already published (1939–59) and even to eleven of the quartos yet to be published! But properly speaking these and most of the other texts for which he was responsible are not editions. The only editions of plays which he did are those of *The Elder Brother* and *The Faithful Shepherdess* done for Bullen's Variorum edition of Beaumont and Fletcher (1905, 1908), of *The Sad Shepherd* for Bang's *Materialien* (1905), and of *Respublica* (1952) for the Early English Text Society, on the Council of which he once served. His *Respublica*, while it would do credit to most men, is not creditable to him. He had not that command of classical and especially Renaissance learning and of English popular writing which makes McKerrow's *Nashe* so outstandingly good, and he was too dependent on the *Oxford English Dictionary*. With the parallel-text edition of *Marlowe's 'Doctor Faustus' 1604–1616* (1950) the case is altered. He was at pains to explain that it is not a critical edition in the sense of reconstructing the original text[2] or supplying a complete exegetical commentary, yet his commentary is not wholly limited to the justification of text, and on questions of date, authorship, and text he gave information that any future editor must consider. He turned to the play because it fascinated him and because the relationship between the two substantive texts of 1604 and 1616 was the chief unsolved problem of Elizabethan bibliography. As always he approached the

---

[1] 'The Function of Bibliography', p. 6.

[2] In a separate publication (1950) he supplied a conjectural reconstruction in modern spelling of the play as he supposed it to have been first produced, an excellent example of his adventurous scholarship. This is a text to be recommended to the notice of all producers of the play.

problem without *parti pris*, letting the facts force the solution upon him. He thought himself that it was the best piece of work he had done, and with that in mind inscribed it 'To my wife who has made my work possible.' He was right in that the work called forth *all* his powers and *all* his learning and experience, as the Bibliography did not. In the tact with which he separates the gold of Marlowe from the dross of his collaborator he shows that sense of his author's style without which a textual critic is but a poor cripple. So too in the essay on 'The Damnation of Faustus' (1946), an essay which, as Miss Helen Gardner has said,[1] recovers 'the full horror and beauty' of the scene in which Faustus embraces Helen.

This edition may one day be superseded, though it can never be ignored. His *Bibliography of the English Printed Drama to the Restoration* can never be superseded, though it will be corrected and supplemented. In four handsome large-quarto volumes, published respectively in 1939 (1940), 1951, 1957, and 1959, he gave full descriptive bibliographies of all printed dramatic works together with much valuable information of a miscellaneous kind. To the sorrow of his many friends and admirers in America he never crossed the Atlantic, and for his knowledge of the great collections in the United States he depended upon reports, always unstintingly offered by men and women eager to repay something of the debt which they owed to him. The long Introduction in volume IV in which he explains the scope and limits of the work and gives a justification of its method is very characteristic. 'Sixty years on a job' he says here, but we have seen how many other 'jobs' he turned to. He felt no complacency, he tells us, about the manner of the work's execution, and

I here admit that I can hear the caustic critic who ever sits like a familiar imp at my elbow maintaining that my problem in writing this introduction has been threefold: first to discover what in fact I have done, next why I did it, and lastly how best it may be defended.

Yet the points that established themselves in this work without consideration must be very few indeed. The system of collation, for

---

[1] *Essays and Studies of the English Association* (1948), p. 33.

example, he arrived at after long years of trial and error and many a talk with Pollard and McKerrow, and it is a system that has come to be accepted as the most precise and economical possible. This and other matters he explains with unfailing clarity and acuteness and a pertinacity of logic which allows and accounts for every possible peculiarity that may arise. He did not live to see the publication of this last volume and to 'take his bow', but long before the end of the performance he had heard the applause of all lovers of the great period in English drama.

In 1942, at the end of a history of the 'new bibliography' from the beginning of the century, particularly as it related to the work of Shakespeare, I added an epilogue repeated below, in which I claimed Greg as the hero of the whole movement.[1] If what I wrote then was true how much truer is it now when all or almost all his harvest is gathered in. He was blessed with long life, good health, and a mind always at concert pitch; and in the annals of scholarship there can be few men who have put a life of 'leisure' to better use.

The movement of which this chapter has given an outline is one in which many men and women on both sides of the Atlantic have played their part, but if the writer's point of view is accepted, and if one man is to be chosen as the hero, then it is clear who that man is.... Again and again he has published work which has directed the development of Elizabethan textual studies in the way they should go. The timeliness of his publications is to be remarked as well as their quality. Perhaps he did not always realize how timely they were and sometimes worked by instinct—yet 'instinct is a great matter'—but often he worked deliberately with a sense of direction that enabled him to see how knowledge was best to be advanced. Nor are his achievements to be judged merely from the sale of his books and articles, for this would be to omit his personal influence and his reviews. A company of younger scholars at home and abroad is glad to acknowledge the value of his advice and assistance, and as a reviewer he has worked for forty years 'without envious malignity or superstitious veneration' to raise the standards of English scholarship. If the reviews of his later years lack something of the severity of his early ones, they still expose the errors of sciolists, but with a mellowed animosity; while to be praised by him is counted praise indeed. He

[1] See p. 233 above, note 1.

has never been tempted to overrate the importance of the studies in which he has employed himself. As Johnson said: 'They involve neither property nor liberty: nor favour the interest of sect or party.' But to these studies he has brought exceptional qualities of mind and a patience that does not flag. A distinguished contemporary has praised his friend for the pertinacity which will not neglect to follow up the slightest trace of evidence and an integrity which contantly refuses to rate evidence at more than it is logically worth.[1] As do men of science, he has worked by analysis and synthesis, combining a minute vision for significant detail with a power of erecting hypotheses that fit and interpret the available evidence; and whether in analysis or synthesis he has worked with caution yet without timidity, and with a daring that does not pass into temerity. His fault is that since he wrote on the pastoral many years ago he has neglected a gift for writing literary history for work that has less popular appeal yet is perhaps more likely to endure.

There is little to record of his life between the wars except the births of his two sons and his daughter. In 1932 he accepted an honorary lecturership in Bibliography at University College, London, and when he faced a class for the first time found that his difficulty was not to know what to say or how to say it but to stop. In the summer of 1939 he went with his family to Switzerland by car, a mode of travel the pleasures of which he had not before experienced. They drove back through a mobilizing France reaching home in the last days of August.

Park Lodge had become too large and too expensive to keep up, and it was sold. They rented a small house, Standlands, in the village of River between Petworth and Midhurst in the downland of Sussex. The fine library at Park Lodge which he had been collecting for over forty years had to be sold,[2] and in the hurry he parted with some books the want of which he was to regret. But he minded the loss less than many men, and soon built up a useful working library. The sale of his books led to a belief that he was dead; his name was removed from the electoral roll at Cambridge and only restored when he turned up at Trinity and confronted the Registrary in Hall.

[1] E. K. Chambers in *M.L.R.*, xxviii (1933), 96.
[2] See Hodgson's Sale Catalogues for 1941, nos. 2, 3, 4, and (lots 104–8) 6a.

In the spring of 1946 they left Standlands, at first reluctantly, and bought Tanners Knap, a larger house in the same village where there was more room for his books. His study was on the first floor and his desk next to the window, and in summer the house-martins in the eaves were busy with their nests or their young a yard from his head. The view looking north-west over the valley to Lodsworth and Blackdown, the highest point in Sussex, was as peaceful as any England can now offer. I reminded him of what Aubrey had said of Walter Raleigh's study in Durham House and its view of the Thames as it sweeps round from Westminster, a prospect 'pleasant perhaps as any in the world, and which not only refreshes the eyesight but cheers the spirits, and ... enlarges an ingenious man's thoughts'. But of course he had been just as ingenious at Park Lodge.

In later years he worked in the mornings and between tea and dinner. When he wrote his letters I do not know. His answers came so promptly that his correspondents were seldom out of debt. There were certain fixed habits. One was the nine-o'clock news, and it was advisable not to come down to breakfast till 9.10. Another was the *Times* crossword, and truth to tell he did not excel at it. For the theatre in his London days he had a passion. In his Sussex days he was one of the most constant attendants at Saturday Night Theatre the B.B.C. can have had; plays good, bad, or indifferent he listened to them all; but he never discussed them. When he was not reading tougher books, he relaxed over a detective novel, especially if by Dorothy Sayers or Michael Innes. His favourites (e.g. *Hamlet Revenge*) he read again and again, submitting them to the same kind of scrutiny he gave to the variants in the first quarto of *King Lear*. In the late nineteen-forties he stayed several times in Merton, and surprised some of the Fellows by his nightly addiction to rummy and liar dice in the rooms of H. W. Garrod, then the College Casino.

There is (as Samuel Smiles said) 'a place for everything, and everything in its place'. His desk never seemed untidy. Rows of his own books and bound articles faced him on the shelves attached to his desk, and beneath them were many drawers and niches each with its special variety of paper, pencils, and whatnot. There was a niche for a little notebook labelled 'Wise Saws', one of which was

Henry Bradley's 'A hypothesis ought to be a one-storied building only.' Under the window to his left stood the *Oxford English Dictionary*, but for Arber he had to take three paces to the rear. In whatever he did—whether carving the Christmas turkey or wrapping and sealing a parcel—there was a touch of elegance. Miss St. Clare Byrne in her admirable portrait[1] recalls 'the casual elegance of his personal appearance, so correctly informal in dress, so individually distinguished, carrying off without any trace of affectation the gold-rimmed magnifying-glass on its watered-silk ribbon and the handsome heavy seal ring... a challenging combination of the fastidious and the robust'. Of his handwriting I have already spoken. I should have said his handwritings, for he had two, one known to his correspondents and one used for transcription, adopted, I suppose, because it enabled him to keep his eye on the document. Both were beautifully neat and elegant, sign of an inner accuracy. In his style, a model for all bibliographers and textual critics, he aimed first at expressing his meaning as exactly and as lucidly as possible. 'If one achieves that one is half way towards good writing. But even in a mathematical formula there may be and should be a quality of elegance, which is something beyond mere comprehensibility and correctness.'[2]

If he could be severe with others, he was very severe with himself. Some scholars have been known to defend their views long after they are tenable, but not Greg. True, he stuck to the view that the first quarto of *Lear* was reported by stenography as long as he could, but in the end he abandoned it 'cheerfully'. In his *Bibliography* he dated a play (no. 89) 1587 although the date in the imprint followed the legal reckoning: 'I don't know how I came to overlook this—or rather I know only too well—sheer incompetence.' On another occasion—I am mentioning one of the very few disputes when I was left in possession of the field—he argued that at *Lear*, II. iv. 136

> I pray you, sir, take patience. I have hope
> You less know how to value her desert
> Than she to scant her duty

---

[1] See p. 228 above, note 1.
[2] A letter of 1 June 1946 kindly communicated by Professor Geoffrey Tillotson.

Shakespeare was making Regan say exactly the opposite of what he meant her to say. Six weeks later came the postcard 'You were right. The meaning is "Little as she [Goneril] knows how to scant her duty, you know even less how to value her desert". I must have been very dense.'

In his youth unusually handsome, he was still in old age an impressive figure. Redoubtable in print he was sometimes so in person, and when angered by pretence or arrogance or slipshod writing or thinking his aspect made a man realize that the reading of the second quarto of *Hamlet* (III. iii. 5)

> The terms of our estate may not endure
> Hazard so neer's as doth hourly grow
> Out of his brows

is in no need of emendation. But the many visitors who enjoyed his and Lady Greg's generous hospitality do not think of him so, but of his courtesy and the pains he took to be of service to them. To a Canadian scholar, F. M. Salter, who shared Greg's interest in the Chester plays, he represented not only exact and far-reaching scholarship, and not only hospitality 'and a helping hand to the stranger within the gates, but Magnanimity, the last and greatest of the Twelve Moral Virtues'.[1] Perhaps he always remained (in Howson's words) rather reticent and inaccessible except to his intimate friends, but of these he had many, both men and women, both old and young. They knew they had for life a faithful and affectionate friend.

His services to scholarship earned him many honours. He became a Fellow of this Academy in 1928 and Gold Medallist of the Bibliographical Society in 1935. Oxford gave him an honorary doctorate (D.Litt.) in 1932: 'I was particularly pleased to find myself in company with de Sitter, the Leiden mathematician, whose cosmographical theories fascinated me.' His other honorary doctorate was from Edinburgh (LL.D.) in 1945, a university where his father had studied more than a century earlier. In 1944 he was elected to honorary membership of the Elizabethan Club of Yale University and in 1945 became a foreign member of the American Philosophical

---

[1] *Mediaeval Drama in Chester* (1955), p. vii.

Society, 'a flattering link with a country where I have so many patient correspondents'. He had for many years enjoyed honorary membership of the Modern Language Association of America: it pleased him that he was elected in succession to Henry Bradley, for he thought of Bradley as one of the greatest of bibliographers and regretted that so little of his bibliographical work was included in the *Collected Papers* of 1928. It is natural that much as he valued these distinctions the one he valued most was his election to an Honorary Fellowship at Trinity in 1941, renewing as it did the ties with his old college. In 1950 he was knighted 'for services to the study of English Literature'.

When he came to fourscore years his strength was neither labour nor sorrow. I still found it difficult to keep pace with him as we walked from the Academy to the Athenæum or the Museum, the more so, perhaps, because he seemed indifferent to traffic. Early in 1947, owing to some sudden jerk, he lost the sight of one eye through detachment of the retina, but as before he continued to work without spectacles, so suggesting that secretary hand and black letter are sovereign exercise for the eyes. He spent his eightieth birthday with his wife, his children and 'in-laws', and his six grandchildren, and told them that he continued to think instinctively of old age as of something in the future rather than in the present. He spoke of his exceptionally fortunate life, blessed as he was with the companionship of his wife and growing family; and of that life, he said, the last ten years had certainly been the happiest and most contented and, he thought, the most fruitful.

Death is not a thing to be feared or regretted if it comes in the fullness of time. . . . In the ordinary way I think of death calmly and almost with indifference, and when in the end the fell sergeant does make his strict arrest, I hope I shall 'come along quiet' and without too much reluctance.

The first hint he gave me that his health was failing was when we said good-bye in the summer of 1957. When I returned after a long absence abroad and was about to visit him at Tanners Knap in December 1958, he sent me a letter—'because it is easier, and perhaps less embarrassing, to write than to say it'—warning me that

I should find he had aged a good deal since we met. Mere living had begun to absorb more and more time and energy, and while he was happy and content, still finding plenty to interest him and as active as ever at his work, he had begun to feel that life was rather a burden and that he would not be altogether sorry to lay it down. At the same time he felt his general health to be good: 'I cannot look for any speedy release from service.' But his days of service were nearly over. On 4 March 1959 death came for him, as he wished, quietly and suddenly: *felix non vitae tantum claritate, sed etiam opportunitate mortis.*

[Private papers. Personal knowledge. I am indebted for advice to Miss M. St. Clare Byrne, Professor Herbert Davis, Mr. and Mrs. Peter Newsam, and Professor D. Nichol Smith.]

8

Some English Mock-prognostications[1]

DURING the last twenty years the Bibliographical Society has given much attention to the almanacks and prognostications published in England in the sixteenth and seventeenth centuries. In 1932 it published an article by Mr. Carroll Camden Junior on 'Elizabethan Almanacs and Prognostications' and in 1934 M. René Pruvost's note on 'The Astrological Prognostications of 1583'.[2] But it is above all to the work of Mr. E. F. Bosanquet that any student of this subject, however ignorant or however learned, must turn: to his bibliographical history of English Printed Almanacks and Prognostications to 1600 which the Society issued in 1917,[3] to the corrigenda and addenda to this bibliography (1928), and to his article of 1930 on 'English Seventeenth-Century Almanacks'.[4] And to these benefactions is to be added the facsimile of Buckminster's Almanack and Prognostication for 1598 which he published in 1935 for the Shakespeare Association. This paper is a small pendant to the work of Mr. Bosanquet, prepared by one who pretends to no astronomical or astrological learning, but was engaged, when the request to contribute a paper came to him, in writing notes to Thomas Dekker's comic prognostication, *The Raven's Almanack*.

It is with the comic parodies of astrological prognostications that this paper is concerned, and at the outset a distinction must be drawn—and the distinction is usually clear and sharp—between the prediction which derives from the observance of celestial bodies and the prophecy which is the gift, or purports to be the gift, of divination or revelation.[5] It is not necessary to go back for examples

---

[1] [Read before the Bibliographical Society on Monday, 21 February 1938, and printed in *The Library*, 4th Series, xix (1939), pp. 6–43. Reprinted here with minor additions and corrections.]
[2] *The Library*, 4th Series, xii (1932), pp. 83–108 and 194–207; xiv (1934), pp. 101–6.
[3] Referred to below as *A. & P.*
[4] *The Library*, 4th Series, viii (1928), pp. 456–77; x (1930), pp. 361–97.
[5] A compendious statement of the functions of astrological prediction is given by

to the prophecies of the Old Testament or the apocalyptic visions of the New or to the Delphic Oracles. The characteristic form of English prophecy which disguises men and women under a symbolism of animals and birds began to be influential from the time when Geoffrey of Monmouth in the early twelfth century gave examples of the prophetic gifts of Ambrosius Merlin and of his powers of prophetic interpretation. For centuries dark and riddling prophecies worked like yeast in the minds of credulous and disaffected persons, becoming particularly powerful and dangerous in a time of rebellion.[1] So according to Hall and Holinshed[2] the realm of England and Wales was divided between Glendower, Percy, and Mortimer 'through a foolish credit given to a vaine prophesie'. It was the prophecy with which Shakespeare's Glendower angered Hotspur:

> With telling me of the moldwarp and the ant,
> Of the dreamer Merlin and his prophecies,
> And of a dragon and finless fish,
> A clip-wing'd griffin and a moulten raven,
> A couching lion and a ramping cat,
> And such a deal of skimble-skamble stuff
> As puts me from my faith.

William Fulke in *Antiprognosticon* (1560), D3: astrology 'is ye knowledge by whiche the prognosticatiõs be made, that tell of rayne and fayre weather, sickenes and health, warre & peace, plentie and dearthe, with suche lyke: By whiche also they cast your natiuities, tell you youre fortunes, pretende to gyue you knowledge of things that be lost: and last of all appoynt you dayes and tymes good or euyll, for all thynges that you haue to doo. As, for workes of phisike, to let bloud, to take purgations, and al other medicins for other cõmon matters, to sow, to plant, to iourney by lande, to iourney by water, to bye and sell, to marye, to begynne anye woorke, and fynally to attempt any thyng that men vse cõmonly in their lyfe to doo.'

[1] See George Puttenham, *Art of English Poesy* (1589), ed. Willcock and Walker, p. 260, s.v. the vice '*Amphibologia*'; 'in effect all our old Brittish and Saxon prophesies be of the same sort, that turne them on which side ye will, the matter of them may be verified, neuerthelesse carryeth generally such force in the heades of fonde people, that by the comfort of those blind prophecies many insurrections and rebellions haue bene stirred vp in this Realme, as that of *Jacke Strawe*, and *Jacke Cade* in *Richard* the seconds time, and in our time by a seditious fellow in Norffolke calling himself Captaine Ket and others in other places of the Realme lead altogether by certain propheticall rymes, which might be constred two or three wayes as well as to that one whereunto the rebelles applied it.'

[2] 1587 edn., iii. 521b 60. On this *Prophecy of the Six Kings to follow King John*, written about the middle of Edward II's reign, see the article on 'Political Prophecies in the Reign of Henry VIII' by M. H. Dodds, *M.L.R.*, xi (1916), pp. 279–80. See also Rupert Taylor, *The Political Prophecy in England* (1911), and C. L. Kingsford, *English Historical Literature in the Fifteenth Century* (1913), pp. 236–7.

It was mainly against this sort of prophecy that the sixteenth-century laws against prophecies were directed: whether Galfridian prophecy with its animal symbolism, or Heraldic with allusions to heraldic emblems and devices, or Sibyllic with names mentioned by puns and rebuses, by initials, or by numbers.

Were it not a needles, or booteles labor, to make a special *Analysis*, either of their Abcedary and *Alphabeticall* Spels, or of their *Character-isticall*, and *Polygraphical* suttelties, or of their *Acrostique*, and *Anagrammatistique* deuises, or of their *Steganographicall*, and *Hieroglyphicall* mysteries, or of their *hyperbolicall metaphors*, phantasticall *allegories*, and *heraldicall* illusions, or of their ambiguous *æquiuocations*, interdeux *amphibologies*, and *ænigmaticall* ridles, or finally of any their other colourable glosses, & hypocriticall subornations, in some like prestigiatory, and *sophisticall* veine.[1]

That the prophecy survived into the seventeenth century to be used as political propaganda during the Civil Wars may be gathered from a reference to the many entries under 'Prophecies' in the Index to the British Museum Catalogue of the Thomason Tracts; nevertheless it became of less importance with the increasing popularity of astrological prognostications made possible by the invention of printing.

There were mock-prophecies as well as mock-prognostications. The most famous in English is the Fool's in *King Lear*, beginning

> When priests are more in word than matter;
> When brewers mar their malt with water;

and ending with the comment: 'This Prophecy Merlin shall make; for I live before his time.'[2] To this kind belong also Raleigh's riddling verses 'On the Cards and Dice', the cobbler's song in *The Cobbler of Canterbury* (1590), the paradoxical and satirical verses in Nicholas Breton's *Pasquil's pass, and passeth not* (1600), *Cob's Prophecies* (1614), and many another piece. 'William Terilo's' *A Piece of Friar Bacon's Brazenhead's Prophecy* (1604) is neither prophecy nor

---

[1] John Harvey, *A Discursive Problem of Prophecies* (1588), p. 65.
[2] See also the prophecy 'When this cow rideth the bull' and Wolsey's interpretation of it, with George Cavendish's earnest advice to him to take no thought of dark and strange prophecies; George Cavendish, *Life of Wolsey* (1554–7), ed. R. S. Sylvester (E.E.T.S., 1959), pp. 127–8.

prognostication, for the author contrasts 'The Time Was' with 'The Time Is' and omits Bacon's 'The Time Shall Be' altogether as not being able to go so far. Swift is perhaps the only writer who wrote both kinds: his *Famous Prediction of Merlin, The British Wizard*, I call a mock-prophecy, but the pamphlet in which he predicts the death of the astrologer, John Partridge, and its two sequels, I call mock-prognostications.

My theme is the mock-prognostication, or to speak more precisely, the comic parody of the astrological prognostication, but I have not been able to resist the temptation to say something by way of introduction both about the serious prognostications and about the different kinds of attack, other than parody, which were made upon them.

I

According to Mr. Camden, the prognostication 'made its annual appearance from the time of the predictions of Merlin', but when that time was he does not say. Mr. Bosanquet has shown that very few prognostications of English origin exist in manuscript; that the earliest printed one now known, extant only in two small fragments, came from Pynson's press at the very end of the fifteenth century; that all the early printed prognostications are translations;[1] and that Andrew Borde's of 1545, known only from the title-page, is the earliest that we have of English origin. At first they were published separately, but from about 1540 they began to be added to the Almanack and Kalendar and to be issued annually.[2] Before the end of the century they had settled into a more or less constant form, from which they have not departed in essentials down to the present day.

If we look at the current number of Old Moore's Almanack 'published under the original copyright dating back to 1697' we find much the same information, if not always set out in the same order, as in the original issue of Francis Moore or in the almanacks of his predecessors, Buckminster, Dade, Pond, Bretnor, and the rest. Here are the times of the movable feasts, of the eclipses, and

[1] e.g. *Prognostication drawn out of Ipocras, etc.*, 8°, R. Wyer (1530?), *S.T.C.* 13522.
[2] *A. & P.*, p. 4.

of the tides, which survive from the Almanack proper: that is, in Mr. Bosanquet's definition, 'a table which gives the chief astronomical events of the year and the terrestrial events dependent on them'.[1] The Kalendar still records the chief festivals of the church, although many a saint has been displaced by more secular events. (On 15 January St. Maurice gives place to 'British Museum opened 1759.') Here is the same kind of information which made the almanack an indispensable book to the countryman: sunrise and sunset, moonrise and moonset, weather forecasts for the year, lists and dates of fairs, days and hours when it is fortunate to sow or to do business. 'Froward and unfortunate' days for blood-letting and purging, and for 'entering the bath' no longer figure in the modern almanack, but there is precise information about the days on which it is profitable to back a horse, and medical advice is not spared in the advertisements. Of the twenty 'Omens and their Meanings' given in the current Old Moore five are to be found in the 'Catalogue of Many Superstitious Ceremonies' in J. Melton's *Astrologaster* (1620). Old Moore gives predictions for the year, for the four quarters of the year, and for each month, as did the almanacks of the sixteenth and seventeenth centuries; and his prognostications are almost as gloomy and sinister, and are still presented in vague terms which admit of a wide solution. What has disappeared from the almanack is almost as nothing beside what has remained, but it is a pity that we no longer find the figure of the anatomical man with the zodiacal influences governing the parts of the body. Old Moore with its certified net sale of $2\frac{3}{4}$ million copies a year needs no such adventitious aids to popularity as had to be cherished by John Tipper in his almanack for 1711:[2]

> Should I omit to place this Figure here,
> My Book would hardly sell another Year:
> *What* (quoth my Country Friend) *D'ye think I'll buy*
> *An Almanack without th' Anatomy?*
> As for its *Use*, nor he, nor I can tell;
> However, since it pleases all so well,
> I've put it in, because my Book shou'd sell.

---

[1] Ibid., pp. 1-2.
[2] *Great Britain's Diary: Or, The Union-Almanack.*

II

The grounds upon which astrologers based their predictions were attacked from more than one quarter in the sixteenth and seventeenth centuries. Sometimes the attack was based on religious grounds, as notably by Calvin in a pamphlet translated into English by Goddred Gylby in 1561 as *An Admonition against Astrology Judicial*.[1] Comets, meteors, northern lights, and other unusual phenomena might be interpreted, as many interpret them today, as messages from God to man. So John Evelyn, F.R.S., writing in his Diary on 12 December 1680: 'We have had of late severall comets, which tho' I believe appeare from naturall causes, and of themselves operate not, yet I cannot despise them. They may be warnings from God, as they commonly are forerunners of his animadversions.' But the prognostications of astrologers, it was felt, were false in themselves, encouraged a greedy desire of prosperity and wealth, and argued diffidence in God and neglect of His providence. As John Chamber put it in his *A Treatise against Judicial Astrology* (1601, p. 4): 'if all our actions depend of the starres, then may God haue an euerlasting playing day, and let the world wag'. Other writers objected on scientific grounds. Peter Dacquet, M.D., attacked astrological pretensions to medical science in his *Almanach Novum et Perpetuum*, published by Reginald Wolf in 1556. This was never translated, but a more important book found a translator in 1560 in William Painter of *novella* fame: William Fulke's *Antiprognosticon that is to say, an Invective, against the vain and unprofitable predictions of the Astrologians as Nostrodame, &c.*[2] This is a remarkable pamphlet for a young man of twenty-two who had recently taken his bachelor's degree at St. John's College, Cambridge. Fulke goes to the root of the matter by denying that men know anything about the significance of the stars. For what reason is it said that Jupiter is more

---

[1] The translator signs himself G. G., but at sig. a1ᵛ he acknowledges that he is the translator of Cicero's epistle to his brother Quintus (printed by Rowland Hall, 1561), to which Gylby signs his name in full.

[2] To Painter's translation of his original work Fulke added another treatise especially written 'for the better vnderstandynge of the common people, vnto whom the fyrst labour seemeth not sufficient'. Dacquet is mentioned on sig. A4ᵛ: 'in our tyme (as farre as I haue knowledge) among al men, the most famous and excellent Doctour, Peter Dacquet onely hath both learnedly and playnely declared, that the vse of this fayned art is altogither vnprofitable for the woorkes and practises of phisike.'

wholesome than Saturn? Or why is Mars called hot and Saturn cold? 'Seing you know not what ye stars do signify, you can not by their aspects tell of thyngs to come . . . [it is] impossible for any man to haue any knowledge of thynges to comme by the course of the starres.' And he makes the distinction between astrology, which 'standeth on thynges that most commonlye are false, but alwayes vncertayne and vnconstant', and 'the moste beautyfull and certayne science of Astronomye'.[1] This is an important book in the history of science and of rationalism. It appears to be a lonely book in its time, one of those books which anticipate by years the trend of modern thought, like Reginald Scot's *The Discovery of Witchcraft* (1584), or John Poynet Bishop of Winchester's *Short Treatise of Politick Power* (Strasbourg?, 1560) with its arguments that kings have their authority from the people and may be deposed in the interests of the nation;[2] or the little-known *Temporis Filia Veritas*, printed abroad in 1589, which pleads for the toleration of Catholics, Protestants, and Puritans, and 'for all People that are zelous for Religion & for the Truethsake be they what they be, or dwell they where they shall: so they loue God, and desyer to liue vnder obedience to the King and his good Lawes'.

It would be wrong to write down all astrologers and almanack-makers in the sixteenth and seventeenth centuries as asses or quacks. Some like Leonard Digges and John Dee were learned men acquainted with the most recent developments in astronomical science. F. R. Johnson has pointed out that the almanack-makers, Edward Gresham and Thomas Bretnor, were both ardent supporters of the Copernican theory.

However severely the dramatists might satirize Bretnor as the most prominent astrologer of his day, his scientific contemporaries continued to respect him for his learning. William Bedwell, in the preface to his *Kalendarium viatorium generale* (1614), makes a point of excepting Bretnor and three others from his censure of the horde

---

[1] See especially sigg. A5, A7^v, B8, C7^v, D3, D4. For an interesting account of Fulke's book see an article on 'Astrology and Politics in the First Years of Elizabeth's Reign' (*Bulletin of the Institute of the History of Medicine*, vol. iii, March 1935) by Professor Sanford V. Larkey.

[2] See on this book G. P. Gooch, *English Democratic Ideas in the Seventeenth Century* (2nd ed., 1927), pp. 30–2.

of common almanac makers, saying: 'I speake not of Hoptons, Mathewes, Rudstones, Bretnors, and such like learned ones: but of such, who beside certaine Fustian, as they call it, strange and barbarous termes, (*ampullas, et sexquipedalia verba*) haue nothing worth the reading.'[1]

The almanack-makers themselves deplored the discredit which ignorant practitioners brought upon their craft, Pond complaining in his almanack for 1604 of those who wrote for the meridian of London 'when they immitate Authors (without calculation) which write for *Frankforde* or *Antwerp* &c which causeth grosse errours in their whole worke'.

The satirists did not distinguish between the learned astrologers and the rabble of star-gazers and figure-flingers who wrote 'whole Calenders of lies for bare forty shillings a yeere, (seruingmens wages)'.[2] Sometimes astrologers are attacked in satirical pamphlets, such as W. P.'s *Four Great Liars* (1585),[3] and J. Melton's *Astrologaster* (1620). To these more elaborate attempts to discredit astrologers and almanack-makers by ridicule and abuse may be added the satirical 'characters' of almanack-makers and quack astrologers by Overbury, Braithwaite, and others, and many a chance reference in pamphlets, sermons, epigrams, jestbooks, and plays, as when the Clown in Act V of *The Welsh Ambassador* (*c.* 1623) gives a mock-prognostication. Ben Jonson, a great exposer of the greed and credulity of man, represents his farmer Sordido as having good reason to curse those 'skie-staring cocks-combs' the almanack-makers, for he hoards his grain in expectation of dearth only to find

---

[1] *Astronomical Thought in Renaissance England* (1937), pp. 250–1. John Chamber wrote in 1601 (op. cit., p. 2) that the abuses of almanack-makers had become so gross and palpable 'that euen the offenders themselues are readiest to condemn themselues. In so much that some of them of late haue set out certaine reformed Almanackes, wherein they haue not medled at all with winde, weather, dismall dayes, purges and such like: but only with changes of the Moone, Eclipses, Festiuall daies, both mouable, & vnmouable, and such like. When themselues are ashamed of themselues, what reason haue others to forbeare them?'

[2] T. Dekker, *Work for Armourers* (1609), D4. A passage in Braithwaite's *Whimzies* (1631), cited in *A. & P.*, p. 10, observes that forty shillings is the 'yeerly pension upon every impression' of an almanack-maker.

[3] In the copy at Corpus Christi College, Oxford, the work is attributed to William Perkins, in a hand which the librarian, Dr. J. G. Milne, identifies as that of William Fulman, the seventeenth-century antiquary and divine. For arguments supporting the attribution to Perkins, see H. G. Dick, *The Library*, 4th Series, xix (1938–9), pp. 311–14.

his hopes dashed by the falseness of these weather-prophets. Sordido is doing what Fulke in 1560 and W. P. in 1585 had charged farmers with doing: believing the 'oracles ... of the intemperaunce of wethers [farmers] do so craftily dyspose their wares, y^t in abundaunce of al thynges the common people suffer a greate and greuous scarcity'.[1]

III

Ridicule of the predictions of the astrologers was not unknown in the classical world and in the Middle Ages. The story in our *Hundred Merry Tales* (no. 84) of the herdsman who foretold the weather more truly by the behaviour of his cow than the scholar who had studied the judicials of astronomy is told as an old story by Benvenuto da Imola about 1375.[2] But that particular kind of ridicule which is parody does not seem to have existed until the end of the fifteenth century. It had to wait until the invention of printing turned the almanack and the prognostication into a popular book and so a target for the satire of the scholar or the wit. As printing came to England rather late than soon, it is to be expected that prognostications, and therefore mock-prognostications, will be found earlier on the Continent than in this country. I know of no English comic prognostication before 1544, but the earliest German example of a comic 'Lasstafel', according to Dr. Lutz Mackensen,[3] is dated 1480; and soon after the turn of the century some writers, like Pamphilus Gengenbach and Johann Rausch, turn from serious

[1] *Every Man out of his Humour*, I. iii, III. vii. The quotation is from Fulke, op. cit., B2^v: 'This next yeare there will be much rayne, it will rotte corne vpon the ground, it wil be spoyled, I will keepe my corne vntill the next yeare following: I finde that corne wil be deare about halfe a yeare hence, I will not sell my corne now, but keep it, that I may haue plenty of money for it, and sufficient beside, to maintaine my house.'

[2] In his *Comentum super Dantis Comœdiam* (1887, ii. 90). The details differ. (I am indebted for the reference to my colleague, Dr. C. S. Gutkind.) Herman Oesterley in his edition of *A Hundred Merry Tales* (1866) notes that this story is told of Newton and Scogin; and D. Guerri ('Un astrologo condannato da Dante', *Bollettino della Società Dantesca Italiana*, N.S. xxii, 1915, pp. 222–3) notes the continuation of the tradition associating it with Dante's Bonatti, and the application of the story to another astrologer, Ugo da Santa Sofia, in Novella 5 of Ortensio Lando (1552). In *Lillyes Lamentations* (1652, p. 6) a similar story is told to the discomfiture of William Lilly.

[3] *Die deutschen Volksbücher* (1927), pp. 51–2. See also Adolf Hauffen, *Johann Fischart* (1921), i. 145.

prognostication to comic. The most famous of the German comic prognostications is Johann Fischart's *Aller Praktik Grossmutter* (1572), although it is not one of the most original: for there is the same chain of plagiarism in the German productions which I shall have to expose in the English. The humanists were also attracted to this form of parody. Just as Poggio in Italy and Bebel in Germany had compiled jest-books to indulge their love of satire and to show off the virtuosity of their Latin style, so Jacob Henrichmann von Sindelfingen freely adapted, enlarged, and turned into Latin the Swiss 'Praktika Doctor Johannis Rossschwanz'.[1] Henrichmann's *Prognosticon* was printed by itself in 1508 and was reprinted again and again for a century and a half at the end of the *Facetiae* of his master Bebel, to whom it is dedicated. Soon afterwards Bebel wrote a similar *Prognosticon* 'ex Ethrusco sermone in Latinum traductum ab anno domini M.D.IX. usque in finem mundi'. Henrichmann boasts that his book differs from all other prognostications in that *his* predictions will all come true, and it is no empty boast. 'Vtilius erit pecuniam accipere, quam expendere. Melius erit equitare quam pedibus vadere. Qui vinum non habebit, aquam bibere non spernet.' This is the simple pattern which all later comic prognosticators embroider.

A greater humanist than Henrichmann and Bebel wrote his parody of prognostications. The *Pantagrueline Prognostication* for the year 1533, first printed in 1532, owes little to Henrichmann and to Bebel, most of all to the quiddities of Rabelais himself. A *Prognostication des Prognostications pour tout temps, à jamais* (1537) by Bonaventure des Périers is more a direct attack than a parody, but several parodies in verse, some perhaps earlier than Rabelais or des Périers, are printed in the *Recueil de poésies françoises* edited by Anatole de Montaiglon.[2]

In Italy, from which country we derived so many of our literary forms during the Renaissance, the prognostication does not appear to have become a popular work so early as in Germany. Perhaps the most famous writer of that nation to use the form of the popular

---

[1] Hauffen, op. cit. i. 146.
[2] 1854–77, iv. 36; vi. 5; vii. 204; viii. 337; xii. 144 and 168; xiii. 12. Des Périers is reprinted at v. 224.

Some English Mock-prognostications

giudizi or prognostications for satirical parody is Pietro Aretino. His *Pronostico satirico* for the year 1534 exists in a late-sixteenth-century manuscript which may have been copied from a printed text;[1] and his *Judicio over pronostico de maestro Pasquino, quinto evangelista* gave much offence to the Pope and the papal court.[2]

IV

The earliest English comic prognostication, I have said, is for the year 1544: it is no. xxviii in Mr. Bosanquet's Bibliography, where a facsimile is given of the title-page.[3] The title, like the prediction, is in verse:

> A mery pronosticacion
> For the yere of Chrystes incarnacyon
> A thousande fyue hundreth fortye & foure
> This to pronostycate I may be bolde
> That whan the newe yere is come gone is ye olde.

It is possible that this pamphlet is a translation or adaptation from some foreign source, but I have not succeeded in tracing an original. Like most of these prognostications, earlier and later, it imitates the various sections of its models: 'Of the Eclyps', 'Of the foure quarters of this yere', 'Of the twelue monethes', etc., and the humour comes from saying the most obvious or the most nonsensical things with as much astrological jargon as possible.

The only copy known, formerly at Britwell, is now in the Huntington Library, San Marino, California.[4] The pamphlet, which is in quarto, has three leaves, all unsigned. An uncompleted rhyme at the foot of the verso of the second leaf indicates that it is the third leaf of the sheet which is missing.[5] The context shows that this

---
[1] I know it only from Guillaume Apollinaire's introduction to *L'Arétin* (1922), pp. 10–12. I have not been able to see Alessandro Luzio's edition of this mock-prognostication published at Bergamo in 1900.

[2] I have not seen this libel; it is described by R. and F. Selenzi in *Pasquino* (1932), p. 48. In L. Guicciardini's *Detti et fatti piacevoli et gravi* (1565, 102*b*) and in J. Sandford's English translation (*The Garden of Pleasure*, 1573, L1^v) a prognostication by 'Pasquino di Roma' is cited. It begins 'Questo anno prossimo, i ciechi vedranno poco, o niente, i sordi udiranno mai', and proceeds as inoffensively.

[3] Mr. Bosanquet points out that the cut on the title-page is from that used on f. cxxxvi of Pynson's 1509 edition of *The Ship of Fools*.

[4] Mr. F. S. Ferguson kindly identified the printer for me as William Middleton.

[5] [A]1 recto is the title-page: the prediction runs from [A]1^v to [A]4^v. The missing leaf is [A]3.

leaf contained part of the prognostication of diseases and sicknesses, and the predictions for those born under Saturn, Jupiter, and Mars.

It may be presumed that the contents of this missing leaf are preserved in a mock-prognostication printed almost a century later; for there are few of the extant lines of the prediction for 1544 which are not incorporated somewhere or other in W. W.'s *A New and Merry Prognostication* of 1623.[1] For example, here is the end of the passage with the uncompleted rhyme at the foot of [A]2ᵛ in the pamphlet of 1543-4:

> Thys is bycause of the Eclyps of the Mone
> Some shall supe theyr potage for lack of a spon
> In the[2] somer tyme shalbe suche an heate/

Under the same section of diseases and sicknesses we find in 1623 (C2ᵛ):

> Some say it is by reason of the Moone,
> Many shall sup their Pottage, for lacke of a spoone.
> Others say, because the signes be in such heat,
> The people would fare well, if they could get meat.
> Some shall say truth, and some shall goe by gesse:
> And other some shall goe to bed supperlesse.
> After their first sleepe, they shall be striken with hunger,
> They would refuse neither Capon or Cunger.
> Some ere they be wise, will needes be wed,
> And some wiues shall leade their Mates drunke to bed:
> Other some shall be so sore agast,
> They shall be faine for lack of meate to fast.
> Some shall fast, and some shall pray,
> And some surely cannot tell what to say . . .[3]

The sequence of chapters or sections is the same in both pamphlets, but '1623' has many more sections and treats each section more

---

[1] Reprinted by J. O. Halliwell in 1860. Halliwell notes that the lines of the title of '1544' are 'very similar to those in the first stanza of the address of the Author to the Reader' in 1623.

[2] the the *Q*.

[3] At the top of [A]4 in the prediction for 1544 are the last two lines of the prediction for those born under Mars:
'For Saturne and Mars haue ful wel discust
That in the eclyps Mercury is combust.'
These lines are not incorporated in the twenty lines about 'Marcailists' in 1623.

voluminously. For example, in the section 'Of the twelue monethes' '1544' has twenty-six lines and '1623' has eighty-four lines. There is no difference in style or versification between the lines found in '1544' and the lines not to be found there, and there can be no doubt that the prognostication for 1623 is substantially a reprint of some lost mid-sixteenth-century work.[1]

Between 1544 and 1591 I know of no extant examples of this kind of parody. Many may have perished without leaving a trace, for they would not normally be entered in the Stationers' Register. One or two likely titles of works which were entered but have not survived may be mentioned. There is the ballad entered in the trade year 1557-8:

> Then and in thos days, then, I say, then
> Knaves that be now will become honest men.

But this may have been paradoxical prophecy rather than mock-prognostication. 'A merry prognostication for the year of our lord God 1567 by J. Dernyll' sounds more promising: it was entered to William Pickering in 1566-7. Perhaps this may be the original of the *New and Merry Prognostication* printed in 1623.[2]

One work I mention doubtfully here because it ridicules astrologers by quotation and not by parody: Nicholas Allen's *The*

---

[1] The only attractive thing in '1623' is the drinking song at the end, not to be found in '1544'. The song may well be of about the same period as 'Back and side go bare, go bare'. The refrain and the first stanza are:
> Kyrieeleyson sing wee, now merrily euery one,
>   that honest mirth, is more worth,
> Then Siluer, Golde, or precious Stone,
>   taking thought who list, for I will take none.
>
> All yee which be heere,
>   Vnto vs now draw neere:
> Drinke good Wine, Ale, and Beere,
>   Care not though Mault be deere.
>   Learne this lesson at me first,
>   He that drinketh well shall neuer dye for thirst.
>   Kyrieeleyson sing we, &c.
[See Note 'A Merrie and Pleasant Prognostication (1577)' (pp. 283-4 below), where, eleven years after this article was published, F. P. W. identified and described this 'lost work'. H.G.]

[2] See also 'A new and pleasant prognostication &c' entered to E. Allde on 8 August 1586. The entry of the same book, '*a merry* and pleasant prognostication', to Thomas Purfoote on 5 September 1586 is cancelled. [See Note, p. 283 below, for further discussion. H.G.]

Astronomers Game (1569), a book which escapes the attention of the Short-Title Catalogue but not of Mr. Bosanquet.[1] Allen's purpose is to expose the contradictory statements in the almanacks and prognostications of Thomas Buckmaster or Buckminster, John Securis, and Henry Low, and he does so by imitating exactly the format of the contemporary almanack and prognostication and by printing side by side the information given by these three astrologers about lucky days, what sign the moon was in, and the weather predictions. Here, he says in his satirical preface, they have the advantage 'all together in this one Booke, if they can be content, like good fellowes parteners in the Lotterie, to take their chaunces in common, and put their lucks in hotchpot (as the lawyer termeth it) that lightely one of them will, may, or would hit right: for vnhappy it is if of so many boltes shot, none light neere the mark'. It is odd that in the only known copy, now at Corpus Christi College, Oxford, two openings (four pages) are blank except for the few letters on each page printed in red. Was this done intentionally in order to suggest that a blank page of such nonsense was as good as a full one, or was it merely that the printer of this copy forgot to pass the sheets through again to print the parts which were to be in black?

As if to compensate for the dearth of mock-prognostications before 1591, that year saw the publication of no fewer than three. Only one of them was entered in the Stationers' Register: 'A booke entituled Ffrauncis Fayre Weather' entered to William Wright on 25 February 1591. It is the only one of the three which has not survived, but as Florio refers in his *Second Fruits* (1591, A2) to those that 'pronosticate of faire, of foule, and of smelling weather', it would seem that Fairweather's pamphlet had been printed.[2]

Foulweather's prognostication has the title *A wonderful, strange and miraculous astrological prognostication for this year of our Lord God. 1591 ... Wherein if there be found one lie, the Author will lose his credit for ever. By Adam Foulweather, Student in Ass-tronomy.* The satire took with the town, and was reprinted in the same year.[3] More than a

---

[1] *A. & P.*, 37.

[2] In R. W.'s *Martin Mar-sixtus* (1591, A3ᵛ) the reference is more vague: 'We liue in a printing age.... What publishing of friuolous and scurrilous Prognostications? as if *Will Sommers* were againe reuiued.'

[3] See my note in *M.L.R.*, xiii (1918), pp. 84–5.

Some English Mock-prognostications

century ago it was fathered upon Nashe, and for that reason it has been reprinted three times since 1883; but, as McKerrow observes, 'there is not the slightest reason for connecting it in any way with Nashe'.[1] And with a writer with so distinctive a style, not to be convinced that it is his is almost to be certain that it is not.

Adam Foulweather at once found a follower in Simon Smellknave, 'Student in good fellowship', under which name was published *Fearful and lamentable effects of two dangerous Comets, which shall appear in the year of our Lord,* 1591. *the 25 of March.*[2] Both Foulweather and Smellknave are most allusive writers, and both calculate, rectify, or supputate their prognostications for the meridian and elevation of London, although these also serve universally, without any great error, for most parts of England or indeed of the world. How far they are original must remain in doubt, when so many earlier parodies are lost.[3] The style and the allusions are undoubtedly of their period. It will be seen later that several writers gave the next generation the opportunity of reading Foulweather and Smellknave in a slightly altered form.

The merry prognostication for 1544 differs in several respects from those for 1591 and from later ones. It is in rhymed couplets, whereas all the others printed before 1640 are in prose except the *New and Merry Prognostication* of 1623. Its sole purpose almost is to parody astrological prediction, and it makes little use of the chances this form offers for covert social satire. And it lacks all those particular allusions to places, persons, events, professions, trades, manners, customs, and pastimes which, together with the range and vigour of their vocabulary, are the chief interest of the later productions in this kind. Writing of Shakespeare, Dr. Johnson observes: 'The compleat explanation of an author not systematick and consequential,

---

[1] *The Works of Thomas Nashe*, v. 138–9; see also iv. 476–7. Mr. Carroll Camden (op. cit., p. 103) continues to ascribe it to Nashe, but without reason.

[2] 'Some joking on the days of the week, in which Monday is said to be the best of all, perhaps suggests that Anthony Munday was the author (D2ᵛ).' R. B. McKerrow in Nashe, *Works*, iv. 477.

[3] Both Foulweather and the prognostication for 1544 prophesy that mariners 'shall stick in the sands' and that there will be some who 'shall not be able to change a groat'. The resemblances are no doubt accidental. I am not convinced by the arguments of Huntington Brown (*Rabelais in English Literature*, 1933, pp. 37–41) that Foulweather is indebted to Rabelais.

but desultory and vagrant, abounding in casual allusions and light hints, is not to be expected from any single scholiast.... What can be known, will be collected by chance, from the recesses of obscure and obsolete papers, perused commonly with some other view.' It is the merit of the 'obscure and obsolete' papers of which I am speaking that they sometimes elucidate the meaning of better writers.

Between 1591 and 1604 I know of no book to my purpose, but I would give much to see the 'Gargantua his prophesie' which was entered to John Wolf on 6 April 1592. It can hardly have been the prophetical riddle in the style of the prophet Merlin (really Mellin de Saint-Gelais) of Rabelais's first book (ch. 58), for that is too brief and too obscure; and if it was a translation of the *Pantagrueline Prognostication* why was it called 'Gargantua his prophesie'? Could it be that the parody was transferred from Pantagruel to Gargantua because Gargantua was more familiar to the English public?[1] Gargantua, the hero of the folk-tale rather than of Rabelais's novel, was well known to sixteenth-century England, and is mentioned in an English book as early as 1547.[2] But it is foolish to speculate, for the book is lost, as also is 'the historie of Gargantua' entered to John Danter on 4 December 1594.[3]

Two comic prognostications were published in 1604, but one of these is of little interest. At the end of the jest-book *Jack of Dover* printed for W. Ferbrand in 1604 is *The Penniless Parliament of Thread-*

---

[1] I find that the conjecture is anticipated in Huntington Brown's edition of *The Tale of Gargantua and King Arthur*. By François Girault, *c.* 1534 (1932), p. xxv.

[2] *The book of Merchants* (1547), C3. I am informed that the reference is not in the earlier edition dated *c.* 1534 in *S.T.C.* Brown does not notice this reference. [But see note in the article on 'English Jest Books', published in the following year (p. 299 below), where F. P. W. notes that the unique copy of the first edition in the Huntington Library has references to Pantagruel, excised in the second edition, which show the author had Rabelais in mind. H.G.]

[3] *S.R.*, ed. Arber, ii. 607, 667. On 16 June 1592 an entry of 'Gargantua' not assigned to any publisher is cancelled; ibid. 613. *Gargantua* is mentioned by Laneham (*Letter*, 1575, ed. Furnivall, p. 30) among the many English books which Captain Cox the Coventry mason had at his fingers' ends. For evidence that most of the sixteenth-century English references to Gargantua are probably not to Rabelais but to a lost translation of the *Croniques admirables* of François Girault see Huntington Brown, op. cit., and *Rabelais in English Literature*, pp. 31–3. The 'History of Gargantua' was still a live book in 1626 when the widow of Thomas Pavier assigned the copyright to Edward Brewster and Robert Birde (Arber, iv. 165): and again in 1642 Brewster and Birde's rights were assigned to John Wright, junior.

bare *Poets*. In 1608 it was separately printed for William Barley.¹ From this edition of 1608, of which a copy apparently unique is now in the Huntington Library, it was reprinted in the first volume of *The Harleian Miscellany* (1744), by the Percy Society in 1842 together with a reprint of the 1604 text of *Jack of Dover*, and by Charles Hindley in the second volume of his *Old Book Collector's Miscellany* (1872).² But none of these editors observed that *The Penniless Parliament of Threadbare Poets* is lifted except for the opening and closing paragraphs from Simon Smellknave. The text is divided into seventy-three paragraphs, there is some rearrangement, and what had been a prognostication becomes the enactments of a parliament simply by understanding the word 'shall' in an imperative instead of a prophetic sense.

Plato's Cap. Cast at this Year 1604, being Leap-year. London Printed for Jeffrey Chorlton, 1604, is more interesting and more original, although here too there are borrowings from Simon Smellknave.³ The author, in signing himself Adam Eavesdropper, had one eye perhaps on Adam Foulweather, but he is clearly a skilled and gifted writer, and had no need to borrow his 'prognosticating Comedie, or comicke Prognostication' from other writers. A former owner of the copy now in the British Museum wrote in it in 1728: 'very full of merry Punns &c', and it is not easy to catch this author's allusions or to follow him in all the turnings of his wit. If a paragraph is to be chosen to illustrate his quality let it be one that sorts with the theme and attitude of the satirical comedy of the time. 'Haue amongst you Citty dames?' as Justiniano in *Westward Ho* observes,

---

¹ *Jack of Dover*, Part 2, had been entered to Ferbrand on 3 August 1601, and this may have been *The Penniless Parliament*. On 12 November 1614 Barley's rights in *The Penniless Parliament* were transferred by his widow to John Beale. In 1615 *Jack of Dover* was printed by J. B. and sold by R. Higgenbotham, but *The Penniless Parliament* is not given, although the title-page announces: 'Whereunto is annexed *The Pennilesse Parliament of Threed-bare Poets*'. In 1649 *The Penniless Parliament* was reprinted 'for John Wright, at the Kings Head in the Old Bayley': ten paragraphs were omitted and parts of five others.

² Hindley's text and the comment on the verso of the title-page are from the edition of 1744. The Percy Society text is also from the Harleian reprint.

³ See, for example, Smellknave, 8: 'there shall be warre betweene the foure knaues at cardes for superioritie, and twixt false dice and true for antiquitie'. This is in *Plato's Cap*, C3ᵛ. Or see Smellknave, 10: 'Those that sing bases shall loue good drinke, and Trumpetters that sound trebles, shall stare by custom.' This is in *Plato's Cap*, D2.

'You that are indeede the fittest, and most proper persons for a Comedy.'[1]

And therefore you the Widdowes of rich deceased Marchants, Mercers, and Grocers, whose Husbands in their life-tims haue been large Benefactors to Hospeitalles, and Almes-houses, and eleuated many profitable Bucketts in their Parish-churches, with Armes most quaintly painted vpon them, beside Sixpennie Dole at their Funerals, and the blewe Consort of Hospitall Boyes singing their Dirges: you (I say) their weeping Widdowes, this fearefull coniunction threatens most, for many ryotous Spendals goe about to enquire for you: and therefore all you that loue your selues better than a satten Suite, and preferre your carefull States before a white Feather, lette my prognosticating skill fray you from such briske perfumed Wooers, lette not a newe fashioned prodigall Hat, wast and consume that, which an ould fashioned honest Cappe, carpt and car'd for all his lifetime before.[2]

The title appears to be taken from a jocular reference to Plato's *annus magnus* in Dekker's *The Wonderful Year* (1603): '*Platoes Mirabilis Annus*, (whither it be past alreadie, or to come within these foure yeares) may throwe *Platoes* cap at *Mirabilis*, for that title of wonderfull is bestowed vpon 1603.'[3] When in 1925 I attributed to Dekker the two anonymous pamphlets *News from Graves-end* and *The Meeting of Gallants at an Ordinary*, both of 1604, I pointed out some striking resemblances between these pamphlets and T. M.'s *Father Hubburd's Tales* and *The Black Book* of the same year; and I said that these resemblances are not surprising if we identify T. M., as I think we must, with Thomas Middleton. 'We know that in 1604 at some date before the 14th March Middleton and Dekker were engaged in writing *The Honest Whore*.[4] What is more likely than that they should talk over and show to each other those pamphlets by the writing of which they were earning some sort of livelihood while the theatres were closed for the plague?' *Plato's Cap* was written by one who moved in their circle, who had at his command the same racy and spirited style, and who was as well acquainted with the

---

[1] 1607, B1. [2] C3.
[3] *Plague Pamphlets* (1925), pp. xix–xx and 19. 17–20.
[4] Henslowe's *Diary*, ed. W. W. Greg, ii. 175.

Some English Mock-prognostications 269

wit and scandal of their corner of the town. It is invaluable for the annotator of T. M. and of Dekker: for example, it illuminates more than one passage which has baffled the editors of *The Gulls' Hornbook*. I am not rash enough to attribute *Plato's Cap* to Middleton, still less to Dekker, but the perusal of it is to be recommended to any editor of Middleton. I observe, without attaching very much value to the observations, that *Plato's Cap* was published jointly by Geoffrey Chorlton or Charlton and Thomas Bushell, that *Father Hubburd's Tales* was published by Bushell and sold by Chorlton, that Chorlton also published *The Black Book*, and that Anthony Wood's copy of *Plato's Cap* in the Bodleian is bound up with *The Wonderful Year*, *The Meeting of Gallants*, and *The Black Book*.[1]

From *Plato's Cap* we descend to Anthony Nixon's *The Black Year* (1606).[2] Nixon was a prolific pamphleteer and versifier of whom it might be said more truly than of Shadwell:

> Thou art of lasting Make, like thoughtless men,
> A strong Nativity—but for the Pen.

In his *Lanthorn and Candle-light* Dekker speaks of certain Falconers, as he calls them, who having scraped together some small parings of wit, cut them handsomely in pretty pieces, and of those pieces patch up a book. *The Black Year* is the most blatant example of word-piracy that I know. Granted that the distinction between *meum* and *tuum* in literary property was not so sharp then as now, Nixon's conduct cannot be condoned under any code of literary behaviour. It is a moot point in ethics whether it is more dishonest to steal an author's dedication than to steal his text. The whole of Nixon's dedication to Francis Coppinger is stolen from the dedication to Lord Derby in Lodge's *A Fig for Momus* (1595), except for a long parenthesis thriftily borrowed from Lodge's address to his reader. Fortunately, Nixon does not forget to alter 'your honour' to 'your

---

[1] *Plato's Cap* was entered to Bushell and Chorlton on 21 March 1604: *The Black Book* on the following day to Chorlton. In the Bodleian and Huntington copies of *Plato's Cap* the imprint is 'Printed for Ieffrey Chorlton. 1604'. The British Museum copy lacks the first sheet, including the title-page. Copies of *Plato's Cap* and *The Black Book* were in the Isham find. See *Bibliographica*, iii (1897), pp. 418–29.

[2] A few passages in Marston's *Parasitaster, or The Fawn*, v. i (1606, H3^v and H4) are in the manner of the comic prognostication: e.g. 'A great scarsitie of Lawyers is likewise this yeare to ensue, so that some one of them shall be entreated to take fees a both sides.'

worship'. But this is only the first of his depredations. The pamphlet divides itself into three parts:[1] a comic prognostication (B1–D1ᵛ); a general disquisition upon the world's corruption (D2–D4); and finally a sermon against the church of Rome (D4ᵛ–E4ᵛ) which the author pretends he has been inspired to write by the Gunpowder Plot. In the second section, I regret to say that I do not know in whose snow to track him except for a passage or two in a book from which he borrows in his first section.[2] But rather to my surprise—for I underestimated his effrontery—the third section turned out to be no derelict sermon, but the work of that popular divine Henry Smith. It is all borrowed from Smith's *God's Arrow against Atheists*, printed in 1593 and in 1600 and added to the one-volume edition of his sermons in 1604. Nixon omits much of the facile rhetoric which earned for Smith the epithet 'silver-tongued', and little is left but the dry bones of the argument.

There remains the mock-prognostication in the first and longest section. Any one who reads this with the attention which it does not deserve will notice that it is not all of a piece, for the comic prognostications are interspersed with Latin tags, English verse, and general moral reflections. As for the Latin tags I give Nixon learning enough to use a florilegium.[3] The English verses are mostly from Lodge's *A Fig for Momus* with transpositions of lines to cover up his borrowings and to make things more difficult for the literary detective. One or two of Lodge's verses are transprosed, but most of the moral reflections are taken in generous chunks from Thomas Wright's *The Passions of the Mind in general* (1604), again a known and current book.[4] One of Nixon's borrowings I should have missed if it had not been noted by Malone in his copy of this pamphlet:[5] it refers to the gentleman who discharges 'half a score proper men' in the country

---

[1] The collation is: quarto, A–E⁴. The preliminaries take up sheet A, and the text begins on B1.

[2] There are borrowings in this section from Thomas Wright.

[3] In his *Oxford's Triumph* (1605, A3ᵛ) he claims that he has been a member of the University of Oxford, but his name does not appear in Joseph Foster's *Alumni Oxonienses* or in Anthony Wood.

[4] First printed in 1601, but Nixon uses at least one passage from the enlarged edition of 1604 not found in 1601.

[5] Malone 659 in the Bodleian Library. Malone also noted one borrowing from Wright on sig. B1ᵛ; it is noted too in his *Shakespeare* (1821), ii. 416.

Some English Mock-prognostications 271

and will 'wait at the Court (vncalled) with a man, and a Lackey after him'. This seems to be a solitary theft from W. S.'s *A compendious or brief examination of certain ordinary complaints* (1581): it may have been borrowed from a borrower. Finally, the prognosticating parts of this section are taken, with the exception of a few lines, from Simon Smellknave's work of 1591. Smellknave's order is much jumbled, allusions obsolete by 1606 are omitted, and Nixon puts in occasional references of his own, one, for example, to Marston's *The Dutch Courtezan* (printed 1605).[1]

This is Nixon's only comic prognostication, and it is not my task to expose him in his other works. I could point out that the dedication to his *The Scourge of Corruption* (1615) is borrowed from the dedication to Dekker's *A Strange Horse-Race* (1613), but 'I will not rake the dunghill of his crimes.' Yet two examples may be given of the dangers which writers like Nixon present to literary and social historians and to editors. *The Black Year* has been brought in as evidence of a fundamental gloom, a fear of vague and limitless calamities, which is said to have pervaded England in 1605 and 1606 and to account in some degree for the tragic terror of *King Lear*. Far be it from me on this present occasion to say if Shakespeare's pangs were caused by private sorrow, or were caught from the circumambient air, or were merely artistic. Nixon's pangs, I feel sure, were pecuniary, and the prognosticating gloom of this pamphlet was borrowed from the sixteenth century. My other example illustrates the dangers which lie in wait for editors and the good luck which sometimes attends them. Since Malone it has been customary to cite a passage from *The Black Year* (sig. C2) in illustration of the

---

[1] I give a sample from the first four pages of text of the extraordinary network of borrowings in *The Black Year*. The references to the pages and lines in Nixon come first and are in italics; the sign = stands for 'is borrowed from' or 'is based on'; S. is Smellknave (1591), L. is Lodge (1595), W. is Wright (1604), W.S. is *A compendious . . . examination* (1581):

B1. 10–11 = W. 127. 31–128. 2; *B1. 11–15* = L. B2ᵛ. 4–7; *B1. 15–17* = S. 23. 3–5; *B1ᵛ. 6–8* = S. 7. 10–11; *B1ᵛ. 12–15* = W. 137. 4–7; *B1ᵛ. 16–18* = S. 8. 3–5; *B1ᵛ. 19–20* = S. 13. 11; *B1ᵛ. 21–24* = S. 8. 2–3. 1–2; *B1ᵛ. 25–31* = S. 7. 15–21; *B2. 14–20* = W. 142. 30–143. 4, 143. 26–8; *B2. 23–5* = S. 19. 21–3; *B2. 25–B2ᵛ. 6* = W. 135. 22–136. 3, 136. 12; *B2ᵛ. 7–13* = S. 23. 25, 8. 22–9; *B2ᵛ. 13–17* = S. 8. 14–17; *B2ᵛ. 19–20* = S. 8. 30–1; *B2ᵛ. 20–22* = S. 8. 18–19; *B2ᵛ. 25–32* = W.S. B1ᵛ. 8–14.

Nashe would have called this stealing 'by patch & by peecemeale' (*Works*, ed. R. B. McKerrow, ii. 246).

circumstance mentioned by the Porter in *Macbeth* of 'an English tailor stealing out of a French hose' and as evidence for the date of the play: tailors, writes Nixon, 'where they were wont to steale but halfe a yard of broad cloath in making vp a payre of breeches, now they doe largely nicke their Customers also in the lace, and take more than enough for the new fashion sake, besides their olde fees'. Now the 'new fashion' of nicking customers in the lace is an old fashion, for the passage is in Simon Smellknave in 1591. Yet this piece of good fortune attends the editors, that where Nixon wrote 'they were wont to steale but halfe a yard of broad cloath in making vp a payre of breeches' Smellknave (p. 11) had written 'they were wont to steale but one quarter of a cloak'. The passage remains worthless, of course, for the dating of *Macbeth*, for the practice of stealing cloth from breeches is not referred to as new.

A moral is pointed by that excellent antiquary and naturalist John Ray in the preface to *The Ornithology of Francis Willughby* (1678), and as I believe the passage is little known, perhaps I may be allowed to quote it before returning to my theme. He is referring to a book by Nicholas Cox which had been published in 1674.

Here by the by I cannot but reflect upon the Author of a late *English* Book, entituled, *The Gentlemans Recreation*. For having had occasion to examine and compare Books upon these Subjects, I find that all that he hath considerable concerning *Fowling* is taken out of the forementioned Book of *Markham*, and yet hath he not to my remembrance made any mention of his Author: What he hath of *Hawking* is likewise an Epitome of *Tuberviles* Collections, with some addition out of *Lathams Falconry*, without acknowledgement that all was borrowed. I doubt not but I could have traced him in his other Discourses of *Hunting* and *Fishing*, had I had leisure or will to compare his Book with *Turberviles*, *Waltons*, and other Treatises of those Subjects. I do not blame him for Epitomizing, but for suppressing his Authors names, and publishing their Works as his own, insomuch that not only the Vulgar, but even Learned men have been deceived by him, so that they have looked upon him as a considerable Writer, of extraordinary skill in such Arts and Exercises, and one that had advanced and improved them. By the way therefore it may not be amiss to caution Learned men that they be not too hasty nor lavish in their public commendations of new Books before they have taken the pains to compare them with former Treatises on those Subjects, lest they render themselves ridiculous by publishing those for advancers of knowledge, who are indeed meer Plagiaries and Compilers of other mens Works.

Of the originality of Dekker's *The Raven's Almanack* (1609) I have no doubt: the form is conventional, but the writing is his own. Dekker was not above 'conveying' the work of a contemporary when it suited his purpose, and in saying that I am not thinking merely of *The Bellman of London*, which seems to me a special case. But on the whole, unless my reading is defective, he made few verbal borrowings, and needed to make few. 'His mind and hand went together', and he flowed with such facility in his busy journalism that he must have found it quicker to write for himself than to borrow from others.

It is remarkable that *The Raven's Almanack* is the only original comic prognostication printed in England before 1640 to which we can attach an author's name. It went through three editions in the same year, but its success may have been due less to the comic prognostication than to the four tales or *novelle* with which the parody is diversified: these are the last and among the best examples in English of their kind. Dekker's pamphlet is a prognostication rather than an almanack, but he does not distinguish between the two in his text, and after the fashion of the almanack the title-page is printed in red and black. (The prognostication was always in black, probably because 'it was considered the serious portents of doom contained in it could not be treated in any other ink than black'.)[1] At the head of the text stands the figure of the anatomical man which the printer, Edward Allde, often used in printing serious almanacks for the Company of Stationers; but never again perhaps did he confuse the signs of the zodiac—Gemini changing places with Taurus, Leon with Cancer, &c.,—as he has done for Dekker's comic purposes.

The author's aim is not so much to ridicule the almanack-makers as to amuse his audience by satirizing the poor abuses of the age. There are few classes of men from courtiers to cobblers, few trades and professions from lawyers and merchants to players and fiddlers,

[1] *A. & P.*, p. 31.

few vices and follies to which he does not give a lash of his pen as he takes his incoherent way.

Rupert Taylor in his book on *The Political Prophecy in England* says that Dekker's pamphlet was 'evidently a burlesque' of '*The Raven's Almanac* licensed to Laurence Lyle July 7, 1608',[1] but it is much more likely that it was Dekker's own pamphlet which was entered on that day. According to the imprint of all the extant copies *The Raven's Almanack* was published and sold by Thomas Archer, but it is not uncommon to find that the name of the publisher in the imprint of a book does not correspond with the name of the publisher who entered the book. For example, Dekker's *The Honest Whore* was entered to Thomas Man the younger on 9 November 1604, but it was printed in the same year by Valentine Sims for John Hodgets.[2] There may have been an agreed transfer of copyright without formal assignment in the Register and payment of a second fee, or (more improbably with a pamphlet of this kind) it may be a case of piracy. Certain it is that the almanack Lisle was entering was a comic one. The monopoly of printing serious almanacks and prognostications had belonged to the Stationers' Company since 1603, and it was not customary to enter them as separate items in the Register at this date. If *The Raven's Almanack* had been a serious production it would not have been entered at all, and it would certainly not have been published by Lisle or any one but the Stationers' Company.[3] It may also be noted that the entry in the Register in July 1608 more clearly relates to Dekker's pamphlet because it quotes a considerable portion of Dekker's title-page: 'the Ravens Almanacke &c foretellinge of A. plague, famine, and Ciuil. Warres.'

Although Lisle was no author, he wrote a preface to *The Owl's Almanack* which he published in 1618. This work has often been ascribed to Dekker. A prospective editor of Dekker's non-dramatic

[1] p. 123. See also Carroll Camden, op. cit., p. 105.
[2] Hodgets may have been merely the bookseller; see W. W. Greg, *The Library*, 4th Series, xv (1934–5), p. 55.
[3] At a later date almanacks were entered in the Register by George Sawbridge acting as treasurer for the partners in the English Stock of the Stationers' Company, but this form of entry is not found, I think, before 1652–3. For examples see *S.R.* i. 404 (1652), 417 and 432 (1653), 451 (1654), and ii. 3–4 (1655). The dates on which almanacks for the following year were entered vary from April to October: Dekker's prognostication for 1609, entered in July of the previous year, was entered, then, at much the same time of year as the serious predictions of the astrologers.

works who already has more than enough upon his hands may be suspected of being a prejudiced witness, yet no better reasons have been advanced for ascribing it to Dekker than that the work was suggested by Dekker's *Raven*[1] and that 'an early possessor' noted that it was by Dekker in a copy seen only by the eye of J. P. Collier.[2] The author good-humouredly refers to *The Raven's Almanack* as 'a hotch-potch of Calculations', and mentions *The Bellman of London* and *Candle-light* as 'Two bookes written by T. D.';[3] but acquainted as he was with Dekker's work, he is no imitator of Dekker's sentiment or style. This is the most elaborate of all English comic prognostications printed before 1640, for in its twenty-one chapters it ridicules the whole contents both of almanack and prognostication from the beginnings and endings of the four terms and the annual computations of time to the lists of fairs and highways and observations on good and bad days.

In 1623 appeared W. W.'s *A New and Merry Prognostication*, which I have taken to be a reprint of a sixteenth-century work. More interesting is *Vox Graculi, Or Jack Daw's Prognostication . . . for the year 1623*. Two birds of ill-omen, the raven and the owl, had already been appropriated, and there remained graculus or the jackdaw. Perhaps the author felt that the bird was also suitable because of its thievish habits. Mr. Camden pointed out that 'Several passages have been lifted bodily out of Nashe [i.e. Adam Foulweather], and others have been paraphrased or added to',[4] but this if anything is to underestimate the debt. Except for Foulweather's section 'Of the second Eclipse of the Moone', there is hardly a line of his pamphlet which is not used somewhere or other by Jack Daw. The substance of his dedication, and of his accounts of the eclipses and of the eclipses of the sun is from Foulweather. But when he comes to the four quarters of the year he borrows from other sources as well. The account of each season begins with passages from *The Raven's Almanack* before returning to Foulweather. The borrowings in

---

[1] A work entitled *The Owl's Almanack* is promised in *A Countercuff given to Martin Junior* (1589), but it never appeared. It would have been an attack on Martinists and 'upstart religions': cf. Nashe, *Works*, ed. McKerrow, i. 60. 56, 74. 14, iv. 45. The title of the pamphlet of 1618 was suggested not by this, but by Dekker's *Raven*.
[2] *A Bibliographical Account* (1865), ii. 80.
[3] pp. 1 and 14. [4] Op. cit., p. 107.

'Autumne or the Fall of the Leafe' are especially notable because there he takes several pages from Dekker's *The Dead Term* (1608): the order of his borrowings in this section may be represented by the formula, *The Raven* + *Foulweather* + *The Raven* + *The Dead Term* + *The Raven* + *The Dead Term*. The prediction for the twelve months which follows is based on *The Raven's Almanack* and Foulweather, but at the end of his book he gives predictions for each of the first six months of the year—he is content only to 'discouer sixe of them, and then cast Anchor'—which appear to be his own.

Jack Daw's is a very different case from Nixon's. For one thing he is content to remain anonymous, and for another he shows some ability in the passages which he adds of his own. It is of course possible that some of the longer passages are from some unidentified source, but I give Jack Daw the benefit of the doubt because he shows his quality in the phrases and short sentences with which he ekes out his borrowed matter. Perhaps it is not beneath the dignity of this Society to draw attention to a passage in his prediction for Summer which is not taken from Foulweather or Dekker. It gives a reference, eighteen years earlier than the earliest in the Oxford Dictionary, to bottle-beer: he calls it light-headed 'Because stopt with Corke'.[1]

Jack Daw's most interesting addition to Foulweather and Dekker is found under 'Autumn', and there is a curious bibliographical point about it. The pamphlet, which is in quarto, collates regularly A–I^{4}K^2 except for two leaves which follow sheet E and are signed ee and ee^2. The following passage runs from ee1 to ee2^v:

[ee1] When the issue of the Earth are disroabed of all their Verdures, and the brood of man stript naked of all their Vertues: [ee1^v]

When *Greatnesse* sits pruning her feathers, (and those borrowed too) in the Sunne-shine of *Reputation*, and *Goodnesse* be faine to lie sculking in the shadow of *Contempt*:

---

[1] Sig. E2. *O.E.D.*'s earliest reference to bottle-ale is from William Webbe's *A Discourse of English Poetry*, 1586 (*Elizabethan Critical Essays*, ed. Gregory Smith, i. 246. 29), but the ballad to which Webbe was probably referring, 'A Jest of bottell ale', was entered in the Stationers' Register on 19 August 1583. The difficulty of bottling beer, which was hopped, is suggested by Jack Daw: 'the which being once let loose, will furiously flie in any mans face'. On sig. H2 Daw gives another reference: '[Charity] as colde as the *Harrowes* Bottle-Beere was the last yeare on *Christmas* euen'.

Some English Mock-prognostications 277

When *Flattery* is euery Lords fellow in the Court, and *Honesty* is forced to goe a begging in the Country, because the Citie will not entertaine her: . . .

When Churches shall be empty of sound-hearted professors, and Ale-houses cram'd full of bestiall and pernitious Pot-suckers:

When Murther shall be held but manly reuenge; and the maine act of manslaughter, made but the light *Scæne* of mans-laughter:

When *Vsury* shall be tearmed *Thrift*, and Lechery, a tolerable *tricke of youth: Extorsion, warie husbandrie: Pride, comlinesse*; and *Drunkennesse*, a laudable *recreation*:

When *Hypocrisie* gets on the gabbardine of *Sanctitie*, to goe to Church in on a Sabbath [ee2] day, where he will sit sighing at a Sermon, and turne vp his eyes, as though he would shoote them through the Churches roofe into Heauen; and being returned home, fals to an vndigested seeming-deuout prayer and that so lowde too, as his neighbours round about may heare him: yet neuerthelesse, all the weeke after will practise no worse, then to lie for aduantage, falsifie his promise, filch himselfe drunke, if he can catch it a free-cost, traduce his neighbour secretly, defraud his friend, and then fliere in his face:

When children shall fling vp oathes and execrations against the face of heauen, in the streets, and their Parents sit laughing at their doores, to heare them so forward of their tongues:

When *Iustice* is so troubled with the palsey in her hand, that when she is to poyze her ballance, she makes a solide cause seeme light, and a light cause, heauie and downe-waight; and when she heaues her sword, and strikes more out of rage then right; mad-man like, wounding those that stand neerest vnto her;

When the grafs of *Grace* lie starke deaded in the hearts of men, and *Goodnesse* is excluded from humaine societie:

These, with a supernumerarie multitude of [ee2^v] the same breed, shall bee the vndoubted signals of the *Fall of the Leafe*, or rather of the finall dissolution and desolation of this wide, wilde, and wicked Vniuerse.

The tone of this and of one or two other passages in Jack Daw is very different from that to be found in other comic prognostications. He turns from parody of the almanack-makers, from word-play and scandal, from amusing and light-hearted references to social abuses, and in these brief paragraphs hits hard at the darker vices of society. There is an edge on the writing, a moral ferocity, which contrast with the passages from Dekker which go before or from Foulweather which follow.

But to return to bibliography. How are we to explain the irregularity of the signatures? The passage of which I have quoted a part cannot be explained as an afterthought of the author's sent to the printing-house after the pamphlet had been printed off; for the passage which the author has borrowed from *The Raven's Almanack* runs on from E4^v to ee1, and that which he has borrowed from Foulweather runs on from ee2^v to F1. Nor is it likely that a page or two of the manuscript was temporarily lost or accidentally omitted by the printer, for the catchword at the foot of E4^v coming in the middle of a sentence and a new paragraph beginning at the top of F1, the error would at once have become apparent. The explanation seems to lie in the practice of dividing an author's manuscript among two or more compositors in order to expedite printing. So in Thomas Bell's *The Pope's Funeral . . . Printed by T. C. for William Welby* (1605,*2) is the statement: 'The Booke for expedition sake, was committed to three seuerall Printers, by reason whereof the Pages could not bee distinguished with numbers.' In *Vox Graculi* if a measurement is taken both of the width of a page of type and of twenty lines of type, it will be found that A–E^4 and ee^2 agree together as against F–I^{4}K^2. It will also be noticed that the running-title VOX GRACULI contains a swash letter R down to ee2^{v1} which does not appear after that page. We must suppose that when the author's manuscript came to the printing-house it was divided as exactly as possible into two equal halves and handed to two compositors, compositor X being instructed to begin with signature A and compositor Y with signature F.[2] Y managed with four and a half sheets, but five sheets were not enough for X and he was forced to use a supplementary half-sheet ee^2. The overlap may of course have been due not to any miscalculation in the printing-house, but to an afterthought of the author's which arrived after the

---

[1] Except on B2^v, D1^v, and E1.

[2] There is also pagination from A4(1) to E4^v(34) and from F1(35) to K1^v(68) with I3^v, I4, K1, and K1^v mispaged 66, 67, 69, 70 instead of 64, 65, 67, 68. The preliminaries are simple—with title-page, address to the reader, and a few lines of verse; so that it was easy for X to judge that his page 1 would begin on A4 and for Y to calculate that F1 would be page 35.

Some English Mock-prognostications 279

division of the manuscript. Two leaves were rather more than were necessary, and X had to do a good deal of 'leading' to space his matter over the half-sheet.

V

If any comic prognostications published between 1623 and 1640 are extant I do not know of them. *Martin Parker his marvellous prognostication* entered to Francis Grobe on 31 January 1638 does not seem to have survived. Beyond 1640 they multiply at such a rate that I should not care to attempt an exhaustive list. Those that I have examined exploit the greater opportunities which presented themselves after that date for personal and political satire. Sometimes the satire is grafted upon old material. The alleged flight of the Welsh at the battle of Edge Hill is ridiculed in *The Welshman's new Almanack and Prognostication for this present year 1643*, but the substance of the pamphlet is taken from Adam Foulweather's predictions for the seasons and eclipses of 1591.[1] Similar satire on the same theme is found in *Wonders Foretold by her crete Prophet of Wales which shall happen this present year 1643*,[2] but it is imposed upon material taken verbatim from J. Melton's *Astrologaster* of 1620. More original perhaps is *Shinkin ap Shone Her Prognostication for the ensuing year 1654 . . . Printed for the Author, and are to be sold at his shop at the sign of the Cow's Bobby behind the Welsh Mountain*. In *Now or Never: Or, The Princely Calendar. Being a Bloody Almanack, For the Time present and to come* (1659) the satire is seriously political, and the return of 'that Princely Person Selrach Drauts', that is, Charles Stuart, is foretold before the end of 1662.

> New Gouernours peeps in, Old Ones cast down,
> You'l know in Sixty Two, who'l wear the Crown.

---

[1] Topical allusions are brought up to date: Bull the hangman (Nashe, *Works*, ed. McKerrow, iii. 394, 34) becomes in Jack Daw (F1) Brandon and in *The Welshman's new Almanack* (1643, A4) Gregory (i.e. Gregory Brandon). There was an entry of *The Welshman's new Almanack* in the Stationers' Register on 4 November 1646, so that it was probably reprinted 'for this present year 1647'. A copy of an edition 'for this present year 1648' is in the British Museum with Naseby for Edge Hill and other changes.

[2] Reprinted as *Crete Wonders fortold by her crete Prophet of Wales, which shall certainly happen this present year 1647*. For a reprint of this edition see E. W. Ashbee's *Occasional Fac-simile Reprints*, xxix (1872).

The author of *Jack Adams His Perpetual Almanack* was free to indulge in open abuse of 'the Phanaticks': the satire is undated, but the Conventicle Act of 1664 is referred to as new (p. 19). In *A Merry Conceited Fortune-Teller: Prognosticating to all Trades and Professions their good and bad Fortune* (1663) the satire is more general, and it would not be surprising to discover that it is reprinted from an earlier seventeenth-century work.[1]

Of all the astrologers before Partridge, William Lilly came in for most ridicule. In the many astrological pamphlets which he published between about 1644 and 1660 his prognostications had consistently favoured the parliamentary cause—he was accused of taking a salary from the Council of State[2]—and many a satire in pamphlet or ballad was directed against his astrological pretensions by royalist wits. He escapes lightly in *Strange Predictions* (1652), a single-sheet prognostication in verse foretelling events that could only come to pass if human nature were radically changed; but the satire is more personal in *Merlinus Democritus; Or, The Merry-conceited Prognosticator . . . By W. Liby, Student in Astrology* (1654), a mock-prognostication in ridicule of 'Merlinus Anglicus', as Lilly called himself in his almanacks.

Much the best of the many satires on Lilly is in the dedication to *Pantagruel's Prognostication: Certain, true, and infallible; for the Year everlasting. . . . Set forth long since by that famous well-wisher to the Mathematicks, and Doctor in Physick, Francis Rabelais. Done in the way, and by the Tables, of that Astrologer of the First Magnitude, in the British Hemisphere, Anglicus*, a translation by 'Democritus Pseudomantis' of the *Pantagrueline Prognostication*. The work is undated,[3]

---

[1] Copies of all the pamphlets mentioned in this paragraph except *Jack Adams* are in the British Museum. See also *The Black Dutch Almanack* (1651) and *The Mad-Merry Merlin: or the Black Almanack* (1653). There is a copy of *Jack Adams* in the Bodleian. Of another comic prognostication, *Mercurius Verax: Or the Prisoners' Prognostications for the year 1675* by John Phillips, there is no copy in the British Museum or the Bodleian. I am indebted to Mr. E. F. Bosanquet for lending me this and other volumes from his remarkable collection.

[2] Cf. *Lilly Lash't with his own Rod* (1660).

[3] In the British Museum copy (Huth 146) the imprint is 'London,', and the rest of the imprint is cut away, apparently deliberately; in the Bodleian copy (8° C. Linc. 508) the imprint is 'Printed at London.'. The Museum copy was formerly in the Huth library (Sale Catalogue, Sotheby's, 1 July 1918) and in J. O. Halliwell's library (Sale Catalogue, Sotheby's, 13 June 1859): in both sale catalogues it is wrongly said to be the only copy extant.

Some English Mock-prognostications 281

but it must have been written between 1644, when Lilly took a political side, and 1660. Probably it belongs to the sixteen-fifties when Lilly was in full astrological career.[1] The second English translation—or perhaps, as we have seen, the third[2]—was to be Motteux's in 1708, which owes no debt whatever to the earlier translation and is less literal. The anonymous translator gets in many a shrewd blow at Lilly both in his prose dedication to Lilly and in the Skeltonic verses 'Skelton upon Rabelais'. A short extract from the dedication will show the vein 'ironically grave' and the breeding of the prose:

thou resembles him in this, that although thou art not altogether so good a Droll, yet every man when he reads thee, has a kind of tentation to laughter. And yet thou for thy part seemest so grave and serious that thou wilt easily pardon the Translator of this, having thy selfe so usefully rendred his jest into good earnest: and I know not perfectly whether he were thy Originall, or but an imperfect Type, or faint representation of thee, a greater Prophet to come.[3] Thou hast all along his Style, Figures, and Policy, and all but the profession of Drollery. Thou knowest as well how to wrap thy deceits in a cloud of generalities, that they may not lye open to discovery or reprehension. Do but look upon thy Ephemerides, and thou canst tell us very gravely that some body or other shall dy next month, and as plainly forseest the fall of some great man in August, as we mortalls the dropping of a Pomwater in Autumn. In fine, thy Prophecies are as sure as Death: For Those, as This, are in themselves certaine, but the Time, Place, Manner, and Persons, and such petty circumstances, altogether uncertain.

A vogue for printing a mock-almanack and mock-kalendar together with a mock-prognostication set in about the middle of the century. 'Raphael Desmus Philologist' or Samuel Sheppard[4] produced for 1653 *Merlinus Anonymus. An Almanack, and no Almanack. A Kalendar, and no Kalendar. An Ephemeris (between jest and earnest) for the year 1653.* Early in 1660 appeared *Montelion, 1660*, where

---

[1] W. C. Hazlitt says *c.* 1645: the British Museum Catalogue, ? 1660. W. J. Harris in the *First Printed Translations* (1909) says 1620, an impossible date, for Lilly did not begin to prognosticate in public before 1644 or thereabouts.
[2] See above, p. 266.
[3] Cf. *MacFlecknoe*: Heywood and Shirley were but types of thee,
    Thou last great prophet of tautology.
[4] Cf. Britwell Sale, 30 March 1925, lot 21, and Halkett and Laing (1932), vi. 397.

'Montelion' is the pseudonym of John Phillips, the nephew of John Milton.[1] *Montelion, 1661* is a different production with much post-Restoration satire on puritanism and the Commonwealth: it has been attributed to Thomas Flatman.[2] Similar in mind is *A Yea and Nay Almanack* specially designed to satirize 'the people call'd by the men of the World Quakers'; it appeared in 1678 and earlier. From this ribald tradition descends *The Comic Almanack An Ephemeris in Jest and Earnest* of the nineteenth century to which Thackeray and Cruikshank contributed.

The most famous of these comic annuals and one of the longest-lived was *Poor Robin's Almanack* by William Winstanley and others, which appeared from 1664 and lingered on into the nineteenth century. Like the *Yea and Nay Almanack* it provided a serious almanack and kalendar as well as a comic, and it was therefore printed by the monopolists, the Stationers' Company. On one page it gave 'the Old, Honest, Julian, or English Account' of the Kalendar, and on the opposite page it gave 'the Round-heads, Whimzey-heads, Maggot-heads, Paper-scull'd, Slender-witted, Shallow-brain'd, Muggletonian, or Fanatick Account, with their several Saints Days, and Observations upon every Month'. *Poor Robin* is not to be confused with *Poor Richard*, whose first almanack appeared in Philadelphia in 1733—'Printed and sold by B. Franklin, at the New Printing Office near the Market.' Benjamin Franklin also compiled his almanack partly in jest and partly in earnest, but the serious part with its prudential proverbs and sententious sayings greatly outweighed the comic. How else could the claim be made for *Poor Richard* that it 'is perhaps the one secular work in the world which has educated a people and formed the character of a nation'?[3]

I have said enough to show that the form is not exhausted after 1623, but becomes increasingly popular. And I have not strayed into the eighteenth century to mention the *Predictions for the Year 1708* by Isaac Bickerstaff. There the subject threatens to rise into literature.

---

[1] The pseudonym is from Emanuel Forde's romance *The Famous History of Montelion, Knight of the Oracle*. For the authorship cf. *Mercurius Verax*, 'By the Author of the first *Montelion*, and *Satyr against Hypocrites*,' i.e. John Phillips.

[2] See Wood, ed. Bliss, iv. 245.

[3] William Macdonald in his edition of Franklin's *Autobiography* (1905), p. 210.

NOTE

A MERIE AND PLEASANT PROGNOSTICATION (1577)[1]

In an article on 'Some English Mock Prognostications' (*The Library*, 1938, xix) I gave some account of W. W.'s *A New, and Merrie Prognostication* (1623). This work incorporates most of the lines in the earliest surviving mock-prognostication *A mery pronosticacion* (1544, Bosanquet, xxviii), also in verse; and as there is no difference in style or versification between the lines found in '1544' and the lines not to be found there, I conjectured that 'the prognostication for 1623 is substantially a reprint of some lost mid-sixteenth-century work'.

A copy of this 'lost' work has survived in the Library of Corpus Christi College, Oxford, one of many rare books and pamphlets presented to that College by Brian Twyne. The collation is 8^0, A–C^8. A1 and C8—both presumably blank—are missing, and the title-page (A2) and C7 are imperfect. The date of this edition is given by a line in the verses from the author to the reader 'Fifteene hundred, seuentie and seuen so true' (A3^v), a line altered in the later edition to 'Sixteene hundred twenty and three so true'.

I give a transcript of the title-page. This is in roman and italic, whereas the text is in black letter and italic. Of the missing words supplied within square brackets the only one not corroborated by '1623' is 'pleasant'. The downstroke of the 'p' is visible, however, and the word is supported by the entry to Thomas Purfoot on 5 September 1586 of 'a merye and pleasant Prognosticacon, whiche was an old Copie of James Robotham'. This entry was cancelled, the work being the property of Edward Allde, who had entered 'A newe and pleasant prognostication &c' on 8 August 1586. Allde was the printer and publisher of the reprint of 1623.

A merie and [pleasant] / *Prognostica*[*tion*] / *Deuised after the finest fashion, Made and written for this presen*[*t year,*] / *By fower wittie Doctors as shall ap*[*pear,*] / *Spendall, Whoball, & Doctor Deusac*[*e,*] / *With them Will Somer takes his place*[,] / *They haue consulted all in deede,*/ *To solace them, that this shall reede.* / [Woodcut repeated on C3^v under 'Lunatistes'.] / *Imprinted at London for Iames Rowbo-* / *thom, dwelling at S. Magnus corner,* / *and are there to be solde.* [In ornamental border.]

Rowbotham, who is not known to have been a printer, is given two addresses in the Bibliographical Society's *Dictionary of Printers, 1557–1640*. The address on this title-page is not recorded.

The contents of '1623' are the same, except for textual variants, with those of '1577'. In '1623', however, the only clue to the authorship is the initials 'W.W.' at the end of the Preface. In '1577' these initials appear at the end of

[1] [Reprinted from *The Library*, 5th Series, iv (1949), pp. 135–6.]

the Prognostication (C6ᵛ), and the Preface is signed '*J.D.*' (A4ᵛ), initials which in the Corpus copy have been altered in ink to '*J.B.*' It is tempting to believe that '*J.D.*' is right and to identify the pamphlet with 'a mery pronostication for the yere of our lorde god 1567 by J. Dernyll' entered to William Pickering in 1566–7 (Arber, i. 337) and published presumably in the year 'Fifteen hundred, sixty and seven so true'. Pickering is last heard of in 1571, Rowbotham in 1580, and the property may have descended from Pickering to Rowbotham, as it certainly descended from Rowbotham to Allde. Mock-prognostications, while they may go out of fashion, are so written that they do not easily go out of date.

9

The English Jest-books of the sixteenth and early seventeenth centuries[1]

THE ordinary recreations which we have in Winter, ... are *Cardes, Tables* and *Dice, Shovelboard, Chesse-play,* the Philosophers game, small trunkes, shuttle-cocke, balliards, musicke, masks, singing, dancing, ule-games, frolicks, jests, riddles, catches, purposes, questions and commands, merry tales of errant Knights, Queenes, Lovers, Lords, Ladies, Giants, Dwarfes, Theeves, Cheaters, Witches, Fayries, Goblins, Friers, &c.... *Bocace* Novels, and the rest.

It is appropriate to begin with a quotation from *The Anatomy of Melancholy*,[2] if only because we owe to Burton the preservation of many an ephemeron. Sir Thomas Bodley was for excluding from his library 'Almanacks, plays and an infinite number that are daily printed'. He feared the scandal which might be brought upon it if it were stuffed 'full of baggage books'. Thanks to Robert Burton, and after him John Selden and Anthony Wood, the Bodleian can hold its own in this kind of literature with any other library.

Yet in spite of the zeal of these men, and of later collectors like Edward Capell whose books are among the riches of the Library of Trinity College, Cambridge, the mortality in these 'baggage books' has been exceptionally heavy. A notable instance is the fate of *The Sackful of News*. It was entered in the Stationers' Register in 1557/8 and often later; we know that it remained alive, because it is repeatedly referred to in Elizabethan literature; yet the earliest copy which can now be traced is dated 1673. Boswell was sometimes obliged to run half over London in order to fix a date correctly. He who would consult the early jest-books in the earliest editions must

---

[1] [Read before the Shakespeare Association of London on 26 November 1937, printed in the *Huntington Library Quarterly*, ii. 2 (January 1939), reprinted here with some additions and revisions.]

[2] 1638 edn., Pt. 2, Sect. 2, Memb. 4, p. 271.

travel half over the world—if not from China to Peru, at least from London to Washington and from Göttingen to California.

We owe it to a German scholar, Ernst Schulz, that a path has been cleared through this rather tangled subject. Perhaps his book has been neglected by English scholars. In *Die englischen Schwankbücher* (1912) he gave a list of those jest-books printed before 1640 to which he could obtain access;[1] he described their character and contents, and gave a list of what sources had been traced.[2] And he also gave a reprint of *Dobson's Dry Bobs*, a work of which more will be said later.

It may be argued that to train the guns of scholarship upon so slight a target as a jest-book is in itself a matter for jesting, and there is bound to be some incongruity between the theme and the treatment. Perhaps the incongruity is inevitable to the scholar. It is the same predicament which a lexicographer finds himself in when the exigencies of his craft call upon him to define, say, a simple sport of our childhood as 'a game in which small counters are caused to spring from the table into a bell-like or cylindrical receptacle, by pressing upon their edges with larger counters'.

Schulz classifies the jest-books under three headings: 'Lose Sammlungen', or collections of detached jests; 'Schwankbiographien', or jest-biographies; and 'Novellistische Schwanksammlungen', or collections of comic short stories or *novelle*. In this paper I accept that classification, and stop at 1640, except for an occasional raid beyond that date.

I also follow in the main his definition of the jest-book. It is a collection of comic prose tales or anecdotes designed for the entertainment of the reader. I exclude single jests, whether printed separately or to be found in pamphlets or plays. I exclude collections in verse, such as books of epigrams or a book like *Twelve Merry Jests of the Widow Edith*, and collections in which comic matter is mixed with serious, like the anecdotes and apophthegms which have survived from the ancient world and the *exempla* which have survived from the medieval. I exclude collections with a palpable design upon the reader, like the *Merry Jests Concerning Popes, Monks and Friars* of

---

[1] I attempt a supplement to this list on pp. 313–23, below.

[2] Schulz's list was based on the work of two scholars, H. de Vocht and A. L. Stiefel. For additional information and corrections, see Douglas Bush, 'Some Sources for the *Mery Tales, Wittie Questions, and Quicke Answeres*', M.P., xx (1923), pp. 275–80.

1617, which is a piece of Protestant propaganda. And I exclude humorous passages which do not contain some relic, however rudimentary, of narrative form. These reservations and exclusions may seem rigorous and sometimes arbitrary, but without them the theme becomes unmanageable. If we accept them, we can begin with Poggio.[1] And there is no harm in making the time-honoured statement that the practice of collecting jests into a book began in Renaissance Italy with Poggio, if we do not forget that the jests which he and other early compilers assembled were traditional and dateless and may once have pleased a contemporary of Chaucer or Sir Dagonet.

I

For some centuries Poggio earned more reputation by his collection of *Facetiae* than by his zeal in combing the monasteries of Europe for classical manuscripts. He was over seventy years of age when he finished the *Facetiae*, yet before his death, in 1459, he could boast that the collection was known throughout Italy, France, Spain, Germany, and England, and was read by all who understood Latin. The setting is the society of apostolic secretaries at the Roman *curia* among whom he spent the greater part of his life. In their *Bugiale*, or factory of lies, this most pagan society met to hear the news of the day, and converse on various subjects. 'There nobody was spared, and whatever met with our disapprobation was freely censured; often the Pope himself was the first theme of our criticism, and many people attended our gatherings for fear of being ridiculed in their absence.' Poggio's work was placed on the Index by the Council of Trent, perhaps as much for the sauciness of its jests on churchmen as for its indecencies. In spite of fifty years in an ecclesiastical environment he kept his paganism pure.

When Poggio published his work his old friends—Razello of Bologna, Antonio Lusco, the Roman Cinthio—were dead, the *Bugiale* had come to an end, 'omnisque jocandi confabulandique consuetudo sublata'. We can imagine that he was led to write the *Facetiae* because he wished to live again the days of the *Bugiale* and its merry secretaries, because he had a gift for the humorous and the

[1] At least we exclude some of the early *novellieri* like Sacchetti (c. 1330–c.1400), whose work had little or no circulation.

satirical, and because it was a challenge to his Latinity to translate into a learned tongue these stories of popular and vernacular origin. 'I have wished to try the experiment whether many things that seem difficult of expression in Latin may not be written without absurdity.' A like impulse lies behind the *Facetiae* of the German humanist Heinrich Bebel, who calls attention to the difficulty of writing 'lusus et iocos eleganter'. The same writer defends himself against a possible charge of licentiousness, by pleading that he had told no jest which he had not heard recited 'a grauibus viris in conuiuiis . . . et maiori parte apud matronas'.

Not long after Poggio's death even those Englishmen who could not read Latin were given the chance of sampling his jests. *A Hundred Merry Tales* has always had the reputation of being the first collection of jests in English, but pride of place should surely be given to the twelve 'Fables of Poge the Florentyn' printed in 1484 at the end of Caxton's *Fables of Aesop*. The spelling 'Poge' suggests—as was indeed the fact—that Poggio was known to Caxton in a French version.[1] Caxton called them fables, but only the seventh is a fable, and only the first nine are from Poggio. Of these twelve jests five are about women, and one of them—the third—is so little honest that the nineteenth-century editor Joseph Jacobs was 'fain to omit it'. Perhaps Caxton took more pleasure in the 'Fables of Alfonce', which immediately precede the 'Fables of Poge'. These descend, through many intermediary versions, from the *Disciplina clericalis* of Petrus Alphonsus, a Spanish Jew of the twelfth century. Some of these thirteen fables we should call jests, one or two are fables, but most of them have some tincture of the purpose for which the collection of Alphonsus was designed—the seasoning of sermons.[2] At the end of the 'Fables of Poge', and so at the end of his book, Caxton adds a story of his own, 'whiche a worshipful preest and a parsone told me late'. Its moral application is never in doubt, and the discrepancy between Caxton's tale and Poggio's jests is striking.

---

[1] Caxton's collection of the fables of 'Esope' followed by the fables of 'Auian', 'Alfonce', and 'Poge', descends from Stainhöwel by way of a French translation. 'Stainhöwel's *Äsop* is the parent of all the printed Aesops of Europe' (*The Fables of Aesop*, ed. Joseph Jacobs, 1889, i. 186).   [2] Ibid., pp. 198–9.

early seventeenth centuries 289

No relics of the jest-book have survived for the period between 1484 and 1525/6, the date of the *Hundred Merry Tales*. But the taste and the market were there, and among the pamphlets printed by Wynkyn de Worde are *The Fifteen Joys of Marriage*, *The Friar and the Boy*, *The Smith and his Dame*, and *A Merry Jest of the Miller of Abingdon*, while Notary printed More's *A Merry Jest how a Sergeant would learn to be a Friar*. All these were in verse. Prose at this period was seldom used for fun. Robert Copland complained:

> Olde morall bokes stonde styll vpon the shelfe
> I am in fere they wyll neuer be bought
> Tryfles and toyes they ben the thynges so sought.[1]

It was not until 1815 that fragments of the *Hundred Merry Tales* were rescued from an old binding by the Revd. J. J. Conybeare and edited by S. W. Singer. These are now in the Huth collection in the British Museum. The text of another edition, dated 1526, was well edited by H. Oesterley, in 1866, from a perfect copy discovered in the library of the University of Göttingen. A fragment, less than half a page, of yet another edition is in the Bagford collection in the British Museum (Harl. 5995). There were later editions, as we know from the Stationers' Registers and from the many Elizabethan references to the collection, but they have all perished.[2] It was from this ancient and long-popular collection that Benedick accused Beatrice of stealing her wit.

The extant copies or fragments of copies all come from the press of John Rastell, the brother-in-law of Sir Thomas More. He also published *The Book of a Hundred Riddles*, which we may regard perhaps as a companion piece. Only a small fragment of it survives. Hazlitt conjectured that the *Hundred Merry Tales* was made by John Heywood, with the assistance, possibly at the instigation, of Sir Thomas More. This is mere conjecture, yet the work is of a piece with other work of the More circle, with *Twelve Merry Jests of the Widow Edith* by More's body servant Walter Smith, and with the interludes and proverb collections of John Rastell's son-in-law, John Heywood.

---

[1] Verses in de Worde's edition of Chaucer's *The Assembly of Fowls* (1530), sig. A^v.
[2] There is a very late reference in *The London Chanticleer* (1659), sig. C$^{r\,\&\,v}$, where Ditty, a ballad man, cries for sale 'The seven wise men of *Gotam* [misprinted *Gotma*], a hundred merry tales, *Scoggins* jests'.

We can imagine More rejecting the licentious paganism of Poggio, but not the more honest fun of *A Hundred Merry Tales*. It is significant that the one jest which seems to derive from Poggio (No. 16 in Oesterley's text) can have appropriately attached to it the moral: 'Here ye may se that some haue remorse of conscyence of small venyall sinys and fere not to do gret offencys without shame of the world or drede of god: and as the comen prouerb is they stumble at a straw and lepe ouer a blok.'[1] Of the rest, two or three are traced by Oesterley and Schulz to the collection of Bebel, a few are from fabliaux, four are from the *Summa predicantium* of Bromyard, but the great majority appear to come from the native stock of oral tradition. *Tales and Quick Answers*, the jest-book which seems to have followed soon after the success of *A Hundred Merry Tales*, is much more humanistic in origin, and there are many borrowings from Poggio, Erasmus, More's Epigrams, Brant, Luscinius, and others.

It is not my intention to describe the numerous collections of detached jests published before 1640. Many of them are accessible in the three volumes of Hazlitt's misnamed *Shakespeare Jest-Books*—misnamed because neither Shakespeare nor his Beatrice was at any time reduced to stealing wit from these sources. Some generalizations may be hazarded about them, and if my observations are desultory I shall at least be keeping decorum.

There is little or no attempt at originality. When necessary, old stories about friars and monks are given a Protestant twist, and an outlandish tale may be naturalized by the change of a name. Poggio tells a story of a man who went upstream to search for his drowned wife because in life she was so contrary; in *Pasquil's Jests* (1604) the same story is told of one 'Coomes of Stapforth'. Moreover, jest-book borrows from jest-book, and the same story may appear again and again in slightly different shape. For example, there is the story of the man who hears burglars in his house one night, and cries out: 'I wonder you will lose time to seek anything here by night when I myself can find nothing by day.' It gets into print about 1480, in *Mensa Philosophica*, where it is told of a player,[2] and it is

---
[1] Here and in later quotations contractions have been expanded.
[2] Bk. IV, s.v. 'De histrionibus': 'Quidam histrio videns latrones in domo sua dixit, nescio quid vos hic potestis invenire in nocte cum ego nihil invenire possim clara die.' T. F. Dunn has found this story in *Scala Celi*, fol. 104b, no. 567, in Bebel, *Facetien*,

soon put into English in *Tales and Quick Answers* (? 1532). Here it is told of a 'poore man'. In 1576 it is told of a 'skoffer', in 1577 of a 'scattergood', in 1607 of a country schoolmaster, in 1609, 1614, 1637, and 1638 of a player again, and in 1633 once more of an unthrift.[1] Among the jest-books which have some claim to originality—or, to speak more cautiously, the sources of which have not for the most part been discovered—are Dekker and Wilkins's *Jests to make you Merry* (1607) and the three collections of John Taylor the Water Poet: *Wit and Mirth* (1629), *Bull, Bear, and Horse* (1638), and *Taylor's Feast* (1638). These writers seem to get their jests from the talk of the town. Taylor tells us in *Wit and Mirth* that its jests were 'Chargeably collected out of Tauernes, Ordinaries, Innes, Bowling Greenes, and Allyes, Alehouses, Tobacco shops, Highwayes, and Water-passages'. If some of the jests he got by 'relation and heare-say' are to be found in earlier collections, that is because they were still on men's tongues.

Some of these ancient jests seem capable of perpetual renovation, and the reader is often surprised to find a nineteenth- or twentieth-century jest in an Elizabethan setting. For example, well known— too well known—is the excuse of Midshipman Easy's wet nurse for the unlawfulness of her baby: that it was 'only a little one'. The jest was at least two centuries old when Captain Marryat used it.[2] Again I have always liked, and still like, an episode in Scott's journal which well illustrates his insensibility to what is merely flimsy in feeling—the supremacy in him, at his best, of sense over sensibility. He was visited at Abbotsford by Mrs. Hemans, author of 'Casabianca' and other poems once admired by those who recite in public places. They took a long walk together, tête-à-tête, and she told Scott of the peculiar melancholy attached to the words 'no more'. Here was a chance for a banquet of sentiment.

I could not help telling [he writes], as a different application of the

---

Bk. I, no. 32, in Herbert, *Catalogue of Romances*, iii. 711, no. 21 (a *jongleur* of Modena), and in Hazlitt, iii. 11, no. 23. See 'The Facetiae of the *Mensa Philosophica*', *Washington University Studies*, N.S., Language and Literature, No. 5, June 1934.

[1] See T. T. *The School master or Teacher of Table Philosophy* (1576), T. Kendall, *Flowers of Epigrams* (1577), Dekker and Wilkins, *Jests to make you Merry* (1607), *The Philosophers' Banquet* (1609 and 1614), *The History of Will Summers* (1637), told of Will Summers, *Gratiae Ludentes* (1638), *A Banquet of Jests*, Pt. 2 (1633).

[2] H. L. Oxon., *Gratiae Ludentes: Jests from the University* (1638), pp. 176–7.

words, how an old dame riding home along Cockenzie Sands, pretty bowzy, fell off the pillion, and her husband, being in good order also, did not miss her till he came to Prestonpans. He instantly returned with some neighbours, and found the good woman seated amidst the advancing tide, which began to rise, with her lips ejaculating to her cummers, who she supposed were still pressing her to another cup, 'Not ae drop mair, I thank you kindly.'[1]

The rudiments of the story are in a book of 1595:

A Drunkard passing ouer a bridge, his eies so glar'd, that he thought they were two bridges: and stepping vpon the wrong bridge downe hee tumbled into the brooke: where drinking his bellie full of water, he continued, saying: No more nowe (Hostesse) no more now.[2]

In a version of 1633 a few embellishments are added. A drunken waterman goes to sleep on the riverbank near Tower Wharf, on a moonlight night. And as the tide comes in he murmurs: 'No more drinke I thanke you hartily: but a few more clothes if you please, and then put out the candle.'[3]

It is the habit of every country to poke fun at foreigners and their stupidity at misunderstanding the manners and speech of the country they are visiting. The favourite butt of the sixteenth-century jest-book was the Welshman. Seven of the *Hundred Merry Tales* are jests about Welshmen, only one is about an Irishman. And the one about Scotchmen (No. 61) is mainly about a Welshman. One of the tales about Welshmen (No. 16) is told in Poggio of a Neapolitan shepherd, but of the other six (Nos. 30, 31, 61, 78, 81, and 92) no sources or even analogues are cited in Oesterley's learned edition. They seem to belong to the native stock. The Welshman is still prominent in so late a collection as *Gratiae Ludentes: Jests from*

---

[1] *The Journal of Sir Walter Scott* (1946), i. 96 (17 July 1829).

[2] Anthony Copley, *Wits, Fits and Fancies* (1595), sig. Aa^v. Surtees as well as Scott found the joke still serviceable over two hundred years later: 'When Porter... was making his round some half-hour after, he stumbled over Pigg, lying in the gutter in Duke-Street, muttering, as the dirty water trickled under his nose, "Not another drop, I thank ye. No, not another drop"' (*Handley Cross*, 1854, chap. liii).

[3] *A Banquet of Jests*, Pt. 2 (1633), pp. 130–1. But the story in this form was current much earlier; see Mulcaster, *Elementary* (1582), edited by E. Campagnac (1925), p. 2, who refers to 'that fellow, which will rather ly in a ditch all night & call for more clothes when he feleth more cold, and bid put out the candle, when he seith the moonshine'.

the *University* of 1638, where there are ten jests about Welshmen and none about Scotchmen and Irishmen. Many of these jests turn upon the Welshman's ignorance of English customs or of the English language, or upon his alleged passion for toasted cheese. 'I will rather trust... Parson Hugh the Welshman with my cheese...', says Ford in *The Merry Wives*, 'than my wife with herself.'[1] In some of the jests the Welshman is credited with a gift for ludicrous inconsistency of speech, so that in the early jest-books the Irish bulls are usually Welsh.

One meeting a Welshman carrying a Hare at his backe ask'd him how he would sell it: he answered: I will not sell it, but (hold heer) giue me a shilling, and take it.

One being accused at the Assizes for stealing a Bull, pleaded that he had brought him up from a calfe, defended himselfe, and was freed. A Welchman who was endited for stealing of a sword, was next tryed, and he hoping for the like successe, pleaded that hur had brought up hur sword from a dagger.[2]

In sixteenth-century Spanish jest-books this sort of jest is told about 'Biscains'. 'The Biskains', observed Thomas Wright, 'are not so subtle as the Castilians', and believed the climate was responsible for making them less crafty and wary.[3]

In English the word 'bull' in its modern sense seems to begin to emerge about the 1630s.[4] *The Book of Bulls* appeared in 1636, and in 1638 *A New Book of Mistakes. Or, Bulls with Tales, and Bulls without Tales*. 'There was as much wit shewed in breaking a good bull', wrote the author of *Gratiae Ludentes*, 'so it were voluntarily done, as in the best jest, which speech another confirming, said, that it was

[1] II. ii. 269–72. [2] Copley, sig. V$^{r\,\&\,v}$; *Gratiae Ludentes*, pp. 160–1.
[3] Thomas Wright, *The Passions of the Mind* (1604), sig. a. Copley (op. cit.), following a Spanish original (see below, p. 295), devotes a section to 'Biscayns and Fools'.
[4] In *O.E.D.* the earliest example of 'bull' in the sense of a 'ludicrous inconsistency of speech' is dated 1640, and Tilley's first example is dated 1639. Of 'bull' in the more general sense of 'jest' *O.E.D.* gives an example dated 1630, though in this example the word may carry its narrower meaning. An earlier example of 'bull' in its general sense may be found in Fletcher's *Wit without Money* (printed 1639, but dated by Chambers *c.* 1614): 'wits blasted with your bulls'. John Taylor's lines in *Bull, Bear, and Horse* (sig. A6) suggest that the narrower, modern sense was new in 1638:
  And now of late a *Bull's* a Common Creature,
  For men (with *nonsence*) do speak *Bull's* by Nature.
See an article on 'The Origin of Bulls' in W. J. Lawrence, *Speeding up Shakespeare* (1937), pp. 144–58.

harder to speake good nonsence, than bad good sence.' In the same year (1638), John Taylor gave this example:

A Gentleman riding in the Countrey, attended with one Servingman, they met a fellow that was a stride upon a Cowe, the Servingman said, Master behold, yonder is a strange sight. What is it said the Gentleman? why sir (said his man) looke you sir, *there is one Rides on Horseback upon a Cowe; that's a great* Bull, *said the Gentleman*; nay sir, said his man, *it is no Bull, I know it is a Cowe by his Teats*.[1]

Ease of communication and the lack of it account for the prominence of jests about the Welsh and the rarity of jests about the Scotch. After 1603 we might have expected to find more about the Scotch. But for some time after the accession of James VI of Scotland to the English throne it was safer to break jests upon the Scotch in conversation than in print. The experience of the authors of *Eastward Ho* was a deterrent. When the Scotch do make their rare appearances before 1640, they usually come off best. One of the most familiar jests is that recorded, from Roger de Hoveden, in Camden's *Remains*. Duns Scotus, sitting at table with Charles the Bald, emperor and king of France, 'behaved himselfe as a slovenly Scholler, nothing courtly; whereupon the Emperour asked him merrily, *Quid interest inter Scotum and Sotum*; What is the difference beteene a Scot and a Sot? He merrily, but yet malapertly answered, *Mensa*, The Table; as though the Emperour were the Sot, and he the Scot.'[2] In a later jest-book the story is told about a man called Scot and the jest is spoiled, but as Mr. Fitzherbert says in Boswell, 'it is not every man that can *carry a bon mot*.'[3] More in the modern style is a jest in a book of 1595: 'A Scot was preaching how that all men are one an others neighbour and brother in Christ, euen the Turke, the Iew, the Moore, the Caniball, the farre Indian: and then concluded: Yea and the very Englishman is our neighbour too.'[4]

It may be thought that the jest is international in character, that it crosses seas and frontiers with as much ease as the riddle, the fable, or the proverb. But this is not true of all jests, and particularly

---

[1] *Bull, Bear, and Horse*, sig. B8ᵛ.
[2] 1637 ed., pp. 236–7. That Duns Scotus could never have sat at table with Charles the Bald is of no consequence. The story is also told in J. Parinchef, *An Extract of Examples* [1572], p. 135, 'Ex domino Foxe'.
[3] *Life of Johnson*, ed. G. B. Hill, ii. 350.   [4] Copley, sig. Oᵛ.

of the quibble. An interesting and very full collection of jests, not noticed by Schulz, was produced by Anthony Copley in 1595. *Wits, Fits and Fancies* is in part a translation from the *Floresta Española* of Melchior de Santa Cruz de Dueñas, but in part it is a collection of English jests; and in dedicating his work to the voyager, George, Earl of Cumberland—the Spaniard had dedicated *his* to Don John of Austria—Copley remarks: 'Diuers of them are of mine own inserting, and that without any iniury I hope to my Authour: the which are easily to be discerned from his, for that they taste more Englishlie.' Now, the jests which taste most 'Spanishly' are those which turn upon verbal quibbles. For example, in the section 'Of Equiuocates in Speech', we find '*Roque* in Spanish is a Chesseman so called, and *Dama* is a Gentlewoman, and the Queene at Chesse-play: One *Senior Roque* married a faire Dame and a rich, and a friend of his hearing of it, said: Oh happy *Roque* that couldst giue so faire a *Dama* the mate.'[1] But while Copley says his explanatory grace the jest cools.

In the country of El Dorado, Candide was surprised to find that all the king's *bons mots* still appeared to be *bons mots* after they had been translated. To Addison, too, the best way to try a piece of wit was to see if it vanished in the translation. But Addison and Voltaire were writing in an age when quibblings with words and quibblings with sense had long since gone out of fashion in literary circles. In the late sixteenth and seventeenth centuries they were in their heyday, and, if we put such characteristic collections as Copley's or Dekker and Wilkins's *Jests to make you Merry*, John Taylor's *Wit and Mirth*, or *A Banquet of Jests* (Part 1, 1630; Part 2, 1633), beside such early collections as the *Hundred Merry Tales*, we find that jests tend to depend less and less upon situation and more and more upon wordplay and the turn of a phrase. Quintilian had stated that laughter was concerned in things or in words, 'in rebus aut in verbis'.[2] Dekker and Wilkins seem to be making something like the same distinction when they distinguish between 'a Jest spoken' and 'a Jest done'.[3] They promise both, but they give few that do not depend upon words.[4]

[1] Copley, sig. Y2.   [2] *Institutio oratoria*, VI. iii. 22–3.   [3] Sig. B.
[4] See also Thomas Wilson's *Art of Rhetoric* (1560), ed. G. H. Mair (1909), pp. 144–5.

Of 'Jests spoken' they observe that 'the most sudden is the best', and when wit became fashionable, jests tended to become pointed, sudden, and brief, and the aim was to make them 'cry tink in the close'.

A Gentleman being at Sermon, where a dull fellow preacht almost all his Auditory out of the Church, said that he made a very mooving Sermon.

[A gentleman] complained that the beere at such a Colledge was dead, that may very well be said his Companion, for it was weake when I were here last.

Mr. Popham, when hee was Speaker, and the Lower House had sate long, and done in effect nothing; comming one day to Queene Elizabeth, she said to him, *Now, Mr. Speaker, what hath passed in the Lower House?* He answered; *If it please your Maiestie, seuen weekes.*[1]

Sometimes, as of old, the jest depends on an extravagance of situation or of phrasing, but here too the tendency is towards point and brevity.

A Gentleman sitting at a play, a Marchant by chaunce sate afore him, whose hat was so high and broade, that it hindered his view of the play: whereupon he saide vnto him: My good friend, I beseech you doe off your hatte a while, for I assure you it will greatly benefite my eie-sight.

A prisoner at Newgate, having lost money out of his pockets, looking about on his fellow Prisoners said, how now Gentlemen what have wee theeves among ourselves.

One seeing a Meteor fal down when an Astronomer was taking the height of a Starre with his *Jacobs* staffe, cryed out unto him, O well shot ifaith!

[One] seeing a little fellow with a great bushy beard, askt who it was that stood behind the beard. [This jest is attributed by Aubrey to Richard Corbet, and perhaps rightly.]

A Divine, Preaching a funerall Sermon for one that had lived and dyed very badly, sayd to his Neighbours: how he lived you know. How he dyed I know. And where he is God knowes. Thus much by

---

[1] The last example is from Bacon's *Apophthegms New and Old* (1625), No. 59; the others from *Gratiae Ludentes*, pp. 55, 110.

early seventeenth centuries 297

way of Praeface, now to my Text, [According to Sir George Buc these words were used by Nowell, Dean of St. Paul's in a funeral sermon preached on Sir Richard Sackville (nicknamed Fillsack), father of the poet; see R. C. Bald, 'A Manuscript Book by Sir George Buc', *M.L.R.*, xxx (1935), p. 8.][1]

To our taste many of these jests do not rise above the level expected of a motto in a Christmas cracker. Yet they are just the sort of jest which the intelligent John Manningham of the Middle Temple was hearing from his friends in 1602–3 and recording in his Diary side by side with his shrewd notes upon sermons and preachers.

One said, yong Mr. Leake was verry rich, and fatt, 'True', said B. Reid, 'pursy men are fatt for the most part.'

One Mr. Ousley of the Middle Temple, a yong gallant, but of a short cutt, ouertaking a tall stately stalking caualier in the streetes, made noe more a doe but slipt into an ironmongers shop, threwe of his cloke and rapier, fitted himselfe with bells, and presently cam skipping, whistling, and dauncing the morris about that long swaggerer, whoe, staringly demaunding what he ment: 'I cry you mercy,' said the gent., 'I tooke you for a May pole.' (*Ch. Da. nar.*)[2]

The first is a clinch, and the second a dry bob or a jeer or perhaps a flout, but it would need the precision of a Polonius to make distinctions between Bragardisms, Bulls, Carwhichets, Clinches, Conceits, Dry Bobs, Flashes, Jerks, Mistakings (now called spoonerisms),[3] Quips, Rodomontades, Taunts, Whimzies, and Yerks.[4] Moreover, if I continue to quote the jests of our forefathers I shall lay myself

---

[1] The five jests are from Copley, op. cit., sig. C4; *Gratiae Ludentes*, pp. 151, 20, 171; *A Banquet of Jests and Merry Tales by Archie Armstrong* (1889 edn.), p. 98. Cf. also *A Banquet of Jests*, Pt. I, p. 78.

[2] *Diary of John Manningham*, ed. John Bruce (1868), pp. 48, 53.

[3] Cf. Henry Peacham's *Compleat Gentleman* (1634), ed. G. S. Gordon (1906), p. 231: 'A melancholy Gentleman sitting one day at table, where I was started vp vpon the sudden, and meaning to say, *I must goe buy a dagger*, by transposition of the letters, said: Sir, *I must goe dye a begger.*' Puttenham gives examples under '*Hipallage.* or the Changeling', *The Art of English Poesy*, ed. Willcock and Walker (1936), pp. 171–2.

[4] Erasmus, *Apophthegms*, translated Udall (1542), distinguishes only between 'scornes, taunts, checkes, iestes, or merie conceipted sayings to laugh at'. Puttenham provides examples to help us to distinguish various kinds of mockery: the 'Drie mock' (*Ironia*), the 'Bitter taunt' (*Sarcasmus*), the 'Merry scoffe' (*Asteismus*), the 'Fleering frumpe' (*Micterismus*), the 'Broad floute' (*Antiphrasis*), the 'Priuy nippe' (*Charientismus*) (ed. cit., pp. 189–91).

open to the charge which Quintilian feared, of overloading his book with illustrations and turning it into a common jest-book.

II

Let us pass to those jests to which some semblance of unity has been given by grouping them round the figure of a popular hero. The unity is only that of hero—a structure as primitive as that of the amoeba. Yet it is here, as much as in the *novella*, that we find writers groping towards the form of the modern novel. 'Schwankbiographien' is Schulz's name for them, and there is no harm in calling them jest-biographies if we do not attach any value to them as biographies. If the original impulse to the detached jest-books came from humanism, the impulse to the jest-biography came from the folk literature of Germany and the Low Countries. The earliest English books of this kind are translations. They are among the rarest of English books, for they exist for the most part in unique copies, or fragments of copies. The foul boor, Markolf, who outwits the wisdom of Solomon with his coarse humour and coarser actions, the ingenious and facetious parson of Kalenberg, and that gross mocker and deceiver, Howleglas, who is Eulenspiegel, are the three characters of German folk-humour who were introduced to English readers in the late fifteenth and early sixteenth centuries.[1] The humour of these practical jokers, especially Howleglas, is for the most part scatological. 'We could not read Eulenspiegel', says C. H. Herford, 'but for the light which it throws upon a society which could and did.' Of these three it is only Howleglas who has any appreciable influence on the form and subject matter of the English jest-biographies.

The history of the assimilation of this foreign matter into English story has been fully told by Brie in his *Eulenspiegel in England* (1903) and earlier by Herford in *Studies in the Literary Relations of England and Germany in the Sixteenth Century* (1886). Not so well known to literary historians is the vogue in this country of a piece of folk-humour of French origin. I have said that a notable instance of the

---

[1] Spenser gave Harvey 'Howletglasse, with Skoggin, Skelton, and L[a]zarillo' on 20 December 1578, to be read by 1st of January on pain of Harvey's forfeiting to Spenser his Lucian (*Marginalia*, ed. G. C. Moore Smith, 1913, p. 23).

early seventeenth centuries 299

mortality among jest-books is the fate of *A Sackful of News*, printed in 1577/8 and often later, yet not now to be traced in any copy earlier than 1673. Even more remarkable is the total disappearance of the English translation of *Gargantua*. It is not Rabelais's masterpiece that we have to do with here, but the champion of King Arthur—the hero of folktale whose fantastic exploits had been published in France in two distinct *Croniques* in 1532 and 1534.[1] There would seem to have been an English translation by 1570, for six books (i.e. copies) of 'Gargantua' are mentioned among the books supplied by Abraham Veale, printer and bookseller, to Robert Scott, a bookseller of Norwich, in an action brought by Veale in Michaelmas Term 1571.[2] There is also a reference to Gargantua as a trifling tale in E. Fenton's *Certain Secret Wonders* (1569), and in 1575 Laneham mentioned *Gargantua* among the many books of folklore which Captain Cox, the Coventry mason had 'at his fingers endz'.[3] The notorious John Danter entered *'the historie* of *GARGANTUA'* on the Stationers' Register on 4 December 1594, but what is more striking is that, in the seventeenth century, publishers still thought this pamphlet-chronicle worth the expenditure of a sixpenny registration fee; copyright was made over from Thomas Pavier's widow to Brewster and Bird on 4 August 1626, and from them to John

---

[1] Cf. *The Tale of Gargantua and King Arthur, by François Girault, c. 1534*, ed. Huntington Brown (1932). Brown also reprints the *Croniques* of 1532, and supplies evidence that the English translation was from the text of 1534.

[2] *The Library*, 3rd Series, vii (1916), p. 323.

[3] [I have removed from the text F. P. W.'s repetition here of his discovery published in the preceding year, of the earliest reference to Gargantua in England which he interpreted as a reference to the folk-tale hero; see p. 266 above and note. He noted here that his article went to press before he had seen O. J. Campbell's note on 'The Earliest English Reference to Rabelais' swork', *H.L.Q.*, ii (1938), pp. 53–8. Professor Campbell stated that the first edition of *The Book of Merchants* (1534), of which the Huntington Library owns the unique copy, has the names of Pantapole and Pantagruel on its title-page. The work is a translation of Antoine de Marcourt's *Le Livre des marchands* (Neuchâtel, 1533). Marcourt, a Calvinist, wrote to attack the Catholic clergy and took Rabelais as an ally here; but in the following year Calvin condemned Rabelais, so that in his second edition (1534) Marcourt expunged the names of Pantapole and Pantagruel. The first English translation (which F. P. W. had not seen) translates the first French edition; but the second (1547), in which he found the reference to Gargantua, follows a later French edition, probably the second and omits Pantapole and Pantagruel from the title-page. Their presence there in the first edition makes clear that the later reference to Gargantua is to Rabelais's hero. Professor Campbell noted that this antedates by twenty-one years Huntington Brown's earliest reference to Rabelais in England. H.G.]

Wright, Junior, on 13 June 1642. In view of these late entries it is remarkable that no copy has survived, not even in the debased form of an eighteenth-century chapbook. Nevertheless, Gargantua's substantial form is to be numbered among the popular heroes of English folklore, together with Friar Rush, Tom Thumb, and Robin Goodfellow.

It is in the pleasant pamphlet, *Robin Goodfellow, His Mad Pranks, and Merry Jests* (1628), that the most interesting impact of these foreign influences, and especially of Howleglas, is revealed. One or two of the pranks of this mischievous spirit are modelled on Howleglas—some details of his early life, and his adventures with a tailor—but they are transformed in the telling, and from the 'Once vpon a Time' of the opening words we find ourselves in a world that is far removed from the beastliness of Howleglas. We are in the world of Puck—a practical joker, it is true (like Howleglas), as 'The wisest aunt, telling the saddest tale', realized when she sat 'on a three-foot stool' that was not there; but the Robin Goodfellow of the play and of the pamphlet is no coarse peasant but an honest fairy, whose shrewd and knavish tricks are lightened and adorned by song:

> Within and out, in and out round as a ball,
> With hither and thither, as strait as a line,
> With Lilly, Germander, and sops in wine:
> > with sweet-bryer,
> > and bon-fire,
> > and straw-berry wyer,
> > and Collumbine.
>
> When Saturne did liue, there liued no poore,
> The King and the Begger with rootes did dine,
> With Lilly, Germander, and sops in wine:
> > with sweet-bryer,
> > and bon-fire
> > and straw-berry wyer,
> > and Collumbine.[1]

We are nearer the world of Howleglas when we read the jests attached to the names of Skelton, Long Meg of Westminster,

[1] Sig. C2^v.

George a Greene, Oliver Smug, Tarlton, Peele, and especially Scogin. Of these the least-known and the best is *The Pinder of Wakefield: Being the merry History of George a Greene the lusty Pinder of the North. Briefly shewing his manhood and his brave merriments amongst his boon Companions. A Pill fit to purge melancholy in this drooping age. Read, then judge. With the great Battle fought betwixt him and Robin Hood, Scarlet and little John, and after of his living with them in the Woods. Full of pretty Histories, Songs, Catches, Jests, and Riddles* (1632). It has not the biographical sequence or the topographical detail of the story of that other north-country hero, George Dobson,[1] but in the rich variety of its contents it excels all other books of the kind. Parts of the book are arranged in a rough framework as George a Greene calls upon the company that drinks with him each to 'tell his tale, reade his riddle, sing his song or Catch', or pay a sixpenny forfeit; but the framework is dropped when it suits the author's purpose. Short jests are mingled with tales told at length. Many of the short jests, as we should expect, are ancient, but the tales told at length sometimes preserve authentic news of the manners of a sixteenth-century country town—for *The Pinder of Wakefield*, like *Dobson's Dry Bobs*, is a country book without any tincture of London manners. The most remarkable of the long tales is that describing the adventures of a soldier who spends three nights in a haunted house. The reader cannot fail to be reminded of the tale, in Grimm, of the young fellow who watched three nights in an enchanted castle in order to learn how to shiver.

Riddles, catches, songs, and ballads add to the variety of the book. Among the riddles is that put to Pericles in Shakespeare's play;[2] and among the catches is 'Nose, nose, jolly red nose', sung by Merrythought in *The Knight of the Burning Pestle*. The ballads of *The Jolly Pinder of Wakefield* and *Musselburgh Field* are to be found here in texts earlier than any given in F. J. Child's collection of *English and Scottish Popular Ballads* (Nos. 124 and 172).[3]

Some of the heroes of these books—George a Greene, Long Meg, Oliver Smug—are as legendary as Howleglas, and it is only with

[1] See below, pp. 306–8.   [2] I. i. 64–71.
[3] Child's only text of *Musselburgh Field* is from the Percy MS. There is a text in *Choice Drollery* (1656) ed. J. B. Ebsworth (1876).

reference to their form that we can call them 'jest-biographies'. Even Scogin's historical existence has been doubted, and Richard Johnson's *The Pleasant Conceits of Old Hobson*[1] (1607) is little more than a titivation of *Merry Tales, Witty Questions, and Quick Answers* (1567), which in turn is an enlargement of *Tales and Quick Answers* (c. 1535). Given some turn for humour, some oddity of character, and a dash of espièglerie (a word thought to be a corruption of Eulenspiegel), the snowball of a man's reputation easily collected to itself the jests that lay in its way. But some respect was paid to a man's position in the state. There is no early collection of Sir Thomas More's jests.[2] And I have no doubt that William Fleetwood would have become the hero of a jest-book if instead of being Recorder of London he had been a mere player or poet.[3]

If we could depend upon them the most interesting of the sixteenth-century jest-biographies would be those of Skelton, Tarlton, and Peele, but it is impossible to disentangle fact from fiction. The *Merry Tales* of Skelton were not printed until 1566/7.[4] This is more than a quarter of a century after his death, but one of the jests had already been told of him in his lifetime, in the *Hundred Merry Tales* (No. 41) and another had appeared in *Tales and Quick Answers*. The collection of Tarlton's jests is known to have existed a few years after his death in 1588, and while some of them have been traced to sources older than the jester others are doubtless genuine. More

---

[1] A London haberdasher, not Milton's Hobson, as some have said.

[2] Gabriel Harvey noted five of his favourite Sir Thomas More's 'Jestes reportid in these words unto me'; see S. A. Tannenbaum, 'Some Unpublished Harvey Marginalia', *M.L.R.*, xxv (1930), pp. 327–31. Camden put some of them into his section on 'Grave Speeches and wittie Apothegmes of worthy Personages of this Realme in former times' (*Remains*, 1637 edn., pp. 274–9). He adds 'a few Tales, or call them what you please', from More's works.

[3] Recorder from 1571 to 1591. Isolated jests are recorded in: *The Journal of Sir Roger Wilbraham*, ed. H. S. Scott (under April 1593); Manningham's *Diary*, ed. Bruce, p. 107; Copley, op. cit., sigs. P2ᵛ–P3 (four jests in all); Dekker and Wilkins, *Jests to make you Merry*, sig. B3; *The Pinder of Wakefield*, sig. E4; and Aubrey, *Brief Lives*, ed. Clark (1898), i. 253. See also Dekker's *News from Hell* (1606), sig. E. Fleetwood's reputation was such that it was sufficient for Dekker to refer to him *sine nomine* as 'the old Recorder'. His letters bear out Anthony Wood's description of him as being 'of a marvellous merry and pleasant conceit'.

[4] But W. Nelson, *John Skelton Laureate* (New York, 1939), p. 109 notes that 'among the papers that came into the possession of Thomas Cromwell between 1530 and 1532 is a piece entitled *The Jests of Skelton*' (*Letters and Papers* vii, No. 923 [vii]). Was this a collection similar to the *Merry Tales* or even the jest-book itself?

might be said for the biographical interest of Peele's jests. They exist in an edition of 1607, not so long after Peele's death, and they have not been traced to a particular source. It is possible that this spirited collection of cony-catching stories preserves some authentic information about the dramatist.

On the other hand, the jest-book writers' practice (complained of in the *Female Jester*, 1771–8) of attributing the 'Wit of our Forefathers to their would-be-witty-Sons; . . . by dexterously changing *Ben Johnson* to *Dr. Johnson*, and *Joe Miller* to *Sam Foote*'[1] was also followed in earlier centuries. And so it often happens that the jokes attached to famous men are libels upon the dead. For example, Ben Jonson in tattered dress was refused admittance to the house of Lord Craven, and while he and the porter were at words Craven returned home. 'No, no, quoth my Lord, you cannot be *Ben Johnson* who wrote the *Silent Woman*, you look as if you could not say *Bo* to a Goose: *Bo*, cry'd Ben, very well, said my Lord, who was better pleas'd at the Joke, than offended at the Affront, I am now convinced, by your Wit, you are *Ben Johnson*.'[2] If this had been characteristic, who would have said, 'O rare Ben Jonson'?

III

These jest-biographies do not differ in form from the collections of detached jests, except for the accident that they relate to one person. The emphasis is still on the isolated jest, and there is little or no attempt to link jest with jest or build up character or setting. There were, however, a few collections of comic short stories in prose—'Novellistische Schwanksammlungen', as Schulz calls them —in which comic incident was elaborated after the manner of the *novella*. While the jest-biographies and collections of detached jests tell jokes, the comic *novelle* also tell stories.

It is no use quarrelling with Schulz for placing Richard Edwards's *Comic Stories* (1570) under 'Lose Sammlungen' instead of 'Novellistische Sammlungen'. The existence of the book depends upon the authority of the first historian of English poetry, who claimed to

---

[1] Cited by T. S. Graves in 'Jonson in the Jest Books', in *The Manly Anniversary Studies in Language and Literature* (1923), p. 139.
[2] *Joe Miller's Jests* (1739), No. 45.

have seen it in the library of 'the late Mr. William Collins', together with Skelton's *Necromancer*, printed by Wynkyn de Worde in 1504, and *Fabell's Ghost*, 'printed by John Rastell in 1533'. It is to be feared that all these works, as also *The Children of the Chapel Whipt*, Hake's *The Touchstone of Wits* (1588),[1] and the ballad on Romeo and Juliet,[2] existed only in the mischievous brain of Tom Warton.[3] A book mentioned in a footnote by Warton[4] certainly exists, and can be found in a unique copy in the Capell collection, although I do not know that any writer except Capell has done more than refer to it by title. It is *The Mirror of Mirth, and Pleasant Conceits* (1583), a translation of some of the *Nouvelles recréations* of Bonaventure Des Périers. According to the title-page the translator was R. D., and according to the address to the reader he was T. D.;[5] but R. D. or T. D., he was a bungling translator and he knew it: 'this simpel and rude worke, the grace and beautie whereof beeing strypped from his Countrey guise, and now newly wrapped in this strang attyre, is not onely blemished by meanes of the translators vnskillfulnesse, but as it were spoyled both of fauour and fashion'.

In the first edition of Des Périers, published in 1558, there are ninety 'Nouvelles', and out of the first fifty-nine of these the Englishman translated thirty-nine.[6] Some of the tales which he chooses are of considerable length, so that his book may as appropriately be mentioned among the *novelle* or 'story-books' (the word is Capell's) as among the collections of detached jests. It so happens, however, that the most famous of the tales which he chooses is also

---

[1] Cf. C. Edmonds's edition of Hake's *News out of Paul's Churchyard* (1872), p. xxxviii.

[2] See Halliwell-Phillipps, *Outlines* (1881), ii. 273.

[3] Cf. D. Nichol Smith, 'Warton's History of English Poetry', *Proceedings of the British Academy*, xv. 95–6. The last remaining shred of evidence for the existence of Richard Edwards's *Comic Stories* as the source for the Induction to *The Taming of the Shrew* was disposed of by Charles C. Mish in a letter to the *Times Literary Supplement* (28 Dec. 1951). [4] iii (1781), p. 259.

[5] According to the title-page of the edition of 1592, the book was 'Englished by T. D.' It is not impossible that the translator was Thomas Deloney. In the same year (1583), he published his *A Declaration Made by the Archbishop of Collen* (i.e. Cologne), translated from the Latin: 'this simple translation, faithfully & iustlie done according to the coppy.' See *Works*, ed. F. O. Mann (1912), p. 276, ll. 7–8. Mann (p. viii) gives some evidence that Deloney knew French.

[6] Nouvelles III–VII, XIII, XV, XVI, XVIII–XXIII, XXV, XXVI, XVIII–XXXV, XXXVII, XXXVIII, XL–XLII, XLIV, XLVI, XLIX, LII, LV, LVIII, LIX.

early seventeenth centuries

one of the shortest. It has been preserved in the amber of La Fontaine,[1] and in one form or other is still current in our nurseries. One might think it the invention of the nation which was to give to the world the tales of Mother Goose, were there not reason to believe that it is older than France herself.

> a good wife . . . sometime caried a pale of milke to the market, thinking to sell it, as pleased her, making her reckoning thus. First she would sell her milk for ij.d. and with this ij.d. buy xii. egs, which she wold set to brood vnder a hen, and she would haue 12. Chickons, these chykons being growne vp, she would kerue them, and by that meanes, they should be capons: these capons would be worth, (being yong) fiue pence a piece: that is, iust a crowne: with the which she would buye two pigs, a Sow and a Boare, and they growing great, would bring forth twelue others, the which she would sell (after she had keept them a while) for fiue grotes a piece: that is, iust twentie shillings. Then she would buie a Mare, that would bring foorth a faire Foale, the which would grow vp, and be so gentill and faire, that he would playe, skip, leape, and fling, and crie we he he after euery beast that should passe by, and for the ioye she conceyued of her supposed coult, in her iollitie counterfeiting to show his lustynesse, her pale of milcke fell downe of her head, and was all spilt: there laie her egs, her chikons, her capons her pigs, her mare, her coulte, and al vppon the ground.[2]

Apart from *The Mirror of Mirth* there are only three English collections of comic *novelle*: Tarlton's *News out of Purgatory* [1590], *The Cobbler of Canterbury* (1590; reissued in 1630, with additions and omissions, as *The Tinker of Turvey*), and *Westward for Smelts* (1620). If all comic tales of this kind were included—whether they occurred in collections of comic *novelle* or not—the list would be greatly swollen. Barnabe Rich, Deloney, Dekker, and other popular writers would find a place. Then, there is the translation of the *Decameron* (1620).[3] And there is *The Queen of Navarre's Tales* (1597), a translation of seventeen stories from the *Heptameron*, most of which are

---

[1] *Œuvres*, ed. H. Régnier (1884), x. 145–54, 495–8.
[2] Sig. D4^r & ^{v}. This is the one tale from *The Mirror of Mirth* which Capell quoted in his *School of Shakespeare*. The story also appears in Scogin's *Jests* (1613; sig. E2^v), the compiler of which clearly consulted the translation of 1583.
[3] See W. Farnham, 'England's Discovery of the *Decameron*', *P.M.L.A.*, xxxix (1924).

comic, but not all; for the last tale is the story of Hyrenee, who is Peele's and Pistol's Hiren and Dr. Johnson's Irene. Even so, when the full list had been drawn up, it would be found that the comic *novelle* were never so popular in England as in Italy and in France. Perhaps the censorship did not permit them to be.[1]

The ancestry if not the contents of these three English collections of comic *novelle* is most respectable. They descend from the highly stylized versions of fabliaux and other comic material in the *Decameron* and its many imitations and in the *Canterbury Tales*. While the chief source of the tales in these collections is the *Decameron*, the framework is English: Tarlton's news from purgatory revealed to a gallant sleeping in the fields near the theatre in Shoreditch; a company, mostly of the lower or middling classes, who tell 'Canterbury Tales' as they sail down the river in Gravesend barge; and a boatful of fishwives on their way upstream from London to Kingston. If Boccaccio presides over these tales, Chaucer presides over the framework. But, as the author of *The Cobbler of Canterbury* modestly observes, '*Chaucer* . . . the father of English Poets . . . shot a shoote which many haue aimed at but neuer reacht to.'

There is one work, of unusual originality in form and in subject-matter, which applies to the jest-biography the technique of the *novella*, with a result that is different from either. In sixteen chapters the anonymous author of *Dobson's Dry Bobs* narrates the life and merry jests of George Dobson. When a small boy he is taken under the guardianship of his uncle, Sir Thomas Pentley, a canon of Durham in the time of Queen Mary. He is sent to the reading school at the Church of St. Nicholas, where he is cruelly bullied and put upon by the other children until he revolts against his oppressors and makes them 'cry miserere'. Promoted to chorister in the cathedral singing school, he grows into a sturdy lad, becomes 'Captaine of Schooles' and the ringleader in all sorts of escapades. Among those on whom he breaks his dry bobs are the usher, his

---

[1] There is evidence, of course, that many Englishmen could and did read them in their original tongues. Lodge recommends the *Serées* of Bouchet and the 'Nouels' of Des Périers, together with Rabelais and 'Aretine in his mother *Nana*', as certain means of wasting time and corrupting the soul. See *Wit's Misery* (1596), sig. M4ᵛ–N. Also, John Wolf, a London printer, printed many books in Italian. The *Decameron* was licensed to him but no edition by him has been identified.

uncle, the alewife of Witton Gilbert, his school friends, and his schoolmaster. At eighteen years of age he 'had so well profited in Musike, and in the Latine tongue, that he was supposed fit for the Vniuersity', and through the recommendation of the Dean of Durham he obtains a scholar's place at Christ's College. For three years he behaves himself to admiration, until 'he was called to the publike schooles, to hold his disputes in open audience of the Vniuersitie, when he rushed againe into his olde humours'. Unlike the prolusions of another undergraduate of Christ's College, Dobson's end in horseplay. His first opponent is a Welshman, and the theme 'An aër sit substantia corporea'. Worsted in logic, Dobson discomfits the Welshman with a piece of cheese. The term following, as primate of the northern companies, he is defendant before the University in questions of philosophy against certain Kentishmen, and provokes a fight in the schools by pictorial allusions to Kentish longtails. In his third public act his dry bob is so outrageous that it leads to his expulsion from the University, 'at the very instant when he should haue proceeded Bachelour'. A last chapter huddles his experiences as an ostler and a serving-man, his narrow escape from the gallows, and his last years as canon of Durham Cathedral like his uncle before him.

Dobson's Dry Bobs is not described in any history of the novel known to me, yet it is nearer the novel form than most works of that time. And the book is accessible enough, for it was edited by Schulz in 1912 with an elaborate introduction. The hero's character is developed from boyhood to manhood in a natural biographical sequence, and he is firmly placed in his environment both by the development of the subordinate characters with whom he comes in contact and by the rich topographical detail which displays the author's intimate knowledge of Durham and the neighbourhood and of Cambridge. Starting out to write a jest-biography—he calls Dobson 'Heire to Skoggin'—he has achieved a rogue-novel, and he has done so without borrowing from his predecessors.

It is no forraine translation, but a homebred subiect, nor doth hee desire anie other thing than his patrimony, which is, as being the eldest sonne of Skoggin, to be esteemed for no Changeling, onely by how much the propertie of his father was fitte to be altred, hee hath by so much, in the quantitie of his time reformed: he is to auntient men mirth, to the middle age profite, and to youth nurture, pregnant witte; To conclude, hee is George Dobson, whose pleasant merriments are worthy to be registred among the famous Recordes of the ieasting Worthies: yea, hee hath proceeded farther in degree than Garagantua, Howleglasse, Tiell, Skoggin, olde Hobson, or Cocle.[1]

The author has taken his material from the life about him, but when we ask what quality of life is displayed in this novel we receive no satisfactory answer. We are invited to a banquet of rough practical jokes or the scandal incident to parish gossip. One of the chapters is much ado about the theft of a pudding, and another about the sophistication of a barrel of ale; and the material will not stand the elaboration which the author has given to it. The pity is that Dobson was truly the heir to Scogin who was the heir to Howleglas, and while *Dobson's Dry Bobs* lacks the beastliness of *Howleglas* it does not rise above the same level of practical joking. Here was a form as adequate as *Moll Flanders* for the writing of a novel, if an author 'had a mind to try it'. But in England for more than a century the mind was wanting which could fill this form. I say in England, for in Spain the form had been richly filled half a century before Dobson was created. In *La Vida de Lazarillo de Tormes*, of how little importance are the practical jokes beside the refinement of irony and the mordancy of phrase with which a whole society is brought before our eyes! It was long before an English book of the kind was worthy to become a part of the European tradition.

IV

In conclusion let me ask for whom were these books written and for what purpose. They served for entertainment, of course. They were pretty and pleasant to drive away the tediousness of a winter's evening. While the farmer sat in his chair turning the crab in the fire, he listened to his son reading them, and laughed till his belly ached. In the houses of country gentlemen it made a pleasant

---

[1] 'Tiell' is Till Eulenspiegel, who is Howleglas. Schulz suggests that 'Cocle' may be the puppet-player, Cokely. He is mentioned in Jonson's 129th Epigram and in *Bartholomew Fair*, III. iv. 126.

change from dice or cards or Christmas games, when some 'pleasant madheaded knaues, that bee properly learned,' read to the company 'in diuerse pleasant bookes and good Authors: As . . . the Budget of Demaundes, the Hundreth merry Tales, the Booke of Ryddles, and many other excellent writers both witty and pleasaunt.'[1] But whether it be taken as an indication of our morality or our saturnine humour or our national hypocrisy, the truth is that our jest-book writers often seek some other justification for their labours than that of entertainment. Sometimes they add a rider that their jests are a preservative against melancholy, or they call attention to the wisdom of Solomon, that 'a merry heart doeth good like a medicine, but a broken spirit drieth the bones'.[2] There is nothing in English quite so mercurial and insouciant (if that goes for an English word) as the preamble of Des Périers, of which the burden is: 'Ventre d'ung petit poysson! rions. . . . Ouvrez le livre: si ung compte ne vous plait, hay à l'aultre! . . . Riez seulement.' It is significant that the English translator of Des Périers omits the original prologue and substitutes one which points a moral—that 'moderate pleasure is not only conuenient, but also profitable and necessary for vs.' As the tag in an eighteenth-century chapbook puts it,

> Mirth and morals here are join'd
> To please and to improve the mind.[3]

But a jest may not only be acceptable in itself or for reasons of health or morality: it may be found of use in a man's profession. The medieval preacher had used it to swell the numbers of his congregation or to awaken the slumbering attention, and comic as well as serious *exempla* are provided in the *Summa predicantium*, *The Alphabet of Tales*, and other medieval collections. Says Sir Thomas More: 'He that can not long endure to holde vp his head and heare talking of heauen except he be now and than betwene (as though to heare of heauen were heauines) refreshed with a mery folishe tale, there is none other remedy but you must let him haue it.'[4] The

---

[1] *The English Courtier* (1586), ed. W. C. Hazlitt (1868), p. 57.
[2] Prov. 17: 22.
[3] *The History of That Celebrated Lady Ally Croaker.*
[4] *A Dialogue of Comfort against Tribulation* (1553), Bk. II, ch. I.

practice survived the Reformation,[1] and Hugh Latimer was literally stealing his wit from the *Hundred Merry Tales* (No. 27) when in the sixth sermon before Edward VI he referred to a gentlewoman of London who was asked by her neighbour whither she was going. 'Mary sayed she, I am goynge to S. Tomas of Acres to the sermon, I coulde not slepe al thys laste nyght, and I am goynge now thether, I neuer fayled of a good nap there.'[2]

But Hugh Latimer was an exceptional character, as Richard Corbet and Thomas Fuller of a later generation were exceptional wits, and after the Reformation there were more and more pulpits from which the terrors of hell were thundered without the alleviation of a jest. The attitude of many a preacher is represented by Henry Crosse, who in his *Virtue's Common-wealth* (1603) includes in one compendious curse *The Court of Venus*, *The Palace of Pleasure*, *Guy of Warwick*, *Libbius* ('Libeaus Desconus'), *Arthur*, *Bevis of Hampton*, *The Wise Men of Gotham*, Scogin's *Jests*, and *Fortunatus*. 'What may we thinke?' he asks, 'but that the floudgates of all impietie are drawne vp.'[3]

> By which we note the Fairies
>   Were of the old profession;
> Their songs were Ave Maryes,
>   Their daunces were procession:
> But now, alas! they all are dead
>   Or gone beyond the Seas,
> Or farther for Religion fled,
>   Or else they take their ease.

At the Inns of Court jesting never flagged, but did John Manningham of the Middle Temple, barrister-at-law, record jests in his Diary entirely without thought for the morrow? In this most litigious age, an age when, as Greene says, a man went to law if a

---

[1] Erasmus regarded jests as a lesser evil than foolish tales: 'In sermones percase it is not conueniente to miangle iestyng saiynges of mortall menne with the holy scriptures of God, but yet might the same much more excusably bee vsed, to quicken suche as at sermones been euer noddyng, then olde wiues foolyshe tales of Robyn Hoode & such others, whiche many preachers haue in tymes past customably vsed to bryng in, taken out euen of the veraye botome and grossest part of the dregges of the comen peoples foolyshe talkyng' (*Apophthegms*, translated Udall, sig. ✱✱✱1).
[2] c. 1549; sigs. V2ᵛ–V3.
[3] Sigs. Oᵛ–O2.

hen did but scrape in his orchard, it must have occurred to lawyers that Cicero and Quintilian and all who had written on the arts of oratory had observed how cases might be lost and won with jest. Francis Bacon of Gray's Inn was frankly utilitarian when he compiled his *Apophthegmes New and Old*—jests of the pointed and witty kind, dignified by attachment to famous historical characters. Each one of these apophthegms, it is felt, might become a brick in the architecture of a man's fortunes. 'They serve', he writes, 'to be interlaced, in continued Speech. They serve, to be recited, upon occasion of themselves. They serve, if you take out the kernell of them, and make them your owne.' And in another place he writes of apophthegms that, as former 'occasions are continually returning, ... what served once will serve again; whether produced as a man's own or cited as an old saying'.[1] The trait is hereditary, for Bacon's father before him had been 'abundantly facetious, which took much with the Queen, when it was suited with the season, as he was well able to judge of his times'.[2]

For men of lesser parts the jest-books were a godsend, and to supplement the printed jest a gallant had but to take his table book to the playhouse. It is all very well for Sir William Cornwallis to complain of those 'that neuer vtter any thing of their owne, but get Iestes by heart, and robbe bookes, and men of prettie tales, and yet hope for this to haue a roome aboue the Salt'.[3] Perhaps we should value 'a roome' above the salt chiefly because the pie would come to us before too many fingers had been in it, but in those days rank or degree of favour was awfully marked by a man's place at table. And what was he to do if he lacked facility in facetious conversation, especially if he belonged to that class, very numerous in an age of commercial prosperity, whose fathers had always sat below the salt and whose claims to gentility were dubious? For him were designed the many books on etiquette, home-grown or imported from Italy, which taught him comportment. The difference between

---
[1] *De Augmentis Scientiarum* (1623), Bk. II, chap. 12 (Spedding's translation in works, iv, 1858, p. 314). For the uses of jesting in oratory, see Harvey's *Marginalia* (ed. cit., p. 114), where he refers to Pontanus and Barlandus and says 'ye most compound Jest, ye best... A mixture, and concourse of many Conceytes, jn on'.
[2] Sir Robert Naunton, *Fragmenta Regalia* (1653), p. 40; ed. Arber (1870), p. 38. In 1653 and in Arber's reprint 'facetious' is misprinted 'factious'.
[3] *Essays* (1600), sig. I3.

these books and *Il Cortegiano* has been likened to the difference between Sancho Panza and Don Quixote. Castiglione's second book, it is true, is mostly taken up with wit and humour, but falls into its place in the integration of all the powers of man, both of the body and of the soul, which is the whole work. It is a far cry from Castiglione's fashioning of a 'gentleman or noble person' to Peacham's injunction to his 'compleat' gentleman to improve his table talk by reading Pasquin's epigrams: 'You shall have them all bound in two Volumes',[1] and it is a still further cry from Castiglione's *sprezzatura* (which is a nobler quality than Horace Walpole's 'the beautiful negligence of a gentleman') to the instruction provided by Simon Robson in *The Court of Civil Courtesy*. Gentlemen at a loss for suitable replies to taunting jests he supplied with possible retorts, as, 'Oh finely handled, were you borne so?' or 'Did any body teach you to say so, or comes it of your mother wit?' or (in what seem to be anticipations of a modern American usage) 'You haue made a great speake sir' and 'that is, quoth you'.[2]

It may be thought by those whose reading in this kind stops at 1640, or with Joe Miller at 1739, that the jest-book is now dead. But it still leads an active if subterranean existence, impervious to all the changes of which literary historians make so much. Still these collections aim both at the *utile* and the *dulce*, and still they cater for all the classes of men who need their jokes ready-made. If Swift were alive today he might assure Prince Posterity that there are now in being such collections as *Jokes for the Business Man, Humourous Hits and How to Hold an Audience, Funny Stories for Table Talk, That reminds me! A book of After Dinner Stories, Good Stories from Oxford and Cambridge and the Dioceses*, and *Thistledown: A Book of Scotch Humour*.

[1] Ed. cit., p. 232.
[2] S. Robson, *The Court of Civil Courtesy* (1591), sig. E4$^{r\ \&\ v}$. An earlier edition appeared in 1577. The work professes to be translated from the Italian of Bengalasso del Monte, but W. Lee Ustick maintains that Robson was the author, not the translator, and that the account of the Italian nephew for whom it claims to be written is a hoax. Cf. J. E. Mason, *Gentlefolk in the Making* (1935), p. 371.

BIBLIOGRAPHICAL NOTES

Schulz gives a bibliography of the English jest-books on pp. 18–21 of his *Die englischen Schwankbücher*, in *Palaestra*, cxvii (1921). I mention below the jest-books, and editions of jest-books, printed in or before 1640, and also modern reprints of these, which are not given in Schulz's lists. My list is merely a supplement to his bibliography.

Schulz defines the jest-book in the sense indicated on p. 286, above, groups the pamphlets under the three headings noted on p. 286, above, and within each group arranges and numbers them in the probable order of publication. The numbers given below are the numbers in Schulz; works marked with an asterisk are not to be found in his bibliography.

Where a book is omitted from the *Short-Title Catalogue (STC)*, I note its omission if the book can be traced.

An interesting list could be compiled of jest-books entered in the Stationers' Registers, and presumably published, which have not left a trace behind them. The list would include: *Pleasant Tales of the Life of Richard Woolner* (1567/8)[1] *Mother Redcap Her Last Will and Testament, Containing Sundry Conceited and Pleasant Tales Furnished with Much Variety to Move Delight* (10 Mar. 1595), John Day's *The Mad Pranks of Merry Mall of the Bankside, with Her Walks in Man's Apparel* (7 August, 1610), if this is not a play, *The History of Jack Knight, or the Fools have Best Fortune*, by John Harrison (30 April 1627), *New Bulls or Ignorant Nonsense, First and Second Parts* (6 April 1936). And there must be many a lost work which was never entered in the Registers.

The loss of *The Mad Pranks of Merry Mall* is particularly to be regretted. It was perhaps a little earlier that Moll Cutpurse, or Mary Frith, a notorious virago of the time, was made the heroine of Middleton and Dekker's *The Roaring Girl*. Two pamphlets on her life were published in 1662, but these are clearly of their age. One of them, *The Life and Death of Mrs. Mary Frith*, is of some interest in the history of the novel. It is the shortest of steps from this vigorous and fictitious autobiography to Defoe's *The Fortunes and Misfortunes of Moll Flanders*.

Some of the eighteenth-century chapbooks may have a history which stretches back before 1640. *The Merry Tales of the Wise Men of Gotham* and *Long Meg of Westminster*, together with kindred works like Deloney's *Gentle Craft* and *Jack of Newbury*, certainly persist in chapbook form to a late date. Among the chapbook heroes whose comic deeds may have descended from jest-biographies of the sixteenth or early seventeenth century are Simple Simon, with his shrewish wife Margery, Tom Tram, son-in-law to Mother

[1] John Smyth, *c*. 1600, asks why stationers' shops and some men's shelves should contain nothing but 'Guy of Warwick, William of Cloudeslee, Skeggins, and Wolners jests, and writings of like qualitie'. Cited by W. Haller, *The Rise of Puritanism* (1938), p. 183.

Winter, John Franks, and Tom Long, carrier to the men of Gotham, whose name may derive from the proverbial saying, 'To send by John [or Tom] Long the carrier'—i.e., by a roundabout route. There is also Little Jack Horner, but his exploits, as we still care to remember, were related in verse.

For help in making the list I am grateful to Professor W. A. Jackson, of Harvard University, Dr. J. G. McManaway, of the Folger Library, and Mr. Lyle H. Wright, of the Huntington Library.[1]

I. COLLECTIONS OF DETACHED JESTS[2]

*William Caxton. *The Book of the Subtle Histories and Fables of Aesop*

Caxton printed the first edition of his translation in 1484. For many later editions see *STC*. On the fables of 'Poge', found at the end of this collection, see above, p. 288.

1. *A Hundred Merry Tales*

An imperfect copy of an edition without date is in the British Museum (Huth 31), and a perfect copy of an edition dated 1526 is in the Library of the University of Göttingen. Both editions are from John Rastell's press, as is also a fragment of a leaf from yet another edition (not recorded by Schulz or *STC*) in the Bagford collection in the British Museum (Harl. 5995, No. 190). A fragment formerly in the library of J. O. Halliwell-Phillipps (*Calendar of Shakespearean Rarities*, 2nd ed., 1891, No. 196), and now in the Folger Library, is from the same edition as the Museum copy. (There is a second fragment in the Folger Library.) Comparison of the tears at the side and at the foot of the first fragment with the corresponding portion of the Museum copy indicates that the Folger fragment, like those which make up the Museum copy, has survived from the pasteboard which the Revd. J. J. Conybeare rescued from an old book in 1815. In his reprint of the Göttingen copy in 1866, Oesterley argued that the dated edition was earlier than the undated; A. W. Pollard suggests the reverse conclusion, in a *Catalogue of the Fifty Manuscripts and Printed Books Bequeathed to the British Museum by Alfred H. Huth* (1912), pp. 52–3.

2. *Tales and Quick Answers*

S. W. Singer reprinted this pamphlet in 1814 as *Shakespeare's Jest Book*. Soon afterwards Conybeare discovered fragments of *A Hundred Merry Tales*, and these were reprinted by Singer in 1815 as *Shakespeare's Jest Book*. In 1815 Singer also reprinted the twenty-six jests added to *Tales and Quick Answers* in the 1567 edition of *Merry Tales, Witty Questions, and Quick Answers*. *Tales and Quick Answers* was edited anonymously in 1831 as *The Hundred Merry Tales: Or Shakespeare's Jest-Book*. In 1845 an edition of *A Hundred Merry Tales* and *Tales*

---

[1] There are twenty early jest-books in the Ewing collection at Glasgow University Library; see *The Library*, 1st Series, viii (1896), p. 392.

[2] I have nothing to add to Schulz's bibliographies of: 3. *The Sackful of News*; 15. *A Banquet of Jests*.

early seventeenth centuries 315

and *Quick Answers* was published by George Routledge with the title *Shakespeare's Merry Tales*.

4. A. B. [Andrew Borde?]. *The Merry Tales of the Madmen of Gotham*
No copy earlier than that in the Bodleian Library of the edition of 1630 can now be traced.¹ On 22 July 1616 (*Stationers' Registers*, ed. Arber, iii. 593) the rights of Hugh Jackson in this book were transferred to 'Master Jackson'. Professor W. A. Jackson informs me that, in the Stationers' Court-Book C, fol. 55*b*, under date of 3 May 1619, Eld and Flesher were ordered to pay 'Mr Jackson' 6*s*. 8*d*. for printing this book formerly entered to him. Many examples of the chapbook version popular in the eighteenth and nineteenth centuries have survived. See, e.g., William Garret's *Right Pleasant and Famous Book of Histories* (Newcastle, 1818).

5. Richard Edwards. *Comic Stories*
The book was probably invented by Thomas Warton: see above, pp. 303-4.

6. R. D. or T. D. *A Mirror of Mirth*
Schulz mentions the book under this first group, but I have preferred to discuss it with the English comic *novelle* in the third section. The only known copy of the edition of 1583 is in the Capell Collection at Trinity College, Cambridge. The only known copy of an edition printed by John Danter in 1592 was bought by Dr. Rosenbach at Sotheby's on 15 April 1930 (lot 412), for £880. There is a modern edition by J. W. Hassall, Jr. (Univ. of S. Carolina Press, 1959). For some account of the book see above, p. 304. Neither the edition of 1583 nor that of 1592 is recorded in *STC*.

7. T. T. [Thomas Twyne?]. *The Schoolmaster, or Teacher of Table Philosophy. A Most Pleasant and Merry Companion*
STC mentions editions of 1576 and 1583. This is probably the same work as T. T.'s *A Most Pleasant and Merry Companion* (1576) mentioned in the Roxburghe Sale Catalogue, 1812, lot 6649, and thence in Lowndes and Schulz. [See T. F. Dunn, *The Facetiae of the Mensa Philosophica* (1934), *Washington University Studies*, N.S., *Language and Literature*, No. 5. *The Schoolmaster* is a translation of the *Mensa Philosophica* (printed 1480), in its early editions ascribed to Theobald Anguilbert, but later to Michael Scot. This is a work in four parts of which the fourth is a collection of jests. A different translation, adding fresh material but also abbreviating the original, appeared in 1609 under the title *The Philosophers' Banquet*. This was reprinted in 1614 and 1633. It is Schulz's No. 12. Schulz did not appear to realize that his items 3 and 12

¹ [This is no longer true. Thomas Warton mentioned a duodecimo edition, printed by 'Henry Wikes', *c*. 1568 (*History of English Poetry*, 1781, iii. 73), and J. O. Halliwell described another early edition, printed by Thomas Colwell, no date, black letter, which he dated 1556-66 (*Notices of English Popular Histories*, 1848, pp. 72-3). A unique copy of this last edition is in Harvard College Library and has been reprinted in an edition by Stanley J. Kahrl for the Renaissance Text Society, Northwestern Univ. Press, Evanston, Illinois, 1965. H.G.]

were dependent on the same Latin work. Dunn considers the date and authorship of the *Mensa* and the sources of the *Facetiae* in its fourth book. Only a selection of these jests was included in *The Philosophers' Banquet*. This selection can be found in Hazlitt, vol. iii, as 'Certayne Conceyts & Jeasts'. Dunn erroneously refers to Hazlitt's item as 'a little book published in London early in the seventeenth century', though Hazlitt clearly states the fact that he has taken it from *The Philosophers' Banquet* of 1614. H. G.]

*Anthony Copley. *Wits, Fits and Fancies*

STC mentions editions of 1595 and 1596 and two editions of 1614. For some account of the book see above, p. 295. On the two editions of 1614, see R. B. McKerrow in *The Library*, 4th Series, x (1930), p. 137.

8. *Pasquil's Jests*

STC traces editions of 1604, 1629, and *c.* 1632. An edition of 1609 'Newly corrected with new additions', printed, like the edition of 1604, for John Browne, is described in Egerton Brydges' *The British Bibliographer* (1810), vol. i, pp. 41–2; there is a copy in the Folger Library. According to Brydges, Warton mentions an edition of 1627 in his *History of English Poetry*. The edition of 1629 omits the 'dozen of gulls', and contains a preface and jests not in the edition of 1604. A copy of an edition printed by Miles Flesher and sold by Andrew Kembe in 1635 is in the Capell Collection; the jest which Capell quotes on p. 82 of his *School of Shakespeare* as from *Mother Bunch's Tales* is from this edition of *Pasquil's Jests*.

9. *Jack of Dover*

There was an entry of a second part to William Ferbrand on 3 August 1601, but no edition earlier than that printed for Ferbrand in 1604 has survived. The second part made some stir in the House of Commons on 16 December 1601, as appears from the reports of Hayward Townshend (*Megalopsychy*, 1682, p. 217). Henry Doyley, of Lincoln's Inn, complained to the Speaker and the House of a libel called *The Assembly of Fools*, the printer of which dwelt 'right over Guild-Hall-Gate'. (The imprint on the 1600 edition of Armin's *Fool upon Fool* is: 'Printed for William Ferbrand, dwelling neere Guild-Hall-Gate ouer against the Maiden-head. 1600.') The book was sent for, was well scanned by the Privy Council, and 'was found to be a meer Toy, and an Old Book, Entituled, *The Second Part of* Jack *of* Dover: A Thing both Stale and Foolish. For which, Mr. *Doyley* was well Laughed at; and thereby, his Credit much impeached, in the Opinion of the *House*.' The 'second part' may have been *The Penniless Parliament of Thread-bare Poets*, printed at the end of the 1604 edition of *Jack of Dover*; perhaps in 1601 'The Assembly of Fools' was part of its title. *The Penniless Parliament* is indeed 'A Thing both Stale and Foolish', for it is all borrowed from the mock-prognostication, *The Fearful and Lamentable Effects of Two Dangerous Comets*, published in 1591 under the pseudonym of 'Simon Smellknave': see my article in *The Library*.[1] *Jack of Dover* was an

---

[1] Reprinted above; see pp. 251–82.

appropriate name for jest-book and mock-prognostication, for the expression still retained its Chaucerian meaning of a dish that has been cooked and served up more than once. (Fuller, *Worthies*, 1662, Kent, p. 65.) I am indebted to Mr. Graham Pollard for the reference to Hayward Townshend.

10. Robert Armin. *Fool upon Fool*

In his edition of Robert Armin's works (1880), Grosart reprinted the 1605 edition of *Fool upon Fool* and the additions found in the enlarged edition published in 1608 with the title *A Nest of Ninnies*. Armin signed his name to the latter pamphlet, but the edition of 1605 was published under the pseudonym 'Clonnico del mundo Snuffe'—i.e. Snuffe, Clown of the Globe Theatre. Halliwell-Phillipps owned, and described in his *Calendar of Shakespearian Rarities* (p. 145), a copy of an edition of 1600 in which Armin's pseudonym was 'Clonnico de Curtanio Snuffe', or Snuffe, Clown of the Curtain Theatre. *STC* records *A Nest of Ninnies*, but neither the 1600 nor the 1605 edition of *Fool upon Fool*. Copies of both editions are now in the Folger Library. The edition of 1600 contains descriptions, in verse, of Jack Oates, lean Leonard of Sherwood, Jack Miller, and John of the Hospital, which are omitted from the edition of 1605.

If Armin could be described in 1600 as clown of the Curtain Theatre, it would appear that he did not immediately succeed to the comic parts (e.g. Dogberry) of William Kempe, who left the Chamberlain's men early in 1599 (cf. T. W. Baldwin, *M.L.N.*, xxxix. 447–55). But for what company was he clowning at the Curtain in 1599–1600? It does not seem likely that he was still in the service of William, fourth Lord Chandos (succ. 1594—d. 1602), to whose widow he dedicated a pamphlet in 1604, for there is no evidence that this company of players ever acted in the theatres of London. The first certain reference to Armin as a member of Shakespeare's company seems to be in the patent of 1603. It may be worth pointing out that, while there are Shakespearean echoes in the passages added to *A Nest of Ninnies* in 1608, there are none in *Fool upon Fool*.[1]

This note has long ceased to be relevant, and the digression will continue to the end of the present paragraph. Another pamphlet published in 1600, *Quips upon Questions*, also printed for William Ferbrand, bears the pseudonym 'Clunnyco de Curtanio Snuffe', and may therefore be ascribed to Armin. It is made up of answers, in verse, to such questions as, 'Who's the fool now?', 'Are you there with your bears?', 'Where's Tarlton?' The idea for the book may have come from the practice of giving themes to clowns on which they would proceed to make 'extemporal rhymes', but the feebly satirical or tritely moral verses in *Quips upon Questions* have none of the marks of extempore

---

[1] To the echoes in *A Nest of Ninnies* recorded in the *Shakspere-Allusion Book* (1909) may be added: 'they cry it vp in the top of question' (Grosart, p. 59; cf. *Hamlet*, II. ii. 355), and the interesting use of 'squened' and 'squinies' (Grosart, pp. 45, 48; cf. *King Lear*, III. iv. 122, and IV. vi. 140) to which W. W. Greg called attention in *T.L.S.*, 9 November 1933.

playhouse wit. The attribution of the work to the actor John Singer rests solely upon the authority of Collier. He stated in 1865 that the work is given to Singer in 'a MS. note on the first leaf' of the only known copy (*A Bibliographical Account*, ii. 209). By 1875 his story had become more circumstantial, for he told Ouvry that 'the name J. Singer was written in his own autograph on the title-page of the volume'. But Ouvry, when in that year he reprinted the work, could only say: 'It has been bound since it came into my hands, and most unfortunately, in the process of cleaning by acid, the name has disappeared.' The copy is now in the British Museum, and no trace of any signature can be seen. W. C. Hazlitt gave the work to Singer in his *Hand-Book* (1876), p. 559, but in his *Bibliographical Collections, Third Series, Second Supplement* (1889), p. 119, he gave it to Armin, and regretted that he had 'incautiously' followed Collier. In *STC* it is still entered under Singer. There is no evidence that Singer was at any time associated with the Curtain Theatre. He was an Admiral's man, acting the clown's parts chiefly at the Rose and later at the Fortune. There is a story in *Taylor's Feast* (1638; Spenser Society reprint of works of Taylor not included in the Folio of 1630 [Third Collection, 1876], pp. 66–7) about '*Iohn Singer*, who playd the Clownes part at the Fortune-play-house in *Golding Lane*'. An epitaph in I. C.'s *Epigrams* (1604, sig. C4^v), not noticed in Chambers' *Elizabethan Stage*, also links him with the Fortune (opened in 1600), and helps to fix more closely the date of his death:

> Death was bolde his dayes to shorten,
> Who altogether liu'd by fortune.

11. Thomas Dekker and George Wilkins. *Jests to Make You Merry*

The edition of 1607 was reprinted by Grosart in his edition of Dekker's *Non-Dramatic Works*, vol. ii (1885).

12. *The Philosophers' Banquet*

See No. 7. The Britwell copy of the edition of 1609 is now in the Huntington Library. *STC* does not record a copy of this edition.

13. *A Help to Discourse*

STC mentions (s.v. Basse, W.) editions of 1619, 1620, 1621, 1627, 1628 (the seventh), 1635, 1636, 1638 (the thirteenth). Dr. Rosenbach possesses a copy of a seventh edition with the date 1629. An edition of 1623 (the fifth) was advertised in the catalogue of the London booksellers, Messrs. Myers and Co., in January, 1936 (catalogue 310, No. 43). Copies of editions printed for Leonard Becket in 1630 and 1631 and of an edition printed for Nicholas Vavasour in 1640 are in the Folger Library. Hazlitt (*Hand-Book*, p. 300) mentions an edition of 1633.

*Francis Bacon. *Apophthegms New and Old*

To put Bacon among the compilers of jest-books is to be guilty of *lèse-majesté*, yet, as I have said above (p. 311), his apophthegms are jests of the pointed and witty kind, dignified by attachment to famous historical characters. They are *Mucrones Verborum, Pointed Speeches*. *Cicero* prettily cals them, *Salinas, Salt Pits*; that you may extract salt out of, and sprinkle it, where you will.' The book was entered to Hannah Barrett and Richard Whitaker, on 20 November 1624, and was available before the end of the year. John Chamberlain, writing 18 December 1624, refers to 'the collection of the Lord of St. Albans Apothegmes newly set out this weeke, but with so little allowance or applause that the world sayes his wit and judgement begins to draw neere the lees' (*Letters*, ed. N. E. McClure, ii. 592). Another edition followed in 1626. Many transfers of the copyright are recorded in the Stationers' Registers.

14. H. L. Oxon. *Gratiae Ludentes*

The British Museum and the Rosenbach copies are the only known copies. The imprint is, 'Printed at London by Tho. Cotes, for Humphrey Mosley. 1628.', and in both copies the figure 2 has been altered to 3 in ink. As the book was entered to Moseley on 16 December 1637, it is probable that the date on the title-page is a misprint for 1638.

16. John Taylor. *Wit and Mirth*

STC notes editions of 1629 and 1635. A copy of an edition printed for H. Gosson in 1628 is now at Harvard. There is also the reprint in the Folio of 1630.

**A Banquet of Jests*, Part 2

STC mentions editions of 1633 and 1636 (title only). Part 1, Schulz's No. 15, was printed in 1630 and often later.

* *The Book of Bulls, Baited with Two Centuries of Bold Jests and Nimble Lies*

The book was entered in the Stationers' Register on 8 and 11 April 1636, and was printed for Daniel Frere in the same year. It was 'Collected by A. S. Gent'. The R. C. who signed verses 'To the Bull-Reader' is said to be Robert Chamberlain. A copy was sold at the Huth Sale on 5 June 1912, lot 1453, and is now in the Widener collection at Harvard. The book is not recorded in *STC*.

**A New Book of Mistakes. Or, Bulls with Tales, and Bulls without Tales*

STC mentions an edition of 1637, printed for Nicholas Okes; see also the Huth sale catalogue, 5 June 1912, lot 1454. The book is said to be by Robert Chamberlain. Can it be the 'booke called *Mistakes Clinches Tales &c*. by Master *HAYWOOD*', entered to John Okes on 18 November 1636? Nicholas Okes and his son John were partners at this time.

*John Taylor. *Bull, Bear, and Horse*

STC mentions the edition of 1638. It was reprinted by the Spenser Society, op. cit.

*John Taylor. *Taylor's Feast: Containing Twenty-seven Dishes of Meat*

STC mentions the edition of 1638; see also the Huth sale catalogue, 8 July 1919, lot 7265. It was reprinted by the Spenser Society, op. cit.

17. **Robert Chamberlain.** *Conceits, Clinches, Flashes, and Whimzies*
Schulz mentions the edition of 1639. *STC* also records the enlarged edition of 1640, entitled *Jocabella. Or a Cabinet of Conceits*; see also the Huth sale catalogue, 5 June 1912, lot 1458.

*R. Cox. *The Conceited Humours of Simpleton the Smith* Edited J. O. Halliwell (1861).

* *The Jokes of the Cambridge Coffee-houses in the seventeenth century* Edited J. O. Halliwell (Cambridge 1841).

II. JEST BIOGRAPHIES[1]

A. Translations

1. *Salomon and Markolf*

Schulz does not mention *The Sayings or Proverbs of King Salomon, with the Answers of Marcolphus*, printed about 1530 by R. Pynson. The Heber-Britwell-Huntington copy (*STC* 22899) appears to be unique. It is translated from a French version, whereas the translation printed by Gerard Leeu in 1492 (*STC* 22905) is from a Latin version. See *The Dialogue or Communing between the Wise King Salomon and Marcolphus*, ed. E. Gordon Duff (1892), pp. xxii ff.

2. *The Parson of Kalenborow*

The English exists only in a fragment in the Bodleian Library (Douce K. 94), printed by Doesborgh of Antwerp, *c.* 1520. I cannot find that the book is recorded in *STC*. In 1887 it was reprinted by Edward Schröder in the *Jahrbuch des Vereins für niederdeutsche Sprachforschung*, xiii.

B. Original or Adapted Works

1. *The Merry Jests and Witty Shifts of Scoggin*

STC does not record the fragments of an early edition, in the Bagford collection (Harl. 5995, Nos. 210, 328–31, and 332). They may belong to an edition of 1565/6, in which trade-year Thomas Colwell entered the collection in the Stationers' Register. The text corresponds to that of the edition of 1626 (reprinted in Hazlitt's *Shakespeare Jest-Books*), not to that of the different collection of 1613. See F. W. D. Brie, *Eulenspiegel in England, Palaestra,* xxvii, pp. 82–3 and W. E. Farnham, 'John (Henry) Scogan', *M.L.R.*, xvi (1921).

3. *Robin Goodfellow, His Mad Pranks and Merry Jests*

Schulz places the work between the *Merry Tales* of Skelton, registered in 1566/7, and *The Pleasant History of Friar Rush*, registered in 1568/9. But while a great deal of the material is traditional there is no evidence that the pamphlet is much older than the earliest known edition, of 1628. It was entered to John Spencer on 25 April 1627, and on the same day was made over

---

[1] I have nothing to add to Schulz's bibliographies of: A3. Howleglas; B2. *Merry Tales of Skelton*.

by Spencer to Francis Grove, who published the edition of 1628. Further transfers are recorded on: 23 March 1631 (Grove to H. Gosson), 8 October 1633 (Gosson to J. Wright), and 9 November 1633 (Grove to R. Cotes). Cotes printed an edition dated 1639—to be sold by Grove—of which the only known copy is in the British Museum. It should have been recorded in *STC* as another edition of the pamphlet of 1628.

4. *The Pleasant History of Friar Rush*

STC records copies of the editions of 1620 and 1626. The Hoe-Huth copy, described by Esdaile in his *List of English Tales and Prose Romances* (1912), p. 122, is now in the Folger Library. It contains the title-page of an edition of 1629 and a complete copy (but lacking the imprint on the title-page) of an edition of 1659. The most recent reprint is in *Some Old English Worthies*, ed. Dorothy Senior (1912), pp. 237–68.

5. *Tarlton's Jests*

The edition of 1613 printed for John Budge is not recorded in Schulz or *STC*. A copy is now in the Folger Library. I cannot trace an edition of 1611 from which Halliwell reprinted the jests for the Shakespeare Society in 1844.

★*The Life of Long Meg of Westminster*

The pamphlet was entered to T. Gubbins and T. Newman on 18 August 1590, and there were transfers from E. White to T. Pavier and J. Wright on 13 December 1620, from Pavier's widow to E. Brewster and R. Bird on 4 August 1626, from J. Wright to R. Bird on 29 April 1634, and from Bird and Brewster to J. Wright, Junior, on 13 June 1642. *STC* mentions an edition of 1635 printed for Bird. Hazlitt also mentions an edition, printed for E. White in 1620, in the possession of the Marquis of Bute, and an edition printed for Bird in 1636. (*Collections and Notes*, vol. i, 1876, p. 286; *Hand-Book*, p. 386.) The edition of 1635 was reprinted in *Miscellanea Antiqua Anglicana*, vol. i (1816), and in Charles Hindley's *Old Book Collector's Miscellany*, vol. ii (1872). A chapbook version is in the Folger copy of William Garret's *Right Pleasant and Famous Book of Histories*, vol. vi, No. 9. *STC* wrongly records an edition of 1582. The British Museum has an imperfect copy printed c. 1650, with a faked title-page taken from C. Desainliens's *French Schoolmaster*, printed by William How for Abraham Veale in 1582. See the British Museum *Catalogue*.

★*Dobson's Dry Bobs*

The only edition was printed by Valentine Simmes in 1607. *STC* records the Talbot-G.Daniel-Huth-White copy; it is now in the Folger Library. Other copies are in the Capell Collection at Trinity College, Cambridge, and in the Pepysian Library at Magdalene College, Cambridge. There is a modern edition by E. A. Horsman (Univ. of Durham Publications, 1955). Schulz gives a reprint of this work, but does not include it in his list. It might as appropriately be placed under the third section, with the comic *novelle*. For an account of *Dobson's Dry Bobs* see above, pp. 306–8.

6. *Merry Conceited Jests of George Peele*
   STC records editions of 1607, c. 1620, and two editions of 1627.

7. Richard Johnson. *The Pleasant Conceits of Old Hobson*
   STC records editions of 1607 and 1610. An imperfect copy of an edition printed for W. Gilbertson in 1640 was sold at Sotheby's at the Halliwell Sale in 1857 (No. 408). It is said to contain additional jests and to differ materially from the edition of 1607. George Daniel of Canonbury, Islington, a great collector of jest-books, owned a copy of an edition, in duodecimo, printed for W. Gilbertson in 1640. This was perhaps Halliwell's copy. It contained additional jests and a large woodcut. The last four leaves were supplied 'from another edition of equal rarity'. See Sotheby's Sale Catalogue, 23 July 1864, No. 903. Lot 902 in the same sale was a copy of another edition in duodecimo, 'a unique edition, but imperfect'. The catalogue gives no date. Hazlitt (*Hand-Book*, p. 303) mentions—with a reference to the Bagford Papers—an edition of 1634 printed for J. Wright.

★Thomas Brewer. *The Life and Death of the Merry Devil of Edmonton*
   STC records the edition of 1631 printed for F. Faulkner. The book was entered to J. Hunt and T. Archer on 5 April 1608. Of the twenty chapters in the edition of 1631, the first three relate to Peter Fabell the merry devil of Edmonton, the rest to Oliver Smug the smith of that town. A play on Smug the Smith is referred to in Jonson's *Staple of News* (1625), First Intermean, l. 71. On 10 February 1631, '*SMUGes Jestes*' was transferred from T. Archer to H. Perry; on 7 April 1635, from H. Perry to F. Coles; on 18 April 1666, from W. Gilbertson to R. White—but this may be a different collection. A reprint of the text of 1631 was published in 1819, for W. R., by J. Nichols and Son.

★*The Pinder of Wakefield: Being the Merry History of George a Greene the Lusty Pinder of the North*
   STC records the Bodleian, Harmsworth, and Huntington copies of the edition printed for E. Blackmore in 1632. The Harmsworth copy (formerly Quaritch's Catalogue 369, of 1922, No. 857; see also *Book Prices Current*, 1900, pp. 484–5, item 5454) is now in the Folger Library; Esdaile is in error in dating it 1633. A copy was sold at the Gordonstoun Sale (lot 1856) in March 1816, and again at Sotheby's in June 1900. The book had been entered to Blackmore on 4 February 1632, but perhaps the two parts of which the book is made up had previously been published separately. The head title of the second part rather suggests that it is copied from a title-page: 'The Second Part of George a Greene: Containing the great Fight between him and Robin Hood, and afterwards of his liuing with him in the woods; full of mery Iests, Tales, Songs, and Catches'. *Tarlton's Jests* and *Jack of Dover* were first published in parts.

   On 4 November 1635, John Crouch entered 'The history of GEORGE A GREENE Pindar of Wakefeild', possibly another work.

early seventeenth centuries

In 1706 appeared *The History of George a Green, Pindar of the Town of Wakefield*, with a dedication signed 'N. W.' This 'bourgeois romance' was printed from a late-sixteenth-century or early-seventeenth-century manuscript at Sion College, and is an entirely different production from the pamphlet of 1632. The relationship of the romance to the play *George a Greene* is examined in *The Plays and Poems of Robert Greene*, ed. J. Churton Collins (1905), ii. 163 ff. The text of 1706 was edited by W. J. Thoms in *A Collection of Early Prose Romances* (1828), vol. ii, and by Dorothy Senior in *Some Old English Worthies*. Surprisingly enough, the more attractive pamphlet of 1632 was not reprinted until 1956, when it was edited by E. A. Horsman (Liverpool Reprints, No. 12). Thoms could find no copy of it in 1828, although the Bodleian copy had already been in the Library for nearly two centuries. For an account of the pamphlet of 1632 see above, p. 301.

III. COLLECTIONS OF COMIC NOVELLE[1]

1. *Tarlton's News out of Purgatory*

The book was entered in the Stationers' Register on 26 June 1590. *STC* records two issues of the edition of 1590—one printed for T. G[ubbin] and T. N[ewman] and one printed for E. White.

2. *The Cobbler of Canterbury*

Schulz and *STC* mention editions of 1590 and 1608. S. De Ricci, in his catalogue of the Clawson Library (1924), mentions a copy of an edition of 1614, with the title *The Merry Tales of the Cobbler of Canterbury*, in the possession of the Marquis of Bute.

3. *Westward for Smelts*

The only early edition known was entered in the Stationers' Register on 15 January 1619/20, and was published in 1620. Steevens, in his editions of Shakespeare (1773 and 1778), and Malone, in his *Supplement* (1780), i. 249, stated that this pamphlet was published in 1603, but the general assumption has been that they were mistaken. The dating is of some interest, because a tale in this work has been thought to be one of the 'sources' of *Cymbeline*. There is a scrap of evidence which suggests that perhaps Steevens and Malone were right, after all. John Hanson, in *Time is a Turncoat* (1604), sig. A2$^{r\ \&\ v}$, after attacking 'proud *Argas*' [Marston?] 'Who ne're durst looke harsh *Horace* [Jonson?] in the face', observes:

> What he, that doth his Braines a begging send,
> For some ragg'd Theame to comment on at large,
> Catching a puddle-wharfe-Discourse by th'end
> Chaunts it, like whore-house tales in western Barge?

---

[1] I have nothing to add to Schulz's bibliography of 4. *The Tinker of Turvey* (see above, p. 305), recorded in *STC* under 'Canterbury'.

A western barge was a barge plying the Thames above (westward of) London. While the epithet attached to 'tales' might fit some of the stories in *The Cobbler of Canterbury*, the tellers of these stories sailed in Gravesend barge, whereas the setting of *Westward for Smelts* was a boatful of 'Westerne fishwives' bound from London to Kingston. If 'whore-house tales in westerne Barge' is a reference to a book, as seems likely, I do not know to what book the line can refer if not to *Westward for Smelts*.

10

Table Talk[1]

Two hundred years ago this paper might have been given the alternative title of 'Books in Ana'. But nowadays the word 'ana' is not so well known as it used to be, and it has suffered great degradation of meaning. For its original and more illustrious sense we may consult Johnson's *Dictionary*: 'ANA. Books so called from the last syllables of their titles; as Scaligerana, Thuaniana; they are loose thoughts, or casual hints, dropped by eminent men, and collected by their friends.'

In this paper I hold fast to Johnson's definition that ana are loose thoughts, or casual hints, dropped by eminent men and collected by their friends. A French critic of the eighteenth century said that there are three classes of ana: those which are ana and are called ana; those which are ana but are not called ana; and those which are called ana but are not ana.[2] To the second class—books which are ana but do not bear that title—belong such notable collections as Luther's *Tischreden* and the conversations of Goethe with Eckermann, and most of the English books which are mentioned below. In the third class—books in ana which are not ana—we must place all the attempts of eminent men to compose their own ana, for these lack the distinguishing interest of ana: that they show us these men, in hours of social ease, expressing without reserve their views on life and letters. We must leave still more severely alone all selections or anthologies from writings or letters—like the *Sevigniana*, which gives titbits from the letters of Madame de Sévigné, or the *Popeana* pirated by the 'unspeakable Curll' from the published works of Pope.

The word 'ana' has suffered the same extension of meaning as the

[1] [The Robert Spence Watson Memorial Lecture, read before the Literary and Philosophical Society, Newcastle upon Tyne, on 19 October 1931; revised for publication in the *Huntington Library Quarterly*, iv. 1 (October 1940), and reprinted here with minor additions and corrections.]

[2] J. B. Michault, *Mélanges historiques et philologiques* (Paris, 1754), vol. i, p. x.

word 'anecdote'.[1] 'Anecdote', of which the earliest use in English cited by the *Oxford English Dictionary* is from Marvell's *Dr. Smirke* (1676), preserved for a century its root meaning of 'things unpublished'. So Johnson in the first edition of his *Dictionary* (1755): 'ANECDOTE. Something yet unpublished; secret history'; and it was not until the fourth edition, of 1773, that he added: 'It is now used, after the French, for a biographical incident; a minute passage of private life.' Similarly, the use of the suffix or the word 'ana' was extended to include a writer's miscellaneous papers, like the *Baconiana* of 1679, or anecdotes about somebody, like the *Addisoniana* (1803), most of which are collected from printed sources, or information about some general topic or theme, like the *Feminiana* (1835), with selections from British authors descriptive of women, or the *Blackguardiana* (c. 1785), which is a dictionary of rogues and cant terms,[2] or the history of Regency bruisers given by Pierce Egan in his *Boxiana* (1818–29). The last stage in the decline and fall of this suffix is shown in its use in works of reference and booksellers' catalogues as a general heading for publications, of all kinds and degrees of merit, bearing on some special author or theme— 'Shakespeariana' or 'Americana' or even 'Railroadiana'. In this paper I return to its primitive meaning of table talk: the conversation of eminent men, in hours of private relaxation, recorded by listeners for the benefit or entertainment of posterity.

The practice of adding the suffix 'ana' to the name of the person whose conversation was reported seems to have originated with the *Scaligeriana* of 1666.[3] Historians of the genre in the eighteenth

---

[1] The *O.E.D.*'s earliest example of the suffix used as a substantive is from Ephraim Chambers's *Cyclopaedia* (1728). An early French example may be found in Pierre de Villiers's *Entretiens sur les contes de fées* (Paris, 1699), sig. a4ᵛ: 'Sur les Ana'.

[2] Really the first (1785) edition of Grose's *Classical Dictionary of the Vulgar Tongue*, with a new title-page and a few leaves and illustrations stuck in.

[3] In 1667 and afterwards *Scaligerana*. The suffix had been used as early as 1508 for Heinrich Bebel's collection of German proverbs. It appeared as *Bebeliana* (Argentorati 1508): W. Bonser, *Proverb Literature* (1930), no. 1534. Was the *Baconiana* of 1679 the first English book to use the suffix? The editor, Thomas Tenison, was conscious of its novelty: 'All these Papers I have put under the Title of *Baconiana*, in imitation of those, who of late have publish'd some Remains of Learned Men, and called them, *Thuana, Scaligerana, Perroniana*' (p. 104). But the book differs from most of the French collections, in that it is mainly a collection of Bacon's papers, grouped under such headings as 'Baconiana Politico-moralia', 'Baconiana Physiologica', 'Baconiana Medica', etc.; it gives few records of Bacon's conversation.

century[1] held, as Bacon held of the essay, that though the word was late the thing was ancient. They ventured to call the book of Proverbs 'Solomoniana' and the writings of Plato and Xenophon 'Socratiana'. With more justice they pointed out that collections were made of the conversations of Pythagoras and Epictetus and that Julius Caesar made a book of apophthegms in which he carefully preserved the memorable sayings of Cicero. Plutarch, too, was rightly mentioned, for more than any other ancient biographer he realized the value and function of ana as materials for biography. 'Very often', he writes—and his sentence is quoted with approval by Boswell[2]—'an action of small note, a short saying, or a jest, shall distinguish a person's real character more than the greatest sieges, or the most important battles.'

During the Middle Ages there were no collections of ana. With few exceptions medieval chroniclers and biographers inherited from the classical historians the practice of inventing set speeches for their characters, and the invention of such orations remained a part of the medieval training in rhetoric. The survival of that tradition is found in Cavendish's life of Wolsey, in Holinshed, in Walton's *Lives*. But the rhetorical 'dialogismus' is one thing—the faithful report of a man's very words another. 'I affect not set speeches in a Historie', Milton says in his *History of Britain*, 'unless known for certain to have bin so spok'n as they are writ'n, nor then, unless worth rehearsal; and to invent such, though eloquently, as some Historians have done, is an abuse of posteritie, raising, in them that read, other conceptions of those times and persons then were true.'[3] Not, perhaps, before the sixteenth century, or in Italy before the fifteenth

---

[1] See, e.g., *Casauboniana* (Hamburg, 1710), with a preface by Johann Christoph Wolf; Michault, op. cit.; Jacques Lacombe, *Encyclopédiana ou dictionnaire encyclopédique des ana* (Paris, 1791); E. G. Peignot, *Répertoire des bibliographies spéciales, curieuses, et instructives* (Paris, 1810).

[2] *Life of Johnson*, ed. G. B. Hill, i. 32. Cf. Bacon, *The Advancement of Learning*, II. xxiii. 19: 'Verior fama e domesticis emanat.'

[3] 1670, p. 66. Cf. Noel (afterwards Bonaventura) d'Argonne, *Mélanges d'histoire et de littérature* (Rouen, 1699–1701; 3 vols.), ii. 332: 'Rien de plus romanesque ni de plus impertinent que ces Harangues directes dans une Histoire qui est un tableau simple et naïf de la vérité.' This collection came to be known, from the author's pseudonym, as the *Vigneul-Marvilliana*. Cf. *Ana, ou collection de bons mots, contes, pensées détachées, traits d'histoire et anecdotes des hommes célèbres* (Amsterdam, 1789–91; 10 vols.), vi. 116.

century, was the interest in the particular and the individual, in what distinguishes a man from his fellows, powerful enough in modern Europe to induce men to make faithful records of the conversation of eminent men.

It would appear that one of the earliest authentic collections of ana is the *Tischreden*, or table talk of Martin Luther, first published in 1566. It was not to be known as *Lutherana* for more than a century. Luther freely showed to his friends the thoughts of his heart, and they reported him in his walks, at his devotions, at meal-times in his house at Wittenberg. They took down what he said on the weightiest matters of church and state, and also his most casual remarks: for example, on witches—'I should have no compassion on these witches: I would burn them all'; on his enemies—'Whenever I pray, I pray for a curse upon Erasmus'; and on his wife—'Never any good came out of female domination'.[1] His arrogance and his hot temper are revealed to us by these faithful admirers as clearly as his humour, his piety, and his courage, and all in plain, homespun speech. Friend and foe have accepted this book as a genuine reflection of the man in his frankest and most unguarded moments.

The *Tischreden* is an early, almost a lonely, example of real table talk.[2] The vogue for this kind of book did not begin until after the publication of the *Scaligeriana* in 1666. From that year books in ana became most fashionable in France. Friends of illustrious scholars collected records of their conversation and published them as tributes to their memory. Some doggerel verses written before 1715, when the vogue was declining, mention thirty-four collections and conclude with the couplet:

> Messieurs, nul de tous ces Ana
> Ne vaut l'Ypècacuanha.[3]

---

[1] Hazlitt's translation ('Bohn Library', 1857), pp. 88, 251, 283, 300.

[2] The compiler of a full list of early ana would have to take into account such collections as the *De Dictis et factis Alphonsi regis Aragonum* (i.e. Alfonso V of Aragon), collected by Antonio Beccadelli about the year 1455; or the *Facezie et motti arguti* (c. 1475), by some (cf. A. Wesselski, *Das Tagebuch des Polizian* [Jena, 1927]) attributed to Poliziano.

[3] The *Menagiana*, reprinted in *Ana*, ii. 215. The *Ana*, in its 1789–91 printing or in the reissue of 1799, remains the most useful collection. See also *Selections from the French Anas* (2 vols., 1797, or 3 vols., 1805).

Table Talk

There was general agreement that the best of the French collections was the *Menagiana* of 1693. It was certainly one of the fullest. Ménage was a scholar and a conversationalist of repute, and his Wednesday receptions, his *Mercuriales*, attracted much good company. He lived in an age that practised conversation as an art, and believed in its efficacy. Of ten things that he knew, he had learned nine in conversation. The rust of philology did not prevent him from shining in the salon of Madame de Rambouillet or from securing the friendship of Madame de Sévigné.[1]

The *Menagiana*, like most of the French ana, reports the conversation of a scholar, and much that it contains is merely grammatical or philological. There are attempts to amend corrupt passages in the classics, speculations on etymology, critical reflections on classical history or literature, epigrams and verses in four languages, severe strictures on the scholarship and books of other scholars. (Ménage was too much of a tyrant in the republic of letters to keep his friends for long, and it was a favourite saying of his that So-and-so 'étoit autrefois de mes amis'.[2]) But the popularity of these French ana in their day, and whatever value they may now be said to possess, lie in the literary anecdotes and critical remarks on contemporary authors and books, and the reflections on the social life of the time. We learn from them, for example, how ridiculous it seemed to the French classicists (as it would have seemed to Sidney and Jonson) that a character in a Spanish play should be born in the first act and be bearded in the last, that early in the seventeenth century French plays were seldom printed till a year after their first performance, that if an author wished his works to be correctly printed he did well to write badly, for then his manuscript would be given to the best compositors; and with Ménage we attend the first performance of *Les Précieuses ridicules*.[3] There is much curious information about literary history. It is stated that about the year 1500 there was a habit of coughing in pulpit oratory—not the cough of importance or endeavour or of want of breath or yet of lapse of memory, but the cough of rhetoric. A sermon preached

---

[1] *Menagiana*, in *Ana*, v. 157.
[2] Ibid., p. 195.
[3] *Fureteriana*, in *Ana*, i. 88; *Menagiana*, ibid. ii. 348, 420, 455.

in French by Olivier Maillard at Bruges, in 1500, has 'hem hem hem' in the places where the preacher intended to cough.[1]

The fashion for ana died out early in the eighteenth century, and by 1750 they were so discredited that collectors of them preferred to disguise their wares under such titles as 'Recueils' or 'Mélanges'.[2] There had been a glut of dull and flat ana stuffed with lies and calumnies and inaccuracies—the work, as Voltaire said, of booksellers who live upon the follies of the dead[3]—and for a time the bad ana spoiled the reputation of the good.

It is odd that the vogue of these books should have been so predominantly French. Few of our scholars have been so systematically reported as Ménage or Charpentier or Boileau. Porson has had his due,[4] yet of Bentley, while there is no lack of anecdotes—true, false, or doubtful—no systematic collection of 'table talk', no 'Bentleiana', exists. But what is lacking in quantity is more than made up in quality. A conversation between Johnson and Boswell will help to bridge the gap between the French and the English ana. They were speaking about French literature. 'Boswell. Their *Ana* are good. Johnson. A few of them are good; but we have one book of that kind better than any of them; Selden's *Table Talk*.'[5]

Selden was a man after Johnson's own heart. He was a scholar with a knowledge of the law so great that Ben Jonson called him the lawbook of the judges of England,[6] but he was also a man of

---

[1] Noel d'Argonne, op. cit. i. 100. The sermon was reprinted by Jehan Labouderie in 1826, and in 1877 by Arthur de la Borderie, in *Œuvres françaises d'Olivier Maillard*. De la Borderie takes the view that the 'hem hem hem' (which is found three times) marks the places where the preacher rested for one or two minutes 'pour respirer et pour laisser à son auditoire le temps de tousser et se moucher'. In other sermons of his, however, the directions 'clama' and 'percute pede' are found. Cf. Labouderie, p. 33.

[2] Michault, op. cit., vol. i, p. i.

[3] Swift also attacked the 'roguery and ignorance of those who pretend to write anecdotes, or secret history; . . . and have the perpetual misfortune to be mistaken'. (*Gulliver's Travels*, Laputa, chap. 8.)

[4] And sometimes more than his due, as when in William Cooke's *Footiana* (1805, iii. 35) he is said to have observed that Gibbon 'drew the thread of his verbosity finer than the staple of his argument' (cf. *Love's Labour's Lost*, V. i. 14), and is praised for the neatness of his remark. A collection of *Porsoniana* was published in 1814 and W. Maltby's collection was printed in 1856, in the same volume with the table talk of Samuel Rogers.

[5] *Journal of a Tour to the Hebrides*, ed. Hill, v. 311.

[6] Ben Jonson, *Works*, ed. Herford and Simpson, i. 149.

affairs who played his part in the political and religious controversies under Charles I and the Commonwealth. His knowledge of life was shrewd and varied, and his intellect strong rather than subtle. Like Johnson he was a man of robust common sense, and he had as little metaphysics in his nature as Johnson. When we add that Selden expressed himself in his talk in plain speech and forceful imagery, we shall understand why Johnson was for once content to admire an Erastian whose opinion of the 'apostolical hierarchy of the Church of England' was very different from his own.

The age was impressed by his immense miscellaneous erudition; 'he was a great Philologist, Antiquary, Herald, Linguist, Statesman, and what not,' says Anthony Wood, and Jonson speaks to the same effect:

> you that have been
> Ever at home: yet, have all Countries seene:
> And like a Compasse keeping one foot still
> Upon your Center, doe your Circle fill
> Of generall knowledge, watch'd mens manners too,
> Heard what times past have said, seene what ours do.[1]

A liberal in politics, a sceptic and clergy-hater in religion, it has been said of him that 'the only thing about which he seems to have had no doubt was the liberty to doubt'.[2] He can be attached to no party except the party which believed in complete freedom of thought. He worked for this liberty by lending his learning in church history, in oriental tongues, in laws and institutions, now to the Royalists, now to the Puritans, according as their policy chimed with his. Fuller's description of his behaviour at the Westminster Assembly describes the man exactly: 'advantaged by his skill in *Antiquity, Commonlaw,* and the *Oriental tongues,* he imployed them rather to *pose* then *profit, perplex* then *inform* the members thereof'.[3] What Fuller fails to indicate is that this employment of his erudition 'in raising of scruples for the vexing of others' was not merely mischievous: he was fighting a losing battle in the interests of liberty of thought.

[1] A. Wood, *Athenae Oxonienses* (1691–2), ii. 107; Jonson, *Works*, viii. 159.
[2] D. Masson, *Life of Milton*, i (1881), p. 525.
[3] *Church History* (1655), bk. xi, p. 213.

Selden's *Table Talk*, known to French readers as the 'Seldeniana', was assembled by his secretary, Richard Milward, for 'twenty Years together', until a year or so before Selden's death in 1654. Milward reports especially Selden's conversation on church and state during these troubled years. Few men are learned enough to follow Selden in all his tracks, and Milward was not one of them. But faithfully and industriously, according to his lights, he transmits to us the wit and wisdom of Selden's talk. Clarendon said that in conversation Selden was 'the most clear Discourser, and had the best Faculty in making hard Things easy . . . of any Man that hath been known'.[1] His knowledge was clearly held in his mind, and plain speech and homely illustration came naturally to him. For example:

The reason of a thing is not to be enquired after, till you are sure the thing itself is so. We commonly are at what's the reason of it? before we are sure of the thing. It was an excellent question of my Lady Cotton, when Sir Robert was magnifying of a shoe, which was Moses' or Noah's, and wondering at the strange shape and fashion of it: But, Mr. Cotton, says she, are you sure it is a shoe?

Preachers say, Do as I say, not as I do. But if the physician had the same disease upon him that I have, and he should bid me do one thing, and himself do quite another, could I believe him?

Preachers will bring any thing into the text. The young masters of arts preached against non-residency in the university; whereupon the heads made an order, that no man should meddle with any thing but what was in his text. The next day one preached upon these words, *Abraham begat Isaac*; when he had gone a good way, at last he observed, that Abraham was resident, for if he had been non-resident, he could never have begot Isaac; and so fell foul upon the non-residents.[2]

Table-Talk: Being the Discourses of John Selden Esq: or His Sense of Various Matters of High Consequence Relating Especially to Religion and State was first printed in 1689, the earliest year in which it was politically safe to print it. But, before Milward took down his

---

[1] *Life* (1759), pt. i, p. 16.
[2] Ed. J. Reynolds (1892), pp. 146, 147, 161. The last story is also told in E. Gayton's *Pleasant Notes upon Don Quixote* (1645), p. 117, and in Eachard's *Grounds and Occasions of the Contempt of the Clergy* (1670), p. 70.

Table Talk 333

first note of Selden's speech, there lay hid in Scotland a record of the observations made by Selden's friend, Ben Jonson, to the Scottish poet, William Drummond, at Hawthornden, about the time of Christmas, 1618. When extracts from these conversations were first printed, in 1711, the severity of Jonson's comments on his contemporaries reminded the editor of *Scaligerana*, the *Perroniana*, and the *Menagiana*.

Jonson's talk with Drummond, over the wine—so inhospitably recorded by his host—does not tell us the whole truth about Jonson's character, but thanks chiefly to it Jonson is the only poet and dramatist of that age of whom it is possible to write a biography. For lack of a Drummond we can only dimly guess—if, indeed, we are entitled to guess—at Shakespeare's friendships and enmities, his religion, his manners, and his views on his contemporaries. Without Drummond's record we should know much less about Jonson's habits, his jests and apophthegms, his comments on his own life and works and on the works of his contemporaries. We might have known from his verses to Donne that he esteemed that poet the first poet in the world in some things, but we should not have known that the same poet, for not keeping accent, deserved hanging. And we should not have known or guessed that Jonson consumed a whole night in contemplating his great toe, 'about which he hath seen tartars & turks Romans and Carthaginions feight in his jmagination'.[1] Or if we had guessed at Jonson's delight in the occult it would have been from the evidence not so much of his plays as of his masques where his fancy and phantasy are given rein:

> Bright Night, I obey thee, and am come at thy call
> But it is no one dream that can please these all;
> Wherefore I would know what Dreames would delight 'em;
> For never was Phant'sie more loth to affright 'em.
> And Phant'sie I tell you has dreams that have wings,
> And dreams that have honey, and dreams that have stings.[2]

Drummond is not a very good Boswell. If he makes no attempt to record the flow of conversation, that may not have been his fault;

[1] Jonson, *Works*, i. 141.
[2] *The Vision of Delight*, Jonson, *Works*, vii. 465.

there may have been as little chance for the sprightliness of animated dialogue in Jonson's presence as in Coleridge's.[1] It is more serious that he is out of sympathy with his guest, that he sometimes misunderstands him, and that, by insisting too much on his asperities, perhaps he has made us misunderstand him. But, in spite of manifest deficiencies, Drummond has preserved much interesting news of a guest whom he found a little overpowering and whom he was glad to be rid of.

Jonson and Selden lived in an age when biography was still the servant of church and state, and when the life of a mere man of letters or man of science was thought unworthy of notice. When Sprat published the life of Cowley, in 1668, he felt it necessary to defend himself from the charge of spending too many words on a private man and a scholar. Yet at this very time there were two men busily engaged in collecting all that they could come by about any man (especially any Oxford man) who had once put pen to paper. Anthony Wood lies outside my compass, and John Aubrey falls doubtfully within it, yet an essay on this theme would be notably imperfect without some account of the *Brief Lives*. They are not ana, but brief biographical notes set down 'tumultuarily, as if tumbled out of a sack',[2] yet they touch the fringe of my subject, because so much of his information was derived not from books but from talk—talk in taverns and coffeehouses and country houses and on country roads. 'When a boy', he says, 'he did ever love to converse with old men as Living Histories.' 'Look', Anthony Wood used to say, when they were together in company, 'Look, yonder goes such a one, who can tell such and such stories, and I'le warrant Mr. Aubrey will break his neck downstairs rather than miss him.'[3] The impulse which drove Aubrey to risk his neck was that same impulse which led men slowly but surely away from the general to the particular in the lives of men, from the typical to the individual. It is the spirit which informs Roger North's lives of his three brothers:

[1] Cf. H. N. Coleridge in his preface to Coleridge's *Table Talk* (1835), vol. i, p. xxv: 'As I never attempted to give dialogue—indeed, there was seldom much dialogue to give—...'

[2] His observations on his manuscripts for the history of Surrey. Cf. *Wiltshire, Topographical Collections*, ed. J. E. Jackson (1862), p. vi.

[3] John Britton, *Memoir of John Aubrey* (1845), p. 16; Hearne's *Collections*, iii (ed. Doble, 1888); p. 35.

Table Talk

If the History of a Life hangs altogether upon great Importances, such as concern the Church and State, and drops the peculiar Oeconomy and private Conduct of the Person that gives Title to the Work, it may be an History, and a very good one; but of any Thing rather than of that Person's Life. Some may think Designs, of that Nature, to be, like the Plots of Mr. *Bays*, good only to bring in fine Things: But a Life should be a Picture; which cannot be good, if the peculiar Features, whereby the Subject is distinguished from all others, are left out. Nay, Scars and Blemishes, as well as Beauties, ought to be expressed; otherwise, it is but an Outline fill'd up with Lillies and Roses.[1]

Aubrey was a man of insatiable curiosity in men, manners and antiquities. He is said to have been one of England's earliest archaeologists:

Historians, chroniclers, and topographers there had been before his time; but he was the first who devoted his studies and abilities to archaeology, in its various ramifications of architecture, genealogy, palaeography, numismatics, heraldry, etc. No one before him investigated or understood anything of the vast Celtic temple at Avebury, and other monuments of the same class; and certainly no person had preceded him in attempting to distinguish the successive changes, in style and decoration, of ancient ecclesiastical edifices, or to ascertain, by observing architectural features and details, to what era any particular building belonged.[2]

And more recently Sir Charles Peers, in praising Aubrey's work on Avebury, has said that he had 'this definite merit, that he took trouble to set down what he saw as precisely as it was possible for him to do'.[3] These testimonies are worth noting because Aubrey is often thought of as a mere foolish gossip—'roving and maggotyheaded', in Anthony Wood's words. Credulous he was, and shiftless, indolent in all matters except those of antiquity, and perpetually in debt. The Earl of Thanet was perhaps right to rebuke him for his 'wonted trapishness'.[4] But his genius drove him on to a task of

---

[1] *The Life of the Right Honourable Francis North* (1742), p. 77.
[2] Britton, p. 3. Aubrey knew Stonehenge from his eighth year (ibid., p. 26).
[3] *Proceedings of the First International Congress of Prehistoric and Protohistoric Sciences* (1934), *Presidential Address*, p. 18.
[4] Britton, p. 53. 'Trapishness' is ignored by the *O.E.D.*, though it gives 'Trapish'.

which few in his age saw the value: 'methinks I am carried on with a kind of Oestrum: for nobody else hereabout hardly cares for it [the search for antiquities], but rather makes a scorn of it. But methinks it shews a kind of gratitude and good nature, to revise the memories and memorials of the pious and charitable Benefactors long since dead and gone.'[1]

Aubrey had a 'strong and early impulse to antiquities'.[2] He had noticed that many memorable accidents had for want of registering been drowned in oblivion, and for that reason he determined to be minute. He was also accurate. He wrote of Tom Coryate that though he was not a wise man he wrote faithfully matters of fact. That is true of himself. His 'observables', written many of them with aching head *post hesternam crapulam*, are faithfully reported. A reader of Aubrey is often prepared to doubt the veracity of the witness he is reporting, but never of Aubrey himself. Why should he pervert the evidence? He was gentle, unselfish, good-natured, and open-hearted, he had no axe to grind, and he had the wit to do something that was worth doing and to do it supremely well. Sometimes he cites his authority with all the scrupulosity of a modern historian. For example, when John Denham was a young student at the Inns of Court, 'a frolick came into his head, to gett a playsterer's brush and a pott of inke, and blott out all the signes between Temple-barre and Charing-cross, which made a strange confusion the next day ... This I had from R. Escott, esq., that carried the inke-pott'.

What has attracted many a reader not addicted to antiquities to read in John Aubrey is his eye for bright, significant detail and his gift for sharp, singular phrasing. Quotations from Aubrey have brightened many a dull page and 'refocillated' the wasted spirits. That gift which the rhetoricians called 'energia' was in him highly developed. 'If ever I had been good for anything 'twould have been a painter. I could fancy a thing so strongly, and have so clear an idea of it.'[3] For example, how vivid is what he tells us about the eyes of his characters: Milton's dark-grey eye; Selden's full, grey,

---

[1] *Wiltshire Topographical Collections*, p. 17.
[2] See his Autobiography in Britton, p. 14.
[3] Ibid., p. 15.

and popping; Hobbes's hazel, with a bright live coal shining within it; Denham's a kind of light goose-grey, not big, but it had a strange piercingness, not as to shining and glory, but (like a Momus) when he conversed with you he looked into your very thoughts; Bacon's a delicate, lively, hazel eye, said by circulation-of-the-blood Harvey to be like the eye of a viper; and the eyes of Ralph Kettell, president of his own college (Trinity, Oxford), sharp and grey, which helped to make his aspect terrible and so keep down the *juvenilis impetus*.[1]

Of the notable talk preserved by Aubrey, here are two examples, the one illustrating literary history, the other character. 'He haz often sayd that way (e.g. Mr. Edmund Waller's) of quibling with sence will hereafter growe as much out of fashion and be as ridicule as quibling with words.' Aubrey is reporting Samuel Butler, the author of *Hudibras*, and the accuracy of his report is corroborated by a passage in Butler's character of 'A Quibbler', first printed in 1759.[2] We must suppose Butler to be speaking soon after the Restoration. Quibbling with words looks back to the pun of Elizabethan times and to their fashion of amplifying words into rhetorical patterns. Quibbling with sense is almost as brave an attempt to crowd a description of 'metaphysical' wit into a phrase as is Davenant's 'wit is a remoter way of thinking'. And when Butler prophesies the decay of this kind of wit, he might almost be prophesying the shift in Dryden's poetry from *Annus Mirabilis* to *Absalom and Achitophel*. From a particular angle, Butler has given us a short view of the development of seventeenth-century poetry. Quibbling with words gave place to quibbling with sense, but it was for Dryden to establish the propriety of words and sense.

My other example is from Aubrey's voluminous notes on the life of his friend and fellow Malmesburian, Thomas Hobbes:

He was 40 yeares old before he looked on geometry; which happened accidentally. Being in a gentleman's library ... Euclid's Elements lay open, and 'twas the 47 El. libri I. He read the proposition. 'By God' sayd he,[3] 'This is impossible.' So he reads the demonstration

---

[1] *Brief Lives*, ed. Clark, i. 72, 220, 348; ii. 17, 67, 223.
[2] *Genuine Remains* (1759), ii. 207-8.
[3] 'He would now and then sweare, by way of emphasis.' (*Brief Lives*, ed. Clark, i. 332.)

of it, which referred him back to such a proposition; which proposition he read. That referred him back to another, which he also read. Et sic deinceps, that at last he was demonstratively convinced of the trueth. This made him in love with geometry.

It took an exceptional man to question the truth of Euclid's proposition or to make such crablike progress in establishing it.

The many intimate lives, of the sixteenth and seventeenth centuries, in which conversation is reported, lie beyond the scope of this paper. In two of the most famous, the conversation was reported from memory, yet it could not have been preserved with more felicity. Roper in filling his life of More with vivid talk was not following precedent but the desire of his heart to preserve to posterity the image of his father-in-law as it existed in his own mind. He wrote twenty years after More's death, and regretted that many of More's 'humble and wise sayings' were 'not now in my memory'.[1] And Burnet, writing shortly after Rochester's death, did not pretend 'to have given the formal words that he said, though I have done that where I could remember them.... I am not so sure of all I set down as said by me, as I am of all said by him to me'.[2]

To the modern reader the least interesting of the early collections of table talk are those which consist entirely or in the main of apophthegms or 'sentences'. An apophthegm 'delivering much in a little, discovering a man by a word, as a Picture in a Tablet',[3] is acceptable, but in some of these collections the apophthegms are mere commonplaces, throwing little or no light upon character and useful only to an age which delighted in 'sentences' as rhetorical embellishments. Characteristic collections are *Worcester's Apophthegms or Witty Sayings of the Right Honourable Henry (Late) Marquess and Earl of Worcester* (1650) and the 'Essays and Discourses Gather'd from the Mouth of my Noble Lord and Husband' in the fourth book of *The Life of William Duke of Newcastle* (1667). A sentence with some spice in it, recorded by the Duchess of Newcastle, sounds as if it

---

[1] *Life*, ed. E. V. Hitchcock (E.E.T.S.), pp. 4, 39.
[2] *Some Passages of the Life and Death of the Right Honourable John Earl of Rochester* (1680), pp. 162–3.
[3] *Comes Facundus* (1658), pp. 171–5: 'Why Apophthegmes do more move and affect others, then set and continued speeches.'

Table Talk

might have escaped from the book of maxims which La Rochefoucauld had given to the world two years earlier: 'That he had observed, That seldom any person did laugh, but it was at the follies or misfortunes of other men, by which we may judg of their good natures';[1] but the sentence is at odds with the magnanimous person whom she had lauded in the preceding books. The man whose table talk was most persistently reported in collection after collection and edition after edition was the Solomon of Great Britain, James I. The title of the earliest collection sufficiently indicates its contents: *Flores Regii. Or, Proverbs and Aphorisms, Divine and Moral. As They Were at Several Times upon Sundry Occasions, Spoken by His Most Excellent Majesty, James, of Famous Memory King of Great Britain. Collected by J. L. S.* (1627). Another collection, *King James His Apophthegms; Or, Table-Talk*[2] (1643), was made by his servant, Benjamin Agar, 'assiduously collected, as well at his Majesties own standing houses, as also in his forraigne progresse both in England and Scotland, with the sundry times and places, when, where, and upon what occasions, or arguments they were uttered'. These were not the only collections of his talk,[3] and in the later half of the century his apophthegms were sometimes published, in one volume, with those of Charles I, the Marquess of Worcester, Bacon, and More.[4]

---

[1] p. 177.
[2] An earlier example of 'table-talk' (in the sense of 'the conversation of eminent men especially as reproduced in literary form') than that given by the *O.E.D.* from Selden's *Table-Talk* (1689). The *O.E.D.*'s earliest example of 'table talk' ('conversation at the dinner-table') is dated *c.* 1569, and of 'table-talker' ('one who talks at table'), 1846. But 'table-talker' is in Camden's *Remains* (1605), p. 27: '*Athenaeus*, in his supper-gulls, table-talkers, or *Deipnosophistae*.'
[3] I have not seen *Witty Observations* (1643) and *Regales aphorismi* (1650; edited by W. Stratton?), both in the Thomason Collection in the British Museum. [The Thomason Collection was not available in 1940 when this essay was published. H.G.] For the apophthegms printed in *The Prince's Cabala* (1715)—in the main, it would seem, a conflation of earlier collections—it is claimed that they were collected by Sir Thomas Overbury, had never been made public before, and were '*really genuine*'!
[4] Thomas Bayly edited such a collection in 1658— *Witty Apophthegms*—a copy of which is in the Thomason Collection. I have not seen it, but presumably it is the same as an edition of 1669 with the same title. Bacon's *Apophthegms* was compiled by himself (cf. *Huntington Library Quarterly*, ii. 145, 153), and some of the additions to the authentic collection of 1625 found in the collection of 1669 were condemned by Tenison (*Baconiana*, 1679, p. 59) as 'too infacetious for a Ploughman's Chimney-Corner'.

The taste for collections of table talk was now firmly established, and the task of enumerating the collections of the eighteenth century would be arduous. Of the many books of ana made in that century, Spence's *Anecdotes*, which Spence once thought of calling 'Popiana', and the *Walpoliana* seemed to the early nineteenth century to be outstanding. John Pinkerton, the compiler of *Walpoliana*, has left us a useful description of Walpole's manners and habits in the last years of his life, but his record of Walpole's conversation is disappointing. The fault may be Pinkerton's, or it may be that only when Walpole spoke through his pen was he able to give to his gossip that spice which flavours the lightest trifles in his letters. Spence's *Anecdotes* is a much more important book. Spence was an agreeable man, not a clever man; a pretty scholar, not a great scholar;[1] and it is his merit to be a medium through whom the conversation of Pope and Bolingbroke and others is transmitted, apparently without distortion. The talk he reports is not wholly about letters; there is much about Spence's pet subject, classical art, and sometimes the talk turned on kings and statesmen. (Here is the report of William III's first speech to the English people, when he landed at Torbay in 1668: 'We are come for your good, for all your goods.'[2]) But the chief distinction of Spence's collections is the conversation of Pope or about Pope. For once, we find Pope speaking his mind without 'his reputation in his head',[3] as we rarely find him in his letters, and from this record of his hours of social ease there emerges a kindly benevolent Pope whom we must do our best to reconcile if we can with the equally genuine Pope with whose hatreds and stratagems his critics used to be too exclusively concerned. There emerges too, a Pope who is a discerning critic of some of the older poets, like Chaucer, Spenser, and Milton.

Later than the eighteenth century there are few systematic collections of table talk. The nineteenth century began well enough with the table talk of Samuel Rogers, a survival from the eighteenth century, with Hazlitt's record of the conversations of the painter, James Northcote (Hazlitt's flair for remembering the conversation

---

[1] Cf. Boswell, ed. C. B. Hill, v. 317; Walpole's *Letters*, ed. Toynbee, xi. 175.
[2] *Anecdotes*, ed. Singer (1820), p. 337.
[3] Cf. *Lives of the Poets*, ed. G. B. Hill, iii. 160.

Table Talk

he had heard in one company and repeating it 'with syllabic exactness' in the next must have caused much pain and embarrassment to his friends),[1] and with the table talk of Coleridge. But we must seek for anecdotes and conversations of eminent Victorians, not in collections of ana but in glancing references in diaries, letters, autobiographies, books called 'Memories', 'Reminiscences'—in a hundred scattered places. If we seek for a reason, we shall say, I suppose, that conversation was no longer esteemed as the art which the seventeenth and eighteenth centuries regarded it, and that less and less time was devoted to its cultivation. (Statistics could perhaps be collected for the common rooms of Oxford and Cambridge—the number of hours spent there, over his wine, by the Senior Fellow in Thomas Warton's essay in the *Idler* for 2 December 1758, bears, perhaps, some resemblance to the reality.) But, above all, there was the feeling that it was not a gentlemanly thing to report the conversation of one's friends in their unguarded moments. The loss to a biographer is considerable. If FitzGerald and Spedding had taken a record of the ante-laureate days when Tennyson 'flash'd his random speeches' at the Cock Tavern, Tennyson might have called them 'literary leeches' or lice that live upon the locks of literature, but it would have been easier today to think of him more as a man and less as a laureate.

Dr. Johnson fancied that in time mankind might come to write aphoristically, grow weary of weaving anecdotes into a system, of making big books.[2] But the man he was speaking to, the author of *the* life of Johnson, was supremely right in waiting to weave his ana into a system. If Boswell had accepted the invitation of the bookseller, Dilly (which he received the day after he had heard of Johnson's death), to prepare an octavo volume of 400 pages of Johnson's conversations, he would have produced the best of all collections of table talk and perhaps failed to write the best of all biographies. He told Dilly that he would write Johnson's life deliberately, and he held his hand for seven years.[3]

[1] C. Lamb, *Letters*, ed. Lucas (1935), ii. 43 (12 Jan. 1808).
[2] Boswell, v. 39.
[3] F. A. and M. S. Pottle, *The Private Papers of James Boswell from Malahide Castle* (1931), no. 94. The *Johnsoniana* of 1776, which accompanied Boswell and Johnson on their trip to Oxford and Ashbourne in that year, was a bookseller's venture and, said

Boswell, like Johnson, was interested in ana. Among his private papers is a collection of his own sayings, called 'Boswelliana', and another recording the caustic comments of his wife—'Uxoriana'.[1] He defends himself from the charge of ungentlemanly behaviour, in reporting private conversations, by pointing to the usefulness of the French and English collections of table talk.

How delighted should we have been, if thus introduced into the company of Shakespeare and Dryden, of whom we know scarcely any thing but their admirable writings! What pleasure would it have given us, to have known their petty habits, their characteristick manners, their modes of composition, and their genuine opinion of preceding writers and of their contemporaries! All these are now irrecoverably lost.[2]

Again, when Boswell towards the end of the *Life* seeks for a parallel to the range and force of Johnson's conversation, he finds it in the *Menagiana*. Ménage and Johnson were scholars whose learning did not prevent them from sustaining conversation upon any topic presented to them. 'If you shew the *Menagiana*', Boswell quotes Bayle as saying, 'you distinguish him from... [other] learned men. There it appears that he was a man who spoke off-hand a thousand good things. His memory extended to what was ancient and modern; to the court and to the city; to the dead and to the living languages; to things serious and things jocose; in a word, to a thousand sorts of subjects.'[3] And we know how Johnson could talk politics with Burke, poetry with Goldsmith, law with Boswell, small talk with Mrs. Thrale, runts with a countryman, and how he made a very good figure before the officers at Fort George by his talk on the granulation of gunpowder.[4]

Johnson, 'a mighty impudent thing'. (Cf. Pottle, no. 576.) *Dr. Johnson's Table Talk*, which Dilly published in 1798, was selected from Boswell's *Life*, during Boswell's lifetime and with his approbation.

[1] Pottle, nos. 289, 293; *Boswelliana*, ed. C. Rogers (1876), pp. 203 ff., 329. Boswell used the suffix more loosely when he indorsed as 'Divryana' a wrapper for the letters of 'the gay little Parisienne', Mlle Divry. (Cf. C. C. Abbott, *A Catalogue of Papers Found at Fettercairn House*, 1936, no. 1384.)

[2] Boswell, v. 414-15.

[3] Ibid. iv. 429. Cf. *Boswell Papers*, ed. Scott and Pottle, viii. 115-16; 'there should be half a dozen of *Ménages* in every age to preserve the remarkable sayings which are often lost'.

[4] Cf. Boswell, iii. 337; v. 124.

Table Talk

Selden once said that 'no man is the wiser for his learning; it may administer matter to work in, or objects to work upon, but wit and wisdom are born with a man'.[1] Johnson's talk is better than the talk of Ménage, because it has less learning and more wisdom. The conversation of Ménage, like that of Macaulay, depended for its effect upon the stores of a tenacious memory. It is said that one day, after he had been entertaining Madame de Rambouillet and other ladies with the many agreeable things he had met with in his reading, she said to him: 'tout ce que vous dites est très-beau, monsieur, mais dites-vous quelque chose de vous présentement.'[2] Everything that Johnson said had become his own. 'Scarce ever any concocted his reading into judgement as he did.'[3]

Johnson's talk is also better than the talk of Ménage because it is better reported. It was a lucky chance that brought together our best talker and our best reporter. The stars are not likely to repeat the conjunction. Not every great man is a good talker, and some good talk, like some good wine, will not stand the carriage. Lockhart could not have Boswellized Scott, even if he had thought it lawful to do so. Scott's conversation was overflowing with good sense, but it was lacking in point and opinion, too dependent upon the geniality and manner of the speaker, the telling gesture, the sparkle of the eye, the lift of the eyebrow, to bear reproduction.[4] Johnson's talk has bottled well,[5] and perhaps under Boswell's care it has not lost much of its bouquet.

In leading the thoughts into domestic privacies, in displaying the minute details of daily life, Boswell is following Johnson's own biographical principles. Johnson was all for the general in poetry, but in biography he stood for the particular. The particular, however, must be characteristic. 'I know not well what advantage posterity can receive from the only circumstance by which Tickell has distinguished Addison from the rest of mankind, *the irregularity of his pulse.*'[6] Tickell made two mistakes: he gave only one particular,

---

[1] *Table Talk*, ed. Reynolds, p. 102. [2] *Carpenteriana*, in *Ana*, vii. 101.
[3] Part of an extract from Baker's *Chronicle*, which Boswell prefixed to the *Journal of a Tour to the Hebrides* (1785).
[4] Cf. Lockhart (1837), iv. 151 ff.
[5] The image is Boswell's: 'We were very hearty, but there was no conversation fit for bottling.' (*Boswell Papers*, x. 164, 30 March 1775.)
[6] *Rambler*, no. 60.

and it was not significant. The irregularity of Addison's pulse sets up no train of associations, for it is at variance with all that we know of Addison's moral or intellectual character. Coleridge's devious walk from one side of the footpath to the other can be related, as Hazlitt relates it, to his instability of purpose, but Addison, of all persons, should have had a normal pulse.

Johnson 'diversifies and enlivens' his *Lives of the Poets* with many particulars, but they appear scanty, as the particulars of all other biographers must appear scanty, beside the rich documentation of Boswell. 'By how small a speck does the Painter give life to an Eye', Boswell observes.[1] Every speck in Boswell helps to give life and adds another touch to the portrait. Since the discovery and publication of the Boswell Papers, we know how Boswell was able to preserve so much of Johnson's conversation.

It is no exaggeration to say [wrote Geoffrey Scott] that Boswell regarded his Journal as the principal duty and aim of his existence; life unrecorded was not life. He goes so far as to make this singular pronouncement: 'I should live no more than I can record, as one should not have more corn growing than one can get in. There is a waste of good if it be not preserved'. Boswell did not feel he *possessed* an experience till it was written down; the *res gestae* were mere preliminaries.[2]

It is now possible to compare the conversations in the *Life* with the reports which he had made ten years and more ago in his Journal or rough notes. In expanding he had, of course, to invent phrasing round the key words and the meaning. 'Men without restraint are insufferable. Were a woman to put out her legs as you do, you'd be ready to kick 'em in', was smoothed out and impersonalized into, 'A man without some degree of restraint is insufferable; but we are less restrained than women. Were a woman sitting in company to put out her legs before her as most men do, we should be tempted to kick them in'; and 'Ease of behaviour comes imperceptibly' is amplified and rounded into 'An elegant manner and easiness of behaviour are acquired gradually and imperceptibly'.[3] But Boswell's mind was so 'impregnated with the Johnsonian aether' that he is

---

[1] *Boswell Papers*, viii. 112.   [2] Ibid. vi. 65; xi. 150.
[3] Ibid. vi. 49; *Life*, iii. 53.

Table Talk

always in character, whereas Mrs. Piozzi with her underlinings and occasional debility of diction sometimes makes Johnson speak like herself.[1]

The rough materials for the life of Johnson are in Boswell's Journal. 'My journal is ready', he writes, 'it is in the larder, only to be sent to the kitchen, or perhaps trussed and larded a little.'[2] It tells the story of his friendship with Johnson but also, with a frankness and minuteness only equalled by Pepys, it tells the whole story of his life. His Journal has left him 'embowelled to Posterity', as his wife (who hated his journalizing) told him it would.[3] But the discovery of his private papers has authenticated his record of Johnson's conversations and established more certainly than ever the claim of his biography to be the most authentic as well as the fullest and most intelligent of all collections of table talk—'The Ana of all Anas'.[4]

[1] I am thinking of such reporting as, 'one has *so* little pleasure in reciting the anecdotes of beggary' or 'I really never mentioned this foolish story to any body except Dr. Taylor, not even to my *dear dear* Bathurst' (*Anecdotes*, in *Johnsonian Miscellanies*, ed. Hill, 1897, i. 148, 158); but a friend tells me it is unfair to compare Mrs. Piozzi or any other reporter with the Incomparable.
[2] *Boswelliana*, ed. Rogers, p. 299.
[3] *Boswell Papers*, x. 254.
[4] Southey, *The Doctor*, vii (1847), p. 347.

PRINTED IN GREAT BRITAIN
AT THE UNIVERSITY PRESS, OXFORD
BY VIVIAN RIDLER
PRINTER TO THE UNIVERSITY